Georgia Toffolo is a broadcaster and British media personality. *Meet me in London* is the first book of her quartet. It is her second book and first fiction novel. She lives in South West London with her dog Monty.

Meet me in London

Georgia Toffolo
with Louisa George

MILLS & BOON

Mills & Boon
An imprint of HarperCollins*Publishers* Ltd
1 London Bridge Street
London SE1 9GF

This paperback edition 2020
4

First published in Great Britain by Mills & Boon,
an imprint of HarperCollins*Publishers* Ltd 2020

ISBN: 978-0-00-837585-0

MIX
Paper from
responsible sources
FSC
www.fsc.org   **FSC™ C007454**

This book is produced from independently certified FSC™ paper
to ensure responsible forest management.

For more information visit: www.harpercollins.co.uk/green

This book is set in 11/15.5 pt. Bembo

Printed and bound in Great Britain by
CPI Group (UK) Ltd, Croydon, CR0 4YY

For Bertie Toffolo,
You are the peregrine falcon in my sky!

MEET ME IN LONDON

CHAPTER ONE

OLIVER RUSSELL COULD WRANGLE a wayward balance sheet back into the black, take failing stores apart and breathe new life into them, make difficult calls on staffing and personnel issues, make his shareholders happy and very, *very* rich. But he had never managed to curb his mother's meddling in his private life.

Some things were just impossible.

Earth to Oliver. This is your mother asking about your Christmas Day plans. Will I need to set an extra place at the dinner table? Hint, hint. Your mother xx

Sitting on a stool at the bar in the upmarket wine bar The Landing, Oliver groaned as he interpreted the 'hint' as yet another badly veiled attempt to discover his relationship status. *Great one, Mum. Way to put pressure on a guy.*

Could this week get any worse? He threw his mobile phone onto the sticky, beer-stained counter, gripped the tumbler in front of him and took a sip of a much needed fifteen-year-old Scotch. As the honey-coloured syrup oozed down his throat and hit his stomach with a warming buzz he silently counted all the ways things had gone wrong in such a short space of time.

First mistake; allowing his mother to believe he was finally settling down when in reality his love life could only be described as… non-existent. And now having to think up all the ways he could appease his parents over the holidays without going quietly insane.

Whereas other families had jolly traditions of games and church on Christmas Day, his parents' idea of fun was to corner him in the lounge, pin him down with laser stares and interrogate him for signs of commitment, a potential wife and progeny. A grandchild, or preferably many grandchildren, to spoil and give meaning to their later years, someone to carry on the family name and also an heir to entrust the business to. As an only child Oliver was expected to do so, as his father had done before him.

Trouble was, after his last romantic failure, settling down was not on Oliver's bucket list. At least, not for a very long time.

Second mistake: in the spirit of keeping the family business afloat he'd agreed to clean up the mess his cousin was making of the new build. Ollie should have let him fall on his sword, but that would have meant his parents suffering too and there was no way he was going to allow that. So, here he was in a rowdy bar in Chelsea at ridiculous o'clock at night – or was it early morning? – having only just finished work, with the prospect of another seventeen-hour day tomorrow and the next day, and the next…

He took another sip of whisky but almost choked as someone bumped into his hip, jolted his arm and sloshed the Scotch, rich but burning, down his throat.

'Hey, gorgeous.' A woman old enough to be his mother – and even though deep down he loved his mum, Lord knew he didn't need two of them – appeared at his shoulder and beamed at him. Her eyes were wine-glazed and the lipstick smudged over her mouth almost up to her nostrils made her look like a startled fish. 'I've got mistletoe, you know what that means, right?'

'That it's time I left?' Scraping his stool back he stood, steadying the woman as she swayed, and then handed her into the waiting arms of her friends who were all dressed as… well, he wasn't entirely sure, but there were glitter wings and feathery haloes involved, so he imagined they were supposed to be Christmas angels. In November?

As if knowing all about his work stress and family dilemmas even the music in the bar seemed to mock him. Too loud and too cheery and all about being home and in love at Christmas. He shuddered. *No thanks.*

Which brought him to his third mistake: choosing the bar from hell to drown his sorrows in. It wasn't even December and yet here they all were screeching Christmas carols at the top of their tone-deaf voices. Christmas was everywhere. In the glittery tinsel that hung in loopy garlands across the ceiling and the fake tree in the corner. The soundtrack to the evening. The clothes people were wearing. Christmas was hurtling fast towards him and he was running out of time. He had so much to do to fix his first mistake before the doors of the new Russell & Co department store opened, way behind schedule, but in time for the busiest, and therefore most lucrative time of the year.

He just needed some kind of miracle to make it happen.

On the counter his phone vibrated. He picked up and grimaced at another text, knowing what was bound to be coming but also knowing if he ignored her it would only get worse:

Oliver? It's a simple question. Blink once for yes. Twice for no. Are we finally going to meet your new girlfriend? Your mother xx

Uh-oh. She was dropping the veiled interest and taking a more direct approach. This was serious.

He flicked a text back:

When your message flashes onto my screen it identifies you as my mother. There is also a little photo of you smiling at me at the top of your texts. You don't need to tell me who you are.

He added two kisses, because, well, she was his mother: *Ollie xx*

A pause while he watched three grey dots dance on his screen and then:

Not a single blink. How do I interpret that? We just want to see you happy. Your mother xxx

By happy, she meant married. As if you couldn't be otherwise. Although he knew just as many people who were married and miserable as married and happy.

How was he even meant to send a blink by text anyway? He rolled his eyes instead. Nothing confirmed as yet.

Before he could say 'Baa Humbug' her reply flashed on his screen:

When will you know? Your mother xx

I don't know.

If he told her the delightful Clarissa had moved on to a more malleable boyfriend his mum would be trying to arrange dates for him.

As if on cue another text arrived:

Is there something you're not telling us? Is it over? So soon? Again? Oh, Oliver.

He could feel the disappointment coming through the airwaves as her next text quickly followed:

Perhaps I should invite the Henleys over on Christmas Day.

4

I heard Arabella's back from her Indian ashram trip and
SINGLE. And stop rolling your eyes at me. Your mother xx

He couldn't help but laugh at that, despite his growing frustration. He tried to stay noncommittal. Apparently, according to his ex, noncommittal was a strength of his:

Do NOT set any more dates up for me. Nothing's confirmed
re Xmas. I'll let you know when I know.

At the new store opening then?

Just a matter of weeks away. She clearly wasn't giving up. She never gave up. She wouldn't give up until she was holding his first child. Or maybe his second – his second set of triplets.

That was the problem; she wasn't giving up. He just needed to appease her. Or ignore her. So, he chose the latter.

Realizing he hadn't finished his drink and grateful that the bar staff were now shuffling the off-tune singers outside he sat back down and resumed his contemplation of the whisky in front of him. At some point the staff would shuffle him out too, but for now he craved this brief peace and quiet, save for his mother's infuriating but well-meaning texts and a muted conversation between the servers coming from a little room off to the side of the bar.

He could hear Paul, the guy who'd served him earlier say, 'Hey, Vicki, are you OK to close up tonight? I promised Amanda I'd get home early. It's our anniversary.'

'Of course,' a soft voice filtered through. 'You helped me out by taking the early shift so I could teach my class, so I'm more than happy to hang around here for the stragglers. Sara said she'd stay on and help me clear up.'

Stragglers? Is that what he was now? Ollie looked around the bar at the three other solo drinkers – all male, all staring hopelessly into glasses of alcohol. He laughed to himself. Yeah, damned right he fitted that description; moving slowly. He didn't want to hurry because the sooner he went home, the sooner tomorrow would arrive bringing with it all his problems.

'So how did class go today?' he heard Paul ask the owner of the soft voice. 'Any more visits from the local cops?'

Police? Interesting. Ollie leaned forward to hear mystery woman's answer.

'Oh, that was all just a misunderstanding. Her brother gave her the iPad, Jasmine didn't know it was stolen.' A pause. 'Um. By her brother.' A rumble of soft laughter that sounded so free and bright had Ollie straining to see who the voice belonged to. It wasn't the other woman who worked here because she was now collecting glasses from empty tables and her accent was Cockney through and through. This Vicki woman was from somewhere else. South-west maybe, a tiny hint of something he recognized from holidays down in Cornwall. Laughter threaded through her intonation. 'We sorted it out. The police dropped the charges against her.'

'So, one of the kids you're teaching is harbouring stolen goods. Great. You really need to stay away from trouble like that, Vicki.' Paul came back into the bar and started to wipe down the counter with a dishcloth.

The woman followed. 'If I stayed away there'd be even more trouble for her, I'm sure. She's so talented. You should see her designs, they're stunning. Really fresh ideas. She could go a long way with the right guidance. I'm pulling out all the stops.'

'You're too good to those kids.' Paul frowned. 'Instead of

focusing on your own career you're spending all your energy on a bunch of no-hope teenagers who probably have never even heard the word *gratitude*.'

The Vicki woman turned and put her hands on her hips, giving Ollie full view of her face. *Wow.*

She was wearing a dress that looked like it had come straight out of the nineteen fifties; all slash neck and cinched waist in a fabric of cream and scarlet flowers. Her glossy, dark hair was loosely tied into a ponytail that was pulled forward over one shoulder. She had bright red lipstick on full lips – not smudged in the slightest, and the most intense dark eyes he'd ever seen.

In stark contrast her skin was pale, he wasn't sure whether it was make-up or natural and he didn't care. Oliver Russell had known a lot of beautiful women in his time, but she was next level. Quite simply, she was the most beautiful woman he'd ever seen.

That gorgeous red mouth curled into a smile, but a little frown appeared over her eyes. 'Paul, honestly, they're struggling in so many ways. They have so much hope and potential and no one else seems to care. If I don't help them then who will?'

'I'm just saying, be careful, that's all. Your heart's too soft, Vicki, you're going to get hurt.'

'It's a fashion design class for underprivileged kids, Paul. Not target practice in the 'hood. Trouble is, we're fast running out of opportunities for them to showcase their work. All the design schools have organized shows already and we're lagging behind. I'm going to have to be creative with my thinking.' Her eyes wandered over the bar and settled on Oliver, just for a moment.

Instinctively, he smiled. She gave him the faintest of smiles back and didn't look away immediately. A look of surprise flickered behind her eyes. Even from here he could see the flush of her cheeks as their gazes met and, as if someone had flicked a switch, a rush of heat hit him too. Interest. The flicker of awareness. Brief. So brief he checked himself; maybe he'd imagined it?

All too soon she dragged her eyes away. Swallowed. She turned to her workmate and took the cloth from his hands. 'Right. Well. Things to do. Off you go, Paul, we've got this. See you tomorrow.'

With that she bent to stack more bottles into a small fridge behind the bar, giving Ollie a front-row view of her graceful, slender neck, the gentle slope of her shoulders, the pearls of her spine trailing into that curve-enhancing vintage dress. Even the back of her was more interesting, more alluring than anything he'd seen in weeks. Months. *Ever.*

In his peripheral vision he sensed movement. As Sara put a fistful of dirty glasses next to him on the counter, she caught him looking at Vicki and grinned. Her eyes widened in something he could only interpret as mischief and he could almost read what she was thinking. Yeah, he was checking this Vicki out. *So sue me.*

But damn, the last thing he wanted was to make anyone uncomfortable. He drew his eyes away but there was something about her that made him want to take a second glance and keep on looking. She was stunning, had a gentle confidence about her, and was helping poor kids in her spare time… his kind of perfect.

Not that he was interested in perfect. Or anyone at all right now. He had far too much to do to save the family business to be distracted by a woman. Still, a guy could look, right?

Vicki was oblivious. Vicki? She was more a Victoria, he thought. Victoria smacked of gravitas and class and she had both in spades.

Sara was still grinning. She opened her mouth, no doubt to say some smart-ass comment, but right on cue his phone vibrated again. *Phew.* Saved by the ringtone. But sadly, saved by his mother was way more of a crush to his ego than being caught admiring a beautiful woman.

How about Jecca Forsythe? She's lovely. Just come out of a messy divorce, so I imagine she's keen to get dating again.
Your mother xx

The latest in the line of single women his mother kept parading in front of him. They were all perfectly nice women, all fitting his parents' ideal of what a Russell wife should be like; preferably the daughter of business associates to strengthen the Russell brand, clever, pretty but not showy, happy to support him in his business, keen for a family. But none of them made him feel… whatever it was he was supposed to feel. The kind of thing his grandparents had had. The laugh together, play together, grow together love. That wasn't something they shared in his Russell household. Loyalty, yes. Proximity… if necessary. Closeness, not so much.

No, Mum. Not Jecca. Or Arabella. Or anyone else for that matter. I can sort out my own love life, thanks.

Another ping on his phone. He didn't want to look, but he had to, because ignoring her wasn't working.

Well, from where I'm sitting you obviously can't. You need an intervention. I'm worried about you, Oliver. It's not good to be alone. Your father is so invested in your future, we both are. We miss you. Your mother xx

Oliver read it twice and cursed while his heart crushed at the mention of his father. The reason for this most recent intense interest in his love life suddenly crystallized: his parents had so much to worry about – too much – that they were looking for a distraction. And why the hell not? They didn't have much else to look forward to, so a marriage and babies and a rosy future for their son was all they could hope for.

Annoyed at himself for his surly replies, and rightfully humbled, Oliver flicked another text to his mum:

How is Dad?

A couple of moments passed, during which guilt shivered through Oliver's gut. Then:

Oh, you know. The same. But his doctor says there's some experimental treatment he wants to try.

That was where they'd got to, experimental treatment when everything else had failed so far.

Give him my love.

His mother was trying, he knew, to forge a better relationship between them all at this difficult time and he welcomed that, but sometimes it could be suffocating. He'd tried I'm fine on my own. He'd tried I'm not ready to settle down and none of it convinced her he was OK. But now she wanted to meet this special woman. Who didn't exist. Who'd got bored of waiting for commitment.

He didn't want to let his parents feel that bitter tang of disappointment, not again when they had so much to battle already, but he didn't want his mother setting up surreptitious dates over Christmas either, inviting the very nice but not for him Arabella or Jecca or any other woman she believed would be a perfect match.

He wanted them to have something to look forward to.

What to do?

Oliver? We're so looking forward to meeting her. Your father in particular.

So without thinking too much about the ramifications Oliver sent a text straight back:

OK. OK, Mum. I'll bring her to the opening day.

Oh! Ollie! Love. Ollie! Finally! See, that wasn't too hard, was it? I'm so excited. Your mother xx

He stared at the screen for a minute and let his actions sink in. Hell. He'd just lied to his mother about a non-existent girlfriend. Great stuff.

He took another gulp of whisky. He had time. Time to find a new girlfriend. Or time to think up another excuse to tell his mother on opening day.

Damn. Because if he didn't come up with a plan his mum would be hounding him then too. If only he could find someone who was open to a mutually beneficial arrangement of *pretend girlfriend* then he could get Mummy Dearest off his back.

'It's last orders.' That voice again. Vicki was close enough he could smell her perfume. A playful, flowery mix that made him want to lean closer and breathe her in. As she spoke her hands moved, fluttering over the glasses. 'Is there anything you want before I close the till?'

So many things but none of them would be found here in this bar.

Unless… Kind. Beautiful. *Perfect.* The germ of an idea started to form in his head. He looked across the bar into dark caramel eyes that swirled with fun and, if he wasn't mistaken, a little heat. 'Actually, yes. There is something.'

She smiled, holding his gaze in a way that made his gut curl in desire. 'Sure?'

'Will you marry me?'

* * *

Not again.

'Absolutely not.' Victoria tried to hide her smile as Mr Tall, Dark and Dangerous' hopeful grin withered under her death stare. Too often – because she was petite and kind of pretty – she'd been underestimated as being a push-over, but she had a backbone made of steel. She'd had to, just to survive. It served her well dealing politely yet firmly with alcohol-soaked guys. But this one was different, definitely a level higher than the usual punters.

'If I had a pound for every marriage proposal I got at the end of a boozy night I'd be a rich girl indeed. But a word of advice, mate – as proposals go it needs work. Next time, maybe do some sort of grand romantic gesture like… oh, I don't know, find out the woman's name before you ask her to spend the rest of her life with you?'

'I take it that's a no, then?'

He grinned and she had to admit that, in another life where she wasn't jaded and burnt by relationship failure, she might have found him a teeny-weeny bit attractive. There was something about his grey-blue eyes that made her want to keep looking at him, despite his ridiculous question. Something about the scruff of his messy hair that made her want to slide her fingers in and smooth it. She wasn't even going to think about his strong jaw and stubble. He was dressed in the usual uniform for people working in offices in the Chelsea area – dark suit, white shirt, brown leather boots. He'd hung his suit jacket on the hook under the bar, and sat with his shirt neck open, no tie, and sleeves rolled up. Dressed down for Friday-night drinks.

The linen shirt caressed well-honed muscles. Broad shoulders. A fine body. He had a crystal-cut voice that was as deep as the trouble he'd just got himself into. So OK, maybe he was extraordinary compared to the usual suited and booted or trendy wannabe King's Road hipster guys that came in after work.

Oh, and then there'd been that deep, low burn she'd felt as her gaze had clashed with his. Something totally elemental and primal. A prickling awareness over her skin. Something she hadn't felt in a long time, and she had to admit it was happening again as he smiled.

She shook her head. 'A definite no. Sorry, not sorry.'

'Way to break a man's heart.' He shrugged.

'Oh, I'm sure you'll survive. There are plenty of women looking for what you're offering.' Ignoring the tingles zipping through her, Victoria printed his bill and put it on onto a saucer. She pushed it towards him. 'Here's your tab. Sara will ring it up for you.'

Then she turned away and busied herself with wiping down the optics. But out of the corner of her eye she watched him scrape back his stool and take out his platinum credit card, pay, then stride confidently towards the door. She pretended not to be gaping when he turned and gave her a woefully sad smile and playfully tapped his 'broken' heart before he disappeared into the night.

When the door closed she felt her body sag on a sigh, as if she'd been holding her breath through the whole interaction. Wow. That connection when they first saw each other had been… weird.

Her friend Sara, standing next to her, gave her a nudge. 'Whoa. Victoria Scott, he is one hell of a hot dude.'

Yes, he is. 'Says the woman with the uber hot girlfriend.'

Sara laughed and raised her palms. 'Sweetheart, just because I don't work that way doesn't mean I don't know talent when I see it.'

Victoria allowed herself to enjoy the fizzy feelings inside her, just for a moment. Because it had been fun and playful but that's all it was. Then reality – fuelled by her doomed romantic history – slid into her brain, so she put those feelings in a box and closed the lid. 'Gorgeous, but drunk. He must be to propose to a stranger.'

'Hmmm.' Sara's mouth twisted. 'He nursed one Macallan the whole time he was here.'

'A cheap drunk, then.' Victoria laughed. 'That's even worse. What a blow to my ego.'

'Not at all. He seemed entirely in possession of all faculties, as you would agree, having not taken your eyes off him for the whole time it took him to pay and walk out the door. Maybe you should have taken him up on his offer?'

Victoria whirled round to look at her friend. 'What? Seriously?'

'Hypothetically speaking. At least, you could have chatted a bit more and seen where it could have gone… drinks, dinner? Bed?' She grinned and Victoria wasn't sure whether she was being serious or not.

Sara was relatively new to the bar and they'd started to develop a friendship that was fresh and fun, but with new friendships there was always that lag time of developing a bond, learning to trust, knowing what to say and what to keep secret.

With her tight group of old friends from Devon, Victoria always knew exactly what they meant, what they were thinking, what they were about to say even before they said it. They'd shared years of closeness, had been there for each other during amazing times, bad times and worse, and although they were all spread across the world now – and she missed them so much it made her heart hurt – they still talked as often as they could on group chats. They'd talk her off the ledge or encourage her to take the next step in anything she was considering, even dating, if ever she felt ready to do it again. Sara was great but Victoria knew it was going to take a little more time before she felt as close to her as she did to Zoe, Lily and Malie.

'Sara, he asked me to marry him, not go on a date. No drinks, dinner or bed. Just cut straight to the 'til death us do part stuff. No thanks.'

'He looked more like the for richer *not* for poorer type, though and he might have been fun, which is just what you need right now.' Sara appeared to be more excited than Victoria was over this. Which was strange, given that proposals did indeed come thick and fast at the end of a drunken night and normally Sara rolled her eyes and bit her tongue. 'You never know, he might even be The One.'

'I do know. He isn't.' There wasn't such a thing.

'Your loss.' Sara shrugged. 'All I'm saying is—'

'It's time to mop the floors and then we can go home?' Victoria closed off this conversation about her hapless love life and looked at her watch. Her feet hurt from standing all day and her brain hurt from teaching lovely but demanding teenagers and then managing the bar into the small hours.

'On it, boss lady.' While Sara filled the bucket with hot soapy water Victoria looked at the empty seat where the hot guy had been sitting and something in her belly kind of imploded at the thought of him. Which was irritating, because even though her head could rationalize how someone good-looking could have a physical effect that was purely instinctive, her body was going along with it as if he was the answer to her recent sex drought. He wasn't.

'I'm not interested in The One who proposes to a random stranger in a random bar on a random Friday night in November. I'm not interested in anyone, you know that. I'm off men. Off relationships. Off getting my heart stamped on. For good. Right now, all I'm interested in is keeping this job so I can fund my design business and the night classes for the kids. Accepting marriage proposals or dating is lower on my to-do list than getting a root canal.' She hit the reconcile button on the till and frowned. 'And we're twelve pounds seventy-five pence down.'

'Ah, yes.'

She felt Sara's eyes on her. 'Ah, yes, what?'

Her friend nodded and her eyes grew sad as she leaned on the mop handle. 'Peter.'

'Oh, and here I was thinking you were going to give me a rational explanation as to why we're over twelve quid short' – Victoria shuddered at the mention of her ex's name – 'not bring *him* up. What about him?'

Sara's hand was now on Victoria's back, gentle. Supportive. 'He did a number on you, sure, but why you let that sleazebag have such an influence over you even now I don't know.'

'Er… because he taught me a very good life lesson: never trust anyone.' And never tell them your innermost secrets and doubts, because they'll use them against you when you least expect it.

'You were hurt, love. But you have to forget him and move on.'

'I am well and truly over him. To be honest, I don't think I ever really loved him, but just when I think I'm over all that – the expectation and the lost time – he parades his new fiancée in front of me as if he's just won the lottery and all I was to him was some sort of temporary booby prize.'

'Sleazebag. Although you do have a damned fine rack, girl-friend.' Sara laughed. 'And that is something I do know a lot about.'

'OK, enough already.' Laughing, Victoria caught a quick look of herself in the mirror behind the bar. Hair smooth, shiny and still in place. Lipstick also still in place. Cat eyeliner… perfect. Boobs enhanced by the dress she'd finished making this morning. Yes, she was looking good today. But she tried to look her best every day in the clothes she fashioned for herself – as a kind of walking showcase of her design talents. She wanted people to look at her clothes, to enquire about her dresses, maybe commission some vintage-inspired pieces.

And *he'd* been looking. She should probably take a proposal from a gorgeous man as a compliment, right? Just a compliment. 'I'm done talking about men. Past or present.'

'What about future?' Sara winked then laughed at Victoria's warning scowl. 'OK, OK, I get the message. No more men talk.'

Although, as Victoria finished closing up, her mind kept flashing back to the stranger's smile. The confidence in his stance. The way the linen shirt clung to his well-toned biceps…

And it occurred to her that she may be done *talking* about him, but she sure as heck wasn't done *thinking* about him.

CHAPTER TWO

THERE WAS NOTHING BETTER, Victoria mused as she sipped her takeaway coffee and felt the late-autumn sun gently warm her back, than mooching in Portobello market on a rare afternoon off.

Sure, she loved working in Chelsea, with its neat white terraces, and feeling of grandeur from the myriad high-end houses and guarded foreign embassies. She loved the sense of history from the three-hundred-year-old red-brick Chelsea hospital. Loved the new and the old of chain-store shops rubbing shoulders with quirky clothing stores, the sometimes daring offbeat clothes choices. The shock factor and yet the reassuring solidity of it all. Chelsea was her place. Her fit. She felt as if she was destined to have a shop right there. Had almost had one. But now she was back to square one with that plan. Thanks to Peter.

No. She wasn't going to ruin this lovely day with memories of plans gone awry. She was simply going to make new ones and put them into action instead. Starting today, by focusing on her designs and growing her vintage-inspired portfolio.

And while Victoria loved working and renting in Chelsea, she also adored exploring and shopping in Portobello market. A more earthy, gritty place with its diverse stores, hippy buzz and exotic smells of cuisines from around the world. To her, Portobello was the mischievous anti-authority younger sister to Chelsea's grown-up older sibling.

Walking down the hill from Notting Hill Gate she could barely control the fizzing in her stomach at the prospect of finding some amazing fabric or cute notions for her designs. At this end of Portobello Road, antique shops lined the street – their mysterious wonders spilling onto the pavements – before giving onto the beginnings of the outdoor market with back-to-back fruit and vegetable stalls brightened by flowers and gaudy Christmas decorations. Then, further along, at the gutsy, grungy Ladbroke Grove end, was the treasure trove of second-hand stalls and bric-a-brac. Also known as her kind of heaven.

The chatter of tourists and locals, the call of the stallholders and the hum of traffic combined to make an upbeat white noise, interspersed with the tinny blare of Christmas carols. She was in her happy place and the sun was shining.

She just wished she had Zoe, Lily and Malie – her oldest and dearest friends – here to share this. Her heart squeezed a little at the thought of them spread out across the world chasing their individual dreams. They rarely had a chance to be geographically close these days. But when they did, they always had such fun shopping together, laughing, getting ready for nights out.

That night.

Her throat tightened. That night had started just like any other. Four girls getting ready. The conversation was all about the make-up and dresses. Who had the highest heels, who could walk in them. It was about the laughter, the anticipation, about living. Oh, the excitement of a summer ball.

A chill peppered her skin. That night had changed everything:

who they were, what they wanted from life, who they'd become. Funny how one blindsiding split second could change you for ever.

Absentmindedly running a hand across her belly she pushed those thoughts away and, now desperate for some seriously uplifting retail therapy, quickened her pace to the first shop she was heading for – The Fabric Store. Popping her now-empty reusable cup into her handbag she pushed the door open.

Betsy, the willowy shop owner, looked up from her phone screen and smiled as Victoria walked in. ''Ello, love,' she growled in a deep voice that Victoria imagined was borne from years of chain-smoking or whisky-drinking, or both. 'Back again so soon? Looking for something in particular?'

'Not really, thanks, Betsy. Just browsing.' Yes, she came in here so frequently she was on first-name terms with the owner. Victoria's eyes settled greedily on the bolts of fabric stacked in rows and rows, lining the walls. 'And drooling.'

'Don't blame you. It's my slice of paradise is this place.' Betsy ran her palm over some quilting fat quarters as if they were her beloved offspring. Victoria sympathized. Only people who loved fabric, sewing and crafting could understand the allure of a pretty pattern or the soft stroke of well-made silk. Not even Malie, Zoe or Lily understood. But Betsy beamed, knowing she was talking to a kindred spirit. 'Not got your kids with you this time?'

Victoria's cheeks flushed. 'Oh, they're not my kids. They're my students. I'm teaching a fashion design class.'

'I knew you weren't old enough to have teenagers, but… well, you never know these days, do you? They seemed a nice bunch. Polite enough and didn't maul the goods with sticky fingers like some people do.'

What a refreshing attitude, compared to Paul's careful, warning one. Although, Victoria had schooled them in manners and fabric store etiquette before she'd taken them in there, hoping they wouldn't run amok amongst the shantung silk. In the end they'd done her proud.

'They are lovely kids. But some of them can't afford to buy fabric so I'm looking for any cheap samples, offcuts, any cute notions to brighten up some of the recycled clothes they're using.'

'Have a look through these.' With a grunt Betsy pushed a huge cardboard box out from behind the counter into the middle of the room. 'I'm just having a sort out, making room for a new delivery on Monday. There's lots of out-of-season ribbon, end-of-line and clearance stuff. I can let you have it on the cheap if it's for a good cause.'

'That would be amazing.' She looked at the box, overflowing with summery offcuts, Halloween fabrics and Easter-themed ribbons, and calculated a cost of well over thirty pounds for the lot. Not much to some people, but a big enough dent out of her salary – which wasn't much after rent on both her flat and design studio, and once living expenses were taken care of. She wobbled a little but then thought of how much those kids deserved a chance. 'I'll take it all.'

'Give me a tenner. I'm glad to see it go to a good home.'

'Wow. Thank you so much. That's very generous.'

'You spend enough in here as it is.' Betsy waved a hand as if it was nothing, but to Victoria's students it would mean the chance to realize their designs. Which in turn would give them the pride of achievement, of seeing their dreams and ideas become reality. More than anything she wanted them to learn they could dream big.

'This is gorgeous.' Victoria let a swatch of softest pale-blue cotton with a wispy white swirl pattern run through her fingers. In her mind's eye she saw her friend Malie wearing a simple halter-neck beach dress made of it as she lounged in the last rays of sun after a day's teaching at her surf school in Hawaii. One day, Victoria promised herself, she'd be successful enough to be able to afford to fly out there and have Malie teach her some surf moves.

She let the fabric drop as something deliciously sparkly caught her eye; the most exquisite double-weight ivory satin. The perfect tone for a wedding dress. She imagined it as a strapless bustier bodice embellished with light-catching crystals and the sheerest lace overlay, giving onto a waist-enhancing silhouette with floor-length skirt and train that glided as the bride floated down the aisle. Dramatic. Simple. Sophisticated. Modern yet timeless. It came to her as a fully formed idea, all she needed to do was sketch it to make it real.

'Oh,' she sighed. The satin was so shimmery and stunning it took her breath away. 'How much is this?'

'Lovely, isn't it?' Betsy's eyes grew almost as hungry as Victoria imagined hers to be. 'One hundred and thirty quid a metre.'

'A bit out of my price range right now.' Like, totally unafford-able. Victoria put it back quickly. But she snapped a quick photo of the label so she could put it on her vision board at home along with the design, once she'd done it – something to save up for. Something else. Along with the Hawaii trip to see Malie, paying for time off to go home to Devon to see Lily, and sticking a pin in a map and trying to meet up with globe-trotting Zoe.

'Vicki, love?' Betsy's gravelly voice distracted her from her reverie. 'Can you mind the shop while I nip upstairs to the loo? I'm the only one here at the moment and running close to desperate.'

'Sure thing. Grab a cuppa while you're there. I'm happy to stay a while. In fact, you're going to have to manhandle me out when it's closing time.' She made her way to the counter and found a little antique cigar box housing vintage hair accessories. A clip made from pearls set in a platinum petal shape caught her fancy. That would be perfect for Lily to hold her hair back while she worked in the restaurant.

Next she rummaged through some reduced-price fabric rolls and found some Italian white linen. It was cool to the touch, perfect for a floaty summer dress or... She swallowed at the image that had flitted through her head more than once, or twice, over the last few hours. A man's shirt.

His shirt.

The man she'd not stopped thinking about since last night. Which was stupid. So, so stupid. It wasn't as if they'd had much of a conversation.

And who proposed to a stranger like that?

And why? He hadn't been drunk. He hadn't looked desperate – far from it.

She needed a distraction. For the first time in for ever the creative mind suck wasn't working. She needed her friends. What time was it in... where was Zoe these days? It was hard to keep up. Mexico somewhere... She checked her world clock app. It was too early for Malie, but two out of three was better than none. A flutter of genuine pleasure floated through her as she tugged out her digital tablet and pressed the group chat button.

Lily answered immediately. Probably because she was in the

same time zone. More likely because, at two o'clock in the afternoon, things hadn't busied-up in her restaurant yet. Or were just quietening down after the lunch rush.

Her happy but slightly pink-cheeked face filled the screen. 'Hello, V! How come you're out and about on a Saturday?'

'It's only for a few hours. I'm back at the bar later. It's lovely to see you. How's things?'

'Er… Hello?' Zoe's green eyes came into view, then a cheek, her rosebud mouth. 'This had better be good. It's the middle of the night.'

'Oh. Sorry, I thought it was nine in the morning your time. Maybe my app's wrong.'

Zoe blinked, smoothed down her blonde hair and squinted at the screen. 'Nine. Yes. Also known as the middle of the night.'

'Sorry. Forgot you're an owl.' Victoria strained to see if there was someone in bed next to Zoe. The pillowcases were crisp white with embroidery on the edges. Expensive. Could Victoria see a shadow? An arm? Or was it just wishful thinking that Zoe would ever allow someone to see past her scars? Past the wheelchair?

Lily's eyes narrowed. 'Where are you, V? It looks dingy.'

'In a fabric shop in Portobello Road market. It's not dingy, it's heaven.'

Zoe rolled her eyes. 'I should have guessed it was going to be either material or the bar. You need to get some fresh air, my girl, you're starting to look like the living dead.'

Victoria laughed, but frowned. Was she pale? Maybe she should tune down the pale-but-interesting make-up a little. It was all part of her vintage vibe, but maybe she'd overdone it?

'I get fresh air. I've just walked up from Notting Hill Gate Tube station.' She eyed Zoe's grin and shook her head. 'We can't all flit from exotic beach to exotic beach reviewing hotels and resorts and getting paid for it. '

'Tough job, but someone's got to do it, eh?' Zoe yawned. 'Jealous much?'

'Only a little. I actually wouldn't want to do what you do, and you'd hate my job. You don't know one end of a sewing needle from the other.'

Zoe frowned, pretending to look bemused. 'There are ends?'

'Yes, and the pointy one is sharp. I love that we're all off doing what makes us happy.' Because there'd been a time when being happy had seemed a long way off for all of them. They'd all had to fight, in their own way, to grasp some kind of new normal and she was so proud of how far they'd come. 'Speaking of sewing, which I know we weren't, but humour me… Zo, here's some gorgeous hand-beaded rose-pink lace. I could make you a lovely dress for a soiree or dinner with the captain… or whatever it is you have to do.'

'That's on a cruise ship. Captain's table. Yes, please. Floor-length as always. Perfect. Anyone heard from Malie recently? She's not on this chat, is she? I can only see green dots on my screen for Lily and V. And Lily, are you outside somewhere?'

Lily laughed. 'No. I'm in my restaurant. We've been experimenting with the layout. Currently we're trying a living wall.'

Victoria squinted to look more closely. 'What on earth is that?'

'It's a wall of herbs behind the counter. Only, I'm not quite sure about the irrigation.'

'Irrigation?' Inside? This was all just a bit too confusing for Victoria's brain.

'The watering! OK, that's it, I'm moving into the kitchen.' There was a blur of movement and then Lily reappeared, as gorgeous as ever with two chopsticks pinning her dark hair up in a messy topknot, her eyes shining. 'That's better. Malie is fine. It's the real middle of the night in Hawaii right now, but we spoke yesterday after I'd closed up the restaurant. The surf school is going well. She seems happy out there.'

'So, V, what's happening in Chelsea these days?' Zoe stifled a yawn.

Proposals. Victoria leaned against a high stool behind the shop counter and mentally batted away the image of that gorgeous body gift-wrapped in white linen, although she couldn't hide the smile.

'Oh, the big gossip is that there's a new department store opening at the end of my road. All the locals keep coming into the bar to complain that it's going to take their business away. It's all doom and gloom which we don't need right before Christmas.'

'Maybe it'll be a destination store, bringing new customers to the area and everyone will win?' Lily, with her business head on, always saw the positive in everything.

'That would be great. Apparently, the owner's a real jerk and winding everyone up the wrong way. There's been problems with rubbish clearance or rather, lack of. That end of the street has looked like a bomb site for months. And any cars parked anywhere near their site entrance are clamped by some private firm that charges extortionate rates to release any vehicles – people have seen the owner popping out, looking at car number plates and then talking on the phone. Five minutes later the clamper arrives. Anyone wanting information receives a load of abuse.'

'Sounds like a nice guy. Not.'

'Well, it was Peter who was complaining, so maybe he was economical with the truth. Or, being Peter, he may just have rubbed the owner up the wrong way.' Victoria thought for a moment and grimaced. 'Two alpha-holes as neighbours. Great.'

Zoe sat up. 'You still see Peter? Why?'

Victoria shrugged, trying to stay upbeat. 'I don't have much choice. His shop is across the road from the bar.'

'You were supposed to have space in that shop to sell your amazing designs. Didn't he promise you that? That you'd go into partnership with him? Then you caught him making out with the retail assistant. Sleazebag. You should sue him for breach of contract.'

'It was only a verbal one.'

'And Lily should sue Alistair too.'

Victoria glanced quickly at Lily knowing this conversation was veering a little too intimately for Lily's liking. Her ex had run off with some of her cash and she'd never recovered it.

Lily shook her head, embarrassment infusing her cheeks. 'No way. I can't afford to go to a small claims court. Besides, I feel such a stupid fool, I don't want anyone else to know about it. Can you imagine how much gossipy Mrs Whittaker in the village would love to hear all about it? No. No way. Al's gone, as is the money. They're both sleazebags.'

'Seems to be the general opinion.' Victoria nodded, grateful for her friends' unwavering support. 'Yes, funny though, the bit that broke my heart wasn't catching him with another woman so much as seeing all those plans we'd made go down the drain. I finally thought I'd have retail space for my clothes – in Chelsea. Every fashion designer's dream. Oh, did I tell you he's now engaged to the girl he cheated on me with?'

'No! That was quick.' Zoe seemed wide awake now.

'Apparently, so he tells me – because he seems to think that I care – when you find The One, you just know.'

First Peter and then Sara going on about The One. So many people thinking The One was the be all and end all of their lives, Victoria thought, with a little pang in her chest. As if being single was such a problem. She liked it. She liked the freedom, liked not having to compromise or worry about what the other person was thinking. She liked making decisions for herself, doing what made her happy. Even if sometimes she did feel a bit… lonely.

'After six months together you deserved so much more,' Lily said.

'It took him that long to find out I wasn't The One. Go figure. Or maybe it was the fact that when I finally told him all about our accident – and I mean *all* and what that means for me, he couldn't run away fast enough.'

Stupid thing was, she'd come to terms with not being able to have kids. It had taken some time but she'd processed it. She'd thought she'd found someone who she could share a life with because he didn't want babies… until he did. And everywhere she'd turned she'd seen babies and bumps and she was left trying to process it all over again. The reminder of what she couldn't have hurt her hard.

'Oh, honey.' Zoe's voice softened. These women were the only ones who truly understood. They'd been there. They'd shared all of this, lived through it together. 'Shallow doesn't come close. You should be enough. You are enough.'

She was and she knew it. Victoria didn't measure her worth by whether or not she could have kids. Shame that someone else did. 'The thing is, I don't blame him for feeling blindsided. If I had an idea of a future all mapped out and I met someone who didn't fit that picture I'm not sure I'd stay with them.' Better being occasionally lonely than risking another heartbreak, or let down, or being made to feel... less.

'He could have been kinder. He shouldn't have cheated on you.' Zoe was always willing to go into bat for Victoria even after everything.

'I'm good. It's fine. Men are off the menu.'

'Amen to that.' Zoe nodded.

'Absolutely.' Lily picked up a wine glass and started polishing it. 'But what a low thing for Peter to do. V, if he doesn't like you for you and only for what you can give him, he's not the right person for you. Not being able to have children shouldn't matter a damn.'

'I do kind of feel like I'm an adoptive mum to all the kids I teach, though. My life is rewarding, it's full. I have fun. It's fine.' The more she said it, the more she'd believe it. But having a relationship end in such a spectacularly gross way as finding her boyfriend *in flagrante* with someone he'd really only just met, on Victoria's cutting table in her studio, had bitten into her ego a little. It felt as if he'd planned it somehow, to prove she wasn't *enough*. Inadequate. Defective.

Afterwards, he'd said Victoria had been the one in their relationship who hadn't been truthful and that she'd led him on and made him believe they had a future together and then she'd snatched it away when she'd confided her truths.

So, she couldn't have kids. Not everyone could. She wasn't the only person in the whole universe who couldn't. Although, he'd made her feel like some kind of defunct freak.

She dug deep to find more positives. 'And I have to say, the prospect of a new store stealing their customers has been driving all the shopkeepers to drink, so business has been booming. I haven't had time to think about Peter and any of that. I don't think we've ever been so busy. Well, that and the fact it's Christmas soon so we're getting a lot of office parties too.' Her mind travelled back to last night.

Proposal guy hadn't been with an office Christmas party. Maybe he'd been stood up? Maybe he'd just broken up with someone. Maybe… why did she care? He was only going to be like all the rest, in the end.

Men are off the menu. But window shopping wasn't.

Lily's mouth twitched. 'Is flirting off the menu? Because God knows, I miss that.'

'Ooh? Anyone in particular?' Victoria asked, grateful the attention had swung from her.

'Not yet,' Lily said. 'In a town where I know every single thing about every single man and their mothers? Not likely!'

Zoe nodded, eyes wide. 'Flirting is OK. Fine, in fact. Yes. Flirt away.'

'What about sex?' Lily asked as her cheeks pinked up again, and Victoria wanted to enquire as to why she was asking that specific question. Did Lily have something to share? Her friend smiled secretively. 'Just future-proofing.'

Victoria laughed, at least one of them was believing in a sexy future. That was good. 'I reckon sex is OK, too. But anything emotional or deep… not so much. Avoid hurt at all cost. Live for the moment, because we don't know how many moments we have left.'

'Hey! We have many, many, many moments left.' Zoe's face came into full focus, along with the spectre of her touch-and-go past. They all knew that life could be literally flipped in a second. 'We're going to keep on doing amazing things.'

Just at that moment the internal door creaked open and Betsy sauntered back in. 'Righty then, Vicki, what have I missed?'

Victoria jumped up, blew a kiss to her friends. 'OK, squad, got to go. I have serious shopping to do. Wish me luck.'

'Luck! Don't forget the lost hours!' they called together as she flicked her tablet off. The lost hours. Their code for *call me whenever you need me*. Good or bad. Emergency, excitement or exhilaration. A code born of an ill-advised trip to Ibiza before the accident, where they'd lost Zoe in a foam party for three hours. Ever since then they'd used it to mean… *we're here for you*.

She wished they were all here, and fit and healthy and not scarred from an accident she'd always feel guilty about.

She paid Betsy for the treasure trove of goodies in the cardboard box, reluctantly leaving the double-weight satin for another day, another life where she was rich and successful and deeply in love with a faithful man who loved her completely.

A woman could dream.

Huh. Maybe lugging a huge, heavy box across the market – and adding to the contents, just a little, as she passed interesting stalls with more sparkly things that seemed to call her name begging to be bought – down the Underground steps, onto the packed Tube train, then juggling it back up to fading daylight on an escalator in the middle of the crush of Saturday shoppers wasn't such a good idea. As she reached Sloane Square station's exit her fingers were going numb and her left bicep was starting to cramp.

Not far. Not far. All she had to do was make it to the bar, up the steps to her flat and then she'd be able to stretch those aching muscles.

She slowed as she turned the corner on to her street and came up alongside the huge building to her left, wrapped in white plastic, that had been the bane of the locals' lives for the last few months. A huge sign advertised *RUSSELL & CO GRAND OPENING DECEMBER 1ST!*

With rubble, construction debris and overflowing skips littering the pavement, and torn white plastic flapping in the gentle breeze revealing dirty windows, the new department store didn't look close to being ready for then, and secretly she hoped the grand opening might be delayed just a little longer – until the new year perhaps, so her neighbours could have decent pre-Christmas sales. OK, maybe not Peter. But she couldn't let her bitterness over him taint her friendship with the other shop owners.

She tried lifting the box higher in her arms to relieve the weight from her wrists, but it was so big it almost obscured her view. She raised her head and stuck out her chin to peer over the top but out of nowhere something big and hard *whapped* her in her side, forcing all breath from her lungs. The box in her arms lurched hard right, tipping her with it and suddenly her legs were whirling out of control and she was falling… the pavement coming up to meet her far too quickly.

Her breath caught tight in her lungs as she fell. 'Noooo!'

CHAPTER THREE

'Whoa! What the hell?' Heart thumping like rapid gunfire against his ribcage, Oliver flung his arms out, fighting to keep upright. Just. Adrenalin pumped through him and he twisted to see what had hit him.

To his left a squeaking, giant cardboard box juddered upwards and sideways – almost in slow motion, but not slow enough for him to stop it – then crashed into the gutter spilling its contents across the ground, spools of bright yellow ribbons wheeling into the road causing a black cab to brake hard, tyres screeching and crunching the plastic flat into the tarmac. The air filled with the smell of burning rubber. The driver tooted his horn and shouted something unrepeatable that would give Oliver's mother apoplexy.

What the hell? Chaos. Utter chaos.

Over in the gutter the box squeaked again. Oliver stepped closer to investigate. Sprawled underneath was a woman in a long, bright-blue winter coat and dark hat, her face obscured by a mask of cobwebs and skeleton bones.

'Damn. Andrew, I've got to go.' Ending the dysfunctional conversation he'd been having with his equally dysfunctional cousin he shoved his phone into his pocket and stepped over swathes of hideous yellow-and-white fabric decorated with grimacing Easter bunnies. He ignored the pain in his stomach from the collision with what he imagined to be the woman's elbow and called out, 'Hey. Hello? Are you OK?'

'No. No, I'm not.' Her voice was muffled underneath the Halloween fabric as she lay unmoving on the ground. It was almost dark now and he imagined she must be cold and possibly in pain lying there. So he was surprised when her words lashed out, 'You weren't looking where you were going.'

'I wasn't going anywhere. I was standing quite still on the pavement...' Or had he been pacing? He'd been angry, that's for sure. He'd been clenching his hand into a tight fist, he'd been holding his anger back by a thread, he'd been spitting out words through a very tight jaw. OK, yes, he may have been pacing. But if she knew that she might sue him for damages or personal injury. That was all he needed. A lawsuit on top of his cousin's mess. 'I was quite... still. Having a chat, minding my own business... are you OK? Do you need an ambulance?'

'I think...' Slowly, she stretched out her limbs one by one. Arms first, then legs. Long, shapely legs encased in thick dark tights, and he reminded himself she was an injured stranger so he shouldn't be admiring anything.

'I think I'll live. Just.' Her voice was strained, but a little softer as she tugged the fabric from her face, squeezed her eyes tightly closed and winced.

So did he. *Great.*

As if his day wasn't bad enough already. This was the woman from the bar last night. The one he'd proposed to, like the idiot he was. If she didn't sue him for actual bodily harm, she would probably sue him for psychological damage incurred by an awful, clumsy proposal. He deserved it.

He crouched down, thought about touching her head to check for fractures or grazes, considered that might seem a little forward, so simply said, 'Don't move. We need to check you're OK. Where does it hurt?'

'Everywhere.' Groaning, she put a hand to her hat and sat up, her warm brown eyes flickering open, then darkening in recognition. 'Oh. You. Just my luck.'

'Great. Thanks.'

'What are you doing here?' Her voice was wobbly, but he wasn't sure if there was a hint of insinuation there too. *Are you a stalker?* Or something. Something untrusting. She was wary and she had every right to be after his performance last night. He decided to keep things low-key.

'I work…' He waved his arm randomly towards the family shop. 'Here…'

She followed his arm and her eyes lost a little of their guarded wariness. 'Ah. On this street?'

'Yes.'

'Of course you do. That's why you were in the bar last night. We get a lot of locals in.'

'I popped in for a drink after work,' he explained, even though he didn't need to. She looked so pale he thought shock might be setting in. 'Come and sit down for a minute, get your breath.'

He offered his arm to help her stand but she shooed it off. Slowly easing herself upright she took in the steps to the department store and shook her head, eyes narrowing. 'I'm not sitting here. If the owner comes out and finds us on his steps, he might growl at us.'

I heard he has a terrible temper. I don't want to get on the wrong side of him if he's going to be my neighbour. The bar's just down there. It's two minutes' away.' But she blinked hard and swallowed and then stood stock still, her complexion chalk white. 'Actually, I do feel a bit dizzy. Maybe I need to sit down. I'll take a chance on the owner. He can't get mad at an injured woman, can he?'

Oliver wasn't so sure. If, by 'owner' she was talking about Andrew then he'd probably growl at a smiling baby. Safe to say his cousin didn't cope well with stress, or with things not going his way, or working to a schedule, or working full stop. Entitled didn't come close to describing him.

And now Oliver was fixing his mess. Again.

Something held him back from telling her that he was now in charge at the department store. He wasn't sure why he wanted to keep that from her other than he felt she'd take a stab at him if she knew, and he didn't want that. He didn't want her any more agitated than she already was. She'd hurt herself and needed to sit for a minute. He needed to make sure she was OK. Anything else could come later.

'I don't care what anyone thinks, we're going to sit you down.' Picking up the box he balanced it on one arm and, ignoring her mumbled words of *I'm fine*, which she clearly wasn't, he wrapped his other arm round her waist and steered her to the pale stone steps of the grand entrance. Then he sat her down and patted her back as she put her head between her legs. 'Do you think you need to go to hospital?'

'No. I'll be OK. I just need a minute. My heart's racing and I feel woozy, but that's the adrenalin. Shock. I've had it before.' She lifted her head to look at him. 'It wears off eventually, you just have to ride it out.'

'Oh? You've had it before?'

Her eyes drifted up as if she was remembering something very difficult and he wondered what had happened to her. Then she looked back at him. 'A long time ago.'

But significant enough to make her react like that and to mention it. 'You make a habit of barrelling into people?'

'No, I don't routinely launch myself at a man's feet.'

'Good to hear. Are we saying this was just an accident?' He didn't have the bandwidth of mental space or energy for any legal action. He looked at the mess of fabric and the battered box.

And so did she. Unfortunately. She seemed very attached to her box, he only hoped it didn't have something valuable underneath the hideous material.

'It wouldn't have happened if you'd been looking where you were going,' she threw at him.

'Ditto. It is a very big box. I'm surprised you could see over the top. If you could actually see over the top?' He let the insinuation hang there for a moment.

She had the good grace to look a little culpable and then smiled ruefully, her large dark eyes soft. 'Oh, OK, maybe we're both to blame.' She sighed, twisting round. 'Keep an eye out for the owner, in case we have to make a run for it.'

He hid his smile. 'Sure. What does he look like?'

'I have no idea.' A shoulder lifted. 'I've just heard things.'

Phew. Technically, Oliver wasn't the owner, his father was, although in time – soon, if his father got his way – Oliver would take over the business. 'What kind of things?'

'Apparently he has some deal with a wheel-clamping company and gets my friends' cars towed away on a regular basis. He's got the backs up of the local shopkeepers – everyone thinks this new fancy department store is going steal their business and some of them have approached him for a meeting. But instead of working with them to create community harmony he's refused to answer any calls or put anyone's mind at rest. And just look at the mess. There's rubble and rubbish everywhere. But will he clear it up? No.'

She was right. No matter how much he'd told the builders to clear up after themselves they always left the street dirty and the skip down the side street was overflowing.

He swore silently and made a mental note to try to repair some of the PR disaster Andrew had created. Just another thing to add to the ever-growing list. 'Surely he'd want keep the locals on side?'

'I guess it's just business to him, this fancy building is just another jewel in the mighty Russell crown. I've heard they're worth billions. But to these people...' She pointed to the clothes shop across the road and the jewellers' next door. 'It's their livelihoods, the money they make from selling their stuff puts food on their tables and pays for their kids' clothes. He doesn't seem to understand that. It's just profit and loss to him. There's a good local business network here, a great community spirit and he's stomping all over it.'

'Sounds like a piece of work.' *Sounds like Andrew.*

'Exactly. That's what I heard. Oh.' Her shoulders sagged as she stared over at the bent and broken spools which were crushed on the tarmac. 'My lovely ribbon. It's ruined.'

He hadn't bothered to pick up the dirty spools because they were too damaged. Plus, he couldn't imagine why anyone would be emotionally attached to something so hideous. 'I think you need to go to hospital. You might have a concussion.'

She frowned and ran a hand over her hat. 'I don't think I hit my head.'

'Are you sure? Because anyone who thinks that ribbon is lovely has something not quite right going on in there.' He gently tapped her hat and she laughed. The sound was light and frothy in the darkening night. The air was full of street noise: the hum of car engines, the screech and rattle of a bus, the chatter of shoppers, but he zoned into that bubbly laugh and something in his gut flickered to life.

'Wait.' He ran out into the road, dodging traffic to pick up the grubby ribbons. As he walked back he stole a moment to take her in. She was lit by a streetlight, her face so pale. Last night he'd been drawn to her fair complexion but today her skin was bloodless from shock. Sitting on his step, her knees hunched up, that huge coat swallowing her, she looked almost vulnerable – except for the light in her eyes that mesmerized him, and the sharp whip of her tongue that made him smile. And prickle with awareness. He held the ribbon out to her. 'Do you think it's salvageable? Would you even want to?'

'You're right, it is fairly ugly. But it's all I could afford. It's not for me, anyway. It's for my kids. Not *my* kids, obviously. I don't have any.' She shook her head quickly, then winced again, holding her arm across her belly. 'It's for my class. I teach fashion design. I needed some fabric because they couldn't afford it and Betsy gave me this on the cheap. And now I'm rambling. Great stuff, V. Maybe I do have a head injury.'

He couldn't help smiling. 'You're doing fine. Really. Hey, I saw someone unload a vanload of fabric earlier on and take it into that building.' He pointed to his store. 'I also noticed there's a door wedged open down the side street. Do you fancy sneaking in and seeing if they've left any lying around for you to… relocate?'

'What? Really? Steal some?' Her eyes widened in shock. 'What kind of an example would that be to my students?'

'I was joking.'

'That's a shame. You had me at vanload of fabric.' Her eyes sparkled. 'Does that mean there's going to be a haberdashery department, do you think?'

'Apparently.' *Third floor.* He shrugged, not wanting to give anything away.

'I hope there is. It's so close to where I live, I could pop in for anything I want. Just imagine, damask silk on tap. But that will also mean curtains for my bank balance.' The corners of her mouth tipped upwards at her own joke and she looked gorgeous. Even in the dusky light he could see the colour had started to return to her cheeks and her enthusiasm for bits of material made her eyes dance and shine.

'I'd love to have a sneak peek inside. Guess I'll have to wait until the grand opening.' She made quote marks with her fingers to emphasize the last two words. 'Although it doesn't look anywhere near ready. Maybe the owner's grumpy because he's woefully behind schedule.'

'Probably. It must be a mission to run somewhere like this.' He thought for a moment, wondered, should he? Why not? 'Look, I happen to know the security guard – d'you want to see if he'll let us in for ten minutes to look round?'

She frowned. 'Is the big boss around?'

'I'll check.' He picked up the battered box and walked her down the side road to the security entrance. Had a quiet word with Stan, then beckoned her in past the little security room filled with blank TV screens ready for the security camera system to be operational – another thing on his seemingly endless list of things to do. 'Stan said we're good to go in. He can look after your box too. Just leave it here.'

With an excited smile she thanked Stan, then Oliver led her through the dark, dusty warren of corridors that took them past staff lockers and changing rooms, the huge electricity transformer room and the service lifts.

'Wait, er…' She'd lowered her voice to an excited whisper, her breath on his neck as she closed in behind him. Her scent curled around him, making him inhale, sharply eager for more. Fresh. Feminine. Attractive. Like her. She was pretty, funny and soft at the edges with a sharp tongue. She wasn't guarded, she appeared to be a *what you see is what you get* woman… and he liked what he saw. She also smelled good. Something primal spiked inside him as she bit her bottom lip and said, 'This is embarrassing, but I don't even know your name.'

He took a step away from her, removing himself from the proximity that was causing his body to react. He couldn't admit who he was now, could he? Not when he'd managed to calm her down and promise an adventure that would make her forget the bump to her body and the destroyed hideous ribbons.

He just hoped Stan wouldn't give the game away, because then he'd have to tell her who he really was. And then she'd leave.

And he didn't want that particular refreshing bubble to burst just yet.

CHAPTER FOUR

'SORRY. OLIVER. OLLIE. WHATEVER.' He stuck out his hand deciding not to fill in the surname gap unless she asked.

She fitted hers into his and shook firmly. 'Oliver. Nice to meet you. Do you work here in the store? Is that how you know Stan and your way around?'

'Yes. Yes, I do.' Her hand was warm and the touch of her skin against his made something in his gut unravel.

'So, you know the boss?' Her voice was tentative, possibly regretful as she let go of his hand.

'Yes.' Not a lie.

'And you let me say all that stuff about him?'

'Just letting you vent. He does tend to have that effect on people.' He tried for a smile, looking into her eyes and trying to interpret what she was feeling. Her eyes were dark but not angry. She looked, more than anything, intrigued.

'What's he like?' she asked, her voice still low.

'Like you said. Grumpy.' *Disappointing.* 'But I think he's working on it.'

'Sounds like he needs to.'

Oh, he does. He waited for her to follow him through the door and out onto the ground-floor retail space. It wasn't finished, not even close, but with only a few of the concession stands in place you could better see the crystal chandeliers, the huge windows, the walnut parquet flooring imported from France and the renovated columns. Quite frankly, it was magnificent. The jewel in Russell & Co's crown. Or it would be, once he'd put his stamp on it.

She brushed past him into the floor space and gasped. 'Wow. It's huge.'

'Three buildings knocked into one. Not something that happens much these days, especially in Chelsea… so I understand. Obviously, we have some clearing up to do before the rest of the concession stands set up. But a lot of the other floors are almost ready. We have jewellery and watches at the rear of this floor, fashion on floors one and two. Toys and children's wear on floor three, with haberdashery at the back.' His heart took a punch as she smiled at that. He'd never given fabric a single thought other than what his shirts were made of. Funny how she seemed to be delighted by it. 'Kitchenware and linens on floor four along with a restaurant. The chef's got two Michelin stars.'

'Wow. I didn't think it'd be so impressive. You'd never know from the outside. The windows are filthy.'

'Window cleaning is happening first thing Monday.' Along with organizing the installation of the point of sale computer system, wifi, most of the restaurant fixtures and fittings, setting up the back offices for HR, the training space and meeting rooms, and a million other things Andrew hadn't got around to organizing. 'Oh, and the whole place is almost exclusively powered by solar panels on the roof.'

But Victoria was oblivious. Her mouth gaped as she looked up at the lighting, the myriad different-sized globes looking as if they were floating in mid-air. 'Those chandeliers are stunning.'

'Italian. Handblown,' he said, then winced. He kept giving too much information away.

But she didn't really seem to care. 'How do you know that? Are you involved in the refit?'

'Yes, I am.' That wasn't lying either, he just didn't need to admit exactly how much he was involved. He took her to the main window, currently shrouded in builders' dust. 'We have heavy velvet drapes to hang. Twelve feet... that's a lot of fabric. There's going to be a ten-foot Christmas tree in that corner. And we're doing a fun winter display here.'

'Like Selfridges do every year? I always make a special effort to go there and see what they've done. It's always magical.'

'Something like that. A fairy-tale theme... but that's all I can tell you.'

'Oh' She whirled round to him. 'Why?'

'Trade secrets. I might have to make you sign confidentiality agreements and everything.' He tapped his nose and winked. 'You might be a mole for the competition. And if you are, I could get the sack.' In truth, very unlikely given he was the heir of this empire. The empire he had never wanted.

'I think moles tend to keep under the radar not knock you down on the street and make a huge impression.' She blinked and looked away, her cheeks going a shade of hot pink. 'I didn't mean—'

'Ah, but maybe you're using underhand tactics. You could be double-bluffing me.' She'd made an impression all right. 'And now you admit it was your fault?'

'Not at all. You should have been looking where you were going.' She laughed and raised her palms. 'I'm not a mole for anyone, honestly. Unless you count me knowing all the local business owners. Most of them are regulars at The Landing.'

'Ah. Yes.' For a moment he'd allowed himself to forget that, enjoying, instead, watching her delight in his store.

'It's going to be fabulous.' But she turned a little sad as she took off her hat and scrunched it in her hand. Her hair cascaded over her shoulders. Lush and shiny and a deep rich mahogany that made him ache to touch it. 'What's wrong?'

She looked round the room and sighed. 'It's amazing. It really is, but pretty much everything they're going to sell here is what people can buy on the street outside. Including food from some decent restaurants and cafés. I just wish…'

'What do you wish?'

She walked back to the window and looked out at the street. 'That one business wouldn't detract from a dozen others.'

'A shiny new department store and all its advertising and PR will bring more people into the area.' He stood next to her and rubbed his suit jacket cuff on the dusty glass. The road was a hive of different shops, cafés and retail outlets – some old and established, some new, some standing empty. It had the feel of jaded glory, an area living on the coattails of its past. The place needed as much refurbishment as this building had. 'It will enhance and revive the street.'

'That's what Lily said too.'

'I don't know who Lily is, but she could be right. It's how economies work. It's the way of things.'

His parents and their parents and grandparents before them had worked hard to build this business from a small shop in Manchester to a retail powerhouse with stores in all the major UK cities and in Europe. It had required hard work and astute business sense and he'd taken it all for granted until recently.

Over the last few months he'd watched his parents grow old almost overnight. His father's diagnosis had made Ollie rethink his priorities. He wanted to make this business a continued success. He wanted them to be proud of him. But… he didn't want to put other people out of business.

Victoria nodded. 'Lily's one of my best friends. She's very business savvy. You'd get on well with her.'

He wasn't interested in her friend. But Victoria on the other hand… He stopped his thoughts right there. He couldn't be interested in Victoria either. Could he?

No. After the shambles that was his last relationship, he'd sworn off anything deeper than a paper cut. Besides, he was up to his neck in his cousin's mess and had no time or energy to spend on a relationship. Not even a first date – and he got the feeling she was the whole two point four kids and a dog type. Nothing wrong with that at all, it just wasn't his thing.

But he was going to enjoy this light interlude from his awful day, while he could.

'Right. The show's nearly over but come upstairs. There's something you might like up there.'

She gave him a side eye. 'Oh? Are you sure it's OK? No one's going to growl at us?'

'If they do I'll growl right back.'

'That, I would love to see. I don't want to trespass or get you into trouble. Unless…' She laughed and her eyes shone. 'Is there fabric involved?'

'There could be…'

She nodded. 'In that case, I'm prepared to growl back too.'

'And that's sure to scare them.' He couldn't imagine this kind-natured woman growling at anyone – sure, he'd seen her firm and polite and taking none of his rubbish in the bar last night. But growling? Never. For some reason he had a ridiculous urge to hold her hand. He wrestled back some sadly lacking self-control. 'We'll either have to walk up the back stairs or take the service lift as the main escalators aren't operational yet.'

'Stairs.'

Relief flooded through him. He was starting to think it was safer to be in large open spaces with Victoria than enclosed ones where he could smell her light flowery perfume, and want to breathe it in. Deeply. 'OK, stairs it is. Three floors. You sure about this?'

'Absolutely.'

They walked through the maze of walled-off corridors to the wrought iron staircase that curled up the inside of the building. As he climbed, he ran his hand over the metalwork, shiny from years of use.

She followed, her fingers skimming the iron. 'This is gorgeous. Is that a bird?'

'Search me.' He peered closer to the detail on the balustrade which had been forged into a tree shape with branches reaching from floor to handrail. And sure enough, there were birds of all shapes and sizes. 'Looks like it. I've never noticed before.'

'Mr Observant. Not.' She chuckled and bent to take a closer look. 'I'm a details girl. I love patterns and shapes and colours. I love discovering the secrets the artist puts in their work, a part of themselves. Their wishes, dreams, hopes. And sometimes their difficulties too. Look, here's a sparrow and a robin and... I don't know much about birds, to be honest, but they're beautifully crafted.'

'I hadn't realized there was so much involved. It was always just a stair rail to me.' Had been. Now she'd opened his eyes. What else had he missed? He looked up at the high ceilings and the crafted plasterwork and realized he hadn't noticed them before either. He'd walked through this building countless times, focusing on what they were trying to create, without looking at the gems that were already here.

He put his hand on the rail, but his fingers brushed against hers. Heat zipped over his skin and he turned to look at her. A little breathless, her cheeks pink from the exercise – or something else? Her eyes caught his and something flickered in her gaze. A flash of matching heat?

Had she felt that buzz too?

He didn't wait to find out and pushed open a door onto the third floor and walked through the back of the children's wear department. Racks of high-end clothes lined the aisles. Red and silver gift-wrapped Christmas boxes filled huge baskets for small hands to pick. Thick garlands of silver tinsel hung in loops across the ceiling and silver sparkly reindeer had been strategically placed in groups, for patting. The place smelt of fresh paint, builders' dust and new carpet. There was no one else there apart from the electric gaffer who was fixing the lighting.

'Oh. This is much better than the ground floor. It looks like a proper shop up here. I'm really getting the festive vibe. The kids are going to love it.' Her hand trailed over the back of one of the reindeer and she smiled.

But then she quickened her pace and – almost as if she knew exactly where she was going – raced past the little babygros and bib sets, breezed by the wicker baby baskets and changing tables and headed into haberdashery. She paused at the entrance and breathed deeply, her eyes dancing with light. Her hand fluttered over her chest and she looked as if she was actually going to cry from happiness.

There were more deliveries arriving by the hour but so far the head of haberdashery had managed to set most of the area up, with an emphasis on holiday-themed fabric and glittery balls of wool at the entrance. Further in were dark mahogany shelves of patchwork fabric, bolts of bright colours giving over to pastels. A whole bridal section, sewing machines and books, and at the back was yarn and all the sewing accessories people needed.

In hindsight Oliver didn't think he'd ever even walked in here until now, but it was clear Victoria had found her happy place. 'Now this, Oliver, is going to mean the start of a whole new...' She beamed at him and he wondered what she was going to say. *Friendship? Relationship?* His gut tightened at that thought.

'Overdraft.'

He laughed, only a little in relief. 'I wondered where you were heading with that.'

'Me too.' She confessed with a blush then quickly drew her eyes from his. 'Seriously, the only thing I'd sell my soul to the devil for is fabric.'

Her enthusiasm was infectious, but he didn't get it. 'Sure, the fabric's kind of nice, maybe, but... why?'

'Heathen!' With a sharp intake of breath she softly punched his shoulder. 'What do you mean *why*? Look at it. It's like magic.'

'How? You just sew stuff together, right?' Of course, he knew that wasn't the case. He'd been to enough tailors to know the process… measuring, cutting, sewing, adjusting. But he'd taken it all for granted. Seemed he'd been doing a lot of that recently; this building, his parents, his job, his good fortune.

Geez, suddenly he was getting a conscience or something.

Shaking her head, she picked up a wad of different-patterned squares. 'This is a fat quarter. It's for making patchwork quilts. Nothing special here, right? Just a mixture of blue colours. But look closer; some of the patterns are a bit wavy, some look like bubbles. Some have images of little fish on them. In a few hours of "just sewing stuff" I can turn the dark blues into boats, use the bubbles as the sea, the fish as… fish.' She laughed and rolled her eyes. 'I add a backing and some wadding between the two layers and little Johnny not only has a cute cover to keep him warm, but he can wear it as a cloak and pretend he's the King of the Ocean. Little Julia can be the Queen of the High Seas, a pirate, a mermaid. She can nestle under it when she's sick, when she's watching her favourite movies, she can sit on it with her friends and chat about everything from teddy bears to boyfriends and later, when she's leaving home for the very first time, she can take it with her to her university dorm and slide under it that first scary night, a little anxious, a little homesick. But she has brought with her hours, days, years of memories, of being warm, of being safe, of dreaming. And if I'm the aunty who makes this for them, I sew every stitch with love. I imagine them loving this as much as I love them. I know… *I know* the pleasure they will get from it. The comfort. Knowing he will be safe under this. That she will carry my love with her wherever she goes… in this. This scrap of fabric.'

He blinked trying to keep up as she spoke, her hands moving fast, spreading the fabric out, shaping the squares into a larger square, then a larger one. He imagined she'd done it so many times before, deciding what to make, how much love to pour into this garment, or the next. She turned the mundane into something extraordinary. She was unlike any woman he'd ever met. He breathed out, hard. 'Wow.'

Her hands finally came to rest at her chest. 'Yes, Oliver. Wow.'

'And you do this?'

'As much as I can. I'd love to do it full time, but it doesn't pay enough yet. I have to make the rent and eat and that means I need a steady job in the real world. Hence… I'm a bar manager.'

'I thought you were a teacher who moonlighted in The Landing. I heard you talking last night about a class you taught and something about a stolen iPad.'

'Ah. Yes. That was an issue for Jasmine but we sorted it out. I'm not a qualified teacher, but I teach underprivileged kids in my spare time.' Her eyes flitted over his shoulder and her mouth opened slightly. 'Oh! Serendipity. I just saw this in a shop in Portobello market. It's exquisite.'

Ah, yes. He knew what this was. About the dreams and hopes imbued into this particular material. 'It's wedding dress fabric.'

But her eyes narrowed a little. 'Ooh? Allergic to weddings?'

Had he been grimacing? He hadn't realized. 'It's just not something I see in my future.'

'Me neither.' And was that relief he saw in her features? She shook her head. 'But I'm working on a bridal collection at the moment. This satin would be perfect.'

'Do you have a shop too? How do you sell?'

'No shop. Nearly…' She shook her head, her nostrils flaring and her mouth tightening. 'Nothing. Never mind. I sell online at the moment and by word of mouth.'

He wanted to get to the bottom of what that look was, but he got the feeling she wasn't going to just blurt it out. She'd stiffened at the mention of a shop. Something had happened there.

Her hand hovered over the ivory satin – at least, that was what it said on the label, he didn't have a clue, but thought he remembered from somewhere that satin was shiny. 'Oliver, I don't suppose you get staff discount? *No!* No, I'm being cheeky. That was rude and presumptuous. Sorry. You don't even know me. Forget it.'

'No problem.' He shrugged. 'I do get a discount, though. I can find out.'

'Seriously. No.' But she was still stroking the fabric as if it were her first-born child and she didn't want to leave the store without it.

'OK, but I can still ask.'

'Well…' She pressed her lips together and he knew she wanted to say yes but was trying to be polite, or maybe didn't want to be beholden to him. Just at that moment one of the electricians walked by with a stepladder under one arm. He nodded towards Oliver. 'Evening, Mr Russell.'

And Oliver's stomach plummeted.

'Mr Russell?' She gaped, confusion playing across her eyes. 'Mr *Russell*? You're related to the boss?'

Of course, he wouldn't have kept the pretence up for ever, just a couple more minutes before he told her the truth.

He hauled in a breath to finally come clean, oddly disappointed his undercover stint had to end. He'd been enjoying it, he realized with a shock. It had been so easy not to have the agenda that came with being part of his well-known family. 'Victoria, I am the boss.'

She let the fabric drop from her hand. 'You're the owner? The one who keeps towing cars away? Who's allowed the street to become a rubbish dump?'

'Actually, no, that's my cousin Andrew. I've just stepped in to clear up his mess.'

'You've obviously got a lot of work to do. Wow, indeed. Right. I'll leave you to it.'

She whirled round and started to walk away. The joy he'd seen in her a few moments ago washed away by anger. Or mistrust. Or something he wanted to erase.

'Wait. Please. Victoria. Why are you angry?'

She sheered round to look at him, her eyes sparking fire. 'Because I don't like being made to look like a fool.'

'That wasn't my intention. But who did you think I was?'

'I don't know. A sales manager? Something to do with the building work. I don't know. I didn't think you'd be... You should have been upfront about it instead of acting like we're on a silly adventure somewhere we're not supposed to be. There you are pretending to be someone you're not and now I look stupid and gullible.'

Hell. No. 'Not at all. God, I'm sorry. What can I do to make things right?'

Her hands hit her hips. 'Oh, I don't know. Try being honest?'

'I never lied. You just believed what you wanted to believe. If I'd said, "Hey I own this place, do you want to come and look?" would you have?'

She looked uncomfortable. 'Probably. Maybe.'

'Unlikely, right? After telling me how godawful the boss was? About how hated he is? After complaining about me taking everyone's livelihoods away?'

She shook her head. 'Being economical with the truth is tantamount to a lie in my book. But you don't really care, do you? You don't care about the truth, you don't care about trampling over people. You can hide behind your cousin, but Russell & Co doesn't care about what it does to the little people as long as your bottom line is healthy.'

So much for thinking she wasn't the growling type. He'd misread her and what was important to her. 'You have got it all wrong. We have a strong commitment to the community.'

An eyebrow rose. 'Prove it.'

'But...' *How?* 'We donate generously to charities.'

'Lovely. But you don't get your hands dirty. Prove that you care about *this* community, Oliver Russell. The people on this street. Your neighbours. Prove that you care about making a difference. Here.'

As if he didn't have enough on his plate before opening day and then Christmas, Boxing Day sales, then New Year's... Easter. An image of flattened, grubby bunnies floated through his head and that was exactly how he felt: flattened and grubby. He should have been honest from the get-go. 'How?'

'Oh, I'm sure you'll think of a way.' She turned away and he knew he was going to lose her and this bubble of fun was well and truly burst. What's more, his reputation would be grubby too once she told her friends.

What surprised him the most, though, was that he cared that he'd hurt her. Her back was stiff and straight, her shoulders taut. Her mouth set in a grim line. She meant it. She expected him to do good by her friends and to keep his word. She expected him to be the better guy. And something about that made him want to be.

His mind scrolled through a number of possibilities and ideas. Why it was so important to him to make her happy, he couldn't fathom. But there it was; he felt bad and he wanted to make amends. He wanted to ensure this community she was so fond of didn't suffer just because his family put a store in their street. Damn it, she made him want to care even though all his training had been about what was best for the business. 'Look, why don't we do something on opening day to showcase the community?'

She stopped walking. 'What kind of thing?'

He thought fast. What was popular at the moment? What did they need? A germ of an idea seeded itself. 'Pop-up stalls for the local merchants. A space for everyone to advertise their shops. Guest food stands. Designers. The jewellers' and the bead shop, the florist… anyone who's interested.'

She turned to look at him, her frown softening. 'That might work. It'd be a start at least.'

She wasn't going to let him off the hook and hell, it was going to be a nightmare to organize at such short notice… if at all. 'Great. I'll arrange a meeting with the business network first thing Monday.'

'Excellent first step.' For the first time since she'd found out who he was she smiled. But it wasn't exactly warm, and it didn't reach her eyes. 'After you've cleaned your windows.'

CHAPTER FIVE

YOU SHOULD HAVE BEEN *upfront*.

Victoria put her pencil down, scrunched her hair into a topknot and secured it with a hair tie. She pulled tight, the sharp sting on her scalp mirroring the sharp sting in her gut. It was the sting of confusion. Because she could hardly blame Oliver, really. She'd been pretty vocal about what she'd heard, and therefore thought about the owner, so he would hardly want to introduce himself on the back of her scathing description, would he?

But there she was, being too nice, again, giving him the benefit of the doubt. And that kind of attitude had got her into enough trouble in the past. She looked out of her studio window and tried to breathe in some calm, but she couldn't settle, and she knew exactly why…

You should have been upfront.

Words Peter had slung at her when she'd finally plucked up the courage to admit her deficiencies. She, more than anyone, knew how not being upfront could lead into all kinds of dilemmas and problems and, ultimately, a broken heart and lost dreams of a shared shop, a shared future. All Oliver had been doing had been playing her a little.

Now she almost felt guilty about being cross with him. *Almost.*

But he'd allowed her to believe that he worked there, not that he was the billionaire son of a billion-pound retail empire.

God, what she could do with some of that money; she wouldn't be holding design classes in her flat, that was for sure, she'd be holding them in a proper after-school classroom that she'd set up, she'd be buying decent fabric supplies, she'd be out making contacts with people in the business and getting her students decent internships and proper jobs, with better futures.

She stared down at the designs in front of her. The ones she hadn't added anything to for days. She'd stewed on Oliver all through Sunday and now here she was, Monday morning, with nothing to show for the precious free hours she'd had.

A ring of the doorbell broke her reverie. As it was too early for anyone to be setting up downstairs in the pub and therefore able to answer the door, she sent a silent thank you to the caller for the welcome distraction and ran down. As she flung the door open a blast of frigid air hit her. She tugged her robe around her more tightly and looked outside, but there was no one there. Who had knocked?

'Ah. That's all I need. Designer's block and now some stupid prankster too.' She was just about to shut the door when a package wrapped in plain brown paper, on the step below, caught her eye. 'What's…?'

She picked it up and unwrapped it only to have metres and metres of the beautiful satin wedding fabric she'd adored on Saturday running through her fingers. There must have been hundreds and hundreds of pounds' worth. No message. But she knew exactly who it was from: Oliver Russell.

'Typical! You can't buy me, Russell!' Irritation rushed through her as she leaned out into the fresh air to see if he was there somewhere watching, waiting, or hiding. But no one was there. No one, apart from a huddle of schoolkids shuffling past, looking at her and staring, then laughing at the crazy woman in her PJs shouting at nobody in particular.

An hour later she was outside his office on the fifth floor, a floor she hadn't even realized was there, her lovely black suede heeled Mary Janes making footprints in the dust. Luckily, Stan had recognized her, believed her pretence that she had a meeting with his boss and let her in, or she doubted she'd have made it over the security door threshold. But that didn't mean she was any closer to actually speaking to Oliver.

'I'm sorry…' A pleasant young woman behind a large reception desk smiled, although it didn't reach her pale eyes. 'Mr Russell is very busy. If you haven't got an appointment he won't be able to see you today.'

Victoria put the bolt of satin onto the desk and smiled sweetly at the woman. 'Tell him I have a bad concussion and it's all his fault for knocking me over and if he doesn't come out here soon, I'm going to sue him.'

'What?' The woman blinked quickly.

'Please tell Mr Oliver that I will sue Russell & Co for reckless endangerment. He knocked me over, you see. Outside, as I tried to negotiate the footpath that is littered with Russell & Co's rubbish. I have photographs of the debris. It's everywhere.' OK, it was a bad thing to do, but needs must. In reality, she had no intention at all of suing him, she didn't have a headache and definitely no concussion, but if he could be economical with the truth so could she. And if shocking this receptionist into action was the only way to get her face to face with Oliver then that's what she would have to do. 'Do I get my lawyers to send the papers here or should I just meet him in court? It will be so costly for the business. And for your job, too, I imagine. If they go bankrupt.'

The woman went a shade of green. 'Well… he said not to bother him. He's so busy… but—'

'Of course, I'm sure it could all be smoothed over if I could just speak to him. Two minutes of his time, that's all I need.' Victoria suppressed a smile. Who knew she was so good at acting? 'Or I could give you the number of my lawyer?'

'Oh.' The receptionist jumped from her chair and scurried down a corridor. There was the sound of raised voices, a moment of silence and then Oliver appeared. Dressed in a dark navy suit with a pale-blue linen shirt he looked every inch the heir apparent. Also… drop-dead cologne-ad gorgeous. In a surly kind of way. He wasn't smiling but he wasn't frowning either. In fact, it was hard to interpret the look on his face. Then it came to her… hassled, busy, tired. His features were strained. But still gorgeous. Still compelling her to look.

'Victoria? Oh, you got the fabric. Excellent.'

She bundled it into her arms and handed it to him as her heart squeezed to see it go. 'No. Just no.'

But Oliver handed it back to her. 'Keep it. It's a peace offering.'

'Oh, it's so beautiful, I'd keep it if I were you,' the receptionist said, as she took her seat again, obviously waiting for a showdown about a concussion and not about double-weight satin, given the surprised look on her face as her eyes went from the fabric, to Victoria, to Oliver and back to the fabric.

'It is exquisite.' Victoria sighed. 'But I can't accept it. I just can't.'

If he'd given her jewellery or even money it would have been far easier to return, but he'd hit her right in the feels, where he knew he'd have the most effect. Oh, he was a canny businessman. Astute indeed. He clearly wasn't going to take it from her, so she put the bundle back on the counter and, as she did so, felt the satin stroke across her skin. Divine. Yes. Beautiful. Yes. But she was giving it back. Oh, how stupidly selfless of her. 'Please, take it back.' *Before I change my mind.*

He shook his head sharply. 'It's an apology and a thank you gift. First rule of gift-taking. You can't return it.'

He was right about that. She'd been brought up to accept things in the manner they were given but this was different, she felt as if she was being bought. His economy with the truth wasn't worth this amount of fabric. 'A gift for what?'

'Let me explain. In my office.' His voice was all efficiency and big bad boss as he turned to the side and put his hand out for her to walk ahead of him down the corridor. When they reached a door with his name on, he held his hand out again. She followed him into a vast corner office that was light and airy with views across the city. Almost filling one window was a huge mahogany desk and in another corner two expensive-looking leather couches were separated by a small glass coffee table. So far, so traditionally corporate.

The floor-to-ceiling windows shone and as she looked out she could see two men on a suspended platform one storey down, rubbing away at the grime on the glass. She hid a smile and said nothing.

Oliver offered her a very comfortable-looking plush leather seat to sit on as he said, 'I spoke to the chair of the business network first thing this morning and he's canvassed a few of your friends already. Looks like we will be hosting them on opening day by way of a huge pop-up market stall in the centre of the ground floor.'

She nodded, the smile spreading through her body as she sat. 'You're going to make it happen?'

A curt nod. 'We're going to make it happen. I see it as the beginning of an exciting new partnership.'

'What? Between you and me?' Her heart hammered a little and she had to put a palm over her chest to stop it.

He smiled then and with that one little adjustment the strain in his face seemed to smooth away. He was back to the gorgeous man who'd shown her around the store, looking completely delighted by the birds on the iron railing and who had watched her face so intently as she'd walked into his haberdashery department.

His haberdashery department, *his* iron rail. King of everything here, she reminded herself. He raised his palm. 'Don't look so horrified. I mean a partnership between the business network and Russell & Co. I think it will benefit everyone. In fact, it's going to be excellent PR for us all and it's thanks to you. So please, take the material. It's yours now. Unlike this store I have a zero returns policy.'

'OK. Well, I suppose no one else would want it after it's been cut.' Although there was far more yardage than she needed for one dress. But she could use it as a feature fabric in some of the other clothes in her collection. A skirt for one, a bodice for another. Ideas began to crystallize for the first time since Saturday. She needed to go start drawing them. Excited at creativity returning she stood and turned to go. 'Thank you.'

But his hand was still in the air. 'Actually, there is something else.'

'Oh? What?' For some odd reason an image of him nursing that whisky the other night flitted through her head. The heat of his gaze and that deep unspoken connection they'd had just for a moment washed through her again. And she realized there was a part of her that was hoping for the something else to be more personal.

His fingers steepled. 'The runway show for your students… have you arranged anything yet?'

'How do you know about that?' Still clutching the satin, she sat back down.

'You were talking about it in the bar. How everyone was already booked up and you didn't want to let your students down.'

'You heard all that?' He'd been listening?

He shrugged. 'The awful music had stopped and the place was empty. Your voices carried.'

'I see.' When had she become so mistrusting? But she knew the answer to that… it was when she found her ex with someone else. Having her dreams fall apart just when she'd started dreaming again.

Oliver's eyes widened. 'Have you arranged anything yet?'

'No. I've made more calls, but no one's interested.'

'Then you can hold it here. I can invite some of my friends. Fashion friends,' he explained. 'I know people.'

'Which people?' Despite herself excitement rippled through her. This could be an awesome opportunity. 'Really? Here?'

'We host runway shows all the time in our stores. We have a big commitment to up-and-coming designers. It's good to be at the forefront of the industry and it brings a different demographic in. Russell & Co would like to extend an invitation to your students to bring their designs here.'

Imagining their excitement, she couldn't wait to tell them this news. 'That would be awesome. Thank you. Thank you. That's very kind.'

'It's business.' He smiled. 'I've spoken to the floor manager and we'll get something sorted. Opening day? A gala reception and a runway on the fashion floor.'

But at what cost? 'Everything comes at a price. You've done enough already.'

'No. Really. It's PR.'

It was more than that. It was a chance she had to grasp for her students' sake. 'That's a huge effort… the pop-up stores *and* the runway.' But something didn't quite add up. She'd asked him to prove that Russell & Co cared but this was far beyond her expectations. 'Why do you want to do this for me? Us?' she quickly corrected herself.

'Consider it a first step in repairing the damage my cousin Andrew has wreaked here.'

'But it's too much.'

'So, spread the word about Russell & Co. Please. About the opening day. We need everyone here.'

'Of course. Absolutely. My students will be thrilled.' She imagined a catwalk stretching across a floor, bifurcating concession stands of brands such as Versace and Stella McCartney. And there in the middle of such esteemed designers would be Nisha's designs, Jasmine's, and Billie's. 'This will be so special for them. There must be something I can do in return?'

He glanced at his feet, rocked back on his heels. Then his eyes met hers. Grey-blue the other day, she noticed they changed a little with his mood. Now they were darker, slate. 'Actually, there is something I'd like to ask you, Victoria.'

Ah, now came the crunch. Nothing ever came free and she'd been silly to expect anything different from Mr Retail Mogul. Laughing, she held up her hand. 'For the record, I'm not going to marry you.'

'It's not that.' His gaze held hers and she couldn't read him. 'Not... exactly.'

What the actual hell? 'What do you mean, *not exactly*?'

'I need a favour. I need someone to be my... girlfriend at the opening day.'

A small part of her heart fluttered. The part that belonged to the eighteen-year-old girl before the accident. The one with dreams and hopes. She stamped it out. Those kind of dreams weren't for her.

The laughter died on her lips. He was serious? 'Let me get this right. You need a girlfriend for an event two weeks away? That's a very odd thing to ask. Is it just for the one day?'

'Yes.' He seemed certain about that.

'Why? I mean, if you want to take a woman on a date surely the normal thing to do is just invite them out and see how it goes. Not ask them about a thing in the future. What if we don't like each other? What if we don't get on? I can't commit to something weeks away. Other than you proposing to me, we don't know each other at all.'

She tried not to think about those muscles, or the way his eyes softened when he wasn't trying hard to be a businessman. The buzz of awareness as their fingers had brushed together. She knew enough about him to feel her body reacting.

Which was not a good thing.

'It's not...' He scrubbed his hand across his hair, leaving little dark tufts sticking up. Her hands itched to smooth them down. To run her fingers through that hair. How was it possible he could be so damned officious and yet so ruggedly handsome at the same time? 'Look, Victoria, please don't get the wrong idea. I don't want to date you.'

'Sorry? I'm a bit confused here.' Her heart clenched. Of course he wouldn't want to date her. She wasn't exactly the billionaire girlfriend type with her penchant for vintage – real vintage that had been worn and used for years, rather than new-vintage that was made to look classic, or the totally out-of-her-budget vintage that designers like Chanel kept locked away in air-monitored rooms for celebrities to peruse and borrow.

With her useless reproductive system. With her bijou flat above a pub. He wouldn't want her. Just the idea of her.

Like Peter. He'd loved the idea of Victoria, he just hadn't loved the whole of her. Or, more specifically, the lost parts of her. It had started out as fun, nothing serious, then they talked about going into business and building something good together, but then he'd discovered her infertility and suddenly he hadn't loved the idea of a sterile future with her.

But Oliver wasn't Peter.

And besides, she didn't measure her own worth that way. She had a lot to give – too bad Peter hadn't seen that in her.

Oliver shook his head. 'I don't have time to date. I don't... It's not something I can do at this point in my life. I don't want to date you, Victoria, but I would like you to consider being my girlfriend for a set period of time. When my parents are here.'

Weird. 'Why?'

He stood and walked to the window, hands deep in his suit

pockets, and looked out across town. His voice softened. 'Because my father is sick. And my mother is stressed by that, and by the fact I'm not settling down at my age.'

'Which is?'

'The ripe old age of thirty-two.'

'God. Better book your retirement home soon.' She laughed, trying to make it sound encouraging rather than disparaging. Mostly, she laughed at the ridiculousness of having such expectations put upon you by your parents even as an adult. At least her folks had scaled all that back; they were just happy she was alive.

He wasn't laughing. 'The best way to keep them happy is to pretend I'm settling down.'

'But with me? You want me to pretend to be someone I'm not.' She shook her head. 'Like you did the other day. Is this a habit of yours?'

'Not at all.' He looked at her and shook his head. 'It's for a definitive period of time. Just be you, that would be perfect. I know it sounds far-fetched. But can you pretend to be my girlfriend for one day?'

She didn't want to make any deals with this man who made her react in ways she didn't want. Too much already. Enough to distract her from her work, from her passion. She didn't want to make deals, full stop. She'd made one with Peter and had been let down. 'Is the runway show conditional on my accepting this... proposal? Is that it? You give with one hand and take with the other?'

'Not at all. The runway will happen regardless of your decision. I want to help your students.' Oliver frowned. His eyes darkened but there was a hint of humour there too. 'Is the idea of spending a day with me so repulsive?'

'No. Not at all. It's just totally ridiculous. We're living in the twenty-first century, not Regency times.'

'Unfortunately, my parents very firmly live in the past.' Oliver shrugged. 'I'm trying to make them – my mother, mainly, I suppose – happy. Which in turn gets her off my back and stops her parading every single woman she knows in front of me. I don't want or need dating help.'

'Tell her that. Tell her to get off your back.'

'Believe me, I have. Over and over. But she doesn't listen.'

'It's just so… old-fashioned.'

'Yes.' He groaned and came away from the window, sitting down opposite her. 'She's very old school and traditional. They had me late in life and I'm their only child. It can be suffocating, but I know it comes from a good place. Now Dad's sick she wants him to feel he needn't worry about me anymore. That the business is going to move into a stable, steady and capable pair of hands. To someone a lot like him. Someone who is reliable, who has a partner and is settled. No drama on the horizon. And then he can relax.' He looked sad.

And that made her heart twist in sympathy. Her parents had been distraught after the accident and it had been hard to deal with their emotions along with focusing on her own recovery, but Zoe's parents had been over-the-top suffocating and Victoria had seen first-hand how the weight of that was carried by her friend – how Zoe had felt restricted and tied and eventually had flown as far away as possible from them, just to be able to breathe. Now Oliver was in the same boat. And a single child too, so the weight of every expectation, every hope was on him. 'I'm sorry he's sick.'

There was a moment when Oliver's eyes didn't meet hers and

something dark flickered across his features. Sadness? Regret? Oliver's dad wasn't just a bit sick, she didn't think. Finally, he raised his eyes and looked at her, with a half-smile that seemed to be taking some effort.

'It's one of those things, you know? You expect your parents to be around for ever and then you realize they're fallible. He can't do this job for much longer...' The rest of his sentence was left hanging and she wondered if he really meant his father wouldn't be around much longer. 'That's why I'm here. Stepping up, taking my place at the helm.'

She got the impression he didn't exactly love his job. 'What would you prefer to be doing?'

'Instead of working here? I don't know. This is all I've ever known, to be honest. I can do this easily. But I want... more.' He shook his head. 'More than a billion-dollar empire? More than being my own boss? More? God, that sounds entitled, right?'

'It's honest.'

'But it's not about me right now. I need my father to rest and maybe – just maybe – we'll have some more time. But the only way he'll agree to that is if a Russell takes his place. I can't entrust it to Andrew or we'll be bankrupt by Christmas. Andrew's parents are retired, so it's me. I'm the only one left.'

'You're doing all this for your dad?' She pointed to the walls bedecked with accolades and awards, Oliver Russell MBA, Oliver Russell First Class degree, Oliver Russell CEO. 'All this?'

He followed her gaze to the certificates. 'Wouldn't you?'

Would she? Sure, her parents had been her biggest supporters, especially after the accident that had threatened to take her away from them for ever. They had put her before everything. They had loved her unconditionally and she'd do anything for them, but would she take a job she didn't want? Live a life for them instead of for herself? Would they expect her to?

But Oliver moved in a very different sphere to her, she didn't know or understand his life. The Russells were traditional, they were off-the-scale rich, they knew people she read about in the media. Heck, they *were* the people she read about in the media. Their expectations were probably very different from her family's. She couldn't understand them, but she could help them.

What harm would it do to make his parents stop worrying for a while? What harm would it do to make a deal with him? To swap a runway show for a few well-meant little white lies to his over-doting parents to give them the space to heal? What harm would it do? As far as she could see it was a win all round. She put out her hand. 'OK. You have a deal. I will be your fake girlfriend.'

His hand fit into hers, strong and warm and steady as he shook. 'Fake fiancée would be preferable.'

'Fiancée. Right.' Her throat worked and a slow creep of heat flushed her neck and cheeks. She felt the burn and the warmth of his eyes on her face and a tightening in her gut that was surprising and disarming. And sensual.

Was she completely mad? Not if she kept this strictly what it was – a business deal. 'Oliver Russell, I will play your fiancée on opening day, but not a moment longer.'

CHAPTER SIX

'*WHAT* DID YOU SAY? He wants you to be his pretend girlfriend?' Lily's pretty face, on the laptop screen, was incredulous. She gaped at Victoria as if she thought she was completely out of her mind.

She was probably right. Victoria couldn't stop her hands from trembling as she propped the laptop next to an empty dishwasher basket on the bar, all the better to speak to her friend in Devon. She'd come straight back from Oliver's second proposal and known exactly who she needed to talk to about this. 'I know, it sounds crazy, but it's just for the opening of his store. Basically, his mother is determined to marry him off and keeps foisting dates on him with all her friends' single daughters.'

Lily was walking along the beach at Hawke's Cove, the wind whipping her hair. Her eyes were as dark as the sullen wintry sky. 'I don't know about this, V. It's very sudden.'

'It's not like it's a real engagement. I barely know the guy.'

'Which is not convincing me that it's a great thing to do.' Lily shook her head, then scraped her wayward hair back from her face. Her cheeks were pink and flushed from the notoriously biting sea-salt wind down there. 'It seems like a risky game to play. Even if it is for a good cause.'

'And for his parents.'

Eric Russell was famous for being a hearty and dynamic retail mogul. He was often in the media, and there was often speculation about his business and slick take-over manoeuvres. Was his illness in the public domain too? She didn't know, but it wasn't for her to tell Lily.

But her friend's shock was now morphing into real concern. 'Please be careful, V. They're a powerful family.'

'It's for one night. That's all. It's just a few little white lies for everyone's benefit.' But Lily's caution was making Victoria even more nervous. She wished she hadn't agreed, but she couldn't exactly change her mind now. She wished – for the first time in a while – she was back at the home she couldn't wait to leave and walking with Lily on the beach, living a simple life. Instead of being here walking herself into difficult situations with men she didn't know. A billionaire, for God's sake.

'How will you get to know enough about him before the store opening? Are you going to meet up beforehand and swap stories or something?'

'We didn't discuss details. I don't know. I thought…' What had she thought? Exactly nothing beyond *will you pretend to be my fiancée?* Truth was, she'd been so surprised by his request that she'd turned a bright shade of beetroot and backed out of his room. She'd needed to process it. Like this, with her friend. She'd agreed to lie to a powerful businessman who had contacts in high places in return for her students to get a step up the design ladder. What could possibly go wrong?

Just about everything.

So yes, she probably was quite as crazy as Lily thought she was. 'I'm going to look him up on the internet.'

Lily shook her head. 'There are some things you can only find out by face-to-face contact. What if he isn't a nice person?'

Her values were very close to Victoria's. For them life wasn't about the money, it was about spending time with good people and doing something positive in the world, helping others. Having both been on the receiving end of help after the accident – not physical but psychological, in Lily's case – they wanted to give back.

'I think he is. He seems OK.' Victoria had a bad feeling she knew enough about him to keep her interest well piqued. But knowing he had gorgeous guns, mesmerizing eyes and a smile that did something strange to her tummy possibly wouldn't be enough to convince his mother that she was adequately acquainted to be marrying her son. Otherwise, she might come over as a gold digger, interested only in his bank account and nothing else, and that was not the impression she wanted to give of herself, fake fiancée or otherwise. 'You're right though. We probably need to get together to get our facts straight.'

'If you're going to impress his mother... which, if I'm honest, seems like a weird excuse to me.'

'You know, she does sound like a meddling over-smotherer but the way he looked when he talked about her made me think he doesn't believe that. He cares that his parents are happy. That's got to be a good sign, right? And the best thing is that my students will get to showcase their designs on the runway in front of invited guests, VIPs, people of influence, people who could change their lives.'

'People like you, V. You've changed their lives already. You care, you believe in them.'

'But I can't make their dreams come true, Lils. I can only help them formulate them and take a few shaky steps towards them. That's why I've sold my soul to the devil.' A fake engagement. Honestly. Looking back it seemed ludicrous. But it had all made perfect and reasonable sense at the time. 'I can't wait to tell them about the catwalk.'

'Are you sure, honey? I know how much those kids mean to you, but don't go getting hurt in the process.'

'As if. This is purely business and I have no intention of getting involved with any man, not least Oliver Russell.' Victoria took out her phone and tapped on his name. She'd managed to stutter out a request for his contact details before she'd left, and he'd put them into her phone. 'I'm going to message him right now.'

She typed:

I guess we need to catch up at some point before I meet your parents. Get our stories straight, that kind of thing. And to plan the runway. V.

She hesitated at the V. What was texting etiquette with a man you barely knew and yet with whom you had to play intimate? Certainly not a kiss. Or should it be a kiss? Would she have sent a kiss to any other friends? Yes. To business associates? No. Sighing at her own damned insecurities she kept the full stop and pressed send.

After a few minutes of checking and rechecking she got a message back:

Dinner? Thursday night? I'll pick you up at 7 p.m., O.

'Help!' She tried to control her shaking hands. She would not be intimidated by this situation, or him. 'He wants to meet me on Thursday. Dinner.' How the heck was she going to pull this off?

They, she reminded herself. They'd agreed to do this together. How were *they* going to pull this off?

Lily smiled. 'You look scared as well as just a teeny bit excited at the prospect. Are you sure there isn't something more you'd like to tell me?'

'Like what?' Victoria's heart rate had trebled since the text arrived. Yes, she was scared. It was going to be a huge undertaking. She'd definitely need to know things about him that his mother might ask. They'd need to write a list. She'd need to write a list.

'Clearly he's available and on the market.' The smile grew just a little curious. 'Is he hot?'

Those arms. That smile. That mouth. 'Maybe… just a little bit.'

'V, come on. Would you have gone on a date if he'd just asked you, without the proposal?'

'I don't know. I just don't know. After Peter. I don't want to go there again. I can't do serious. I don't even want to start.'

'You deserve someone a lot better than Peter.' Her friend almost spat the name out. 'Who knows where this might go?'

'To prison, for fraud?' OK, so Victoria was definitely having second thoughts.

'At least if you see him on Thursday, you'll have time to decide if it's going to work or not. So maybe the sooner the better. Get it over with… or? Wow.' Her eyes glittered. 'Victoria Scott, you look excited.'

She wasn't. She was? 'I'm not. What if it goes badly wrong?'

'You're beautiful and funny and amazing. His parents will love you.'

'And then I'll break their hearts when they find out it isn't real.'

'Who knows? It might get real?'

'I can't. You know that.' For all the physical reasons, sure. But she just couldn't bear having her heart stomped on again. She had to keep her distance, if not physically then emotionally.

But Lily was looking at her the way she had so many times when Victoria was recovering from her life-changing injuries; as if she wished she could somehow bestow all the hope and positivity in the universe into Victoria. Make her believe and trust in good things happening. 'You can do anything you want, V. Just be safe. Say yes to the date. And message me when it's over. I want to know every minute detail.'

'It's not a date, it's a meeting.'

'Whatever.' Lily winked. 'Meeting schmeeting.'

Once bitten twice sure she wasn't going to do it again. She had to keep it in the professional realm. 'And please don't tell anyone else about this, Lily. Please. I'm going to look like a right idiot if it all goes wrong.'

'Of course not.' Lily did a zipping motion with her thumb and forefinger across her lip. 'I won't say a word.'

'Not even to Malie and Zoe.' This was a big ask. They shared a lot of secrets.

'OK, I promise. Now text the man back. He's waiting on your answer.'

'You're enjoying watching me squirm, aren't you?' Victoria managed to laugh. It was a ridiculous situation. But whatever happened next this had to be faced head on. She texted:

Thursday. Yes. OK.

He came straight back: See you at 7 p.m.

No kiss. Good. Right. They were on the same page. He wouldn't want to kiss her and she definitely didn't want to kiss him.

She thought about his mouth, the half-smile he'd given her that had made her heart squeeze. The unbidden fizz in her stomach when he'd smiled at her passion for fabric which everyone else thought was a little weird. Kissing might not be such a bad thing to do… just once, to try it?

No. You don't kiss your work colleagues.

'Hello? Victoria?' Lily was watching her with a curious smile on her face. 'I said, don't forget to ask him for a rock the size of the Shard.'

Victoria slid her phone back in her back trouser pocket, all the better not to reread his texts and try to decipher any other deeper meaning there. 'What do you mean?'

'For your pretend engagement ring. You'll need a huge diamond. Or three.'

Hot damn. Victoria glanced down at her left hand and tried to imagine a ring there. Tried to control the panic roiling in her stomach. 'I hadn't even thought of that.'

It seemed silly to be nervous. Heck, she'd met him twice and had been completely herself both times. But now they were meeting on official fiancée business Victoria felt anxiety spiralling through her. What if she didn't pass the test? What if, once he got to know her, he thought she was totally inappropriate to meet his parents' expectations?

But then, what should it matter? It was just research for one night of acting, that was all. But knowing it and feeling it weren't the same thing, she realized as the bar door swung open and he strode in. 'Victoria. You look amazing.'

She looked down at her navy polka dot dress, a relic from the fifties that she'd updated with a more modern neckline. It was quirky, she loved it and felt amazing in it, but she hadn't expected him to say anything.

'It's OK, Oliver, you don't have to start pretending now. These two know we're just in rehearsal mode.' She pointed at Sara and Paul.

Victoria had tried to pass this off as a business meeting but somehow Sara had managed to wrangle the truth out of her.

Oliver waved to her work colleagues as if he knew them personally and as if playing fiancé was a daily occurrence. 'I'm not pretending. You do look amazing.'

'Oh?' She didn't know what to do with that. He looked pretty hot himself. No sharp suit today, just an open-collared white shirt, a charcoal cashmere jumper and a slate grey unbuttoned coat. And battered jeans. Jeans that hugged his legs like a gift.

Whoa. She was the pretend girlfriend, not a real one. She dragged her thoughts from his legs. But they wouldn't budge, choosing to stay fixed on him. On the way the light in the bar picked out golden strands in his dark hair. The way his eyes glittered. Today they were blue like the Hawke's Cove sea on a sunny autumn morning. His hair looked as if he'd pushed his fingers through it more times than he could count today. He was stressed. Stressed by Andrew and his parents and taking a girlfriend to meet them.

Fake. It was fake, she reminded herself.

He wasn't in work attire, so had he been home to change? Where was home? She'd need to add that to her list. She stepped awkwardly towards him, her hands stretched out like a shop mannequin. *Relax.* 'Hi. Er… what's the etiquette? Do we kiss now?'

He grinned, his face alight with the reflection of tinsel that hung low over the bar. 'Tempting, but I think it's better if we get to know each other first.'

'I meant, on the cheek.' Shaking her head she stepped back. 'Isn't that what you usually do when you meet your fiancé's parents?'

'Search me.' He shrugged. 'I've never done it.'

'Me neither.'

'Then we're engagement virgins. Good. Excellent.'

'I'm not sure whether that's something we should be proud about or not.' She laughed, feeling a lot more at ease. 'Right. So…? Should we start? I have a list of questions…'

He looked round at the noisy bar; the quiz teams were arriving and the quiz mistress was setting up her microphone and kept *testing, testing…* 'You really want to do this here?'

Maybe a quiz would dilute the awkwardness. She saw Sara grinning at her while pulling a pint of London Pride and Paul giving her the thumbs up. She was never going to live this down. 'Let's go somewhere else.'

'I'm starving. Food? Know anywhere round here that's good?'

'Aziz down the road does a brilliant chicken korma. Do you like Indian food?'

'I like food. Full stop. Lead on, Macduff.'

Food. Good. Right. Allergies? Intolerances? She'd surely need to know all that, because what fiancée wouldn't know exactly what her future husband could or couldn't eat?

She was starting to feel like a quiz show contestant. Specialist subject: Oliver Russell.

And God, how she was going to fail. *Nil points.* 'Aziz's restaurant was the first place I ate at when I came to live here, and I go about once a week. It's a family-run place. Like yours but, literally, about a billion times smaller.'

She led the way out of the wine bar, turned left and immediately went cold. Across the road Peter was locking up his shop, Emilia was with him, hanging onto his arm as if he was about to scarper and she wasn't going to let him go. Victoria put her head down and added pace to her steps but his irritating nasal voice followed her. 'Vicki! Vicki! Wait!'

She ignored him. The last thing she wanted right now was to have to introduce Oliver to him. Questions would be asked. Questions she didn't know the answers to. Some questions she just didn't want to have to answer. Like why they broke up. Not how. But why.

'Victoria, wait. That man's calling you.' Oliver's hand on her arm stopped her in her tracks. She turned, panic in her chest.

'I don't…' Too late. Peter had crossed the road and was encroaching. 'It's just…'

Oliver took his hand away, concern in his voice. 'What's wrong?'

'Nothing.' She hauled in a breath and dug very deep for something resembling a welcoming smile, not for her ex and his girlfriend, but for Oliver who didn't need to be dragged into her past. 'Hey, Peter. Emilia.'

'Vicki. Hey. And…?' After diving in for an unwanted peck on her cheek Peter looked at Oliver, his eyes narrowed. Funny, she hadn't realized until now just how pinched his features were.

She stepped away from her ex and touched Oliver's arm. 'This is Oliver. Oliver Russell. He works next door to the bar.'

The narrowed eyes got darker and Peter tapped his fingers on his bottom lip. Victoria found herself holding her breath. Peter wasn't exactly known for his manners and he'd been very affronted by having his car clamped. Twice.

'Russell, Russell… of course. Yes, hello. Are you the guy who is trying to organize some pop-up thing at your department store for the opening day?'

Oh? None of the barbed comments she'd expected about the rubbish or the clamping. Just a friendly, measly smile now he was going to get something.

Oliver, totally oblivious to the painful history, gave a brief, professional nod of his head. 'I am. And you are…?'

'Peter Swain.' He pointed to his shop across the road. *Her* shop. Once upon a dream. 'Tailor. Bespoke, obviously.'

'Obviously. Are you on the list? I'll check. Good to meet you, the pop-up is going to be a great opportunity for us all.'

Emilia beamed a too-friendly smile. So different from the face she'd pulled when Victoria had walked in on them. 'Well, we mustn't keep you. We're going to a cake tasting. For the wedding. You know?'

Victoria swallowed and pushed a stray lock of hair behind her ear for something to do with her hands other than curl them into fists of hurt. 'That's lovely. Oliver, Peter and Emilia are getting married.'

'Great. Congratulations,' Oliver said, shaking first Peter's hand then Emilia's. 'Well done.'

But then she felt Oliver's eyes on her. Was he expecting her to say something else? Like what? *No hard feelings?* Because there were some. She turned to look at him and was completely taken aback when he slid his arm around her shoulder and pulled her closer.

As was Peter. 'Vicki?' he said through gritted teeth. 'I didn't know you were seeing anyone.'

'I… er…' What to say? They hadn't practised anything yet, they hadn't decided how to handle things. Oliver's arm was warm and firm, enough pressure to make her feel protected, but not too much that she felt stifled by it. He was tall… she hadn't realized quite how tall until now. He towered over her and there were a good few inches between him and Peter which she was sure her ex would find intimidating. This close she could smell Oliver's scent; a warm buzz of sandalwood, masculine. Clean. Fresh. She leaned against him and breathed.

Why was she inhaling this man?

Acting. Method, obviously. If she lived the role she would be more convincing, surely? What would a fiancée do now? Ah, yes. She leaned her head against his chest and felt the thud of his heart. Steady. Strong. Then wound her arm round his back, brushing his abs as she went.

Big mistake.

The man was buff. Her skin prickled at the contact, giving her a hit of heat low in her belly. What would those hard abs look like? Feel like under her fingers? Stifling an instinctive shudder, she blinked to focus. Oliver. Peter. Right. Yes.

Acting, good. Lust, bad.

'We like to keep things low-key.' Oliver gave Peter and Emilia a rather satisfied smile with just enough intrigue that had Peter leaning closer to hear his next words. 'Paparazzi, you know. Make my life hell. I'd be grateful if you keep it hush-hush for now. Thanks, man.' Oliver stuck his other, non-hugging hand out and Peter had no option but to shake his agreement, with an open mouth and confused stare.

Victoria bit down on a smug smile. This was the first time she'd ever seen her ex lost for words. Peter looked at her with something like regret in his eyes. Regret and interest, even though he had no right to be interested in anything she did at all. 'OK, we'd better get going. Nice to meet you, Oliver.'

'Yes.' Oliver cleared his throat. 'I'll get one of my PAs to contact you. I'm sure it'll be great doing business together.'

One of my PAs. The struggle to stifle her smile was lost. Take that Mr No-PA Swain.

Then she unwound herself from Oliver's grasp, wishing the method acting didn't have to end; she'd been perfectly in the moment. In his arms.

Oh, hell. This was getting a little too hot for her to handle.

CHAPTER SEVEN

As they walked into the restaurant Oliver asked the inevitable question, 'Who was that?'

'Just a neighbour.' Still regretting extracting herself from his arm, but also congratulating herself for doing so, Victoria sat at an empty table and took out her notebook filled with as many questions she could think of, helpfully brainstormed with Sara. 'Right, what do you like to eat?'

'Anything I don't have to cook.' He sat opposite her and handed her a menu Aziz had left on the table, but his eyes were searching. 'He was clearly more than just a neighbour. First off, you pretended not to hear him. Your voice was shaky, your cheeks bright red, and if you'd been able to shoot daggers from your evil death stare that poor woman would be out cold on the floor. Even I was frightened of you.'

'Humph. There isn't much poor about Emilia.' She'd got the guy, the shop, the future.

He put his menu down on the table and studied her face. 'Victoria, what happened?'

'Oh, we had a thing. Now we don't.' She tried to sound nonchalant although she was shaky because of her body's reaction to Oliver rather than about her ex. Oliver was attractive and it was becoming clear that she was attracted to him. But it was basic chemistry and something she could overcome with a little effort. She just needed to get a handle on her wayward hormones. 'Thank you for the arm gesture, though. I think he got the message.'

At least Peter and Emilia wouldn't now be thinking she was going to be staring at a Christmas dinner for one. Even if she was. It felt good to have got an upper hand there at last.

It had felt good to have that arm there, too, she realized with a shock and not just because she got to smell Oliver Russell and see the look on Peter's face, but because the one thing she missed most about being single was physical contact. The encouraging little press of lips to her forehead, snuggling on a sofa. Kissing. But, in order to keep her heart intact, she was going to have to get used to being on her own.

'It seemed like a good time to start our pretend relationship. Witnesses are even better proof that we are an item, should my mother have any doubts. Which she won't. She'll be thrilled to see me with you—' They were interrupted by Aziz for their order. After he'd gone and returned with drinks Oliver grinned. 'Seriously, that tailor guy is your type? Hipster beard? Nordic jumper? *Ponytail?*' Never had such derision been used for such an innocent word. 'That's why you were all weird around him.'

'I was not weird.' She was. She always was with Peter, when they'd first got together she'd liked his rough edginess but these days he just made her anxious. He knew things about her she wouldn't tell another soul. He knew her insecurities and he'd stomped on the part of her that she felt would never heal. The loss that was a dull ache inside her and would never be filled.

But Oliver smiled as if he'd uncovered one of her deepest

secrets. 'Your hands were moving nineteen to the dozen, pushing your hair back behind your ears, messing with your bag strap, smoothing down your skirt. Not weird exactly, but spooked by the situation.'

'I move my hands a lot?' She looked down at them. Perfectly still now. But yes, she was guilty as charged.

He grinned, eyes on her fingers. 'All. The. Time.'

He'd noticed. 'It's one of the things my family laugh at me for doing. One of the reasons Mum encouraged me to draw from a young age.' *Stop those hands moving or you'll damage something.* She slid both palms under her bum to keep them still. 'It's a nervous energy thing. Usually, if I'm feeling worked up about something I busy myself with drawings, designs or making things… creating keeps me calm. It's like meditation. Nothing like sewing a row of blanket stitch to relax you.'

'Being *under* a blanket sounds much better.' His eyes glittered as they held her gaze just long enough for heat to suffuse her skin. His mouth curled into a not-so-subtle sexy smile. 'Sleeping, obviously.'

'Obviously.' She imagined him under the king-size log cabin patchwork quilt she'd made a few years ago. She imagined being in there with him. Pressing close to that hard, toned body.

Wow. That was so inappropriate. Really, the conversation was taking her to places she didn't want to go, in so many directions. Was flirting in the rules? Was it breaking hers? She didn't want to read the wrong thing into this, so she looked down at her notebook. 'I really do think we should start—'

'He hurt you.'

She refused to answer that. 'Oliver, I have a lot of questions.'

'So do I.' He sat for a moment and looked at her pensively.

She wasn't sure what he was going to say next, but she hoped he'd get the message that she didn't want to examine her failed relationships. Her tummy fluttered with anxiety and a mixed-up attraction that she shouldn't be having. Maybe this was a really stupid idea? They needed to get to know each other just enough to fool his mother into thinking they were intimate. They didn't need to tell each other their deepest, darkest experiences.

When he hit her with 'Were you two serious?' she wasn't sure what to do next.

Hedging, she opened the notebook and ran her fingers down her bullet points. 'That isn't a listed question. I think we need to talk about allergies and the agreed story of how long we've been dating and the kind of things your mother will want to know.'

'But I want to know what happened between you and Peter Swain.'

Her heart slowed at his name. She didn't want the past and the present to mix like this. Oliver was discombobulating with his direct questions. 'Is it relevant to our fake engagement?'

'It could be. How will I know unless you give me the details?'

He clearly wasn't letting the subject drop. She blew out a frustrated breath. 'OK. Peter and I had agreed to go into business together and then we broke up and he kept the shop and I lost my dream. For a while anyway. Now I'm just reframing and rebuilding. I'm good. I'm... happy.' She was. 'I work hard but use my spare time to help my students and do my own designs. I have good friends. I can do anything I want without taking anyone else in to account.' And now she'd said far too much and sounded desperate.

'Why did you break up?'

She looked down at the table and drew a deep breath. 'I think I'm going to draw the line here, Oliver. This isn't relevant to our deal.'

He shook his head. 'I beg to differ. You looked upset, frustrated, angry and anxious. There was a definite tension between you and the woman. But he's already applied to use the pop-up stall at my store. I need to know if there's going to be a problem here? I don't want trouble on opening day, especially from my…' His gaze ran slowly over her body which was disarming and… distinctly possessive. 'Fiancée.'

The way his eyes slid over her she felt caught under a spell. Handsome. Possessive. Interesting. Funny. *Make-believe*. 'Fair enough. There won't be trouble, not from me anyway. Basically, he was cheating, and I found him out.' Strangely, the hurt in her chest when she thought of that moment was not as acute anymore. 'Found *them*,' she corrected. 'Together.'

'With Emilia?' He made a sorry face as if he'd been personally injured. 'Ouch.'

She laughed, although it hadn't been funny at the time. 'That's it? I had my heart completely broken by finding my boyfriend having sex with another woman and all you can say is *ouch*?'

'A dent to your pride perhaps, but hell, Victoria, you deserve so much better. Did that man really break your heart?'

'I thought he had.' Time to deflect the attention away from her. 'Is there a trail of broken-hearted women in your wake, Oliver Russell? Are you scared of commitment? Is that why you're still single?'

His eyes narrowed and he glanced at the notebook between them. 'Are these questions on your list?'

'No, this is just conversation.'

'It's hard to keep track. Did you love him?'

'Wow.' This was like a tennis match. The ball bouncing between her heartache and his refusal to drop the subject. 'I don't know. It was serious. At least, I was serious about him. But the more I think about it the more I realize my heartache was about the lost dream and not losing him. He's not worth hurting over.'

'And if he gave you up then he's an idiot too.'

She looked up at him and tried to gauge his expression. Was he being serious? Was this the real Oliver Russell? Flirtatious when unguarded? It took a bit of getting used to. 'And yet you just invited him to set up a stall at the opening day.'

Oliver's eyes rolled. 'Public relations. That's all.'

Like this was… just a PR stunt for his parents. She needed to remind herself of that every time she thought he smelled good, or when he put his arm across her shoulders and she leaned into him. She found him a PR-worthy smile, although this meeting was starting to feel a lot more like a confessional than a getting-our-lies-straight date. 'Have you ever had your heart broken?'

'Not likely.' At her disbelieving glare he shrugged. 'I haven't found anyone I want to commit to. Fifty years is a long time to be with the same person. You've got to be sure. I've never been sure and so now I have to pretend. What about you? Did you and Peter discuss marriage?'

'I'm not the marrying kind.'

She stopped her hand from creeping over her scarred belly. There… *there* was the problem. At least Oliver was never going to see that, so she wouldn't have to watch him trying to rearrange his features in an *it's OK, you're still beautiful to me* kind of expression the way Peter had. Even though it was obvious everything changed as soon as Peter realized he couldn't have the future they'd been planning. The future *he'd* started to plan after he became an uncle and suddenly wanted a family of his own. He'd been outraged when he discovered Victoria wouldn't be able to provide the goods. Worse, he'd believed she'd been holding back from telling him about her infertility, that her silence about it was tantamount to her *lying* to him. In fact, simply, telling him hadn't been at the top of her list because he'd always said he wasn't interested in kids. Who knew men had biological clocks that suddenly started ticking?

Oliver sat back. 'How can you not be the marrying kind? Everyone does it in the end, right? At least I'm open to the possibility of marriage. Eventually. What if you meet the love of your life?'

'I won't. I'll make sure of it.' There was no way she was going to go through another conversation with a man about her infertility.

As if he could read her mind Oliver inhaled, pensively swirling the amber liquid in the pint glass, his eyes piercing and inquisitive. 'OK, we don't need to get too personal. Do you want to have some no-go topics? Things we're not allowed to discuss?'

Hell, yes. 'I just want honesty, OK? I mean, I know this is all a stupid pretence for everyone else, but if this is going to work we need to be honest with each other as we go along. Otherwise it'll be too confusing to keep up with what are lies and what aren't.'

He put his palm over his heart, the way he had that night when he proposed, before she'd found herself mired in this strange deal. 'I promise to be completely honest. I will never lie to you, Victoria.'

'Nor I to you.' But there were some things she didn't even need to bring up with him, things that would stay locked inside her for ever.

'Good, glad we're on the same page,' he said with a soft smile, looking at the pen poised in her hand. 'And you're really going to take notes?'

She breathed out. 'If I don't write things down, I'll forget. I need to revise and practise, so I don't mess up.'

'It's not an exam. Stop stressing.' He peered more closely at the first page in her book. 'What's that?'

'Nothing.' She snapped the notebook closed and put it face down on the table. She hadn't even realized she'd drawn anything. 'Just random doodles.'

Frowning playfully, he picked the book up and opened at the first page. 'Very accomplished doodles. It looks familiar. Is it… wait… I know, it's that handrail in the new store… the birds and the entwined branches.'

'Oh? Is it?' She couldn't remember doing it, couldn't imagine why she'd chosen to draw that particular thing, other than that it had been such a lovely surprise to uncover it and show it to Oliver.

'It's very good.'

She smiled, unused to getting compliments and not knowing what to do with them, other than wear them as a blush. Her body obliged. 'I did art and design at university, if I couldn't draw a bird on a tree they'd have thrown me out.'

'It's *good* good, Victoria.'

'Thank you. I graduated top of my class. Do you draw? Paint? Hobbies?' She looked at his hands. Long, strong fingers.

He shrugged. 'I used to ski and play rugby. Now I run. At least I did. Work is all-encompassing.'

'You need to take time out, enjoy life outside of the office.'

'Sure. I'll put in my diary for... oh, 2045.' He shook his head with a wry smile. 'Not going to happen.'

'Then you'll work yourself into an early grave.' As soon as the words came out she regretted them. She didn't know what was ailing his dad, but alluding to anything like that was insensitive. Her gut tightened. 'I didn't mean – I'm sorry.'

'It's OK. I know you wouldn't mean it. And maybe he is sick from working too hard. It's heart failure... heart stuff is stress-related, right?'

'I don't know, but I wish I could take back what I said.' She slipped her hand over his and patted his skin. Realized what she was doing and quickly drew it back. But not before he caught her fingers in his. Warmth spread across her hand and when she looked up into his eyes she saw the pain pushed out by something a lot like desire. 'Victoria—'

She didn't know what he was going to say, she didn't want to hear it. Didn't want to be drawn into anything more personal, anything that would hurt. Shaking her hand free she grabbed the notebook again and opened her notes. 'So, I googled you.'

'Oh dear.' He paused as the waiter brought their order over. 'What did you find out?'

'That you have a freaking Wikipedia page!'

'Doesn't everyone?' His wide eyes told her he was joking.

She laughed at the thought of anyone being interested enough in her life to put it on the internet. 'As if. What would mine say? Victoria Scott... um... not much happened and then not much happened again.'

Aziz arrived with the food, interrupting the conversation briefly. Victoria slid her notebook back into her bag.

'Ah, but imagine if your page said' – Oliver raised his hand and drew an arc in the air – 'world-famous designer to the stars.'

'I suppose dreams are free.'

'It could become a reality.'

She took a bite of the chicken and groaned at the deliciousness. *This* was real. This little restaurant with Formica tables and wonky pictures of the Taj Mahal on flocked wallpaper. Not being world-famous. 'If I won the lottery, maybe. I could afford to give up work to focus on my collections. Not everyone has the same opportunities you have had.'

'This is the best curry I've had in a long time.' He shook his head, groaning with her at the spicy heat in the food. 'Not everyone has the same talent you have.'

'You haven't seen my designs.'

'But I've witnessed your passion, I've seen your doodles. If your clothes are as detailed as that bird then I'm very impressed.'

'Sadly, impressed doesn't pay the rent.' She stopped there because she didn't want him to think she was a charity case or hinting at needing money. She was perfectly OK with the trajectory her career was on, it was just taking more time than she'd anticipated after the last setback. But she'd get there.

'OK… back to business. Let me remember: you went to Harrow, then up to Oxford, graduated with a first in economics. Very impressive by the way. You played rugby for your college, got selected for England under nineteens. You won player of the year three years in a row. Even more impressive.' She didn't mention *Tatler*'s profile of him as one of UK's most eligible bachelors, and the fact his father made the *Sunday Times* Rich List, but only at number twenty-seven. Twenty-freaking-seven.

And here she was with him, in her favourite local Indian restaurant, slurping a beer and eating the best chicken tikka masala in London. 'Also, that you were recently responsible for opening a Russell & Co in Paris and that the elegant and sublime Clarissa Maguire was seen on your arm a few weeks ago with speculation that you're a couple and settling down. I'm sure your mother would have read that too.'

'Undoubtedly.' He grimaced. 'She likes to keep abreast of all my romantic encounters, unfortunately.'

'Which makes things a bit sticky. I can pretend to be lots of things, but I can't pretend to be half a foot taller, with different coloured eyes, and a champion ballroom dancer. I'm not sure I have two left feet but they're certainly not right.'

'I don't want you to pretend to be anyone but yourself. Mum is used to media reports of me being seen with different women. That's why being my fiancée rather than my girlfriend gives her a stronger message. It's all part of the plan.'

A plan she was starting to regret agreeing to. 'How does it feel to be under the glare of the media spotlight all the time?'

'Restricting. I envy you the freedom to decide who you want to be and what you want to do.'

'Could you just tell them that you don't want to take the helm of Russell & Co?'

He put down his fork. 'And risk making my father work harder to the detriment of his health? No. Not right now. Maybe in a few years. Maybe never.'

'So, you're trapped?'

He frowned. 'It's an honour and a privilege to have a job like mine.'

'Tell that to your face.' She laughed at the way his mouth formed a circle and his nose crinkled. 'You look as if you've just eaten a lemon.'

'It's the chilli. This is hot.' He laughed with her, but they both knew he was lying. 'You really don't care about the job or the money, do you, Victoria?'

'Not if it makes you unhappy. Life is too short to do things you don't want to do.'

'How did you get so philosophical?'

'I learnt a few hard lessons at a young age.' Fighting to survive had made her rethink what she wanted out of life. But being responsible for horrific injuries to her friends made her re-evaluate her attitudes, her actions. Everything.

For a while guilt had prevented her from moving forward but her friends had rallied round and told her she hadn't been to blame for the accident and to live the life the dead driver from the other car wasn't able to. But Oliver didn't need to know that.

The conversation was veering too close to her personal life again and she was wondering how to steer it away, but luckily his phone beeped and distracted him. He pulled it out of his pocket and shook his head and cursed. 'Damn.'

'Trouble?'

With another exasperated shake of his head Oliver ground out, 'Just Andrew. That's always trouble. I left him in charge of a simple job, but he can't manage even that… and somehow that's my problem.' He looked bleakly at the phone screen and exhaled roughly. 'The buck stops with me. It is my problem.'

'You need to go.'

He nodded, scraping his chair back. 'I'm sorry…'

'Business is business. Just like this is. Let's call this meeting to a close.' She tried to keep her tone as professional as she could, given the image of him in her bed still had her body prickling with nervous, excited energy. 'We have a few work-ons for next time. I can email you some questions through if you like?'

'Sure thing. How do you think we've done tonight?'

She'd learnt that she was more attracted to him than she'd planned to be. That he had a core that was hard to penetrate, but she'd seen a chink of it when he talked about his father. That his arms around her felt good. Not to mention his scent being delicious and intoxicating. That she was at a distinct risk of liking him more than she should.

She watched as he wiped his hands on a napkin and then put it on the table. 'I now know you're left-handed and we didn't even talk about that. But I don't think we're much closer to being able to pull this off. I don't know where you live. What you do on your days off... what your favourite colour is... there's still a lot of ground to cover.'

'We have two weeks. That's plenty of time to get to know each other.' He pulled out his wallet and turned towards the counter. 'Trust me, I've had relationships shorter than that.'

'That, Mr Fifty Years Is A Long Time, I can totally believe.' She followed him to pay the bill, insisted they split it and he argued but she won, and then they walked out into the cold night.

Little flakes of snow whirled around them and she caught some in her palm. 'Wow. It's snowing? In November? Isn't that a bit early?'

'For London, yes. It's freezing. Here.' He tugged his coat collar up round his neck and wrapped his scarf around her. It was soft cashmere and smelled of him. She pulled it close to her throat, inhaling and berating herself for doing so. But he smelt so good. Her stomach tugged and heated and she was shocked to feel stirrings of something she hadn't felt in a long time.

The council had hung strings of little lights across the road waiting for the official switch on which coincided with Russell & Co's opening day. Imagining how it would look, she grinned. 'Christmas is coming fast and furious.'

'And I'm running out of time.' He suddenly looked sad, his face was pained, and she just knew he wasn't talking about the store and that his thoughts had wandered back to his father. She wanted to squeeze his arm and tell him it'd be OK, but she couldn't overstretch the relationship they'd agreed on and couldn't make promises she had no right making. What if it wasn't OK at all?

They crossed the road in silence and when they arrived back outside the bar she stopped, not knowing how to end this and not wanting her time with him to finish so soon.

'Before I forget, my students want to meet you, to get the lowdown on what they're meant to do on the opening day, but mainly to say thank you for the opportunity. If you're not too busy. Sometime.'

'Er. Sure.' But he looked a little spooked at the prospect. 'When's the next class?'

'Tomorrow. Seven o'clock. I work the early shift in the bar then teach in the evening.'

He gave a curt nod. 'I'll be there. Wherever there is?'

She pointed upwards. 'My studio… also known as the master bedroom.'

'You teach in your bedroom?'

'It's a studio now. I sleep in the box room. It's just me, so I don't need much room. And the light in there is amazing.'

'Spending the evening in your master bedroom? That will make my mother very happy.' He laughed, his eyes catching hers as something unspoken passed between them. Another image of them in bed slid into her brain.

'Oliver Russell. Do not overstep.' But before she could move he'd leaned closer and grazed a kiss on her cheek. She turned her head awkwardly at the last minute and found herself staring at his mouth.

Oh.

It was a damned fine mouth. If she moved one inch upwards on tiptoe she could press her lips to his, taste him. Feel the pressure of him against her.

No.

She closed her eyes, beating back the ache deep and low in her body that keened towards him. It felt as if there was an invisible thread tugging her closer.

She wanted to kiss him. She couldn't. That would be madness.

But she wanted to.

She dragged her gaze away from his lips and up to his eyes. They were heavy and misted, soft with a longing that pulled at her gut. He was fighting too. Struggling to keep the right side of a line that was blurring with every second they stood here. But it didn't make anything any better knowing that.

'Tomorrow.' He stepped back. Swallowed. His voice cracking with desire. 'Excellent.'

Was it? She was beginning to think this whole mess was a huge mistake. 'Come around seven thirty, the girls should have settled into work by then. Good luck with Andrew.'

'I'm going to need more than luck.' He squeezed her arm and nodded, then walked away leaving her frustrated and confused. One kiss wasn't worth the trouble it would bring. It was blurring the edges, breaking the rules. Breaking her promise to herself. But it was the sultry promise of the touch of his hand, his skin on her cheek, his mouth – God, that mouth, that she couldn't escape.

And now she'd invited him into her private space. They had to pretend they knew each other well enough to want to spend the rest of their lives together. They had two weeks to pull this off. They didn't have enough time to relax into each other.

It was all moving too quickly.

CHAPTER EIGHT

OLIVER HAD BEEN IN many hostile boardrooms and negotiated complex contracts with difficult terms and conditions with equally hostile people, so God knew why his gut roiled at the thought of meeting a bunch of teenagers.

In Victoria's space.

That was the problem, and the drawcard. It felt strangely intimate climbing the stairs to the apartment above the wine bar, the whole place smelling of her; fresh and flowery. Something quintessentially feminine. In response, his gut contracted.

There was the problem; he'd negotiated those contracts with difficult people and had never had the little hairs on his arm raise and his heart rate pick up in what he could only, frustratingly, describe as attraction. He tried to rationalize it. So, he was attracted to her? She was a beautiful woman. He could work with that. He'd worked with plenty of beautiful women before and it had been just fine.

But he'd never had a feeling in his gut like this: half apprehension, half excitement. All sensual. Worse, he'd been anticipating this all day and no matter how many times he'd tried to pull his thoughts away from her he'd found himself imagining her space. Imagining her in it. Imagining her in her bed. With him.

Even though he knew this couldn't go anywhere – the woman was determined never to get married and it wasn't something he was contemplating – his head was getting all carried away. He was off balance and that wasn't something he was used to.

He knocked. No answer. Waited. Knocked again. Then pushed the unlocked front door open and was greeted with chatter ten decibels louder than he'd expected and a whole other frequency level. No wonder they hadn't heard his rap on the door. He followed the noise down a clean white-walled corridor, glancing past a kitchen, lounge, bathroom and neat feminine box room, to the end room.

And his tight stomach plummeted. Whoa. So many women. So much noise. So much colour. It was a huge bright room that, he imagined, in daylight would get lots of light from the large bay window. There wasn't a bed, just shelves spilling fabric and paper and scrunched linens on every available surface. Large rolls of material were propped up against what free wall space there was and on the floor in the corner were school bags and discarded notebooks covered in drawings. He looked over at the huge wooden table dominating the middle of the room, covered with assorted linens and fabric, zips, buttons, tape, scissors and sequins. Way too many sequins.

Talk about out of his comfort zone. He groaned; out-sequinned, out-numbered and completely out of his depth.

As no one had seen him walk in he tried to make himself heard. 'Hello?'

Nothing. No one even noticed. For someone who was used to conversations abruptly ending and everyone jumping up to greet him when he walked into a room this was unnerving. Laughing and chatting, they had their backs to him, all leaning over the table, picking up swatches of fabric, holding each up against themselves, or against... ah, not so many people; six mannequins wearing an assortment of half-finished garments.

But when Victoria's head popped up from behind the table and she smiled at him he felt the tension slink away and simultaneously his pulse rush at the sight of her. Her hair was piled up on top of her head with loose tendrils framing her face. She was wearing a pale pink jumper and cream cropped-at-the-ankle trousers that covered her curves like a dream. She looked as if she'd stepped out of a nineteen fifties film and was just about to hop on a Vespa and explore Florence or Rome. Her cheeks were flush with excitement – with the girls and the fun, he imagined, and not because he was there.

Although – given the way she'd looked at him last night with sex in her eyes – he wasn't so sure.

Which was another reason why he shouldn't be here. The last thing he needed was to have this arrangement spilling into the personal, no matter how much his libido piqued whenever she was near.

'Oliver. Hello.' She beamed at him and, on cue, his libido jumped. 'Girls, this is Mr Russell. The man who has very kindly offered us the first-floor fashion department in the new store next door as a runway for your designs. What do we say?'

His heart thumped against his ribcage. He only hoped they weren't going to hit him with technical questions. Runway. Clothes. Space. That was all he knew.

'Thank you! Thank you, Mr Russell. Cheers. Mint.' One of the girls raised her fist. He looked at it. What the...? But she grinned and extended it towards him. 'Thanks, Ollie.'

Ollie? So soon? Got to love kids. The hallowed boardroom etiquette he was used to was refreshingly missing here. 'Oh yes. Right.' Laughing and feeling the tension shrink slightly he closed his fist and bumped it against the girl's. 'Thought I'd pop in to see how you're doing.'

Victoria walked towards him, eyes and smile bright. 'We're creating our spring-summer collection. The theme is sustainability. In that spirit, and basically because we can't afford anything else, most of the fabric we're using has come from second-hand and charity shops, but there's also the stuff I got cheaply from Betsy on Saturday.'

'In the famous cardboard box?' How strange to think it was that that had led to this.

'The very one.' She bent and picked up the soggy remnants of flattened cardboard and showed him. 'We've used absolutely everything.'

'But surely there wasn't a need for the bunnies?' He couldn't stop looking at her, all breathless and flushed and sharing their own private joke.

'Actually, there was.' The light in her face was ethereal. In this private world of hers she shone. She walked over to fist-pump girl. 'This is Jasmine. She's creating a collection around modern-day fairy tales and how they've changed over the decades from wanting a handsome prince to save us to being self-actuated and independent. Jasmine, you can explain your ideas better than me.'

Fist-pump girl nodded, her neat braids swaying as she talked enthusiastically. 'Yeah, miss, er… sir, like, we're not just shaped by things around us, but we have power, you know? We have agency and we're doing the shaping.'

'That's right.' Victoria nodded. 'Also, it's a look at how urban living and fast fashion has transformed our dreams and desires into something temporary and fleeting. We want it, we get it, then we discard it. The tyre marks on the bunny ribbon is a very dramatic and apt representation. Right, Jas?'

'It's well peng, miss.' Jasmine nodded and bent to secure some bunny ribbon loops around the armholes of a dress on a mannequin dummy. 'See? City people laying waste to nature. We want new fairy tales where we save ourselves and the world.'

'Peng?' He mouthed to Victoria over Jasmine's head. Was this a technical design term?

Victoria gave him a thumbs up. 'Great.'

It means great? He looked at the dress. 'Excellent. Peng indeed.'

Jasmine giggled. 'You're getting the hang of it, sir.'

'I try.'

'Actually, Mr Russell, can you just stand still for me?' It was one of the other girls, she had a tape measure in one hand a very mischievous look in her dark eyes. She stretched the tape up to his shoulders. 'How tall are you?'

'Six foot three. Why?'

'I want to see how this measures up on you.' She held something made out of the skull-and-crossbones fabric against his chest. 'Careful. Pins. Thanks, right. Needs shortening. Don't suppose you'd be our model on the night, sir?'

He took a step back. 'Absolutely not.'

The girl's shoulders sagged. 'Just, we can't get enough guys to help us out. No point making clothes if we can't see how they drape when you're walking or moving.'

God. What to say? She had a point, but he was not the guy for the job.

Victoria took the tape measure from the girl's hand. 'I'm sorry, Nisha, but Mr Russell is going to be very busy that night. It's the store official opening and he has a lot more to worry about than just us. We'll find some male models from somewhere. Or we'll just have to commandeer your brothers, right? I don't suppose your dad will let them have a night off work?'

The girl shook her head. 'He's already got them roped in to do the pop-up stall.'

'Nisha is Aziz's daughter,' Victoria explained. 'From the restaurant last night.'

'Fantastic. Tell your dad I'll be wanting a regular order of that chicken tikka masala.'

It was all fitting together. Victoria was right; he'd moved his business into a tight community where people helped each other out. It was something he'd never really considered when placing a store. Sure, he'd been on community boards as a rep for the Russell & Co firm, but he hadn't ever really contemplated getting involved on a deeper level. Now he was faced with another challenge; he wasn't sure what he was going to do, but he wanted to make the runway a success for these girls.

'We'll work out something for your models, don't worry.'

'Mint.' Jasmine laughed. 'Or we could teach you how to wiggle your bum and walk in a straight line at the same time.'

'Oh, no. No. There is not a chance in hell you will get me on that catwalk.'

'Come on. It's easy, sir.' Nisha put the fabric onto the table and started to stalk across the floor wiggling her hips in an exaggerated fashion. When she got to the end of the – very short – makeshift runway she stopped, put her hands on her hips and posed first to the left and then the right. Then she turned, walked back and grabbed Victoria's arm. 'Come on, miss. Show him how it's done.'

'No way!' Screeching, Victoria shook her head. 'I can't do that. I have no idea how it's done.'

'Yes, you have, miss. You showed us last week.' Jasmine's eyes were wide and glittering. 'Come on.'

He couldn't think of a better thing to see. 'Come on, Victoria, how else will the girls learn? You need to show us how it's done.'

If looks could have killed he'd have been struck dead. She was shaking her head, but it was more out of frustration than refusal.

'Aww, miss. You did it last week.' A third girl who this far hadn't said a word, suddenly piped up. 'You not shy of the guy?'

'Not at all, Billie.' Victoria's back stiffened and he could see the indecision in her eyes. Why not do exactly what she'd been doing for weeks in front of him? Then there was the slightest hint of a smile on her lips. It grew, her cheeks flushed. Her eyes danced. Eventually, as the noise level rose with the girls chanting *Miss, Miss, Miss,* she raised her palms for silence. 'OK, just once. Then it's time for you all to pack up.'

She looked at them all in turn, gaze lingering just a second longer as she looked at Oliver. Her hair was now falling around her face, enhancing her eyes and the smooth curve of her cheek. Her mouth opened slightly, her tongue darted out to lick her bottom lip as she asked him, 'Deal?'

Bring it on. He gestured to the small space in front of her, wishing there weren't three other people in the room and thinking of all the things he'd like to do to her and with her and said, 'Deal.'

'OK. Watch and learn.' Victoria threw her head back, slid her hands low onto her hips and stepped her right foot in front of the left. Her hips swayed to the left, then the right, then the left. He couldn't draw his gaze away and only did so as she turned one-eighty degrees and stopped. She stepped left and right, twisting her body slightly, then walked forward. He was mesmerized. Enthralled. His peripheral vision blurred as he narrowed his gaze to her. To her eyes. To her. She was beautiful. Elegant. Demure yet strong. Fun. Kind. And sexy as hell.

His skin felt tight, his jeans felt tight, he had an urge to whip her into his arms. An ache to touch her as she strutted across the room back and forth, wiggling her backside wearing the defiant sexy expression of the hundreds of models he'd seen in magazines. He'd dated some of them, God knew, but none of them had captured his interest as much as she did. He wanted her.

But the spell broke as she clapped her hands. 'Right, the show's over. Time to go home, you horrible lot.'

'Naw, miss.' Jasmine pouted.

'I know, I know. I love this class too.' But Victoria shrugged. 'Same time next week. And you all need to think how you want your work to be described in the brochure I'm having made to hand out to the audience.'

After another decibel level increase – as they chatted and packed their bags then shuffled off with a chorus of goodbyes – silence fell.

Victoria closed the door behind them and leaned back against it, her body sagging a little in relief. 'I love them to pieces but they're exhausting. I wish I had that much energy on a Friday night. I remember when I was just starting to get ready to go out at this time, now all I'm fit for is sleep.'

Oliver glanced at his watch, amazed at how fast time had gone this evening. 'It's only nine o'clock. But yeah... they're exhausting. And great.'

Pride shone in her face. 'Thank you for coming to meet them.'

'My pleasure.' Actually, the pleasure was being with her, he realized, not for the first time. He couldn't remember the last time he'd wanted to see a woman so badly. He watched as she walked across the room and began tidying up the table. 'You need a hand?'

'I just need to fold everything up and pop it back on the shelves. They're good kids, but they make a hell of a mess.'

'You should tell them to tidy up after themselves.' Embarrassingly, he couldn't remember the last time he'd folded anything at all, but he picked up some denim and made the best attempt he could.

She smiled as she watched him refold it into something that resembled a square. 'I just love to see them so excited by their projects, and then time flies and suddenly they have to go home. I don't want to waste my time with them on tidying when we could be creating.'

'You're going to be such a sucker with your own kids.'

'Never going to happen.' She turned away and put a box onto a shelf.

'How do you know? They'll wrap you round their little fingers.'

Shaking her head, she picked up a fistful of zips in all colours. 'Such a mess.'

And that conversation was closed. No marriage. No kids. What was he missing here? Sure, a family wasn't every woman's dream, but she seemed to like her students, maybe it was babies she wasn't fond of.

Maybe he should just mind his own business.

They worked around each other, circling as they bent and folded and stretched to put things back on the shelves. Every time he caught her eye, she gave him a small smile that reached into his heart and tugged. Whereas she'd been the confident teacher a few minutes ago she was shy around him in here. Interesting.

He was just straightening – after wrestling a bag of feathers onto a full shelf – when he found himself face to face with a notice board on the wall covered in colourful laminated words like *honeymoon* and *wedding day dreams*, and pictures of wedding dresses, beaches, bouquets and smiling couples. It felt deeply intimate and aspirational. And a little surprising given the things she'd said last night.

He studied it for a while. Were these her wedding dreams? Had she spun him a line about not being the marrying type? 'Considering you're not planning to ever get married you seem to have the wedding dress all picked out. And the flowers.' His eyebrows rose. 'And the honeymoon. Hawaii? Does the guy get a say in it? It is his wedding too.'

She came and stood next to him, arms folded, a smile playing on her lips. 'That's not a wedding vision board. It's a collection vision board.'

'And that is?'

'A *design*' – she emphasized the word *design* as if he was an idiot and rolled her eyes in amusement – 'collection has a theme, a colour scheme, specific shapes and forms that inform the styles and ideas around my dresses for a particular season. I might not see myself doing it, but I do like to think I can make each bride's wedding day unique.'

'And Hawaii?'

'That's a little dream of my own. I'd love to go there one day.' She beamed as she turned to him pointing to the pictures of palm trees, white sand and clear blue seas. 'I'm not getting married but I'm not saying I don't put any of myself into my creations. You have to get inspiration from somewhere, right?'

His gaze travelled along the wall to a large framed photo on a shelf of four young women dressed in long, slinky ball gowns and vertiginous heels. They were laughing at something off-camera and looked freer than he'd ever felt in his entire life. 'And this? Special?'

'My friends.' Her hand stilled as he stepped closer to take a better look.

'You look like you're enjoying yourselves. Some kind of celebration?'

'A summer ball. End of school year. End of school full stop.' She blinked, her body language suddenly closed which was at odds with her words. It was a celebratory picture and yet she was so still and her eyes were suddenly sad.

'You all look so young.' She was still the most beautiful woman in the picture. Her arms were wrapped around the waists of a blonde, almost frail-looking girl and a sun-kissed one with wild corkscrew curls. Another dark-haired young woman stood at the end, clasping corkscrew girl in an embrace and laughing.

'It's nearly ten years ago. We were all turning eighteen that academic year. Just about to embark on a new phase in our lives. We were excited to be moving on, excited at what we had in store.'

Why had her manner changed just looking at the picture? Why had she shivered at such a joyful image? 'Which was what?'

'Fashion design school for me. Daredevil Malie' – she pointed to the sporty, wild-haired one next to her – 'is half Hawaiian and half English, and moved over to Maui to explore that part of her heritage. She's still there and teaches surfing.'

Ah. 'Hence the Hawaii honeymoon?'

She laughed softly. 'Two birds, one stone and all that. Zoe is a travel writer who currently lives in Australia but could be anywhere at any given moment and Lily, the only one who decided to stay in Hawke's Cove' – she pointed first to the willowy blonde and then the woman on the end – 'runs a restaurant.'

Judging by the affection in her eyes they clearly all meant a lot to her. 'Invite them to the opening day, as my guests. I'll make sure they get the full VIP treatment.'

'I'd love to, but they won't be able to make it.' She turned back and met his eyes and he saw a world of sorrow settle there.

'Why not?'

'They all live in different parts of the world. Lily may be able to come up from Devon, but the others… no. I don't think so.' She turned away. This seemed to matter to her.

'They mean a lot to you.'

'Of course, we went through so much together.' Her hand went to her belly and she looked a little uncomfortable talking about this. 'Good and bad.'

He tried to push. 'Those teenage years, eh? I would not live them again if you paid me. So much angst. So much trying to find out who you are and what you want.'

'And then plans change and along the way you become a different person.'

Interesting. She'd thrown him a clue. He grabbed it. 'How did plans change?'

'It's not importan—' She blinked slowly, then took a deep breath. 'OK. It's no secret. That night, a few minutes after that photo was taken, we were in a car accident. It was bad. And it derailed us all for a few months. I deferred my college place for a year.'

'God, I had no idea. A car accident? I'm sorry.' He checked her closely, as if it had just happened. There were no visible scars, but she seemed shaken at the memory.

'Not your fault. I'm OK. Look, I'm here. I'm fine.' She gestured to the room as if to show him how far she'd come.

'But what happened? Were you hurt? Is this what you meant when you said you'd been in shock before?'

She nodded, her arms moving from her belly to her chest, wrapping tight around herself like a shield, like armour. 'We got hit by another car, spun out of control. It was...' She shuddered and inhaled deeply. 'The worst thing that ever happened to me. But I'm fine now. Do I look hurt?'

Only sad, regretful and trying hard to pretend she was as fine as she said she was. But something in her guarded eyes told him he couldn't push her for more details. Yet. He wondered how she'd react if he held her, just to soothe that pain away until the memory faded.

She'd probably bawl him out, and she'd be right; they had a deal and she was hellbent on sticking to it. He didn't need to get any more deeply involved with her. He was just finding it hard not to. 'You don't look hurt, you look beautiful, as always, Victoria.'

Her eyes closed for a moment and she seemed to be steadying herself, but then she opened them again and smiled. 'Thank you, but you don't have to say that. No one else is here.'

'It's the truth.' She was quite simply the most dazzling woman he'd ever met in whichever situation he saw her in – when teaching she was bright and focused and so in the moment with those girls that she hadn't even heard him enter the room. When pulling pints she was fun and approachable, and when she spoke about her passions in design and making clothes she literally shone. He didn't have to pretend she was beautiful, he wasn't trying to live in a fiancé role here, he was speaking the truth.

Frowning, she opened her mouth as if to say something more, thought the better of it and stepped away, making him drag his eyes from the photo. But he didn't want to. These women looked so vibrant and carefree and yet he could see the effect the accident had had on her.

'You look shaken up. It must have been hard for you, Victoria. If ever you want to talk about it, I'm here.'

Her back straightened. 'It was a long time ago. Almost ten years, as I said.'

'And yet you're wearing it still.'

She shook her head, slowly let her arms fall from her chest. 'Only when I remember. But we have lots of brilliant memories too. We had a holiday in Ibiza a couple of months before that ball and we had such a lot of laughs. We had to smuggle Zoe out of her house, and she lied to her parents about where she was. For days. They'd always struggled to allow her to be herself and just wanted to wrap her in cotton wool and never let her leave the Cove. She wanted to fly. My mum encouraged my dreams, but Zoe's parents, like yours, didn't want her to have any.'

'That must have been tough on Zoe. Growing up is hard enough without having your wings clipped.'

She smiled, understanding the subtext. 'You weren't allowed that. You had your life mapped out.'

He noticed she was relieved to be changing the subject and shining the spotlight on him, but he would return to it another time. There was something about the car accident and those friends of hers that had affected her greatly. For now, he'd follow her conversational lead.

'Oh, I grew up pretty quickly at boarding school. I had a great time doing everything I was expected to do, I didn't know anything different. I just wasn't encouraged to dream of things like drawing or surfing. It didn't fit the box they wanted to put me in.'

But he was starting to dream now… dream of doing something different, something more. Stretching himself further than spreadsheets and rebuilds. What, he wasn't quite sure yet, but an idea around helping kids who hadn't been as lucky as he had was forming. No details as he hadn't yet found the right fit, but it would definitely be about giving back, paying forward. Which made taking on the family business full-time difficult. But he would do it. Do both. Victoria had made him start to think what could be possible.

She smiled, her eyes softening and lighting up. 'I can't help with the surfing, but I can teach you to draw if you like?'

Her sketches were tacked to the walls, he'd seen her doodles. There was no way he was going to compete with that. 'Not a chance. Creativity is lost on me. But I can definitely make an exquisite spreadsheet.'

That made her laugh. 'Clearly we see the world very differently. My definition of beauty is nothing to do with numbers.'

Sure. But his definition of beauty was standing right here. She was so close her perfume filled the space, her laughter was a gentle song that made his heart lift. Her skin so clear and smooth he wanted to touch it. Touch *her*. He reached his fingers to her cheek. 'Victoria, I've never met anyone like you before.'

He could feel her trembling under his fingertips. 'Lucky you.'

'I mean it. You're amazing.' He ran his thumb over her bottom lip, and she blinked up at him. The connection between them tightened.

She smiled, warily, her heated gaze clashing with his. 'We can't do this. *Shouldn't...*' Yet she stepped closer.

And he couldn't think of a single reason why they couldn't have one kiss. 'We can.'

Her lips parted as he thumbed her bottom lip, a whimper in her throat. She wanted to do this as much as he did, he could see it written over her face, but she was fighting it. 'It's just business, Oliver. Let's not forget that.'

'But—' He wanted to say it was becoming more than business but the shrill ringtone of his phone blasted into the breathy silence. She moved back to look up and meet his eyes. Hers were misted with intense desire that made his gut tighten.

She exhaled on a ragged breath. 'You should get that.'

'No.'

'You really should. What if it's important?'

He cursed under his breath, hating that this moment was broken. 'It'll be Andrew.'

'He needs you?'

'I am so over his problems. I need this. I want to kiss you and I know you want to kiss me.'

'I...' Her hand went to his chest, she gripped his jacket in a tight fist, pressing herself against him as if she wanted nothing more than to touch him, but he could see her consciously erasing the desire second by second.

He'd spooked her. Spooked himself.

His phone beeped again.

'Get it. Please, Oliver.' She turned away, mashing her hands together as if doing something else with them would stop her from grasping his clothes. Tight little fists locked in each other. He'd lost her already, the moment was definitely gone.

Huffing out a frustrated breath he picked up, read the message and his stomach fell. He closed his eyes wishing that when he opened them again the message would not be there. 'Oh. Damn.'

She wheeled round to face him, her eyes locked on his, fading desire mixed with concern. 'What is it? What's the matter? Is it your dad?'

'Kind of. Nothing bad. My parents are here.'

'What do you mean here?' She stalked over to the window. 'They're not downstairs in the bar, are they?'

'In London. They've just landed at the Edmiston Heliport in Battersea and they want to meet you.'

'So soon? I thought we had weeks to prepare.'

'Tonight. Now.' At her fallen face he explained, 'I casually mentioned we had a date tonight, just to get her out of my hair. I didn't know they were going to do this. Apparently, Dad's been called up to see his specialist tomorrow. They're bringing his treatment forward.'

'Can't we pretend I'm working?'

'Not if I've already told them we're on a date.'

Her eyes widened and she shook her head sharply. 'Oh, God.

I can't lie. I just can't. It's not in my nature, I can't – why did I let you talk me into this?'

'You'll be fine.' He put his hands on her shoulders to stop her from pacing, turned her to face him. She looked flushed with panic and he regretted the whole damned thing and what it was doing to her, but they'd started along this path and he couldn't stop now. He needed to convince his dad that his life was settled. 'Fiancée.'

She pulled away and started fussing over her hair, moving so quickly he couldn't keep up. 'Can we not announce the engagement until I'm ready? I need to know more about you before I can commit to that.'

'It's too late. I may have hinted we're already down that track.' Declared rather than hinted. 'But we've got this.'

She frowned but took a deep breath as she ran her palms down her jumper. 'Right. OK. We can do this. Lipstick? Hair? Is it OK? Do I look up to scratch?'

'I told you before. Beautiful. You are, what is it…? Well peng.' And also like a frightened bird ready to fly away from danger. He needed her with him and to do that he had to calm her, make her feel in control. Without thinking he pressed his lips to her forehead. She stopped moving. Froze completely.

'Oliver, we've got ourselves into very deep water.'

He slipped his hand into hers. 'Then let's hold each other up.'

CHAPTER NINE

HE WAS KISSING HER head and holding her hand and it was so lovely she closed her eyes and let herself sink into the feeling of being cared for and wanted. Of being beautiful in his eyes. She couldn't remember a time when anyone had treated her with such unguarded affection. Not even Peter. Their relationship, now she looked back, developed from fun and casual to her trying hard to please him and him making more demands. There hadn't been a mutual respect there, not like this. This sharing of dreams and ideas.

She let herself believe, just for a moment, that this was real. That she was Oliver's real girlfriend. A whole one who didn't have scars and damage and baggage and who could promise him the future he'd want.

He squeezed her hand and she felt the message resonate through her: they could do this. They could fool everyone into thinking they were a couple. But she had a bad feeling she wouldn't need to do much in the way of play-acting, because the affection she was starting to feel for him *was* real.

Not just that... he was a good guy, sure, but he was also a next-level sexy one. As she felt his palm in hers, his mouth on her forehead, skin against skin, desire rushed through her. Despite the trajectory they were on – meeting his parents and play-acting, she wanted to kiss him. Now. Wanted to explore his body, wanted to know how he tasted. Wanted to know what it would take to snap this thinly veiled self-control. The way her body ached for his touch, she didn't think it would take an awful lot.

When she pulled away and saw his smiling face she wondered if he was thinking that too. And if he was, she had to end it, right now, because neither of them could have any dreams of what ifs and possibilities here. She wasn't a good bet and definitely not Russell wife material and she couldn't let him think she was.

She needed to either finish it or make sure they never overstepped the line stopping them from turning from friends into something more. 'Oliver—'

'We've got to get going, we can talk more in the car.' He gave her a wink and tugged at her hand and, as she walked past the mannequins dressed in her students' designs, she remembered the reasons she'd agreed to this. She could wait a little longer before she said something. She just had to make sure she didn't fall into the trap of actually believing the lies.

She walked with him into the frosty night, round to the car park under the department store and climbed into a very sexy gunmetal grey car, relieved to see it didn't have anything remotely *family* about it. Just two seats. Leather. Expensive. She laughed. 'Might have known you'd have a convertible.'

'It's also a hybrid so I'm doing my bit for the environment.' His chest puffed out with pride. He didn't have any airs or graces, this car was just as much a treat for him as anyone, despite the billions in the bank. 'I just need something small to buzz around the city.'

'For when the helicopter is in for servicing?' She laughed,

having never known anyone who took a helicopter as transport. Even Blake Hawkesbury, the richest man in Hawke's Cove, just drove a car. This was a wealth she couldn't even imagine and just the thought of it made her anxious. How would his parents react to her? Just a small-town girl from Devon? Would they take one look at her and be utterly disappointed?

But Oliver laughed too, gunned the engine and eased the car onto the dark Chelsea street. 'We have two.'

She gaped at him. 'Two helicopters? How eco-friendly are helicopters?'

'We pay a lot of money in carbon offsets, trust me. It's just easier for my parents to get around, especially now Dad's sick. Having taken a few steps back from the business already they're now permanently based in Norfolk, so they don't need to come up to London very often, although they do keep an apartment in Knightsbridge for when they do. Driving is a nightmare for them both – Mum gets migraines and Dad can't concentrate for long, so they fly in and out. It's just logistics.'

It was out of her league. She ran her hand over the soft leather and wondered what he'd thought of her cosy bohemian studio above the wine bar. Her nerves jangled all over again. Of all the women he could have chosen, why had he asked her to do this? 'Where are we meeting them?'

'A little Italian brasserie around the corner from my house.' He grinned. 'The house you're thinking of moving into.'

The panic that had abated slightly took over again. 'I am?'

'But not until after the opening, because we're both so busy.'

'OK, that's good. At least they won't expect me to be there all the time. What's it like?'

'Mews. Three bedrooms. I have to admit it's a bit of a man cave, but you're a designer so you can see past that, right? It has potential for a couple. Or we could be planning to buy a different place together? Yes. That should be our plan. Where would you like to live?'

'I like where I am. I love my flat and it's perfect for me. I've never thought about anywhere else, to be honest.'

'Not sure we can both fit in to your spare bedroom.' He laughed, but images of them entwined together in her bed sprang into her head. The sun shining through the wooden blind slats, their bodies glistening with a post-sex sheen. His hair even more messy than now.

How would he look naked? How would he feel inside her? That last sudden thought shocked her. Shook her. Excited her.

She swallowed, pushing the picture from her brain and trying to focus on his words, 'Notting Hill is nice. Or Primrose Hill. Anywhere with a hill really. Or Highgate, that's where a lot of the celebs live.'

Victoria's heart thudded as panic threatened to take over. 'Oliver, this is all wrong.'

Her thoughts, her desires, these plans, their lies. All of it.

'Getting stage fright?' They stopped at a traffic light and he turned and snagged her gaze. He was enjoying this, but he covered her hand with his and squeezed. 'Hey. It's OK. It's for a good cause.'

She couldn't argue with that. Her girls and Oliver's dad. *Breathe.* 'OK. We've got barely any answers sorted. I need to know about your world, and we need to create ours. Where did we meet?'

'Outside work. We literally bumped into each other, right? I think it helps to keep things as true to life as possible.'

That was easy then. 'How long have we been seeing each other?'

'A couple of months. But we knew immediately.'

'We did?

'Sure.' His grin was now cheeky and mischievous. He certainly didn't have stage fright. 'Didn't I ask you to marry me that very first night?'

'But it wasn't real.' She bit back what she was going to actually say, which was a string of curse words. Because driving over to meet his parents was feeling very real indeed. 'So, what's your favourite colour?'

'I don't have one.'

'You must have. Everyone has a favourite colour.'

He looked at her jumper, his eyes smoothing over her like a caress. 'Pink.'

'Pink?' She knew it wasn't, but she went along with him. 'Good.'

'And white spots.' There was a smile hovering on his lips, it hit his eyes and made them dance with fun. He was messing with her head.

'Now you're stressing me out.' But making her laugh.

'Oh, and green. Green's good. Sometimes. If I'm in a green kind of mood. Oh, wait. What's that colour that's a bit brown and a bit cream. Trouser-type colour.'

'Beige?'

He pulled a face. 'God, no. I don't like that.'

Victoria took a deep breath and let it out slowly. 'Maybe you could give it a little thought? Your mother is bound to have an opinion on your favourite colour. It's the kind of thing mothers know. There'll be other things too. I just don't know what they are yet. Food? Maybe food. Oh, we covered that one already. What about favourite places to go on holiday?'

'I don't know, I love skiing but nothing beats a sultry hot Caribbean beach.' He shrugged. 'Nepal was epic. Prague is amazing. It's too hard to choose. Some questions don't have answers, Victoria. Some things aren't just black or white.'

'I think, to pass your mother's test, shades of grey won't cut it.'

'If shades of grey are involved then I definitely want to be too.' He captured her gaze and held it, looking at her the way he'd looked at her up against her back door. Like he wanted to kiss her. Heat skittled over her skin, raising the hairs on her arms, making her heart race. The longing tumbled back hitting her in the chest, her belly, lower. She wanted to kiss him. Now. Hard and fast. To see how he tasted, to see how it felt to be in his arms.

Big mistake. It would be a disaster to get involved with this man. He was too enigmatic, too much for her. She would come out broken at the end. And there definitely would be an end.

She was so shaken with need she could barely find her voice. 'Good acting, Ollie. Award-worthy.'

But the want in his gaze wasn't an act and neither was the struggle she saw there too. Despite the humour their connection was intense and hot and confusing after the hands-off professionalism of the deal. They were so close to stepping over that line. She closed her eyes and balled her hands into fists. This wasn't going well. This attraction was building and building and she didn't know how to handle it.

When she dared look again he was staring out of the car window, concentrating on the driving, propelling them towards his family. She focused on that. 'Right. Quick-fire round. Favourite toy growing up?'

He frowned and thought. 'Sega Mega Drive.' His voice was cracked with desire. He coughed, cleared his throat. Sat up straighter.

'Not a favourite teddy bear?'

'Didn't have one.'

'You must have had one, Oliver.' Really? His doting parents didn't buy him a bear? 'Everyone has a teddy bear.'

'At home, yes. But not at boarding school. I would have been bullied relentlessly.'

'Was it hard being away from your parents?'

'At first. It was different, strange and took a bit of getting used to. But I was an only child to older working parents. I was bored at home, to be honest, and besides, we were all in the same boat at school, so we formed tight friendships. Yes, I missed my parents at first but... things changed. The boys in those houses became family and I preferred to spend time with them in the holidays rather than rattling round my house with no one to play with and parents at meetings or dinners without me. It's probably selfish but it began to feel as if me being home was a burden, I was in the way of their amazing life where they jet-setted all over the world. We... well, became detached, I suppose. We lost touch as a family really.'

And he'd said boarding school wasn't difficult. In reality they'd edged each other out of their lives. 'I can't imagine being away for so long from my parents and my younger brother... even though he was very annoying growing up. Still is, you know, in a brother kind of way.'

Oliver shrugged. 'I wouldn't know. I don't have a brother, just a cousin. But if that counts then I totally get the annoying bit.'

'Your life has been very different to mine.'

'And now look at us. Who would have thought? Engaged to be married.' He pulled into a parking space outside a small restaurant set back from the road. It had fairy lights around the door and the name Antoine's painted on the window.

Oliver turned off the engine and smiled encouragingly. 'Right, time to go wow the 'rents.'

Before she could say anything, he jumped out, ran around the front of the car and opened her door. As she stepped out he took her hand and gave her a soft kiss on her cheek. 'Just be yourself. They will love you.'

She couldn't work out if this was an act or not, so just nodded, her words lost in her throat.

It will be fine. It will be fine. She'd been through worse and survived.

He held her hand tightly as they walked up to the door. Maybe he thought she was going to make a run for it. 'This is my parents' favourite place. They used to come here when they first started dating. It's also where my dad proposed. Where I had my very first outing straight from the hospital, after I was born. It's a family favourite. Special.'

Which made everything worse. Panic wove through her chest and she was tempted to turn and run but she wasn't the kind of person to renege on a promise. 'I don't know enough about you—'

'Ollie!' The door flew open and a cuddly, balding man in chef's whites threw his arms up. He pinched Oliver's cheeks as if he were his own son. 'Oliver Russell! Long time no eat? And who this?'

'This is Victoria. Victoria, this is Antoine, the best pasta chef in the world, and a long-time family friend.'

'*Bella, bella*. Pleased to meet you.' The chef took Victoria's free hand and shook. Then, as he turned back to Oliver, his face fell. 'They are out the back.'

Oliver nodded, the desire in his eyes replaced with concern. 'How is he?'

Antoine shook his head. 'Not good, I'm sorry. He needs to eat. You all need to eat. You all work too hard. But Victoria will be a good distraction, yes?'

Her stomach clenched. For someone who hated being in the spotlight she was going to be the main attraction.

The chef walked them through the cosy restaurant and she was surprised to see it wasn't as upmarket as she'd imagined. It was simple and homely with framed photographs of the Amalfi coast on walls that had been draped with red and green tinsel for Christmas. Classical festive hymns played in the background. The delicious aroma of garlic and rosemary infused the air making her stomach rumble in anticipation – the last thing she'd eaten had been breakfast because somehow, thinking about spending the evening with Oliver had snatched her appetite clean away. But now she wasn't sure she'd be able to manage a mouthful in front of his parents either.

Antoine's was obviously popular as the restaurant was crammed with diners grouped at little wooden tables that filled the room. But everyone stopped and smiled at Antoine as he squeezed Victoria and Oliver across the floor. Then, before she could take another steadying breath, she was in a private room at the back. About the same size as her spare bedroom, it housed a large table and a mahogany sideboard stacked with plates and glassware.

As Antoine led them in all conversation stopped and she inhaled sharply; three pairs of eyes peered up at her. Three Russells. Some of the most influential people in the country, right here.

Oh, God.

'Hello, family of mine. We made it!' Oliver wrapped an arm around her shoulder, likely to show their 'togetherness', but she froze. Completely. Her body wouldn't soften, wouldn't move. They were looking at her and she'd locked in self-preservation mode.

What to do? Alarmed, she looked up at Oliver and tried to tell him telepathically that she couldn't do this, but he squeezed the back of her arm reassuringly and smiled down at her as if she was the best thing that had ever happened to him. 'Here she is. My Victoria.'

And still the eyes were on her. No one spoke.

My Victoria. It had been so long since anyone had talked about her with such longing in their voice it took her a moment to remember it was just an act. He was good at this.

His pupils flared, nudging her to respond.

Right. Yes. Fiancée. She edged into his embrace, felt the strength in his hold, the warmth of his body. He smelled so good as she lay her head against his shoulder and dug deep for her best smile. 'Er… hi, everyone.'

'Victoria, darling.' A trim woman in her seventies dressed in a neat dove grey cashmere dress and pearls stood and came around the table, trembling as she took Victoria's hand in both of hers. 'I am so very pleased to meet you. My dear, you are such a salve to my heart.'

'This is my mother Stella.' Oliver laughed as he tugged his arm away from Victoria's shoulder and air-kissed his mother's powdered cheek. 'Put her down, Mum, or you'll scare her off.'

'Oh, Oliver, don't underestimate her. If she's won you over she must have more balls than Russell & Co's Board of Directors combined. You notwithstanding. That right, Victoria?'

As the grip on her hands lessened Victoria looked into the older lady's eyes and saw so much hope there it almost broke her heart. Despite her wealth and social standing, she was just a mother wanting the best for her boy.

'Oh, I don't know about that. Hello, Mrs Russell—'

'Call me Stella, please, everyone does. Do you prefer Vicki, Vic, Tory, Victoria?'

'Most of my friends call me V, work colleagues use Vicki, Mum and Dad call me Victoria. Basically, I answer to anything.'

'Victoria it is, then. Such a lovely name and also the name of my favourite aunt so that's a very good sign. I've never met any of Oliver's girlfriends before. I just know you're special.'

Too bad she wasn't actually meeting Oliver's girlfriend, then, just a stand-in. 'Lovely to meet you too, er, Stella. I've heard so much about you.'

Most of which Victoria had found online. She tried to remember the details. Stella Russell. Seventy-four. Daughter of an Earl. Married at… what was it? Twenty-five? No children until she was forty-two. Then Oliver. Great support to her husband.

'This is my father Eric.' A steady hand on her shoulder as Oliver edged her away from Stella and towards a frail man in a wheelchair. Victoria disguised her momentary inhale as a cough. He was barely recognizable from the hearty and robust man she'd seen so many times on the television. He pushed down on the wheelchair arms to stand up but didn't look strong enough, so she went over and bent to shake his hand. 'Mr Russell, I am so happy to meet you.'

'Not as much as I am to meet you. Thank God someone's brave enough to take him off my hands.' Despite his frailty his grip was still solid and strong, and she just knew from the determination in Eric's eyes that he was going to fight this illness, which made her feel as if she wanted to fight along with him.

But – on the flip side – also a little afraid at the lies she was telling right now, to his face. What would he do if he ever found out this wasn't exactly the blissed-up romance they were portraying?

'And this is Andrew, my cousin.' Oliver nodded towards a tall, dark-haired man, with eyes that were too small and too close together, sitting at the table. Even though they bore a definite Russell resemblance – with the same proud jawline and dark messy hair – the looks they gave each other were mistrusting and lacked any familial warmth.

Oliver's voice flattened. 'I wasn't expecting you to be here.'

'Your mother thought it would be nice for your girlfriend to meet us all at once.' Andrew nodded towards Victoria, those small eyes cold and searching. The way he put emphasis on *girlfriend* was suspicious and sullen and he clearly didn't think any of this was nice at all. 'He's kept you a tight secret, Victoria. I see him every day and he's never even mentioned you. Not once.'

'I… er… don't know…' How to answer that? Her heart thumping hard against her ribcage, Victoria went for a shrug and clasped her hands together before she started her nervous gesticulating and anxiety-driven verbal diarrhoea or blurting out the truth.

'Ahem. Talking of secrets…' Stella interjected with a steely tone, clearly used to intervening between the cousins. She looked from Oliver to Andrew and back again with ill-concealed concern, then patted the empty seat next to her for Victoria to sit down.

Oliver took a seat on Victoria's right side, next to his father. Victoria grabbed his hand under the table, for strength and support and not because she liked holding it.

Even though she did.

He pressed a gentle kiss to her cheek and squeezed her hand. Her heart sped up a little.

Stella smiled. 'Oliver let slip that your engagement was being kept hush-hush until the opening. I'm so glad you agreed to let us in on it before then.'

Victoria dredged what she hoped was a delighted, excited expression. 'Not a problem. You all know before...' *Everyone.* 'Anyone.'

'Oh? That is so lovely.' Stella pressed her hand to her heart and blinked back a sheen of tears. 'This calls for champagne. Antoine! Bring a bottle of your best bubbles, please. I was beginning to think this day would never happen. It makes me so happy.' With shining eyes Stella glanced at Victoria's left hand, her mouth forming an 'O'.

'He proposed without a ring?'

Victoria clenched her left hand. *Shoot.* They hadn't got around to talking about that. 'Yes.'

'No,' Oliver said at the same time.

Hot damn. This was something they should have discussed.

Stella's gaze moved slowly from Victoria to Oliver, her smile wavering as her voice cooled. 'Yes, or no?'

Oliver coughed. 'It was a spur-of-the-moment proposal, I just couldn't wait to ask her. She drives me crazy, what can I do?' He raised one shoulder nonchalantly as if it was all completely out of his control and he just couldn't understand it.

'We haven't got around to choosing one yet.' Victoria nodded, taking his lead. 'Oliver's so busy, you know, with the store. I said we could wait.' Then she cringed as, from across the table, Andrew's stare bore into her.

He knew. He knew this was all a lie. He knew and he would wait until the worst moment to tell Stella and Eric and it would break their hearts and break the trust they had with their only son.

Antoine appeared, bearing a huge platter of antipasto and the heat around the engagement dissolved into *oohs* and *aahs* at the glistening olives and slivers of Parma ham.

The Russells started to eat but Victoria couldn't face anything and pushed her food around her plate with her fork, hoping they wouldn't notice. She didn't think she'd manage to get anything past the lump of lies in her throat. There were so many facts of their fictional relationship they needed to agree on. So much she needed to learn about him. She was going to resurrect her list of questions and demand a sit-down meeting so they could get their stories straight. If they survived tonight.

Conversation was stilted and interspersed with groans of pleasure at the delicious-tasting food, but presently Stella's focus turned back to the newly engaged couple. 'Oliver works too hard. Like father like son, I suppose. But I know Russell & Co is going to be in safe hands with you two at the helm.'

You two? The panic rose up into Victoria's throat. Did Stella mean Oliver and Andrew? Or Oliver and Victoria? She couldn't tell. Did they expect her to work for the company too? Surely not? The way Andrew's lip curled in response gave her the distinct impression he thought he was being edged out.

But then Victoria almost laughed as she remembered: this farce was only until opening day then she could sneak off and live her own life. Pretend she and Oliver just hadn't been a good match, grown apart… all those usual excuses. And she could walk away, keeping her heart intact and, hopefully, not shattering any of theirs too much. His parents were a successful power couple, they'd get over this in no time and then Oliver would find his real-life partner and Victoria Scott would be a distant memory of some girl he used to know.

Stella was still talking, 'You need to treat her well, Oliver.' She leaned across and tutted at her son. 'You can't keep a girl like Victoria waiting. She really, really needs a ring.'

'On it, Mother. Give me a chance, she only just said yes.' There was humorous censure in his voice, the pained embarrassment of a child in his mother's smothering gaze. But at least the attention was back on him.

Not for long. Stella turned to Victoria. 'And Oliver tells me you're moving in together.'

Oh, yes! Victoria breathed. She knew the answer to this. 'Right, after the store—'

'Opening.' Oliver finished her sentence and she glanced over to him. He squeezed her hand again and she saw the smile in his eyes. Genuine warmth. This was going OK. They could do this.

She chanced another sip of champagne and let it soothe her throat and her nerves. Maybe she needed to loosen up a bit. She took another sip. And another and felt the tension ease away.

Antoine cleared away the plates and she fiddled with the stem of her glass, not sure what to say next, but Oliver gently pressed her thigh with his palm and offered his hand for her to grip again. She took it gratefully.

As she breathed out, his thumb stroked across the base of hers, then over her palm sending shivers across her skin. His touch was like a switch turning on in the depths of her body. Heat rose inside her and she couldn't help but stroke his hand too.

Stupid idea.

Her nerves were a mess, they'd already embarked on this ridiculous journey together and now she was stoking the connection between them on a sensual level too.

Worse, she felt herself instinctively leaning closer to him. It was crazy – madness – that he had this kind of effect on her, but she just couldn't seem to stop her body from reacting. Even here, with his family. She was like a silly teenager with a crush.

Realizing she was still looking at him – and probably drooling – she drew her gaze away, cheeks burning, but Stella clearly thought it was adorable. She clapped her hands. 'Oh, look at you. Do you two lovebirds want a moment alone? He can't keep his eyes off you.'

'No! No. I'm just fine, thank you.' Victoria took a sip of water.

Thankfully, Eric touched his son's hand and all eyes turned to him. 'Wheel me through to the bathroom, Ollie lad.'

'Right you are, Dad.' Oliver stood and tugged the wheelchair back, but it came to a shuddering halt. 'Damn. Bloody thing's caught.'

'It's stuck on the carpet. Wait. I know a trick.' Glad to be able to use some of the excess tension that made her want to move her restless hands Victoria jumped up and pushed her weight down on the handle, which had the simultaneous effect of levering the front wheel up a little, then she manoeuvred the chair backwards and out onto the wooden floor by the service counter. 'You have to get the balance of your weight right so you can tilt it back and then push it forward.'

Eric clapped. 'Thank you, my dear. We're just getting used to it.'

Oliver caught her up and took control of steering the wheelchair as they walked towards the bathroom together. 'Have you got an advanced driver's licence or something?'

She sighed her relief at being away from the table, just for a minute. 'I've had a lot of practice with these pesky things. One of my best friends is in a wheelchair and we've got stuck plenty of times.'

'Best friend?' He frowned. 'Not one of the girls in the photo? The car accident? Hell, Victoria—'

'Don't. Please,' she whispered, shaking her head as her chest tightened at the memory. 'Not here. Not now.'

Hot damn. Bad enough he'd caught her off-guard earlier and she'd told him about the accident. The last thing she needed was to rake all of that up here in front of his family.

The accident was always off-limits as far as she was concerned and the only people who truly understood were Zoe, Malie and Lily. They'd been through it with her. They'd lived the pain and fear. They'd all fought to survive and heal. Victoria's injuries had been bad enough, and she'd had to re-align her hopes and dreams. But Zoe's spinal injury had been the worst thing out of it and Victoria would never, ever forgive herself for that.

Shaking off the memories she smiled over to Eric. 'It's a bit of a learning curve, but usually the problem's caused by the wheels wanting to do their own thing. A bit like shopping trolleys, you know? They all want to go in different directions.'

'I'm sorry.' Oliver ran his palm down her shoulder, oblivious to the fact his dad was probably listening and watching. Oblivious or not caring.

'What for?'

He leaned to her ear. 'The pain you carry around with you. I wish I could help.'

His smile was kind. It seemed to say, *I understand. You've got this.* And it tugged at her heart. He'd been so gentle when they'd talked about that night, encouraging her to talk when she wanted or needed. Like a friend would. He'd be a good friend to have, she thought. Straight up and loyal. And a dangerous adversary to have, too. The Russells had power and money and knew *people.*

'I'm fine. But thank you.' She gave him what felt like a wavering smile in return, then he disappeared into the bathroom with his dad and she turned, taking a big, deep breath in readiness for returning to her audience.

But Oliver was back in seconds. 'Victoria,' he whispered. 'Stop. Dad said I have to wait for him here.' He took her hand and drew her closer out of earshot of the table. 'Just checking you're OK? You know… about all this.'

'We're doing fine, do you think?'

'Brilliantly. They'd never guess we weren't a couple.'

'They're lovely. So lovely.' She looked over to the table and saw Andrew swiping on his phone while Stella sat upright staring straight ahead, worrying a napkin in her hand. What was she thinking? Did she believe them? Was she anxious about her husband? Her son?

Oliver followed Victoria's line of sight and smiled. 'She tends to get a bit over-excited, I'm sorry. But she likes you.'

'Andrew doesn't.'

Oliver's expression hardened. 'I'm sorry about him too and I honestly didn't know he was going to be here otherwise I would have prepared you. But they're right, you might as well meet them all at once and get it over with.'

Victoria couldn't help laughing. 'You make it sound like taking bad medicine.'

'Believe me, dealing with Andrew is worse than a bout of stomach flu.'

'He feels threatened. You're taking his job and now they're talking about me being involved too. He's being edged out and he doesn't like it.'

'He's going to have to live with it. Unfortunately, my cousin's career is about to take a swerve.' Oliver let out a deep breath. 'Right, I'll go get Dad and see you back at the table. Not long to go and we'll be finished.'

As he turned away her heart stung a little at his words. Sure, she wanted it to be over. But she didn't want it to end just yet. Not with him anyway. In fact, despite everything she wanted him to caress her hand again. She wanted to lean into him, to feel his gaze on her, to see the warmth in his face when he looked at her.

Yes, she knew now without a shadow of a doubt, she wanted this thing between them to be real. She wanted him to fall for her. *As if.* As if anyone would do that. Foolish, stupid woman. She knew better than to let herself believe in fairy tales. She needed to get the hell out and put an end to all this as soon as they were alone.

But for now she was going to act out of her skin and make sure she delivered her side of the deal. Unscathed.

Pressing her lips together she made her way back to the table.

★ ★ ★

Despite her ever-present anxiety the evening flew by and the conversation steered away from the engagement and focused much more on business talk. Stella was impressed with Victoria's teaching and keen to hear about the pop-up stalls. Eric was a funny conversationalist and listened enthusiastically to Victoria wax lyrically about her dress designs.

Antoine's lobster ravioli was divine, the champagne delicious. Other than Andrew's dark, sceptical stares and the lack of truth in any of it, it would have been the perfect evening to meet a fiancé's family.

Finally, after the best tiramisu Victoria had ever eaten, Stella leaned over. 'Oh, I must ask. Have you set the date?'

Her appetite had returned just at the end of the meal, probably because it signalled the coming end of the interrogation. Licking her spoon Victoria turned to Stella. 'For?'

Stella blinked, clearly confused. 'The wedding, of course.'

Of course. The damned wine had gone to her head and made her forgetful and careless. She tried to cover. 'Oh. No. We haven't decided yet.'

Stella clearly had. 'August. An August wedding will be perfect. I'll call Barbara and make sure she keeps August free.'

The whole of August? What were they planning? A wedding festival? Did Victoria have a say in this? 'Um… Barbara?'

Had she somehow missed mention of someone important?

Stella gave a sharp nod of her head. 'The dog sitter. If she's not free, then we'll have to do it another time. I can't have anyone but Barbara looking after my girls, Suky and Sali.'

'Mum's dogs,' Oliver clarified. 'Cavaliers.'

Stella frowned as if the use of the word *dogs* wasn't good enough for her girls. 'Pedigree. Suky won "best in breed" at Crufts two years in a row.'

'Lovely.' Their wedding was going to be arranged around the availability of her fake fiancé's mother's dogsitter?

'Excellent. It's settled then. An August wedding.' Stella pulled out her phone and started to tap on it. 'There's a lovely little chapel in our village. I can have a word with the vicar on Sunday if you like?'

This was getting just a little too much. Victoria pigged her eyes at Oliver. *Do something.*

He grimaced. 'Mother, I think you need to back off a little. We have a lot to work out.' Oliver glanced over to his father. 'And Dad's looking a bit peaky. It's getting late and he has treatment tomorrow. He needs his rest.'

An August wedding. Would Eric be well enough to attend it? Had anyone thought about that? Would he even be here? Victoria's heart lurched. She liked this old man, she really hoped she'd see him again.

Stella fixed a smile. 'Yes, of course, I'm sorry, it's your wedding, I was just trying to be helpful, but I get carried away. Eric's always telling me off about it, Oliver too. Can't help it.'

'It's fine. Honestly.' It clearly was the most hopeful thing Stella had in her life right now and Victoria didn't want to take it away from her just yet.

'We should go. It was delightful to meet you, Victoria.' With a warm smile Oliver's mother dropped her phone into a large Louis Vuitton handbag, stood and signalled for Antoine before kissing her son on his cheek. 'Let me know the date soon, though, darling. We need to get it into the diary, you know how busy we get in the summer.'

An August wedding in a village chapel. Right. Only if Barbara was free. Stella was delightful but formidable. Victoria summoned a smile and silently wished the best of luck to Oliver's future wife. She'd need the diplomacy of a hostage negotiator to wrangle a wedding she actually wanted. But, dogs and chapels on a warm summer's day did sound lovely.

If she was getting married anywhere – and she couldn't imagine a scenario where it would ever happen – it would be back in Devon surrounded by her friends and family. Zoe, Malie and Lily would be bridesmaids just like they'd always promised each other from way back at primary school. She'd make the dresses, she'd choose a bouquet very similar to the one on her vision board; cascading white roses and baby's breath.

There she was with that fairy-tale thinking again.

The bill was paid, Oliver wheeled his father out and secured both parents in a taxi that purred at the kerbside. Andrew stood a few feet away, his coat collar pulled up tight, his eyes fixed on Victoria. The car wasn't moving, Andrew wasn't leaving, and they were all back to staring at her. She felt as if she was the monkey in a circus and they were expecting her to perform again.

'What are we all waiting for?' she side-mouthed to Oliver. But when he tugged her gently to face him and put his palm to her cheek her heart rattled hard. His face was so close, his eyes had that soft look he'd had earlier.

And then she knew. They were expecting The Kiss.

At the thought of kissing him her nerve endings burned. But how much harm could one little kiss really do? He'd kissed her cheek earlier and it had been fine. Sensual as heck, but she'd managed to keep control.

She edged towards him, those dark eyes drawing her nearer and nearer. His mouth was tantalizingly close. So close her heart beat out a desperate rhythm forgetting this was all make-believe. *Yes. Yes. Yes.*

Then his lips slid across hers.

Oh God. Just the softest of touches was enough to make her body quiver. He cupped her face, his fingers at her temples, his touch a torch to a flame that ignited inside her.

Without thinking she wound her arms around his neck and pressed against him. Everything around them seemed to blur. All she knew was his scent, his touch, those eyes glittering with desire, that invisible thread tugging them closer.

She leaned into him, opening her mouth. He tasted of wine and something quintessentially male. Sex. Heat. Need. It was supposed to be make-believe, but she didn't have to act. It was as if her body had been made to do this. Instinct took over, her breath coming in soft stuttered gasps. A deep longing melted into her limbs, hot and liquid. She couldn't have stopped if she'd tried.

Clasping her face with both hands he deepened the kiss, nipping at her bottom lip. A moan escaped her throat and she pressed closer against him feeling the hard ridges of his body. He wanted her.

She wanted him. Wanted this. Wanted more.

From somewhere behind her the taxi tooted, crashing her back to reality and she dragged herself away from his arms, only to catch his mother waving triumphantly from the car window as it disappeared into the darkness. Andrew had skulked away into the shadows.

Which left just her and Oliver out in the crisp night air, hearts racing, breath ragged. The aftermath of that kiss hovered over them like a sultry cloud. She hadn't wanted it to stop. She wished they hadn't.

She was glad they had.

This was all a huge mistake.

With shaking limbs, she stepped away, putting distance between them, to stop herself from going straight back into his arms for a rerun. 'Oliver. I have to go. Early, you know… I mean it's late. I need to get up early.'

'Hey, what's wrong?' Oliver held his hand out to her, his dark expression heated with lust, stealing the breath from her throat.

'Ollie. I have to go.' With every ounce of effort she could muster she waved her trembling hand towards another approaching black cab. She needed to get away from him before she got even more carried away.

Before she started to believe in this romance as much as Oliver's parents did.

CHAPTER TEN

DAMN. WHAT THE HELL was he doing?

Oliver watched Victoria's cab disappear around the corner and huffed out a deep breath. That had been no ordinary kiss. It had been a melding of wants and needs. The summation of the attraction growing between them. It had been pure and raw, and he hadn't wanted it to end, and neither had she if the way she'd pressed herself against him and moaned into his mouth was anything to go by.

But they'd crossed a line they'd agreed was sacrosanct.

What the actual hell? It was supposed to be an act but every fibre in him wanted to take that kiss to its logical and inevitable conclusion. His house was mere yards from here. If she hadn't stopped them he'd have suggested they go there. Asked her to stay. Asked her for more.

And then?

He'd have his eye off the ball. He'd derail the plans he'd put in place. He'd do something he'd never done before and allow himself to start thinking of a future, to start caring for someone.

Someone who had made it clear she didn't want what he had to offer, so the last thing he needed to do was fall for her. He wasn't prepared to waste emotions on someone who didn't want him the way he'd felt his parents had when he was young. So he needed to follow their lead; withdraw, step away from connection, draw that line in the sand again and stay the hell on his side.

'Lils, I'm a bad person. I've done a terrible thing.' Within five minutes of getting home Victoria had video-called her friend, and, true to form, Lily was there for her, despite having to clear up after a busy night at the restaurant.

Victoria lay back on her bed and stared up at the ceiling, trying to put the feelings she had whirling around in her chest and low down in her belly into a metaphorical box. But they wouldn't go in. She couldn't close the lid. Even now, her body was trembling and her skin was alight at the memory of his touch.

Lily gave her a reassuring smile. She was good at steering her friends back on course. 'You? Never. I can't imagine you ever doing anything terrible, V.'

But they both knew differently. 'Don't go there. We both know I have.'

Lily shook her head as she sat back on her tall stool. Behind her Victoria could see the familiar shiny stainless-steel kitchen, pristine as always and closed down for the night.

'Oh, honey. How many times do we have to tell you? The accident wasn't your fault. The coroner's verdict cleared you of any wrongdoing. Claudia was both high and drunk when she slammed into us.'

They'd been over and over this, their school friend had been trying to overtake them and had lost control of the car. Victoria had been absolved of any blame. On paper at least. But she wasn't convinced. Had she been too distracted? Had she paid enough attention? Had she braked too late? Too early? Had she steered the wrong way? There had to have been something she could have done to prevent the accident.

'There was nothing you could have done, OK?' Lily asserted. 'So, no, you have never in your life done anything terrible. What happened?'

'I just met his parents.'

'Oliver Russell's?' Her friend's eyebrows rose. 'So soon? I thought V-day wasn't until the first.'

V-day. Victoria laughed, Lily was a hoot and always so upbeat. 'It was a total surprise. They're in town for...' Victoria didn't want to mention Eric's medical treatment because it was no one's business but his. 'They sprang a quick visit on us.'

'How did it go? Did they believe you were dating?'

'I think so.' Judging by Stella's triumphant fist pump, then yes. 'Totally.'

'What's Eric like? On the TV he looks a bit unapproachable and aloof. But I guess that comes with the territory, right? You can't be a hard businessman without being ruthless.'

Victoria thought about the frail man she'd spent the evening with. How he'd winced as the wheelchair had bumped over the carpet. The way he'd patted her hand. Her heart squeezed. Her feelings were getting all jumbled up inside her. The weight of wanting, willing, longing for Oliver to touch her had been almost too much to bear, but when his skin burned against her could he see the affection in her eyes? Did she hide it enough?

Did it fool him and his parents? Did it make them believe she was the doting girlfriend who wanted to spend the rest of her life in the Russell fold? Strike one to her if it did. Strike a million against her if she started to believe the lies too.

Because, she wasn't fooling herself. She liked him. Almost too much. Liked his parents too. Enough to make her heart hurt at the thought of walking away. And the thought she might hurt them by doing that made her too sad.

How could they stop this pretence from spiralling out of control? 'No, not at all. Eric's lovely. They both are. Very down to earth and friendly.'

'So, the problem is?'

'I'm lying to them.' Victoria's stomach tightened. 'It seemed OK when they were strangers I'd read about in the media, but they're genuine and nice and interested in me.'

Lily nodded. 'And you're worried you'll hurt them?'

'They were talking about an August wedding. Stella is set on the idea and I don't want to lead her on, but I don't want to jeopardize their happiness either. And there's more.'

Lily smiled softly. 'You're worried *you'll* get hurt?'

Bingo. Victoria wasn't sure whether she wanted to admit to her friend that she'd not only kissed Oliver but that she was at serious risk of falling for him.

'Yes. I am. He's kind and funny and…'

Her lips tingled at the thought of the kiss. Her heart thumped. She pressed her fingers against her mouth where his lips had been.

Lily's smile grew a little more suspicious… and mischievous. Almost like she knew what had happened. 'Come on, V. There's more to this. Spill the beans.'

Victoria thought that if she didn't just say it out loud, she was going to burst. 'I kissed him!'

'Oh, I knew it! I could just tell by your smile.' Lily's eyes grew wide as she peered into the camera. 'And...? Was it terrible? Is that why you're panicking? Because you're going to have to do it again to keep your side of the deal?'

'No. It was amazing. And it's all wrong.' And too hard. Victoria ran her hand across her forehead. Kissing someone who was terrible at kissing would be bad enough, but kissing someone who was the best kisser she'd ever known was a whole lot worse. 'We've agreed to pretend until the first of December then we go our separate ways. Even if I wanted anything more to happen – and trust me, that would be a very bad idea – there's no way any of it could work. I am so not ready to go down that track again.'

'Maybe you're putting up barriers when you don't need to. Not everyone's like our exes. There are some good men out there...' Lily gesticulated randomly in front of her. 'Somewhere. Give him a chance. If you keep putting up barriers, you'll never give yourself the chance of more amazing kisses.'

'How do I know if they're real, though? Or if he's just acting?'

'You'll know, V. You'll just know.'

Would she though? He'd seemed to be enjoying himself and surely no man could fake what was going on in the trouser department. Yes. She definitely didn't imagine that! But... *oh*, she didn't want to make a fool of herself. 'God, Lils, I'm so rubbish at relationships. Real or fake.' It was so messy and they always ended in her heart hurting. 'Tell me something nice to cheer me up.'

Lily frowned as she thought, then her smile grew. 'It's Malie's birthday next Thursday so all four of us will be together for a Lost Hours call. It's too long since the last time.' No matter what they were doing, or what time zone they were in, the four friends always made sure they had a get together, virtual or real, on each other's birthdays.

This was the best *something nice* and Lily's smile was infectious. Victoria sat up and put the laptop on the bed, her heart happy for now. 'Oh, yes! That makes me so happy. Especially for Malie. I always feel sad for her on her birthday, with her brother gone and things between her and her parents being so difficult, it's nice if we make a special effort for her.'

When Malie's brother's cancer became so far gone that he couldn't surf, her parents closed their surf school. Their idea being that if Koa couldn't surf then none of them could.

But surfing was Malie's passion and therapy so she'd started to sneak out and do it behind their backs. As soon as she could escape Devon she'd borrowed some money and gone travelling, ending up in Hawaii working at her godfather Kailani's surf school. Feeling as if they had now all but lost a second child, her parents were heartbroken by Malie's actions and things had become difficult between them all.

Lily shook her head. 'I never did understand why they're so upset with her, just because she's following her passion. I mean, who wouldn't want their kids to be who they want to be and do what they want to do?'

Like Oliver. Who had never been given a chance to decide who he was or what he wanted and instead had been pushed into the family firm. And, just like that, Victoria's thoughts tumbled back to him. And the kiss.

Hot damn. That kiss made her ache for him. Her breasts felt heavy and she could almost taste him again.

'Ahem.' Lily's voice came from the laptop.

'Oh?' Victoria's cheeks burned as she tried to push those thoughts back into that box. 'Sorry. Yes. Oops. Listen, on Thursday don't mention this thing with Ollie, please. No one's meant to know about it until… V-day.'

'My lips are still sealed.' Lily did a zipping motion with her thumb and forefinger then yawned. 'I've got to finish clearing up now, V. It's getting late. Sweet dreams.'

'You too.' Taking a huge, deep breath Victoria flopped back onto the pillow. Sure, she was going to dream tonight. But she wasn't sure how sweet they were going to be. Not with the memory of Oliver Russell's hot and sexy kiss still on her lips.

★ ★ ★

She didn't hear from Oliver the next day, or the next, so tried to forget the kiss by burying herself in work. In the hours between her shifts downstairs, and with the designs all finished on paper, she'd been able to cut the beautiful silk fabric and tack it into her collection statement piece: the enchanted wedding dress.

The silk was a pleasure to work with; it draped like a dream, there were a few alterations she wanted to make to the neckline and the bodice but it was shaping up exactly the way she'd imagined it. She'd also found time to finish making paper patterns for four more bridesmaid dress styles, all with little details that cohered the collection together, but different enough for women with individual personalities and body shapes.

With the five pieces she'd worked on over the weekend and the other ten dresses she'd already finished, her collection was complete. Or at least, complete enough for her to give her clients choices. Now all she needed was to have them photographed and put up on her website. Let the orders commence!

She stood back, watching in awe as the light caught the silk and made it shimmer. Her heart filled. This was what she was meant to be doing with her life and she was so grateful everyone had still encouraged her to chase her dreams after the accident. She needed to thank Oliver for such a wonderful gift of silk… even though it had been a bribe of sorts. A peace offering, he'd said.

But… the kiss. She didn't think she could face him again.

What if she'd read the whole thing wrong?

Heat rushed through her until she felt she was probably shimmering as much as the damned dress. It seemed that no matter what she did, she just could not forget the kiss or the way he made her feel.

It was now Monday afternoon and the silence had dragged on to the point that she had to touch base to find out where they stood.

She flicked him a text:

Hey, just wondering how your dad's getting on?

After an hour where she'd checked and double-checked her phone a million times he came back with:

V, sorry. Been a mad weekend. I'm here at the hospital with him. He says hi. Mum sends her love.

Which didn't tell her anything about how Eric was responding to the treatment. She didn't want to intrude and ask directly so just replied:

Say hi from me.

Another pause before:

They're waving. Look, we need to talk.

I know. When? she texted back.

This was it then. His kiss-off. That was why he'd been silent all weekend. He was having as many doubts as she was.

He came straight back with:

Are you free now? Visiting's just finishing and I have a couple of hours before a meeting.

His text made her suddenly embarrassed. How self-absorbed was she to think he'd been avoiding her or even thinking about her at all when his father was so sick? Oliver was trying to be all things to all people. He was at the hospital, he was trying to work and, now, wanting to meet her. After that kiss they definitely needed to talk and the most decent thing she could do was listen.

She looked down at the pyjamas she hadn't even changed out of because she'd been so consumed by her work. Hmmm. She needed to get clean too. As she stood she glanced outside. A weak November sun was trying to peek through a cloud. She desperately needed some fresh air and even Zoe had told her she was getting too pale. Plus, it would be better seeing him outdoors where there was lots of space and no opportunity for up-close and personal. She sent him a quick:

Fancy a walk?

He answered Sure. Tell me where and when.

Her heart rate picked up at the thought of seeing him and she didn't know if it was excitement or embarrassment or both.

Meet me at the entrance to the Chelsea Physic Garden on Swan Walk in 30 minutes.

Oliver replied:

Where? Don't worry, I'll find it. Ox

And a kiss!

What did that mean?

Twenty-nine minutes later she was showered, dressed and waiting outside the garden entrance. When Oliver strolled up exactly on time her heart gave its now automatic little Oliver-leap. Like an over-boisterous puppy jumping against her ribcage.

His hands were stuffed deep inside a dark-blue overcoat, his grey-and-white-striped scarf tied round his neck. Even though his coat hid his body she remembered it all too well from the other night. The heat in it. The feel of it. Nervous energy welled up inside her at the memory.

As he spoke his breath plumed out like smoke. But damn, it was cold. He grinned as he looked at the garden entrance sign. 'You are full of surprises, Victoria. I had no idea this place existed.'

He leaned over and brushed her cheek with his lips. She tried not to read anything into it. It was the kind of thing anyone did with a friend. But the immediate rush of need through her body made her jittery. She wanted to sink her hands into his hair and pull him close. Taste him again.

Consciously dampening down her physical response to him she smiled and stepped away to push open the wrought iron gate, flashed her season ticket to the staff member and walked down the bush-lined pea-gravel path. Frost kissed the tips of the bushes, and lights twinkled in the tree branches giving it a magical, festive feel.

'It's my little secret. A bit of sanity from the city, tucked away here. It's so peaceful, you'd never think you're in the middle of one of the most vibrant cities in the world. Most people walk past and don't even know it exists, but I try to come here once a month and follow the plants and trees through the seasons. The cherry blossom trees in the spring literally bring a smile to your face.'

When she turned, she realized he was looking at her and still grinning. 'I can tell.'

'Oh, ignore me, I get a buzz from all the colours.'

'It's enchanting.'

For some reason she didn't think he meant just the idea of the blossom. After two days of not seeing him she thought she'd got a better hold over her attraction to him, but no. *No.* His sexy smile still made her limbs feel like liquid and she was trembling like an idiot, even though she knew why they were here – to end it.

End something they hadn't even started. 'You just missed autumn. Oh, wow, that was a riot of russets and crimsons, like an amazing red carpet – you know, like at the BAFTAs or something.'

'I do know, yes.'

'Of course you do, because that's the kind of thing you do in your life: awards and dinners and helicopters.'

'And walks in the park when I get a chance. Stop trying to point out how different our lives are and look at the similarities. We both live in London. We're both trying to work out what we want, who we are. Not so different after all.' He shushed her rebuttal with a shake of the head. 'Tell me more about the leaves.'

'Red stretching as far as you can see. So beautiful I almost didn't want to stand on them, but then I'd have missed that wonderful crunch that reminds you of being five years old and running through mounds of leaves.'

'And then collecting them all up in your arms and throwing them in the air.' He stopped, a puzzled expression on his face. 'Why did we do that?'

'I don't know.' Victoria laughed. 'It's just what you do when you're a child, right? You don't even think about it, you just do it. You eat ice cream without worrying if it's going to make you fat. You eat the uncooked cookie dough without caring if it'll make you sick.'

'When did we lose that innocence and pure joy of just being? Now we have to work things out. Be sensible and responsible. Have all the answers.' He looked at the frosty ground and she just knew how heavily everything was weighing on his shoulders. After a moment he raised his eyes and looked at her. 'Damn. Now I want to crunch and there are no leaves. Or ice cream. Where's the uncooked cookie dough when you need it?'

'I'll make some one day and then we can indulge our inner children.' She laughed, wishing she could really ease his troubles somehow. 'One of my teachers at college was always talking about using nature as inspiration for our designs. So, I try to look at the plants from that kind of angle too.' She pointed to a huge gnarly old tree a few feet away and framed it in a square with her hands. 'The even sweep of the majestic tree trunk… look. Or the delicate nod of snowdrops in the breeze, like tiny pearls. In the summer the clash of blooming bright reds and dazzling oranges is jarring but also beautiful.'

'I cannot believe you look at the world like that. It's so alien to me.'

'And your world is alien to me.'

He nodded, his expression suddenly flat. 'I know. You keep saying that.'

'It's true.' She couldn't allow herself to think differently. That she might get used to his world, or want to spend more time in it than she should.

The trees absorbed the hum of traffic until it was discernible but distant. No one else had been brave enough to venture into the gardens at dusk, so it felt as if they were the only two people in the whole world. But there was a gulf between them and in the middle of it loomed that kiss.

She picked up the pace and pointed to a flower bed on their right. 'Try it. Look at that bed there, what do you see?'

He stopped and frowned as he peered at the trees and the bushes. There wasn't a lot of winter colour but the differing heights of the plants, the miscellaneous leaf shapes and different hues of green crusted in jewel-white frost were still beautiful. 'Spiky things, feathery things, some droopy things that don't look very happy to be there.'

'Because it's winter and they don't like the cold. Like me.' She stuck her hands deep into her coat pockets and started to walk again. Yes, she knew she was distracting him from the real reason they were here – to finish it. But she just wanted to grasp another five minutes with him before those words were said and the only time she'd see him again might be if they bumped into each other on the street or in his store. Her heart tightened at that thought. She tried to think of something positive to talk about.

'They also have the best Christmas market here in the gardens, but I double-checked the dates and they don't clash with our' – her cheeks burned at that *faux pas* – 'I mean, *your* opening day.'

And with that she'd brought their reality tumbling back into full focus. He took the lead. 'Look, Victoria. About—'

'I know.' This was it, then. She didn't want to hear him say the words so she just jumped in. 'It's fine, it was a stupid thing to do. I agree, we should stop it all now. I just hope they won't be too disappointed. Tell them we decided it wasn't going to work?'

His eyes grew wide and he shook his head. 'You're joking? Stop it? No way. You're the only thing my dad's talked about the whole weekend. Meeting you gave him a real boost. He's actually looking forward to something good for the first time since his diagnosis. He's got hope. You gave him that.'

Oh. That wasn't what she'd been expecting. 'But – didn't they think it strange I didn't surface all weekend? Weren't they expecting me to be around, if we're such a loved-up couple?'

'Not at all. They know we have busy lives and don't expect us to be joined at the hip. I told them you were working in the bar all hours and thought it best not to visit as the treatment might be gruelling for him. He agreed, saying he didn't want you to see him at his worst. They've decided to stay in town until the opening, so there'll be plenty of time for them to see you.'

Double oh. How could she spend more time with Oliver and not kiss him? It was going to be pure torture. But how could she take a sick man's hope away too? She had to keep this pretence up a little longer, especially if Mr and Mrs Russell were going to be around until the first. 'How is he doing?'

'He's had a pretty rough couple of days, to be honest, but the doctors said the first few days are the worst. They won't know how well he's responding for a couple of months.' Oliver looked out at the feathery and spiky things and smiled grimly. 'He'd love it here, I might bring him when he feels up to it.'

'That would be lovely, but make sure to wrap him up warm.' She started walking again but Oliver touched her arm, steered her to a park bench and made her sit down. 'There is one thing, though.'

'Oh? What?' Was he going to say it was all a mistake, or that he'd enjoyed the kiss as much as she had?

'I have something for you.' He dipped into the inside top pocket of his coat and pulled out a small turquoise velvet box.

Was this…? Panic sent her gut spiralling.

No. Please, no. This was far too much.

'It was my grandmother's,' Oliver explained, pride lacing his voice. 'My father's mother. My grandfather had it made for her. They've been keeping it for you. Well, for my…' He swallowed. 'Wife. Mum insisted I give it to you. Offer it to you at least.'

He flipped open the lid to reveal an exquisite solitaire diamond. Huge. In a six-prong setting and sitting on a band of what looked like platinum. Or white gold. He held it out to her. 'I said you might not like it. That we'd probably buy you a new one. That you'd like to choose something for yourself. I tried to fob her off but—'

'It's beautiful.' She ran her fingers over it and realized how shaky she was. This was a dream of a ring, glinting in the fading light. The most beautiful thing she'd ever seen and made for a woman who was clearly adored. A lump settled in her throat. This had been forged out of a deep love between two people. 'Oliver, I can't take it. Not even temporarily. It wouldn't be right.'

'I thought as much. It's OK, don't worry.' He closed the box. 'I did try to put her off, believe me, but she said I had to offer. She wants you to love it.'

'I do love it, but I can't wear it. It's too much.'

'I'll tell her.'

But break Stella's heart? Right now, in the middle of Eric's treatment? God, this was awful. She was stuck in the middle of this big fat lie. Her own heart hurting too.

What harm would it do to appease them a little while longer? It wouldn't cost Victoria anything. Better to make two people happy in the short term, right? Just until Eric was out of hospital or until Oliver could break it all gently to them after opening day.

'No. It's OK.' Victoria put her left hand out. 'I'll wear it. Until we tell them we're over.'

'She'll be thrilled.' He took the ring from the box then thought for a moment. 'If she asks, tell her I did this, OK?' He got on to one knee and said, in a hushed voice that she had to strain to hear, 'Victoria Scott, will you marry me?'

'At least this time you know my name.' She couldn't help but smile. He looked ridiculous. The whole thing was ridiculous. 'OK, then. Yes. For the next what? Ten days? Now stand up, before your knees freeze to the ground.'

But he solemnly slid the ring on to her finger. As he did so she risked a glance at his face, got caught up in the heat of his gaze. He was the most handsome man she'd ever known and he was down on one knee in her favourite park. Her heart jolted. To anyone watching they'd see a beautiful man proposing to a pale, anxious-looking woman. Expecting them to kiss any moment. And she wanted to. Ached to. Longed to slide into his arms and never leave. But then what?

Just a whole lot more complication and confusion and blurring of edges.

'Does it fit?' he asked with what looked like genuine concern.

'It's a little tight, but it's fine. Your grandma must have had tiny hands.' She couldn't stop looking at him as he stood and stretched out his back. It was time to say it. 'Look, Ollie, about the kiss—'

'Ah. Inspired.' He sat next to her on the bench and winked. 'Convinced them, right? Worked like a dream. Great move.'

'Oh.' Something drooped inside her. Lily had said Victoria would know if it was real. She'd thought it had been. Perhaps she'd convinced herself as much as they'd convinced his parents, but the kiss had meant nothing to him. Sure, he'd been turned on, she'd felt that. But as for anything deeper? Clearly not. She'd stepped over the emotional line but he'd just played his role and kept it physical.

Swallowing hard she recovered her disappointment.

'Yes. Great… er… move.' Inspired? It had been everything she'd ever hoped for in a kiss. At least, until now. She glanced at her watch. 'Look, you have a meeting, you have to go.'

He stood and sighed. 'It's with the stallholders about the opening day, do you want to come? We can work out the positioning of the runway so you can tell your girls on Friday. And you'll need to tell me what kind of backstage set-up you're going to want.'

Straight back to business, then. Her mind was in a whirl, the ring heavy on her finger and in her heart. The kiss tormenting her as much as his presence. 'I could do. Yes.'

It would give her a distraction from all this. Remind her of her real world and not this fairy tale turned nightmare she was living in. 'I just need to pick up some notes I left in my flat.'

'Great. I'll walk you there.'

CHAPTER ELEVEN

OLIVER FOLLOWED HER UP the stairs to her apartment, relieved he'd managed to bluff his way through all of that without showing how much he was spooked by the emotion in his chest. Putting the ring on her finger had made his heart rattle, stealing breath from his lungs. Watching her face light up as she saw the ring – before she had a chance to mask her real reaction – had been like watching a kid at Christmas. She loved it. She just didn't want to show him that.

And he'd loved watching her too.

Ironically, he'd never proposed to a woman before in his life. Now he'd proposed to Victoria twice. He wasn't sure how he felt about that – confused, mainly. At risk of wishing it was real?

Well, hell, when he'd kissed her the other day he definitely hadn't needed convincing. And despite knowing all the reasons why they shouldn't do it again his body was straining for her. Especially now as she walked up the stairs ahead of him, her backside swaying in her jeans. It wouldn't take much to just reach out, span her waist and pull her to him. Kiss her up against the wall – but, to prevent any risk of getting carried away or losing control, from now on kissing would remain limited to her cheek and only in public.

'Here we are.' She smiled as she stood back to let him go through the door into her flat.

'This is very different to the other day.' The studio was ordered and neat. Organized. In the middle of the room stood five mannequins wearing an assortment of dresses, some finished, some half made and one standout one that looked like something he'd sell in his store. It seemed to pull him to look closer. 'Is this the fabric I gave you?'

'Yes. See, it's a rework of the design on my vision board.' She pointed to the wedding dreams board. Yes, it was similar, but hers had a longer train, a narrower skirt, a different neckline. More sophisticated and elegant.

'This is so much better. Your design?'

'Yes.' She blushed and looked away to fluff the skirt. Clearly, she wasn't used to receiving compliments about her work.

'How come I didn't see these the other day?'

'I've been working hard on them all weekend. I only just finished that dress yesterday. I keep all my collection pieces on a rack in my bedroom for safekeeping.' She edged in between two of the dresses and adjusted a pin on one of them. Lifting a fold – or was it a pleat? He had no idea. Allowing the fabric to fall in a different way. 'You really think I'd let those girls anywhere near this beautiful fabric?'

'Good point. Jasmine would make it gangsta somehow. Put rips in the skirt? Tyre marks? Evil Easter bunnies?'

She laughed, her eyes lighting up. 'Then I would congratulate her on her unique creativity. But this is the Victoria Scott bridal collection and I'm a little more traditional.'

'Shame. I think bunnies would look great on that neckline.'

'Then do your own collection.'

'I don't know anything about this kind of stuff, but your designs are next level as far as I'm concerned. Do you sell them? Where?' How had he missed that?

'I don't yet. When they're finished I get Sara from the bar to take photos – she's a part-time photographer – and put them up on my website.'

'For online sales?' He thought quickly, his words catching up, blurting out. 'You need to showcase these, Victoria. On the runway. At the opening day.'

'No. I couldn't.' She walked around looking at them. Evaluating them. Judging them. Shaking her head. 'They're not finished. Not quite right.'

'They look pretty damned good to me. I won't take no for an answer. These can be the main show.'

'Does anyone ever say no to you, Oliver?' She laughed, kneeling and starting to pin a hem. Giving him a good view of her hips, her luscious long hair, her butt. He fought to control his innate reaction to her, the pull of desire that wound through him urging him to plunge his hands into those curls, cup that butt with his palm and kiss her again.

More.

But she'd say no, the way she just had. 'Never. I don't know the meaning of the word.'

'Then let this be a lesson. No, Oliver Russell.' She rocked back on her heels and pushed a stray lock of hair behind her ear, pinning him with a look of pure defiance. 'They. Are. Not. Finished.'

'Is this our first argument? This is fun.' He watched as she absentmindedly ran her fingers over her engagement ring. This assertiveness was a side of her he'd forgotten about – but it was just like that first night in the bar and made his blood heat. Made him want to push her up against the table and make love to her, right now.

But instead, he laughed at the suggestion anyone dared refuse him a request. 'So finish them, Victoria Scott.'

'Really?' Her eyes pigged at him. 'You think it's that easy? I don't have the time.'

'Make time, I'll help you. Whatever you need.'

'You'll make time?' she scoffed. 'What, with going to see your father and working all hours to get the store ready? Do you have a secret machine that conjures up hours like magic?'

'If I like a project, I make time for it. I like this. I'd like to help if I can.'

'Unless you're any good with an overlocker I don't think so.'

'Think about it, OK? You can have the finale spot.'

'No.'

He knew the problem wasn't about finishing the clothes or about time. When she was assessing her designs she was judging herself too. It wasn't the right way to do things, but everyone pinned their worth to their job. 'Victoria, what are you scared of?'

Her pretty, kissable mouth flattened into a line. 'I'm not scared.'

'Yes, you are. You don't think you're good enough.'

'I do.' She shook her head – an action at odds with her words. 'I am.'

'I've seen that same look you have in your eyes many times over the years with my less confident junior managers. You don't want to put yourself out there. You don't want to take a risk.'

'It's just…' With a sigh she ran her hand over the wedding dress. 'I love them. But Ollie, what if…?'

'It's my job to get the best out of people, to push them a little out of their comfort zone. So, I'm going to ask you again.' He lowered his voice, put his hand on her arm, making her turn and look directly into his eyes. He knew what was wrong because he saw it swimming there. 'What are you scared of?'

'That… oh, for God's sake, Ollie.' He saw the moment she decided to trust him enough to say it out loud. It was a big step for her but a punch to his heart too. She was vulnerable and yet sharing those fears with him. 'I'm scared no one will think they're any good.'

Bingo. He'd finally drummed down to the problem. It had taken guts to admit that.

'Great. Now we're getting somewhere. They are good. I told you that. But, yeah, yeah, what do I know? I'm not your creative peer, I'm not a client. But what if I told you, you couldn't fail?'

'What if I do? What if people laugh?'

How had she got such a low opinion of herself? 'Who did that to you?'

She frowned. 'Did what?'

'Who destroyed your belief in yourself? Was it Mr Ponytail? That tailor guy?'

She walked over to the window and looked outside. It was dark now, a cloudy night punctuated with streetlights and an eerie orange glow coming from the little shops along the road. She fixed her eyes on one of them. 'We were going to share his shop, I was going to have a real space for my designs. But when we broke up he said he'd only offered to have my clothes in his shop because he didn't want to hurt my feelings. And that he didn't think my designs were up to much.'

'I've told you before. The man's an idiot. And I do not listen to idiots.' He didn't know it was possible to feel such animosity towards someone he barely knew, but hell, there were a few choice words he wanted to say to Mr Bloody Ponytail. Oliver took hold of her shoulders, managing not to kiss some sense and self-belief into her. Just. 'Listen to *yourself*. Listen to your gut. What would you say to Jasmine or Nisha if such an opportunity arose? In fact, what did you say to them about my offer for the runway?'

She smiled at the memory. 'I told them it was a once-in-a-million opportunity and they needed to grasp it, because no one knew where it might take them.'

'So, if you don't want to listen to me, can you please listen to your own advice? These clothes are amazing. You're a talented designer with an opportunity that could take you to the top.'

'I – But…' Her shoulders sagged in defeat. 'You do wonders for a woman's ego, Oliver Russell.'

'I'm not stroking your ego. I'm ring-fencing something I want for my opening day. It's purely self-interest. Business.' They both knew it wasn't just that. He believed in her and he wanted her to believe in herself. 'Or do you have other stores clamouring for you to hold a show there?'

'No.'

'Do you want to keep them online in case you get a better offer? If that's the case then, sure. I totally respect that. Business is all about competition. But if there's no one knocking on your door then what do you have to lose by showing them for that one day?'

'Oh. OK.' She pressed her lips together. Her eyes were suddenly alight with hope. She moved away from him, her hands alive with excitement as she straightened down a bodice on one mannequin and repinned a sleeve on another.

'I don't need to think about it. I'll find time, I'll make time. I can't pass this up. Who knows where it might get me?' Her eyes darted to the photo of her friends. 'Oh God, my first proper show. I mean, we had them at college, but this is *real* real. People will be looking at my designs. VIPs. Wait until I tell the girls. This is dream-come-true stuff. See those dresses in the photo? I made them.'

She was actually giddy with the idea and it was entertaining to watch. He couldn't remember the last time he'd felt as invigorated as she was by work. All he wanted to do was smack a kiss on her mouth and feel the joy emanating out of her. He looked at the intricate designs of the dresses in the photograph. Each different and all perfect for the women's individual body shapes and, he imagined, their personalities. 'Even then you had real talent.'

'I think it's just the whole ten thousand hours thing. I've done my apprenticeship. I always made things; it started with clothes for my dolls when I was little. My gran showed me how to copy clothes by making patterns out of newspaper. They were woeful with huge clumsy stitches, but I was very proud. Then as I got older, I made things I could actually be seen wearing out in public. My friends liked them, so I made things for them. Not just clothes but accessories too.' She picked up a hairclip from a basket on a shelf. It was made out of pearls and velvet. 'I don't like things to be too matchy-matchy but it is fun to echo a theme in a hair grip or hat.'

'You're a machine.'

'I was. Always making things and trying to sell them.' Her eyes lingered over the photo.

'And then?'

She breathed out and the joy seeped out of her. It seemed that, for Victoria, there was always something that pulled her back from wallowing in pure joy, as if she didn't deserve to stay happy for long. 'The accident happened.'

He let her curl into herself for a minute, but waited, knowing if he didn't say anything then she'd fill the gap. And, eventually, she did. 'I couldn't bring myself to do anything that made me happy. I was punishing myself, I think.' She blinked and gave him a smile that was definitely brave. 'Sorry, stupid me. Shouldn't talk about that and bring the mood down.'

'It's part of your life. Don't hide it away. Punishing yourself for what?'

She shook her head, but at the same time the words streamed out of her, 'Oh, Ollie, I was driving the car.'

'God, you poor thing. You have to live with that.' He picked the photograph up and looked at the four of them, so happy and innocent and oblivious to the horrors the next few minutes would bring. His heart hurt for them. But most especially for the girl in the middle with the soft dark eyes and shiny dark hair who was staring into the camera with such a lightness he doubted she'd ever felt since.

'It wasn't my fault, apparently. The coroner blamed Claudia, the other driver – who was a friend of ours, too. She died at the scene.' Victoria briefly closed her eyes and breathed in a ragged breath. 'It was a terrible time for the whole village. Families broke up over it. Claudia's boyfriend – who had no idea she'd been drinking that night – was so distraught he left town soon after and hasn't been back.'

But Oliver was stuck on the detail she'd just given him. The weight she'd been carrying for the last decade. 'Someone died? Hell, Victoria. You didn't say before.'

He tugged her into his arms wanting to share that weight with her, to take some of her burden but she pressed her lips together and shook her head. Fighting tears. Holding back.

'She never had a chance. A waste of a wonderful life, a lost future all for one stupid mistake.' She shook her head again as if trying to erase the memory, tell herself it hadn't really happened. 'I couldn't even go to the funeral because I was still recovering myself. It was all too hard and everything hurt. My heart mostly. And, truth is, I couldn't face the stares and everyone's grief.'

'You had enough to face, you had to focus on yourself.' He pulled her close, wrapped his arms around her so she knew she didn't have to relive this on her own. As she talked he stroked the back of her head 'You were all so young.'

'The four of us grew up very quickly after that. Grew tight together, the accident sealed our bond. We survived and we knew just how lucky we were to have come out of it but... well, Claudia didn't. Every day after the accident that we had was one less she'd had. It was... truly heartbreaking.'

Victoria looked up at him and blinked, her voice cracking as she spoke. 'No one else understood what we went through, what we felt, so we four clung to each other. Hard. Malie and Lily weren't hurt but they were scarred. Zoe's still in a wheelchair—'

'The pretty blonde?'

'Spinal injury.' She ran her fingers over her friend's image. 'She was so beautiful, like a little wisp of air, ethereal. And then broken.'

Ah. The question from the other night was answered. 'The wheelchair. Now I understand.'

'It was tough for her to get used to it at first but now you should see her. She won't let her injury stop her doing anything.' Her eyes softened with sadness. 'Almost anything. She had so many plans.'

'And you put yours on hold too.'

'I was bruised physically.' She spread her palms across her stomach. 'And it was guilt, you see. I spent hours reliving that night. Trying to think of ways I could have prevented the crash, but no matter what, I couldn't turn back time.'

'Your friends didn't blame you?'

'No. Never. We tried hard to still do the things we'd always loved doing together. Stealing away to our secret bay in a borrowed rowboat. It wasn't really our bay; it belonged to Blake Hawkesbury who owned the sprawling estate around Hawke's Cove, but he let us chill there drinking bubbles and cooking freshly caught mackerel on the beach. It wasn't our boat either, we just borrowed it. But it was definitely our happy place and we kept on going there, trying to rebuild what we'd broken. What I'd broken. And I tried, I really did.' She shivered. 'But the guilt. Can you imagine? If I hadn't been driving maybe none of it would have happened.'

He put the photo frame back on to the shelf, reluctant to let go of her for even just a second. 'Or something worse might have? If someone else had been driving, you all might have died.'

Her eyebrows rose as if this was something she'd never thought of. 'I suppose so.'

'You can't live on what ifs, Victoria.'

'That's what my mum said too.'

He realized then that he knew little of her family. 'She sounds amazing.'

'She is.' Victoria found a smile and he was glad he'd managed to distract her from the pain she'd suffered. 'I'm very lucky when it comes to parents.'

'You haven't told me anything about them.'

She shrugged and walked over to another photo tacked to the wall of two adults and two small children playing on a beach. 'There's not much to know. Dad – David – is an accountant at a small firm in Hawke's Cove. He was born and bred there, and met my mum – Ellen – when she came down on holiday with a group of friends. She's an art teacher at the school I – we all – went to. Which was a bit embarrassing at times, but we coped.' She identified the couple in the picture as her parents, pointing to each of them as she described them.

'That's why she was so good at encouraging you with your designs.'

'She's a brilliant teacher, although she drove my brother, Charlie, mad every summer holiday when she wanted him to do a visual diary every day.' Victoria grinned at the memory. 'All he wanted to do was drive around in his old banger with his friends. He doesn't have a creative bone in his body and now works in the same firm as my dad.'

'Sounds like you're a tight family.' Oliver wondered how that would feel. And felt a pang of envy at the warmth in her voice and the security she had knowing how much she was loved. Seeing her mother every day at home and at school, not once a term if he was lucky. So different to his experience.

Her smile turned a little sad. 'I had my folks very worried for a long time after the accident. I just couldn't face doing anything that made me happy, not when Claudia was dead and Zoe was learning how to live again, but badly changed. But after a few months of me sitting staring into nothing Mum bought me some new fabric from Liberty, my favourite shop in the whole world.'

'What?' He put his hand to his heart. 'Not Russell & Co? I'm wounded to the core.'

'Don't be. That was before I stepped into Russell & Co, Chelsea.' She gave him a side smile. 'She made me sit at the table and make something. I didn't want to at first, I just sat and stared at it and couldn't think of what to make. But she brought me more and more from my stash and from the store and eventually I used it as therapy... creating new things, putting hopes and dreams into something new, something fresh. And finally, she pushed me to take up my deferred place at university here in London.'

Without thinking he put his palm to her cheek. 'I'm glad she did.'

'Me too.' Victoria didn't mention his hand, didn't look shocked or surprised or uncomfortable with his touch. Instead, she angled her head into his palm as if seeking out comfort. Damn, he needed to hold her again. He ran the back of his hand down her throat, trailed his fingers down her shoulder until she quivered and curled into his embrace. He stroked her hair and held her tight. 'And now you get to show the world.'

She swallowed, heat in her eyes. 'Looks like it.'

She'd showed so much courage and resilience, so much fight. What had he ever done that had been so brave as to pick himself up from something like that and make a better life for herself and those she came into contact with?

They stood for a few moments clasping hold of each other. He wondered what she was thinking or expecting, and he told himself not to expect anything at all. It was good just to have her in his arms for as long as she'd let him.

He felt her hands run over his shoulders and down his back, was one hundred per cent aware of the way she pressed herself against him. But he did nothing to encourage her, just kept on stroking her hair and soothing down her spine with his fingers.

Even if not kissing her was driving him crazy.

She looked up at him. 'Oliver, this is intense.'

'Yes.' It was also insane. He ran his thumb down her cheek, traced over her lips.

She shivered, her eyes closing as she rested her forehead against his throat. Everything in her stance, in her eyes, told him she wanted him. Felt the same tug, the same need and desire, and was wrestling with her self-control. 'Oliver, we said—'

'I know.' *And it's killing me.* No kissing. No overstepping the line. But she was letting him into her world more and more and with every step he felt more connected, more intimate. More *wanting* to be intimate.

He picked up her left hand and kissed her knuckles one by one, stopping at the engagement ring. Once again, she was saying things to push him away but her actions belied that sentiment. She was struggling with this and fighting. And so was he. He wanted her. Liked her. Admired her. Cared for her.

What did that mean? For him? For them? Hell. He was in uncharted territory here.

But it wasn't his place to push her into doing something she didn't want to do. So he held her for a moment longer, breathing in her scent and wishing they could stay like this all night.

When she breathed out and stepped away her smile was back in place. 'Right, I have my trusty notebook. Let's go.'

CHAPTER TWELVE

THE TRAFFIC EDGED SLOWLY along the road as Victoria slipped and slid with Oliver on the sleety pavement. Her feet kept disappearing from under her and more than once she had to grab him to keep upright. Seemed she was doing that a lot today. It didn't help that sensual overload made her legs like jelly.

It was a beautiful clear night, a silvery full moon hovering low over the city, with a shimmer around it as if its edges were leaking into the sky. 'Look at that. It's a stunning evening.'

'It is.' His neck tilted as he looked upwards. 'But that is damn near my favourite colour.'

'Finally, he decides! Check. Another thing ticked off the list.'

Her heart was pounding. She'd told him far too much about herself, droned on about her past, leaving her feeling vulnerable and yet strangely animated. Something about his gentle questioning had made her feel safe in a way she hadn't felt when talking to others about the crash. He'd pushed her to say what she was feeling and instead of clamming up she'd taken a risk and it hadn't backfired. He hadn't laughed, in fact, the opposite: he'd bolstered her. Made her feel as if she could take on the world.

She curled her hands into fists against the cold, stuck them into her pockets but the fabric snagged on something… her engagement ring.

Wow. It had been one hell of an intense afternoon. Engaged. Brutal honesty about her deepest fears. Sadness at her memories. Then hope. Shiny, happy hope that made her heart light for the first time in years.

And a hug that had felt so warm and comforting. Safe and… loving. And he'd held on too, as if he didn't want to let her go. Ollie was more than a businessman, he had a heart that was aching to share and she felt he was starting to do that. She'd let him into her world, but he was breaking down some barriers of his own too.

The kiss might not have been real but the friendship they were developing was and that was something new. If, at the end of it all, she came out with Ollie as a friend then she'd be halfway to happy.

Perhaps she could relax a little more into this and see where it took them. After all, there couldn't be a future, but there could be a present. She didn't have to tell him everything but she could explore what they could give each other for now…

She glanced at him now as he strode along, determined to keep upright, the tenderness of a few minutes ago hardening into professional mode the closer he got to work. He was a man of many sides, Oliver Russell. Mostly, he saw the best part of her and shaped it into something better. A catwalk with her name on it! Her heart skipped to the rhythm of their hurried steps.

He walked her up the marble steps as if it was perfectly natural for them to be together. All heads turned as the doors swung open and right there in a huddle of chatter and discussion were Aziz and his sons, and Jakob and Aleksander from the bakery on the corner along with many other familiar faces from her street. And, to her dismay, Andrew, who was talking to a group of workmen.

Great. Let the acting commence. She nodded her greeting and

173

walked into the huge room, her senses suddenly assaulted by the wonderful smell of pine mixed with the expensive perfumes that staff were putting onto shelves.

Then she stopped and stared at the incredible fir tree in the corner and took a breath. 'Wow, Ollie, you said it was going to be big, but I didn't expect this.'

'I like the element of surprise.' He grinned, clearly proud at how far the fit-out had progressed under his leadership.

The tree skimmed the midnight-blue ceiling and was decorated in swathes of silver tinsel and silver decorations. Large, sparkly baubles with pictures of the Russell & Co stores around Europe... Newcastle, Paris, Manchester, Prague, Berlin, Edinburgh, Dublin and one for here, where she was standing; the flagship shop he was responsible for. Underneath the tree were piles of gifts of all shapes and sizes. All ready for excited children and adults alike.

How long to go? Ten days. Nine? She had her work cut out to get everything completed in time, but not as much as Oliver. Some shelves were stocked, but some weren't even built yet. There were wires still hanging from the walls and from here she could see straight up the escalator cavity, through the glass panels lining the second floor and it was all in darkness.

But they had decorations down here and some stock. That was something. A grand entrance at least.

'Hey,' Oliver said as he edged in next to her in the huddle of gawpers. 'Look up.'

'Why...? Oh!' She did as she was told and suddenly thousands of tiny white lights strung across a midnight-blue ceiling flickered on, like myriad twinkling stars. 'It's beautiful.'

Christmas was hurtling fast towards them. As was the opening. The show.

And the end.

'We got here just at the right time. Testing the lighting. We want to iron out any issues in good time. The last thing we need is a fire or a blackout on opening day.'

He gave a thumbs up to a man in a hard hat at the top of the escalator in the middle of the floor. The guy nodded and spoke into a radio. Within seconds the fairy lights were snuffed out and normal strip lighting resumed to a chorus of *nos* and groans.

Then Oliver took command of the meeting. 'Right, gather round everyone. I'm delighted you've all made a commitment to what I believe is going to be a great day for all involved. Let me run through the plan. We have a brass band starting at ten o'clock, playing Christmas carols and repeating again at twelve, two and five. The Santa Claus grotto will be on the third floor in front of the toy department. That should mean any excitable children will be whisked up there and returned tired and hungry to you. I've hired Swiss-style wooden stalls for each of you, creating a village atmosphere here in the middle of the atrium. I think it's important we have you all together. Jewellery and gift items can be down…'

'Vicki?' A voice in her ear. One she knew too well and made her gut go into freefall at the memories. She turned and came face-to-face with…

'Peter. Hello.'

He nodded. No smile. 'Surprised to see you here.'

Given this whole thing had been prompted by her? Although she didn't expect him to know that, or to get thanks for it. She did, however, remember to twist the engagement ring round so the beautiful diamond wasn't advertising her recent agreement with Oliver. 'I'm helping on the day with the fashion show. Where will you be?'

'Men's. Second floor. There isn't an in-store alterations here, so the aim is for men's wear to funnel any alterations over to me across the road. I'm hoping that while I have their attention, I can interest them in some quality handmade suits instead of the off-the-rack ones here.'

Of course he would. And why not? This was business after all. Although, judging by the suits she'd seen Oliver wear she imagined Russell & Co only dealt in quality. 'Great idea.'

But Peter was still catching up. 'Wait. What fashion show? I don't know anything about it.'

'It's… er… nothing really.' Her heart hammered. She really did not want to get into this here. Or ever, actually, not with Peter. Why did she always feel like she had to tone things down with him? As if he was always somehow better than she was, more deserving? Oliver would never treat her like that. She lifted her chin and looked her ex straight in the eyes. 'We're putting a show on for my students. And me.'

'You're having a catwalk here? You?'

Oliver had taken the food-stall owners over to the back wall to discuss electricity logistics, so that left just a few stragglers here. She watched Oliver gesticulating, talking, laughing and giving each person he interacted with his time and consideration. Unlike Peter, who just wanted to feel superior. What would she tell her students in a situation like this? *Own it. Never let anyone make you feel inferior.* She lifted her chin and looked him directly in the eyes. 'Yes, Peter. I'm showing my designs here on opening day. In fact, my bridal collection is going to be the finale.'

His mouth moved but no sound came out. Certainly, no congratulations. 'I presume it's only women's wear designs,' he managed, having gone from looking pleased with himself to the unattractive colour of envy. His voice rose and he shook his head. 'Typical. I could have made good use of that.'

'Is there a problem?' Andrew, who had been watching the interaction, stalked over.

'Not at all. I was just telling Peter about the catwalk.'

'Oh. Oliver's little side show.' There was derision in Andrew's demeanour. 'I assume you're to blame for that?'

'What? It's a fabulous idea. The girls are so excited.'

'It has disaster written all over it.' Shaking his head, he turned to Peter and stuck out his hand. 'Andrew Russell.'

'Russell? As in this place?' Suddenly Peter's shoulders went back and he found a smile. Avaricious. 'Good to meet you. I'm Peter Swain. Tailor from across the road. Great to have the big guns on our street. Hope you're settling in.'

What? He'd been shouting his mouth off about Russell & Co development since planning permission was given.

Andrew nodded. 'Ironing out a few kinks, but otherwise all going to plan for the opening.'

Victoria felt extremely protective of Oliver. *He* was ironing out the kinks that Andrew had put there. And now taking all the credit. And clearly winning Peter on side. Her ex leaned towards Andrew. 'I have some ideas I'd like to run by you. If you're free for a pint after this?'

'Don't tell me you're interested in the fashion show too?' Andrew almost spat the last few words out. 'Because that's not my department.'

Peter shook his head. 'I don't need that kind of publicity. I have enough business to keep me more than busy.' *Then why are you here?* 'Just something I think could be of mutual benefit.'

She couldn't believe how much bluster and self-importance these two men had. 'Well, I think it's going to be a fabulous opportunity. The whole day is going to bring in lots of attention for us all.' She pointed over to Oliver and the rest of the group. 'Look, the stalls are in a perfect place for maximum footfall. This store is a destination shop, bringing people in from all over, and when they're here they'll hopefully explore everything the street has to offer. It's a win-win for everyone.' Now she was sounding like the Russell PR machine.

'Nice ring.' Andrew's lip curled as he stared at her hand. It wasn't a compliment, it was an accusation.

'Oh.' Damn. It had twisted back and was now on full show. She couldn't exactly hide it again. Damn her stupid wild gesticulating. 'Yes.'

'Nana Norma's.' Andrew was looking at her expectantly.

Was it? Had Oliver even mentioned his grandmother's name? She couldn't remember. She'd been so distracted by the on-one-knee gesture she hadn't paid much attention. 'Um. Yes?'

'Oliver did tell you about her, didn't he?'

'Oh…' Victoria inhaled. There was clearly a family story here that she surely would have heard if she'd known Oliver in the deeper truly-in-love sense. Was Andrew trying to trick her into admitting she didn't know enough about Oliver to be engaged to him? *Note to self, ask about Nana Norma.* 'Um…'

'Vicki? You're engaged?'

She breathed out. Never, ever had she been grateful for Peter liking the sound of his own voice. Until now.

'Yes.' Reluctantly she held her finger up to save him bending and peering. 'I am.'

'To the other Russell guy?'

'Yes.' She knew her eyes were darting from Andrew to Peter while she wished the world would stop and she could slide off and hide. She willed herself to slow down. Being engaged to Oliver was something she would be proud of. 'Oliver... Oliver Russell.'

Did he have a middle name? Should she know about that too before anyone asked her?

'That was quick.' Tugging at his goatee beard Peter looked over to Andrew. 'Your brother?'

'Cousin.' Andrew's expression had turned dark. 'Older by two years, so he gets first pick of everything. Right, Victoria?'

'I wouldn't know.' Wow. Talk about a family feud. How did Oliver surmount this kind of hostility on a daily basis? 'But he works hard. Long hours.'

'We all do. He doesn't have a monopoly on that.'

That was the crux of the matter: Andrew worked hard too, he just didn't always get it right the first time. Or the second, according to Oliver. And in a global business like this everything needed to be right. He was simmering because he felt he deserved reward, not side-lining.

Looking beyond Andrew's shoulder she saw Oliver watching the two men, and frowning. She sent him telepathic *help me* messages. *Turn your head to the left. See me.* This was worse than the dinner. At least Eric and Stella wanted to get to know her and she'd had Oliver stuck to her all night.

Stroking her thumb. Kissing her.

Her body reacted to the memory, making her hot. She wanted him. So much. Too much.

She didn't know how long she was expected to hold court with these two failed jesters and hoped it wouldn't be long enough for them to see the way her body reacted to Oliver. The hope and longing she knew was in her eyes. Although, then at least they'd all be convinced that this relationship was legitimate.

As if he'd actually received her telepathic messages Oliver turned his head a fraction more to the left and caught her eye. He must have sensed her discomfort, because he said something to the group and then sauntered over.

She breathed out as he slipped his hand into hers and squeezed, grazing her head with a kiss that cemented her as his. His fiancée. *His*. Her heart contracted at the possessiveness in his gaze and the way he wrapped his arm round her shoulder as he nodded greetings to Andrew and Peter. The two men were left in no doubt that she was taken... not that that was ever likely to be an issue where they were concerned.

After a few strained but polite words Oliver drew her away to discuss the catwalk. They made their way across the shop floor, back to the escalator and started to ride up.

The more distance between her and Peter the better she felt. 'Thanks for rescuing me, Ollie. It was getting a bit tense there.'

He glanced over his shoulder down at the two men who were deep in conversation. Occasionally one would look up towards Oliver, or her? And then they'd chat again.

A shiver skittled down her back. 'Talk about feeling like you're the subject of gossip.'

'It looks like an interesting combination: my cousin, your ex. A match made in hell. Not sure I approve.'

But she didn't care. They could elope together for all she was concerned. 'If it means they're both off my back then they can have each other. I hope they're very happy.'

'Sadly, I'm not sure I can ever use the words *happy* and *Andrew* in the same sentence. He's always been in competition with me, ever since we were kids. Don't know why and I've never encouraged it. We just never hit it off and now I've been promoted over him he's worse than ever.'

They stepped off the escalator and walked through the semi-darkness past empty concession stands. Voices wafted upwards from below, but essentially they were all alone up here. It was a cavernous space, but eerie and intimate at the same time.

'I'm thinking we'll put the catwalk across here.' Ollie paced out a long diagonal line. 'I've arranged for a runway that's about thirty feet long. We'll have chairs either side. The models can start over at the back as it's nearest the changing rooms. You're going to have to sort out the timing and the music, I wouldn't dare suggest anything that wasn't peng or mint.'

She laughed. 'You've really put a lot of time and thought into this – honestly, thank you so much. But yes, leave the music to the students. You're too old to choose anything they'll approve of, we're positively ancient in Jasmine's eyes.'

'God, I'm past it at thirty-two. I just hope they can relax and enjoy the whole thing.' He shuddered as he ran his hand through his messy hair, looking handsome and ageless in the subdued light. She fought the urge to copy his gesture and sink her hands into that glossy hair.

'There won't be any relaxing. I think we'll be at excitement level warp ten by then. It's building already; I'm starting to get texts about everything from where we'll store the clothes, to who's doing the make-up, to how much they should sell each item for. They're going to be giggling messes. It's honestly the best thing that's happened to them.' Even so, she couldn't get Andrew's suspicious stare out of her head. 'Andrew hates the whole idea.'

'Then he's short-sighted and can't see past his own self-importance. That's always been his problem. He's too closed off to ideas. It's not all about the money, it's about building relationships with the community. Look at what we're achieving here.'

Victoria smiled to herself. Had Oliver always thought like that or was he falling in love with her community? Although, the way Andrew and Peter had been cosying up, it looked like his cousin was building allies too. 'What's going to happen to him?'

'Once this place has opened he's being sent up to Edinburgh to manage the store there. It's been ticking over reliably for years so he shouldn't be able to stuff it up. Too much, anyway. God, it's a decent job he's walking into. Good prospects. He'll be the top guy with plenty of people to do his bidding. Is it too much to ask that he enjoys it, settles down, meets a half-decent woman and suddenly finds happiness with his lot?'

'He's jealous.'

Oliver's pacing came to a screeching halt and turned to her. 'Because I have you?'

'Don't be ridiculous.' Although it was a punch to her pride that she was the first thing Oliver thought of. He had her. Yes. She knew it. He had her captivated. Had her aching to spend time with him. Aching to kiss him again. 'The fact you're older and the favourite. That you're fixing his mess. And that you gave me his grandmother's ring.'

'He actually said that? If he has a problem, then he can take it up with me. Not you. We share a grandmother, she wasn't only his. The ring was passed down to me from my father. From his mother. And it will be passed down to my kids and then on through the next generations of Russells.'

His kids. Victoria's blood slowed. He assumed it was just going to happen, that in his future was a family. That it was as easy as that. And it wasn't. She, more than anyone, knew that. The thought of having a baby with him – how their child might have looked – pricked at her, rubbed at the wound she'd thought was healed. And suddenly here she was, reeling from the loss of a family sometime in the future all over again.

OK. Should she tell him… everything? No. It didn't matter; it wasn't as if her infertility was ever going to affect him. She reminded herself that this was a friendship and nothing more and she didn't need to parade her imperfections in front of him. 'Tell me the story of Nana Norma.'

'Ah.' The mention of the name brought a smile to Oliver's face. 'Andrew talked about her?'

'He seemed to expect that I knew all about her.'

Oliver leaned against a railing, opposite a white plinth where, she imagined, a mannequin would be advertising some upmarket clothing brand in a few days' time. 'I would have told you eventually, you can't be in this family and not know about Nana Norma. She was a firecracker of a woman. She had a backbone of steel but a huge capacity to love too. She flew Spitfires in the Second World War and by all accounts had some hairy near misses. There's a story about her working with the Resistance in France, although I don't know if that's just exaggeration.'

'She sounds amazing.'

'She was. After the war she met my grandfather, fell in love and had two sons.' Judging by the look on Ollie's face Nana Norma had captured everyone's hearts. 'But she had so much energy that looking after a family wasn't enough to keep her busy, so she went to work for Russell & Co. It had been Russell & Sons until that point, but she made grandfather change it in case they had daughters. And because, no matter what Grandpa thought, she was pretty much at the helm. He didn't make any decisions without consulting with her first.'

'Go, Norma.' Victoria did a fist pump.

Oliver laughed, low and deep. 'She was formidable all right, but all I remember is a little old lady – yes, she was tiny – who swore like a trooper, chain-smoked and drank whisky over one cube of ice. Never two. She used to sing the old war songs as lullabies. She told me she'd flown those planes for me. For my future. She'd put her life on the line for children and grandchildren she hadn't even had. Hell, have you any idea how that feels? To have someone love you like that before you're even born?'

'I get pretty close with my parents. Sometimes I complain that they're over-protective, but it's their way of saying *I love you*.'

'That's what it's about, right?' His eyes burned with belief. 'For ever, the future. Love.'

He said it almost as if the concept was foreign to him. Had he never fallen? Never spent sleepless nights thinking about someone's caress, or a kiss? Had he never planned a future with someone else?

He scuffed his shoe on a floor tile as he spoke. 'My parents have it. My Nana Norma and Grandpa had it. Back then they didn't know if they'd survive the war, so they learnt to live fully, love deeply and fiercely. They knew life was precious and that love is a gift you grab when you get the chance. They spent fifty years together.'

He wanted it so badly, she could see. But he'd never found it. His successful, powerful family had shown him a bar so high he doubted he could do it justice. What if he bet on the wrong woman and the Russell ideal came tumbling down? What if he destroyed what his family had created?

She realized that was why he'd asked her to do this. So he didn't have to give himself wholly to another person who might not fit the Russell ideal. Was he ever going to take a risk on love or was he going to keep on pretending his whole life?

She didn't know. She wanted to know. Wanted to know every-thing about him and the Russell history. 'Do you think you'll ever find it?'

'I haven't been looking.' He shrugged. 'No one's held my interest long enough to think of a future with them.'

'You've been dating the wrong women then.'

He turned to her and gave her a look she couldn't read. 'Clearly.'

'So what would you look for in a potential wife?' Although, really she didn't want to know because then she'd compare herself to his ideal woman and she knew she'd come out lacking.

His eyes narrowed. 'I don't know, Victoria. That's exactly why I needed you to help me out.'

At least he hadn't said tall and blonde and clever with spread-sheets. That was probably the kind of woman he'd fall for. A peer in his field. A beautiful peer.

Her chest constricted at the thought of him being with another woman, even though she knew it would inevitably happen. One day she'd open the gossip pages and see his wedding photographs.

He'd find someone who held his interest far more than she did. Or could. And a part of her heart would shrivel up.

'But then, after this, won't your mother be on your back again? Pressuring you to settle.'

'I don't want to just settle. That's the point.' He scuffed his hand over his hair. 'I'm just buying more time, that's all.'

'Settle *down*, I was going to say. Even Nana Norma did that.' Victoria leaned against the railing next to him feeling the warmth and strength of his body next to hers. Her arm brushed against his and she didn't flinch away, wanting the feel of his skin on hers to linger just a little longer. All her nerve endings fired and she felt dizzy with a sudden need to be closer to him. And closer still.

Behind them was nothing but air, and a long way down to the ground floor. The building was magnificent. A legacy to his family. But she wasn't thinking about the Russell family and its past, she was thinking about now, here, so close to him his aftershave scent wove around her like smoke making her belly contract, her breath stall in her chest. She held on to the railing to steady herself. 'I wish I could have met Nana Norma, she sounds extraordinary.'

'Legend has it she was a ruthless businesswoman and it's thanks to her that we expanded the way we did when rationing came to an end and people had more cash in their pockets. But it must have been pretty dull running a retail business after all that excitement in the war.'

'Oh, I don't know.' *Not if her husband was like you.* 'I reckon there's plenty to be excited about.' *Aargh.* She realized how that might sound like a woeful attempt at flirting. 'I mean – you know, it must be a fascinating business.'

'It is, V.' He cracked a cheeky smile as he twisted to face her, interest in his eyes. So, yes, he'd thought she was flirting. 'There's never a quiet day.'

'V?' He'd used her nickname. Her chest flooded with warmth. 'Ol?'

He laughed. 'No way, Ollie is fine. Or Oliver. Never Ol.'

The noise level below was receding. People were leaving. The workmen had downed tools and disappeared. And here they were, suddenly alone.

'Do you have a middle name, *Ollie*? I can't believe we've got this far before we talk about this. But at least it's something else I can tick off the list of things I need to know for your mother.'

'Edward, after my grandfather.'

'I like it. Regal.'

'Like Victoria. Middle name?'

'Elizabeth. I think my parents were covering all possible future queen options. Although, sadly, I missed my chance with William and Harry.'

'Still, always good to have goals.' His eyes lit up and he gave a very regal bow. 'Your majesty.'

'Idiot.' She gently hit his arm and was rewarded with a smile that was at once mischievous and deliciously heated. He shifted a little closer to her and that simple movement caused a riot of excitement inside her. A tantalizing thrill of anticipation. Was he going to touch her? Should she touch him?

But he made the connection first, the brush of his fingers on her cheek. A light touch that had the tiny hairs on her body standing to attention and heat pooling deep in her gut. His eyes locked on to hers. 'Do you like being called V?'

'Totally.' The pathetic truth was, she'd liked it more when he'd called her *My Victoria*. 'Victoria's a bit of a mouthful. But Mum and Dad were determined to keep it the full monty long-winded name and never once called me anything different. The girls call me V. You can too. Just never Vicki…' She shuddered at the thought of Peter and the way he whined her name.

'If you were to choose, which would you prefer?' He hadn't taken his eyes off her and the chemistry between them was becoming off-the-scale hot as his fingers trailed to the back of her neck.

'Pretty sure I like Norma best of all now.'

'That wouldn't work for me.' He stepped even closer. 'Not sure I can kiss a Norma the way I want to kiss you. That just wouldn't be right.'

His laughter faded and a seriousness took over. Dangerous intent flickered in his eyes.

Her mouth went dry. And wet at the same time. He wanted to kiss her. Desire spiralled through her sharp and intense. 'You can't. Not here.'

'At your apartment, then? Or my house? Somewhere, damn it, Victoria… anywhere.' He closed the distance between them, squeezing his knee between her legs, capturing her against the railing.

'I…' Her senses were so swamped by his touch, his scent, his lust-filled voice she could barely find words. 'I… thought it was just an act. You said it was inspired. A great move.'

'It was inspired, but I sure as hell wasn't acting. And I want to do it again. Do you?'

Her body flooded with urgent need. They could do it again. Right here, if they wanted. The whole place had fallen silent but for the hum of electricity and the dulled traffic noise. They could kiss here, they could take it up to his office. To her bed.

God, she wanted him in her bed, so badly. To feel him naked beside her, on her, in her. Just one night. Just once. One perfect night with him.

But then he'd see her scars, there would be questions. Pity. Words.

Oh, why couldn't she just gloss over all that and kiss him hard? Forget the questions, forget over-thinking.

She looked up into his dark mesmerizing eyes, he was still waiting for her answer. Did she want to kiss him again?

Yes. But, no. 'My head is all over the place with this, Ollie.'

'Mine too. My body has a mind of its own. We can take it slow. Your speed.'

'My speed is not even touching the ignition, Ollie.' This was agonizing. The subdued light caught the tips of his hair making them golden. His eyes burned with a stark need. The air was filled with his scent. There was nothing more she wanted now than to slide into his arms. The temptation was overwhelming and she was struggling to keep control. Truth was, she was utterly and completely lost, in him.

He brought her hand up and held it against his chest in a move that was almost unbearably chivalrous and tender. She could feel his heart hammering hard.

'V, is it me? Am I reading this wrong? The kiss was real. I'm blown away by the chemistry between us. Pretty sure you're feeling it too?'

She could barely find her voice. She'd never felt such a heightened connection to someone. Never known that having someone close enough to kiss, but not being able to, was such complete agony. 'Yes.'

'Then why not?'

She should have moved away then and broken this deepening intimacy. But she didn't. 'I'm not looking for anything long-term.'

'I'm not asking for fifty years or even fifty days. But you're the only woman I've ever met who's held my interest for me to want more. So, I'm asking for a few minutes, Victoria. Enough for another kiss. Enough to see where it might take us.'

She didn't know what to say. They'd agreed to always be honest with each other and he was expecting that. But did she need to give him a full run-down of her injuries and an explanation of the long-term prognosis? That she wouldn't be able to give him the children he hoped for. That her belly had scars... faded and silvery, but still visible.

For one more kiss? No. That would be attaching too much significance to what for him was probably only a fling, and for her couldn't ever be more than that. Besides, he'd lose interest in her in no time. The only maths she understood was working out her pattern measurements and fabric needs.

But, hell. Another kiss? She'd give anything for that. In fact, it would be good to explore a relationship without worrying about any future.

She'd never felt more turned on and more confused in her life.

Her hand went to his chest, the soft linen of his work shirt under her fingers.

His fingers curled round her ponytail and he tugged, letting her hair fall over her shoulders. He breathed in sharply and picked up a strand, let it flow through his fingers. Then cupped her cheek. 'Beautiful.'

Oh, hell. She'd been thinking he was never going to take

a risk, but she was the same. Stuck in an ever-decreasing cycle of fear of being rejected and hurt. But he wanted to kiss her, he'd just freaking well said it out loud. And she wanted to kiss him. And more. She wished she had the nerve of Nana Norma. The ability to jump in and act. To live fiercely and not worry about the consequences, or think about tomorrow.

She looked deep into his eyes. Saw the truth there, the desire. Saw this chance to grasp something she wanted. For five minutes. Or fifty. For now, at least.

Maybe it was time she took a damned risk and lived for the moment instead of always thinking about protecting herself from the future.

What would Nana Norma do? With an uncertain future and a chance for some fleeting joy?

Live.

So, she gripped his shirt in her fist, tiptoed forward and slid her mouth over his.

CHAPTER THIRTEEN

THE FIRST TOUCH OF her lips was enough to send Oliver's lust into super-drive. She made him forget everything else, but her. Made his focus laser-sharp on her, and blind to everything else. He pressed her against the glass railing, moulding his body to hers. He could feel her curves, the press of her breasts against his chest. The gentle parting of her legs to let him closer and closer still.

He imagined stripping her clothes off, item by item, taking his time to unwrap her. He imagined how she would look in his bed, her dark hair flared on his pillow, her eyes heavy with sex. He imagined tracing his fingers, and then his tongue, across her body, kissing her most intimate parts.

'Oliver,' she moaned as she opened her mouth to him, her tongue dancing with his as she wound her fingers into his hair. His hands went to her waist, fingers sliding under her sweater to the soft silk skin underneath. Her lips were still cold from the November night but hot from need. She tasted of hope and freedom, of lush desire unfolding under his touch. She moaned against him, urging him on. He traced butterfly strokes up her ribcage and she curled into him, twisting her body so her breast met his palm.

The kiss was fire. Breath. Heat. A melding of wants and needs, a desperate exploration. Possession. The minute he'd seen Andrew and Peter talking to her he'd felt a feral need to claim her as his. And ever since that hug in her apartment he'd been desperate to taste her again. And more. God yes, he wanted all of it, all of her.

She moved against him, pressing hard against his body, kissing a hot wet trail from his mouth to his neck in hungry gasps, making him writhe against her. An image of Peter and the way her ex had looked at her flashed through his head. Oliver cursed and found her mouth again, using her desperate kisses to wipe away the picture, wanting to brand his name on her lips, on her skin. No one else would ever kiss her like this. Want her like this. No one.

'My Victoria,' he growled as he crushed her against the railing.

But when he slipped his fingers underneath the lace bra cup she went completely still. Reluctantly, he drew his mouth from hers, his breath ragged. 'You OK with this?'

She nodded and shook her head at the same time. Her eyes were wild with desire, a rough swelling of her lips. She looked utterly and thoroughly kissed. She swiped the back of her hand across her mouth. 'I… we have to stop.'

'Yes, of course. Anyone could be watching.' Any of the board members could come in, his staff. His mother. Andrew. It wasn't exactly a private place.

She leaned her head against his chest. 'I mean, it's all happening so quickly. We need to slow down.'

'Got you. Yes.' She wasn't saying no. She just had a different gear to him and that was OK. But for him it was never going to be just a kiss. And it was never going to be enough. No matter how much he fought it, this thing they were developing was more complex than just physical attraction.

And she was right to make them consider their actions. She'd been hurt before by a man who'd broken promises and betrayed her. It would take time to grow that trust again. Oliver had time. He was a patient man when it came to getting what he wanted. He could do the long game in business so why not in his personal life?

When she'd asked him earlier what his perfect woman would be like he'd almost blurted out her name, her qualities. *My Victoria.* Which had rattled him to the core. But talking about his grand-parents' relationship had made him understand how precious it was to grab a chance at something. No matter how fleeting. To grasp joy when it came.

She stroked his jaw and looked up at him with lust-soaked eyes that he wanted to dive into. 'I'm sure you have things to do tonight? Go visit your dad. Tell your parents I love the ring and am honoured to wear it. And that Nana Norma sounds like one hell of a woman.'

'It will make their night to hear that.' He wasn't going to push it any further. She wasn't running scared so that had to be a good thing. 'When— ?'

She understood the subtext. 'I don't know. Call me. I'll text you. Something.'

But she was smiling. There was no regret in her voice. She wasn't running away, or trembling.

She looked almost in control, which was more than he could say about the way he felt when he was with her. He wanted to press her against the railing, strip her naked and make love to her. He wanted to wake up with her. He didn't know if he wanted it for fifty years, but tomorrow morning would be fine. And the next day. And the day after that.

But his Victoria wanted a slow burn. She needed to develop trust, he got that. She didn't think this could be real.

He just had to make her believe it could.

'How are the show plans coming along?' Sara asked a few days later in the quiet lull in the bar just after opening and before the lunchtime rush.

'I've just had Nisha on the phone in a panic about not being able to find any black buttons the right size for one of her dresses. Jasmine's gone so quiet I think she's scared half to death and has gone to ground.' Victoria laughed, although it was a little on the hysterical side. 'And Billie's mother's rung three times to confirm timings. I could sort it all out with them on Friday, but everyone wants answers now. So, in a nutshell we're moving from excited to fever pitch. God help me by next Saturday. I might need some tranquillizers.'

'Or alcohol?' Sara brandished a miniature bottle of tequila she was about to hang on one of the branches. 'Need a shot?'

'Not while I'm working.' Even though their contract said they were allowed to drink within reasonable limits while behind the bar she didn't think it was a good look to be more drunk than her patrons.

'How's his lordship?'

She assumed Sara meant Oliver. 'Fine. Lovely, in fact.'

She hadn't heard from him in a few days and that was absolutely fine. They both needed some time apart. That last kiss had been better than the first but had complicated things. Man, it had been good but it had pushed her so close to the edge she could have made love to him right there in the store. The way her body responded to him, even just the little things like his smile, or the fleeting touch of his skin set her on fire.

Nana Norma had a lot to answer for.

But even so, Victoria couldn't wipe the smile from her face. Having a handsome, good man wanting to kiss her had been a real boost to her ego. She just had to work out what to do next. Could it even be possible that things could work out between them? Somehow?

Hell, Norma wouldn't let anything stand in the way of what she wanted. The trouble was, Victoria didn't know what Oliver wanted and whether it was completely at odds with what she could actually provide.

'Yes, love, what can I get you?' Sara asked a customer who had just walked in.

Victoria had her back to the door but the second she heard the voice she didn't have to turn to see who it was. The hairs stood up on her neck. And not in a good way. 'Hello, Vicki.'

'It's Victoria,' she replied and turned around to give Oliver's cousin the kind of greeting he was giving her: a cold stare. 'Didn't think this was your kind of place.'

Andrew looked round at the wine bar with its dark wood floor, grey pigmented walls and edgy industrial vibe. And scowled.

'You're not wearing your engagement ring.'

She looked down at her finger and at the little circle of indented skin the ring had made. 'It's not safe to wear something like that in here. I could lose it. It could get damaged.'

His eyes met hers and she saw a sad emptiness there. 'It's not real, Victoria.'

Her stomach tightened. He knew. As she'd feared. He was going to out her as a liar. Or a con merchant. Maybe he thought she was stringing Oliver along? That she'd duped him into proposing. Ha. If only he knew.

'Of course it's real. We're a… couple. Oliver is lovely. Whirlwind… romance.' *His favourite colour is not green or blue, it's the colour of the moon on a cloudless night. He hates his job but he's doing it for his family. For you, Andrew.*

He shook his head, a snarl on his mouth. 'I meant the ring. The one they gave you is just glass. The real one's in a safe at the bank. They're just playing a game too. They wouldn't risk giving something as valuable as that to a barmaid.'

'Designer.' He really was trying to unsettle her, and she refused to allow him the satisfaction of seeing that he had. She tipped her chin up. If she was going to get anywhere in her dream career, she had to start believing in it and that started with claiming it. 'And it's not a game, Andrew. Not to me. Now, can we get you a drink?'

'No. I just came to find someone, but they're not here.' He turned to go, but looked back, his eyes piercing her. 'It is all a game, Victoria. And you're going to lose.'

'God.' Her hands shook as she put an empty glass onto the bar. 'He knows, Sara. He knows we're pretending and he's going to blow the whole thing.'

As their friendship had grown Victoria had confided in Sara about what had happened in the accident and the legacy she'd been left with; her inability to create a genetic legacy of her own.

Sara smiled reassuringly. 'Calm down. He doesn't know anything. He's just messing with you. He's jealous and he's trying to cause trouble.'

'It was a warning. Maybe I just need to tell Oliver the truth.'

'And what's that, my dear?'

'Huh?' Victoria whirled round.

Stella put her white Chanel goatskin clutch on the bar and smiled warily. For a diminutive woman she had an aura of gravitas and presence. It seemed she always looked immaculate. Her hair was groomed and neat and there was a slick of lipstick on her lips.

Today, she was wearing a lemon cashmere sweater and beige trousers, and had a very expensive-looking cream coat hanging from her shoulders as if she'd effortlessly slung it there without thinking. Victoria estimated that just the jumper would have cost the equivalent of her week's wages, never mind the designer coat. Stella pinned her with a look. 'What do you need to tell my boy?'

Well, wow. Victoria's gut clenched. Was this a revolving door of Russells today? She was so not ready for this and couldn't tell Stella any truths without discussing everything with Oliver first. She needed to make sure Eric wasn't going to be upset, because the last thing she wanted was to make him relapse.

'She doesn't want to admit to you and the family but basically, Vicki's nervous about the opening day.' Sara jumped in and Victoria could have kissed her. 'I'm having to talk her off the ledge. She doesn't think she's good enough. But we all know she is, right?'

Inspired. It wasn't a lie and hinted about the real anxieties she had.

'Oh, my dear, I'm sure your designs are every bit as good as Oliver says they are. And I imagine if you work here you'll be equipped to herd a group of teenage girls into order.'

'You don't know the girls.' Victoria laughed, grateful that Stella and Sara had so much faith in her. 'How's Eric?'

'You can always tell when a man's getting better, they stop being compliant, and start complaining and giving orders. That man has a serious grump at times.' Stella shook her head, her mouth set in a grim line. 'I needed a break before I did something bad, like increasing his dosage of laxatives. So, I thought I'd take a trip to see the store and then found myself here.'

She was deadpan. But funny.

'Are you meeting Andrew?' Victoria asked as nonchalantly as she could. 'He was just in here, said he was looking for someone. I wasn't expecting it to be you, to be honest.'

'Andrew? No. But I think I saw him further down the street crossing the road.'

Heading to Peter's? 'Maybe he's meeting someone about the village stalls.'

'That boy has an agenda all of his own. Don't mind him, he's all about the grump too. Russell side of the family – forewarned is forearmed, Victoria. Don't take any of their crap.' Stella looked down at her hands and then back at Victoria. 'My dear, I wondered, I know this is rude of me, but – no.' She shook her head decisively. 'No, you wouldn't. Silly of me, really.'

'What?' Victoria's heart clattered. What the hell was she going to be asked to do now?

'I used to love making clothes when I was younger. Could I have a peek in your studio?'

That was all? Relief spread through Victoria's body. 'Oh, yes. Of course you can. Sara, can I…?'

'Sure, we're not exactly busy. Why don't you take your time owing and have the rest of the day off? You can get on with your sewing, then too.' Sara's eyes widened in encouragement.

'It's upstairs. Come on up. You'll have to excuse the mess. With opening day just around the corner I've left my things out so I can work on them whenever I have any spare time.'

Victoria led the way up the stairs silently thanking the fact she'd woken up this morning, realized the place was pigsty and whizzed round with the vacuum cleaner and cloth.

Stella walked through the flat with the air of an estate agent doing an inspection. Victoria wondered how she was going to handle it if Oliver's mum ran her finger over the mantelpiece and tutted at the dust bunnies.

But she needn't have worried. Stella's eyes softened as she walked into the studio. Her hand went to her chest. 'Oh, it's just how I hoped it would be.'

She rushed over to the table and smoothed her hand over a bolt of lace the way Victoria did when she found something she coveted, and instantly Victoria's heart made a space for Oliver's mother. Someone else who appreciated fabric as much as she did.

'You have a good eye for quality material, Victoria.' Stella walked to a mannequin and inspected a dress. 'I made myself something like this when I was newly married. Well, I say it was something like this, that was the plan. I spent a fortune on the best fabric I could get from Liberty—'

'I love it there.'

'Me too. I convinced Eric I was saving us money in the long run by making my own clothes. Remember, we didn't have eight fashion seasons a year, and throwaway clothes like we do now. Eric liked that I was trying to be frugal… he may be rich but he's astute and doesn't like wastefulness.' Stella smiled.

'One of the reasons I like vintage clothes is because they're so well-made and designed to last.'

'Exactly and they suit you.' Stella's laser gaze appraised Victoria's pin-curled updo hairstyle and her floral rockabilly dress. She nodded her approval. 'But I was a terrible seamstress. The hem was uneven and the sleeves didn't fit right. They were too blousy and puffy.' She laughed at the memory. 'I wanted a dress *à la* Coco Chanel. But Eric said it looked more like something Coco the clown would wear. It ended up in the dog basket. Most expensive blanket that dog ever had.'

Victoria laughed at the thought of a dog in puffy sleeves. 'I've had a lot of failures of my own, trust me.'

'I seriously doubt that and I bet none of them ended up as dress-ups for the dogs. Damned pooch dragged it everywhere until it fell to pieces. Oh, I love this.' She'd moved on to the next dress.

'That's for the bridal collection I'm showing on opening day. Bridesmaid, or ball gown or party wear'. It was the dress she'd imagined Lily wearing. Simple but classic shift shape with an accentuated waist and soft frill round the hem. The fabric draped beautifully and it perfectly suited Lily's approach to life: simple and natural.

'It's stunning.' Stella walked round examining each piece, but when she came to the wedding dress she stood and gaped. 'This is divine. For… you?'

Victoria was not going to fall into the fairy-tale trap and start to dream and hope for something so completely unattainable. This thing with Oliver was moving fast but it was not going to end with a bouquet and a nice dress and her father walking her up the aisle. 'It's my design, yes.'

She hoped that would be suitably vague but enough to stop further questioning. Stella was already completely wedded to the idea and was, as people often did, making up her own answers in her head.

'I can see you in this, walking towards Oliver. But it's probably bad luck for me to see it.' Even so the woman couldn't take her eyes from it.

'Don't worry, it's going to be in the show so everyone's going to see it in a few days.'

'But they won't know it's uniquely yours… for you. You are so talented.'

Stella certainly knew how to say all the right things, but Victoria hadn't missed the way the older woman's eyes wandered to Victoria's left hand more than once. Looking for the ring, she supposed.

'Oh, and thank you so very much for the ring. It is absolutely stunning. I hope Oliver mentioned how much I love it? I don't wear it for work in case it gets damaged. My hands are in and out of hot water too much and I have to move the furniture to mop the floors.'

'Good girl. Practical too. Nana Norma would love you to have it.'

'She sounds amazing.'

'I'm sure she exaggerated half those stories, but they entertained the boys when they were growing up.' The older woman walked along the room peering at the shelves of fabrics and patterns. She beamed at the wedding dreams vision board and nodded as if she'd found a clue in a puzzle.

Score one to Victoria.

'This is wonderful. Are you planning a honeymoon in Hawaii? Go to Maui. Not as brash as Oahu, less touristy and some divine restaurants.' But Stella's smile slipped as she scanned the wall. 'No pictures of Oliver?'

The swift subject change made Victoria feel slightly off-balance. She considered lying and saying she had a picture in her bedroom but thought better of it. No doubt Stella would want to check. 'I just haven't had time to print any up. I'll do it after the opening day. Everything has to wait until then.'

'Naturally. You're both so busy.' She stopped at the picture of before the accident. Which had become the defining moment of Victoria's life. Before and after. Hope, innocence and a clear, bright blemish-free future. Then confronting her guilt, her scars and redefining her dreams. 'And these are…? Not your sisters? No. You're all so different.'

'My friends from Devon. School friends, we're spread over the world now, but we still keep in touch. Birthdays, Christmas… you know.'

'It looks like summer. I love summer by the sea.'

'It is amazing. So much space and light. When you looked out at the horizon you always felt as if there was space and opportunity out there. It was fun. We used to take a little rowing boat round to a private beach and while away the summers sunbathing and laughing, gossiping.' Victoria felt a pang in her solar plexus at the memories. Wished they could go back to that time when everything was so innocent and simple.

'Always make time for your friends, Victoria, never give them up for a man. They'll keep you sane… and trust me, being married to a Russell feels a little insane at times.' This was all Stella's excuse for a mother-in-law chat, then. She was scoping Victoria out. 'This is lovely. I just wanted to… oh, dear, you're going to think I'm terrible, but I just wanted to see you.'

'Here I am.' Victoria's hands flapped at her sides. She felt like a prize bull being inspected for sale. But at the same time her heart went out to a woman who was desperate to see her son happy.

'It's all been so quick, you see. I know we have years to get to know each other but I wanted to… this sounds awful of me. I wanted to check you out. Am I a bad person?'

No. I am. 'If my son was getting married, I'd probably check the woman out too. Maybe not as obviously, but I'd probably Facebook stalk her or something.'

'Oh, I hadn't thought about that. Good idea. Unfortunately, I'm not good with social media.' Stella winked. 'So, you're off the hook on that one.'

Victoria felt a rush of relief. Oliver's mother could at least joke about what she was doing even though it was obvious and a little intrusive. She was starting to realize what a force Oliver had to deal with and why he was trying to keep his parents at arm's length when it came to his love life.

Victoria decided she might as well play this game. 'Do I pass the test?'

'Flying colours. I'm so pleased to see Oliver so happy. You've made a real difference to him.' Stella drew a little closer and grew more serious. 'I also wanted to talk to you. Really talk, Victoria.'

Uh-oh. She'd passed level somehow and had progressed to level two of the daughter-in-law test. The last thing she wanted was a heart-to-heart but the woman was taking a break from her sick husband, Victoria could hardly refuse her a little chat. 'Do you want to come through to the kitchen? I can make us some tea.'

'No. I can't stay long. I need to get back to Eric. I just wanted to say, darling…' She covered Victoria's hand. 'Not everyone's like Nana Norma.'

'I don't understand.'

'She thrived at Russell & Co. She built a good life and a very good business which we all benefit from. But her children barely saw her. I think she realized later in life what she missed out on, which is why she spent so much time with her grandchildren.'

'That happens. We all have to work. It's hard to get the balance right sometimes.'

'There is no balance for a Russell. Eric was groomed to take over the business, he didn't question it, but I know it wasn't what made him happy. If he'd had his life over, he'd have done something else. Medicine, perhaps, or engineering. But it was his family duty and he couldn't bear to be the one that walked away or broke up what his parents and grandparents had worked so hard to build. And I know he's done the same to Oliver. It's a legacy thing, they feed each other.' Stella sighed. 'Don't let him turn into his father. Put your foot down, draw a line at him working all hours. Please.'

'I'm sure we'll work it out between us. Things are different these days.' Although they weren't for Oliver. The whole family needed to sit down and just talk.

'I got sucked into the firm too and we ended up forfeiting the one thing I wanted more than anything – a family. More babies. Eric was so busy, and I helped share that load, being available at all hours for business dinners and trips schmoozing investors and shareholders. But we put it off and I regret that so much. We should have had more fun and now… now it's too late.'

Victoria didn't know what to say. 'I'm so sorry. I really am.'

'Thank you, my dear. I know you are. I can see it in your eyes.' Stella's own eyes misted. 'My boy is right; you are perfect for him. For us. Just enjoy each other and your babies when they come. Make him take time off and don't send your children away like Eric made me.'

Victoria couldn't hide her shock. 'He *made* you send Oliver away?'

'Don't be so surprised, it's Russell family tradition. Same school, same university. And I went along with it... all that stiff upper lip, refusing to hug him before he disappeared into the school hall because it would make him soft. And make me cry. So I held it all in and sobbed on the way home. I did cuddle him, you know, when he was little. I used to hold him for hours. But Eric said our son needed to learn how to be a man. His type of man. So I worked hard to hold myself back when Eric was around and then... well, Ollie went off to school and when he came back he was independent and didn't seem to need me anymore. Didn't seem to want me around. We grew apart. He grew up and now... well things are difficult, and I don't know how to get them back on track without looking like I'm interfering.'

This was so sad. All of them hurting, none of them knowing how to take the first move towards healing. 'Talk to him. Tell him how you feel.'

Stella shook her head. 'I don't know if he'd listen. He's a grown man now. But you can break the mould, Victoria. Don't make my mistakes. Keep your babies close.'

Babies.

This time she couldn't ignore the word. Victoria couldn't help run her hand across the gnarled and scarred skin on her belly. There would be no Russell babies for her. For the first time in a long time Victoria felt sorrow and longing swell through her. A baby. Yes. Over the years she'd convinced herself she didn't want one, that she had enough to offer without producing children. And yet recently she'd begun yearning for what she couldn't have, since her reality had been brought back into sharp focus by Peter and now.

But it didn't matter what she felt, there was no legacy for Stella from this damaged body.

It hit her then that this poor woman was laying out her hopes and dreams for Victoria to trample over with her and Oliver's silly deal. Things were going too far. She didn't want to play this game anymore. She didn't want to develop a relationship with this woman or this family, but it was already too late.

She was going to have to talk to Oliver and make it stop.

CHAPTER FOURTEEN

HER FIRST TEXT CAME during a meeting with his father's cardiologist. Oliver had to ignore it, but it was the first time he'd ever been distracted from something this important by a woman. First time he'd ever wanted to hear someone's voice so badly it was to the detriment of everything else, too. But he figured she'd understand if he later explained why he couldn't reply right away.

And here was the thing: it shouldn't matter what she thought, she was a temporary made-up girlfriend – who was getting under his skin. But it did matter. She mattered. Their kisses mattered, more than he wanted to admit.

He'd learnt, from his parents and from being at boarding school, to keep his emotions in check, to keep a distance and not get entangled in feelings. He'd thought it was the right thing to do, the best course of action to keep a clear head and get through life without being hurt or broken or distracted. But clearly he'd been very mistaken to avoid emotion at all cost, because he didn't know how to handle the deluge of feelings he was faced with now and that was affecting everything. He couldn't get her out of his head.

The next text came as he was cajoling his father to eat something. She wanted to talk. He couldn't right now. He was torn, but not enough to make him walk away from his father's bedside.

Although, if he didn't get a decent polite word out of his father soon he'd be tempted to take five minutes outside for sanity's sake. But he'd promised his mother he'd stay until she got back from her errands, so that's what he was going to do.

'Come on, Dad. The doctor says you've got to eat something, or he'll have to keep you in here until you put more weight on.' As his dad grumbled and shook his head Oliver thought he'd try to appeal to his father's miserly tendencies. 'You know that every day in here costs money.'

'Stop mollycoddling me, Oliver. It's bad enough having your mother doing it, but not you as well. It's like you're a nagging tag team. Why can't anyone understand that I'm just not hungry?' The curmudgeonly man threw his spoon onto the grey tray narrowly missing the stew and dumplings he was refusing to eat, even though he'd ordered them from the private hospital menu. 'Don't you have work to do?'

'Of course. It's Russell & Co, there's always work to do. '

'Then bugger off and do it. Leave me alone.'

Oliver bit back a smile. He'd almost preferred it when his dad was too sick to shout orders because he was managing to get his job done without interference, but he liked it more that Eric was getting some of his fighting spirit back. 'Don't worry. I'm not staying here all day. I'm heading to Paris this afternoon for a meeting with the accountants.'

His father perked up at the mention of business. Seemed that was all that had ever given him a purpose in his life. 'Tell Pierre not to accept the offer from Galeries Lafayette. Russell & Co is not for sale.'

'He knows. He's been batting them back for five years.'

'And tell him—'

'I'll tell him you said to sell the lot.'

'You wouldn't dare.' His old man stared up at him through red, watery eyes. He'd lost so much weight he was barely recognizable. He was a shadow of his formidable former self and Oliver missed it, missed his old dad. The one who'd taught him how to fight in a boardroom, how to remain steely calm under pressure. How to never give up on a deal you believed in. The one who'd taught him to always, *always* steer with your head not your heart.

Bloody heart failure. Oliver hadn't really thought about it before, but his father's heart had a huge capacity for loyalty and trust and Ollie never wanted to jeopardize that. Was he doing his parents a disservice with this make-believe relationship? Victoria was becoming important to them all, if his parents' endless questions about her were anything to go by. What had started as a bit of fun to get his mother off his back was getting out of hand.

But who knew? Maybe Victoria might be around for a while longer?

He thought about the way she'd moaned at his touch, the way she'd tasted and the way she made him hard and hopeful at the same time. Maybe he could convince her to stay around past the deadline they'd agreed on…

His father coughed and readjusted the nasal cannula that pumped oxygen into his lungs. 'Oliver, we need to talk about the Madrid contract. I've been thinking—' Eric pushed the tray table away from his bed as if it was somehow offensive. 'This food is terrible.'

'You need to eat.' When it came to his father, Oliver had learnt to use stealth tactics. While his father grumbled and muttered and looked out of the window Oliver surreptitiously pushed the tray table back over the bed inch by slow inch. 'Thing is, Dad, you're not coming to the meetings, so I don't have to listen to a word you say.'

The unwritten message was there in the congealed gravy and two unappetising lumps of stodge. He had to eat it to get strong again, then and only then could they talk business.

For a few minutes there was a Russell stand-off. Two alpha males staring each other down, neither of them willing to give in. The old guard versus the new. The parent versus the child. The mentor and mentee. At what point had the baton been handed over?

Oliver was not going to give in. His father was going to put on weight, he was going to get better. Or as well as he could.

Eventually, his father tore his eyes away from his son, picked up the spoon and started to eat. Alpha place relinquished. For now. Oliver felt a pang of discomfort. But sometimes tough love worked. God knew, his father had used it with him often enough.

Eric took a second mouthful of food, forced himself to chew. Swallowed. 'I'll make damned sure to be at the next meeting and you'll damned well listen to my advice.'

'Excellent, we're finally making progress. The next scheduled Paris meeting after today isn't until next year and you will be more than welcome to come if the docs say you're fit enough to travel. But if you put on a few more kilograms in the next few days we can talk about you coming with me to the lawyers next Tuesday for the sign-off on Madrid. And, of course, there's the opening. You have to be strong enough for that, right?'

'I'll be there.' Eric looked as if he was eating a lemon, but he was eating. That was something. 'Sounds like you're far too busy to be wasting time here, Oliver. You'd better go to the office and do some damned work.'

And with that Oliver was summarily dismissed. He could wait outside until his mother came back.

'OK. I'll come back tomorrow and let you know how Paris went.' Oliver patted his father's shoulder, reeling from the fact the parent–child roles had reversed. Aware that he had still to allow his dad to be the father if not the boss. And wishing he could do something to make Eric as strong physically as he was mentally. Watching him fade to nothing was too damned hard.

Once outside in the fresh air he called Victoria. 'You OK? You texted twice. Sorry, I was busy with my dad.'

'I hope he's OK?'

'He's getting there.'

'Good. Look, we need to talk.' She sounded distant and tense. His heart kicked hard. Had something happened? Unease snaked through his gut.

'Sure. What is it?'

'I mean, in person.'

OK. He chose not to push her for more because, evidently, she needed time to explain. He would have cleared his diary for her if it wasn't for the Paris meeting; that was long overdue and time critical. Maybe he could delay it. 'I have some meetings later that I can't get out of. What are your plans?'

'I've just finished an early shift and I should be sewing.' She sounded tired, too. 'But my back hurts from bending over to peer at my stitches and my fingers are bruised with needle pricks, so I could do with a night off, to be honest. I think I deserve a break. But I have to pop out and get some more things from a haberdashery somewhere so I can finish my dresses tomorrow.'

An idea crystallized. Maybe…? 'Give me a minute.'

He called Pierre and Claude, then called her back, stupidly relieved to hear her voice regardless of the subtext in her tone – *this is going to be a difficult conversation*. 'OK. I'm good to go. I've pushed back a meeting 'til later. Can you come over here and we'll grab the car?'

'Of course. Where are we going?'

'I'll explain en route.' She'd said she needed to learn more about his world. It was time to show her what being a Russell was all about.

★ ★ ★

Oliver Russell had a chauffeur. That was news. She'd been expecting his little open-top and privacy, so this new turn of events made opening her heart to him and calling this whole thing off rather awkward. What she wanted to say didn't need an audience, especially not one employed by the powerful Russell family. But it could wait until they got to the restaurant or wherever it was he was taking her.

She hadn't heard Oliver give instructions to the man in the hat in the driver's seat, so she had no idea where they were going, so when they pulled up outside Edmiston Heliport her tension morphed into an adrenalin rush. 'Wow. Where are we going?'

'It's a surprise.' Oliver grinned. 'Forgot to ask; do you have photo ID with you?'

'Driver's licence OK?' Somewhere out of the country then. Despite her misgivings her heart did a little dance. A helicopter!

'Excellent. Right. Here we go.' He tapped the back of the driver's seat and the chauffeur nodded, turned off the engine and got out of the car and opened Oliver's door for him.

This was wild. 'But, Oliver. Where?'

Oliver waved the man away with a thanks and a handshake then opened Victoria's door. 'Your majesty, your carriage awaits.'

'Idiot.' But instead of hitting his arm like last time she slid her hand into his and walked through the heliport doors. This was the stuff of daydreams. *A freaking helicopter!*

Once inside, Oliver went to talk to the pilot and complete paperwork, then he walked her out to the huge H sign painted on a platform that extended out over the river. He guided her into a sleek silver machine with six seats in the back. Plush cream leather, chrome fittings. There was a little armrest in between them. Flash.

With the rotorblades going it was difficult to hear anything the pilot and Oliver were saying to each other, but Oliver kissed her cheek and handed her what looked like souped-up headphones. 'Here's a headset and mic. Martin will talk you through all the safety stuff, but basically sit back and enjoy.'

So, she wasn't going to get a chance to talk to Oliver properly now either. It was going to have to wait a little longer. She pushed the guilt and the worry out of her head and listened to Martin, learning that they'd be flying at two thousand feet. Flight time was ninety minutes.

Ninety minutes to where? Prague? Dublin? Paris? Her heart danced some more.

Martin told her he would point out things of interest that… whoa! She looked out of the window, they were already airborne. 'Oh, wow. I didn't even notice we'd left the ground.'

'It's disconcerting going straight up, right? No dramatic take-off. Look out the window.'

Oliver was back to holding her hand again and it was warm and strong and safe and she didn't want to let go. She promised herself she'd hold it when she broke the news to him later that she was cutting their deal short. And when she did finally let go, it would be for ever.

For now she'd relish the heat and the promise as his thumb stroked lazily and very sexily over hers, stoking a need she was failing to ignore or subdue. She looked out of the window and tried to find her balance again.

Below them the architecture she'd come to love in the city she now called home shrank to miniatures. They followed the River Thames, a sparkling silver ribbon threading through London, out towards the south coast until there was nothing below them but sea.

Once they'd left England behind Oliver twisted in his seat to look at her, his eyes warm and kind. She could see the joy in his face as he watched her reaction to the flight. He pressed a kiss to her cheek. 'Are you OK?'

'This is beyond exciting.' And unbearably difficult. She liked him. Maybe even more than that. *No.* Her stomach tightened. She most certainly was not going to allow herself to fall that deeply. But he was everything she'd ever wanted.

He pushed a lock of her hair back behind her ear. 'You wanted to talk to me about something?'

Not here. More ears listening. 'It can wait. How was your dad, really?'

Oliver grimaced. 'Grumpy. But that's probably a good thing. He's got a bit of spark back, but not enough. He's not eating properly and he's very weak with the new treatment. But the doctors are optimistic. Which is good, because he still has a lot to hand over to me.'

'Are you scared? Of taking control of… everything?' The family, the business, the legacy they were all so keen on preserving.

'No.' He looked out of the window and swallowed.

They were all about the stiff upper lip and not showing emotion, she'd never known a family so staunch. Was it really a weakness to admit to feelings? She couldn't live like that but it wasn't her business and she was going to cut ties soon enough, so she let the subject slide. She squeezed his hand. 'Where are we going?'

'You'll see.' He let go of her hand then lifted the armrest between them and pulled out a bottle of champagne and two glasses. 'Fancy a drink?'

Well, yes. 'Why the heck not? It's not every day you get to fly in a chopper and drink bubbles.' She laughed. 'Oh. But it is for you.'

'Don't worry, I made sure to pay the carbon offset for you.' Smiling, he popped the cork, poured and then handed her a glass of champagne. She tipped her glass to his and met his gaze, the familiar tug of affection catching her off-guard. As he looked at her his lips curved into a wicked smile. Everything inside her heated at the thought of that mouth on hers. Of that mouth on her skin.

Nerves ruffled, she dragged her gaze away. Didn't matter what she told herself, that dangerous spark of attraction was always there between them. The champagne bubbles tickled her throat and she sank back into the soft leather running her hand over the armrest, trying to find her equilibrium again. 'This is amazing.'

He was still looking at her, his gaze still burning. 'Yes.'

'It's probably just second nature to you.'

He shook his head. 'Every single time I step into one of these I'm in awe of the technology that builds them and keeps them in the sky and the fact I get to use them to go to work. It's never routine. Look at it. Look out here.' He pointed to the cloudless sky. 'So much space up here.'

She understood the sentiment. Up here she felt cocooned from everything she'd been worrying about. Behind them the sky was a riot of reds and pinks as the sun was starting to set in England. Below them the cross-channel ferries and boats were like children's toys dotted over a calm and vivid-blue sea.

'It's like another world.'

He nodded. 'Respite for ninety minutes, away from work, from thinking. You get to breathe.'

'And drink champagne.' She giggled. 'It sounds like you need a holiday, Oliver Russell.'

He turned to her, suddenly serious. His gaze wandered her face, settled on her mouth. 'I don't need a holiday. I need...'

She put her glass down, mesmerized by his eyes and the desire there wiping all other thoughts from her brain. She didn't want to look anywhere but him, imagined kissing him again. Unable to resist touching him she reached out and skimmed his jaw with her fingertips. Heat rushed through her, making her giddy. 'What, Ollie... what do you need?'

'This.' He tipped her face to his and slid his mouth over hers.

She should have pulled away, should have told him then and there about her reservations, about his cousin's visit and his mother's dreams. Should have put her hand to his chest and pushed him away, but instead her fingers sank into the linen and she tugged him closer.

He was addictive, this man. A drug to her senses that she didn't have the strength to fight it. If this was going to be their last kiss she was going to savour it, remember it, make it count. Bring it out later, in old age, play it over and over in her head. That amazing kiss at two thousand feet with a handsome man who had a wonderful heart.

Their last kiss? She couldn't bear to think about it not happening again. So, she allowed herself the realization of one of her dreams – of being cared for, of being kissed, of being made to feel beautiful and wanted, even if only for now. And let herself sink into it.

It started gently, an exploration as if they had endless time in this new private world. He nibbled her bottom lip, playful at first making her giggle and beg for more. But as the kiss deepened it became a mashing of needs, a lifeline. He clasped her tight against him, kissed and kissed and kissed her until her thoughts muddled and blurred and then coalesced into one thought. This man. Oliver Russell.

She brushed her hand over his hair and looked deeply into his eyes, falling just a little bit more for a man who said he needed her kisses to make him feel better. 'Tough day, huh?'

He pulled away, breathless. Thumbed her bottom lip. 'Not anymore. I've been thinking about doing that all day. All last night. You drive me crazy.'

She was starting to think she was going mad too. He lulled her with every action, every touch. Stole her thoughts with his kisses. He was bewitching. He was everything.

And she was falling. Falling. She needed to save herself before she slipped completely under his spell and ended up hurting not just herself but him and his lovely family. Maybe now was the best time to say it. Cut the ties before they bound them together too tightly. 'Look, Oliver—'

Her phone pinged and she glanced down. A message from Lily: Don't forget it's Malie's birthday. We said we'd chat at six o'clock our time.

Oh, God. Of course. She'd remembered this morning and been so looking forward to chatting with her friends, but with the Andrew and Stella visits it had completely skipped her mind. How was she going to do the Lost Hours call today? 'Erm, Ollie, what's the plan timing-wise?'

'We should get there soon. You need to put your watch forward an hour.'

'Where exactly is there?'

'Look down.'

'Oh! It's beautiful.' The low winter sun bathed pale stone buildings with a soft golden light. Like London, it was another city bifurcated by a sparkling river. A white citadel on a hill, an arch in the centre of a star-shaped intersection. A tower that was the most iconic building in the world. Maybe it was the champagne or the kiss, or just being here with Oliver, but she felt in this moment as if she was the luckiest woman alive. The view took her breath away. Literally. 'I love Paris.'

'I hoped so. It's one of my favourite places.'

'I've never seen it like this. I've only ever been by train.'

'There's no better way to see it than from the sky.' He grinned. 'Look, I have a short but necessary meeting between five and seven, but then we can do dinner. I hope that's OK?'

The call was at six UK time. Which meant seven in France.

Maybe she could bring the chat forward? Damn. But then Malie might not be awake, or being an early bird, she could already be out.

She must have looked concerned, because he cupped her cheek and smiled. 'Hey, I won't be long. I've looked up the nearest fabric shops to the store and there are two close by that don't close until seven. Hopefully they'll have the things you need. I can get Claude to take you if you like.'

'Claude?'

'My PA in Paris.'

She spluttered the remains of her champagne. 'You have more than one PA?'

'You mean you don't?' He deadpanned genuine confusion.

She laughed. 'I don't even have one. A girl can dream.'

'A man can too.' He kissed her again then. Hard and fast. 'I have an apartment here overlooking the river. I'm sure you'll love it.'

He was asking her to stay the night. The thump of reality slipped in between her ribs, but it was overtaken by the shimmer of excitement. He was asking her to stay. He wanted her in his bed, and she wanted to be there. And she was so bewitched by him that the first answer in her head was *yes*.

Her body prickled in anticipation of a slow, sultry seduction and she slipped her hand into his. Closed her eyes and kissed him again. And again. And again.

But. The reality was still there. This was taking everything to another level. Falling deeper and deeper under his spell.

She was getting tired of *buts* when he was so delicious and attentive and thoughtful. When he was offering her a chance of something she'd never experience again. Blurring her thoughts with his kisses until all she wanted was to feel him around her, inside her.

She tucked her doubts away as he said, 'Paris was my first store and it's very special to me. I lived here for two years and I got to know it well. But if I'm completely honest, I have no idea where these shops are or whether they're any good – it's not like I've ever stepped foot in them.' He gave a very Gallic shrug of his shoulders. *'Je suis desolé.'*

The mere fact he was taking her to Paris for dinner was enough. But that he had spent time and consideration in researching stores she'd like made her chest fill with light and warmth.

'Don't worry, my superpower is having a fabric-shop radar. I'll just love mooching through the streets and I'll find them and will be in absolute heaven until your meeting's finished.' She needed to fit the birthday call in. 'Um. Don't hurry, I'll be just fine.'

'Oh, yes, I wouldn't want to interrupt your happy day.' He tilted her chin up and pressed another kiss full on her mouth, making her heart stop and her limbs melt.

Happy? More like ecstatic. Elated. That was what she felt like when she was with him. When he made gestures like this or even just when he held her hand. He wanted to make her happy and that was the difference between him and any other man she'd ever met. By breaking this off she'd be purposefully putting a stop to this feeling inside her. She didn't even want to think about that.

Later. Over dinner.

Or tomorrow.

She'd tell him then.

* * *

The shop was only a couple of minutes around the corner from his office and she found it as if she'd been magnetically drawn there. The window display was a riot of pinks and tweeds that made Victoria's stomach fizz in excitement. And it fizzed a zillion times more when the diminutive sales assistant whispered to her that they wove for Chanel.

OMG! The designer she admired most in the world; she almost had to pinch herself. It was a treasure trove she wanted to dive right into and not surface from for hours. There were offcuts of patterned wool for coats and jackets, and scraps for accessories and decorations as well as cones of different coloured yarn. And even though she couldn't afford to buy much she figured she deserved something to commemorate her trip here. Her arms were full by the time her phone chimed and she silently prayed her credit card wouldn't explode as she paid for them. It didn't, but she'd need to do a few hours' overtime in the bar after the Opening Day madness had settled down.

'Hang on! Hang on!' She laughed as she paid the bill and danced outside with a bag filled with treats she couldn't wait to show Oliver. Even though she knew he wouldn't understand *why* she was so excited by them, he'd definitely understand her excitement. The birthday girl's face appeared on her tablet first and Victoria felt a wave of love. 'Hey! Happy, happy birthday, gorgeous Malie!'

One by one her friends appeared on the tiny screen. Could this day get any better?

She found a bench a few metres up from the shop and sat. 'Malie, what do you have planned for the day? Tell me it involves sun, surf and…' She was jokingly going to say *sex*, but Malie was notoriously quiet about her relationships. Like the rest of them, she hadn't forged anything lasting or meaningful with a guy since the accident, and they'd been too young to really commit before it. They'd all just focused on their own healing, stuck together as such a tight unit they'd not let anyone else in.

Victoria laughed. '. . . And sex on the beach? I mean the cocktail, obviously.'

'Of course! Nothing else entered my head. Apart from the fact that sand gets everywhere and can be... exfoliating on sensitive parts. So I've heard.' The birthday girl winked, beaming all the way from Hawaii. She looked so well with her glowing bronzed skin and bleached curls. Her Devon accent was tinged with the teeniest USA twang. 'It's so lovely to talk to you all. I've already done my most favourite thing today.'

'Let me guess.' Zoe drummed her fingers on her chin as if trying to work out a very difficult puzzle. 'Surfing?'

'You got it.' Malie stretched out her arms as if she was doing a yoga pose. She was wearing a zipped-up pink rash vest and bikini shorts, her hair was still damp after her swim and she looked simply gorgeous. Behind her the sea sparkled. It looked like paradise. 'After this I'm going to teach some classes with Kailani, then drinks with friends.' The way she said *friends* didn't sound like anyone special.

'No foam parties planned?' Lily laughed.

'If there was, I'd be fine. Not like some people I could mention, Zoe Tayler.' Malie's smiling eyes widened accusingly.

Zoe's crinkled. 'Hey! I had a great time. Too bad you all got lost for three hours.'

'We were looking for you,' they all cried at once, the way they must have said it a hundred times before.

'Good times.' Victoria squinted at the screen. Oh, to be that young and innocent again. 'Hey, birthday girl, how's the teaching going?'

Like Victoria, Malie's way of healing from the accident had been to throw herself into helping others. The surf school she ran with her godfather Kailani had specially adapted boards and equipment for kids with special needs. Victoria didn't really need to ask her friend if she was enjoying it because the moment her job was mentioned her face lit up.

'I love it. It's the best thing. Ever.'

'No sexy city boys over for you to give lessons to?' Lily chimed in, wiggling her eyebrows suggestively.

'I've no need for city boys when the surfer dudes are all hot, hot, hot and up for fun! Besides, lessons are for teaching, I would never be so naughty as to mix up...' Malie's face came closer to the screen, her wild curls coming into full focus. 'Where are you, V? It looks different to usual.'

'Oh! Let me guess! It's not Chelsea. Is that... are you in France?' Zoe peered closer. 'That looks like a French street sign.'

Victoria turned ninety degrees, trying to get the tell-tale sign behind her out of view, but it was too late. Typical that the travel writer could discern the French vibe no matter how careful Victoria had been at trying to shade the phone screen. She tried to sound nonchalant instead of as excited as a child at Christmas.

'It's just a work thing. Yeah. Paris.'

'What kind of wine bar work takes you to Paris? Oh, are you doing a tasting? Isn't it Beaujolais nouveau season?' Zoe's eyes were wide and bright, and Victoria felt a pang of wistfulness. It was so good to catch up with them even if she was keeping a little part of her life secret. She pushed away the guilt. This wasn't the time to go into details about him and their deal, especially as it was ending. How had life become so complicated that she was keeping secrets from her friends?

But she needn't have worried, Zoe was still in full travel-guide mode. 'Whereabouts are you? I know a fabulous place in the eighteenth *arrondisement*. They do the best *confit* in Paris. Locals only, no tourists filling it up and you won't find it in a guidebook.'

One of the great things about having a travel writer as a friend was that she always knew the best eating and drinking spots the locals frequented. 'Brilliant. Message me the name and I'll check it out.'

'And then there's this gorgeous bistro in Montmartre… give me a sec I'll double-check the name.' Zoe disappeared from shot. Lily wasn't saying anything now. She just looked at the screen with an emotionless expression and Victoria wondered what she was thinking.

Please don't say anything. Please don't say anything, Victoria silently prayed. Then she felt bad about having asked her friend to keep her secret.

'It's just a day trip, you know. Next time I come over I'll get a list of recommendations from you, Zo.'

'*Eez* there a sexy Frenchman in your future?' Malie laughed, putting on the worst French accent ever.

'Hang on, I'll check.' Victoria pretended to look around as if she'd lost one. 'Nope. Not a single one.'

'Shame. A Frenchman in your stocking would have been a great Christmas present. But oh, by work, do you mean you have a design commission there or something? Please say yes. That would be brilliant.' Malie was combing her fingers through her crazy curls to waft the water out. 'That and *le* sexy Frenchman would show sleazebag Peter.'

Victoria thought about the look on Peter's face when he'd seen the engagement ring. She'd thought she'd feel righteously smug but actually she didn't care. Not at all. Peter was in the past and she had zero feelings for him now.

In fact, talking of sexy… a certain very English, very gorgeous man sprang to mind. A man who should be arriving any time soon to whisk her to a fancy restaurant. To his apartment. To his bed. Her breath stalled at the thought. Anticipation fluttered through her. And nervousness too. She hadn't said yes. But she hadn't said no either. Truth was, she was so torn and so turned on. Whenever she was with him she was incapable of rational thought. She looked around, hoping to see him, but he was obviously still caught up in his meeting.

'No sexy men around here.' *Yet*. 'But I have just been into an amazing haberdashery that makes fabric for Chanel, which is Christmas come early, as far as I'm concerned.' Another one to tick off her list of things Oliver had made happen. 'And I am having a runway show. Like… soon.'

'Oh. My. God,' Malie squealed. 'That's brilliant! Where?'

'You remember the department store I told you about? Next to work? The owner has asked me and my students to do a fashion show at the opening day. I'm showing my new bridal collection.'

Lily was still looking at her with a guarded expression.

'And I promise I'm going to send you all email invitations so you can celebrate with me long distance. I know you won't be able to make it, but I just wanted to… well, show off.'

'Go, you! That's fabulous. It's about time.' Zoe gave the thumbs up. 'You so deserve this.'

'I'll be able to come up for the afternoon but I'm struggling to take the evening off work. It's mad busy here at the moment. Should I carpool with your parents?' Lily finally said. 'Can't wait to cheer you on.'

'They can't make it. They've already booked a trip to the German Christmas markets, but they're thrilled for me,' Victoria said, then felt bad because her parents were the most supportive people she knew, but she couldn't say the same about her friends' families.

Her friends. These three women on her screen were all smiling at her good fortune, but she wasn't being honest with them and that hit her hard. They'd shared everything together, they'd fought for each other through very dark times. She couldn't have a conversation with her closest friends and not be totally honest about why she was here in Paris, she'd never forgive herself. And they'd probably never forgive her either.

She took a deep breath and cleared her throat. 'OK, listen. I've got something to tell you guys. Just don't… don't judge me, OK? Before anyone says anything, I want you to know I have good reasons for doing what I'm doing.'

'Victoria Scott, I have no idea what you're talking about. And I would never, ever judge you. But you're starting to worry me.' The birthday girl's happy smile turned south.

'It's nothing bad. Well… no. It's nothing bad.' Was it? Not bad, but definitely serious. She'd somehow become embroiled with Oliver and she didn't want to un-embroil herself. Victoria's eyes flicked to the little square with Lily's face in it. Her friend nodded encouragingly, and with a certain amount of relief, possibly that she wasn't now the only one carrying Victoria's secret. 'The thing is… I'm in Paris because I'mpretendingtobesomeone'sfiancée.'

'Say what?' Zoe's eyes widened. 'Pretending to blah blah fiancée?'

As if they'd let her get away with that. How to even explain the ridiculous situation she'd got herself into? 'So... there's this guy I met... he needs someone to be his fake fiancée for a few days and he asked me and I said yes.'

Shocked silence. Then:

'Be careful.'

'Go you!'

'Why didn't you tell us?'

Victoria wasn't sure exactly who said what, although she could probably guess.

'"Some guy" being Oliver Russell, the billionaire boss at Russell & Co,' Lily chipped in, making quote marks with her fingers. 'Because his father's sick and wants to see Oliver settled, so Victoria's obliging and making them happy. Right, V? It's for a good cause.'

'Lily, you knew and didn't say anything?' Malie asked incredulously.

'I'm sorry! I promised V I wouldn't,' Lily said with an apologetic shrug.

'I thought we didn't keep secrets,' Zoe said quietly, hurt evident in her expression.

'We don't. I am so sorry, you guys. Lily's right, though, it is for a good cause and that's part of the reason I asked her to keep it quiet.' *Thank you, Lils.* Victoria knew how hard it had been for Lily not to say anything about this to their friends and for that she was immensely grateful. God, she loved these women. No matter what, no matter how insane her ideas sounded, she knew they would always support her. 'He brought me to Paris in a helicopter for dinner and I'm having my show at his store.'

Zoe's eyes narrowed, the hurt still there, but Victoria could see her friend was trying to understand why she hadn't told them about her and Ollie's arrangement. And that made everything worse because they were all right; they didn't keep secrets. Ever. 'You swapped an acting role for a helicopter. Like your style. It sounds like one of those movies like *The Wedding Date*, or *The Proposal* or something. Is he Ryan Reynolds hot too? Please say yes.'

He's more than that. And kind. And lovely. Victoria swallowed. 'A bit. I suppose.' She felt Lily's gaze on her and the truth came tumbling out. 'Look, don't read anything into this but I kissed him. Or rather, we kissed.' More than once... in fact, so many times she'd lost count.

Her words were met by a loud *whoop!* 'Go, you. Finally, one of us gets some action,' Zoe said, but Victoria knew they were all scared of anything that went deeper than a little action, and that none of them had managed to hold down a serious relationship. Ever. She didn't know if that was related to the accident but she thought it could be. They were all scarred and scared in some way or other.

'There's no bed involved. And yes, he kisses well, but it doesn't mean anything.' *Liar.* More silence. 'Somebody say something.'

'I am genuinely in awe.' But Zoe's mouth twisted a little and her voice softened. 'Just be careful, OK. I've seen the way those movies end and it's all great in make-believe and I really hope it all turns out well, but...' They all knew that reality was harsh and didn't always come with a guaranteed happy ending. They knew that better than most people. 'Just be careful, please.'

'I will. I'm fine. But thank you.'

Lily smiled too. 'It is a bit crazy, but you know that whatever happens we're here for you.'

'But it could work out, right? We need regular updates, OK? K-I-S-S-I-N-G, Victoria and Oliver sitting in a—' Malie's excited grin fell at Victoria's warning but half-joking stare. 'OK, Pretend. Right. Got it. But if anything happens… I mean you never know, right? I want the lowdown in a Lost Hours call, OK? And, if he's seriously a billionaire can you get him to fly you over here?'

'I wish. Our deal's only for a few more days so I'm enjoying the high life while I can. A helicopter! Champagne!' Victoria knew she'd like Oliver if he had a bicycle and a bottle of fizzy water. It wasn't the trappings of wealth that attracted her. It was him.

It was him. And for the millionth time she wished, just wished she could be telling her friends it was real.

But Lily, always softer, quieter than the others just nodded. 'We love you, V. If you think it's the right thing to do, then go for it.'

Malie stuck her thumbs up. 'Got your back, OK?'

'Thanks, guys.'

It was past seven now and she wondered where Oliver had got to. She turned and scanned the dark street. There, in the distance, was a figure huddled against the icy wind walking towards her. As he got closer she realized his face was ashen. The easy-going manner from before had been replaced with a stern expression.

Her heart went into freefall. What had happened? She looked back at her friends. 'Hey, squad, he's coming back. I've got to go.'

'At least turn the camera round so we can see him!' Malie shouted.

'No way. Have the best day, Malie.'

'Don't go yet! We need more details!' A chorus of voices chimed as she slipped the tablet into her bag and ran to Oliver feeling relieved and supported and loved by her friends. She'd call them later and explain more. She grasped his arm and leaned in to kiss him, as if kissing this man in the street was the most normal thing to do. But she just couldn't help herself and he looked like he needed it. 'Hey! What's the matter? Did you give yourself the sack?'

He shook his head. 'I need to go back to London. Now. The helicopter's on standby. I'm sorry about tonight. We can grab something to eat back in London.'

'I'm not hungry.' Her appetite had taken a dive the minute she'd seen his grim expression. 'What is it? What's the matter?'

'My dad's taken a turn. Mum called and asked me to go back immediately and I know she fusses but even she wouldn't do that if it wasn't necessary.'

She understood the subtext. Eric was already sick and receiving revolutionary new therapy. Something had gone wrong.

'I'm so sorry, Ollie. We'll go straight back.' She rubbed her hand up and down his shoulder. He turned away. She tugged him back to face her. 'I don't want any of that Russell stiff upper lip stuff. Come here.'

'I'm fine.'

'You are not. I imagine you're scared. You're hurting and that's OK, Oliver Russell. You are allowed to be human.' She spread her arms and waited, all thoughts of what she'd been planning to say to him forced to the recesses of her mind. She couldn't do that to him today when both he and his mother needed her support. She'd do it tomorrow, or once things had settled down a bit. Another time. Right now, she was going to be the friend he needed her to be. The friend she'd be to Lily and Malie and Zoe if they were going through this. 'You don't have to carry this by yourself. I'm here for you.'

He just looked as if she'd handed him a lifeline and he didn't know what to do with it. 'There's not enough time.'

Maybe there wasn't and he'd have to deal with that too. But she wanted him to know he didn't have to do any of it alone. She wrapped her arms around him, spanning the ribbons of muscles and tendons that were primed and tense. It felt as if every cell in his body was tight. This was Oliver in self-preservation mode. She needed him to know that he wasn't alone, he didn't need to have carry this all himself. She kissed him gently. 'I'm here, I'm here. I'm here.'

She clung on.

And held tight.

CHAPTER FIFTEEN

EVEN IN A HELICOPTER it took too long to get to the hospital, as far as Oliver was concerned. Time was running out. He had too much to do, too much to say to his father and he went over and over it in his head on the flight. But now they were here his words fled. He steadied himself for bad news. Whatever happened, he would not lose control.

His mother ran up the corridor towards him and gripped his arm, her features hollowed out by worry. 'Ollie, Victoria. Thank God you're here. The doctors have been with him for hours and they won't tell me anything.'

'What happened?'

'We were just talking, then he suddenly went pale and limp and I called for help. Then the staff rushed in with extra equipment, shooed me out of the room, and left me here.'

Here, being the plush waiting area at the side of the ward. It looked more like a hotel with its lime green and pale wood decor, individual side rooms and personal menus, but inside the bedrooms the patients were as sick and frail as in any other hospital.

Oliver looked round for a member of staff, but they were all in other rooms caring for patients. He wrapped his mum in a hug, pressing a kiss to her head. It wasn't something they usually did and she looked up at him, confused by his sudden, uncharacteristic affection, but he hung on the way Victoria had held him, knowing it would make his mother feel better.

'They're focusing on him, Mum. I'm sure they'll come and give us some news as soon as they have any.'

'Two hours, Oliver. I've been standing here for two hours.' His mother's voice was cracking, and he could see she was nearing breaking point.

'I'll find out what's happening.' He let her go and knocked on his father's door.

A nurse came out of the room pushing a trolley. 'Sorry it took so long. You can go in now. But please be quiet as Eric's sleeping. The doctor's going to – oh, here he is now.'

Dr Malik came out of the room and closed the door quietly behind him. He opened his mouth to speak but Stella got in first, 'Is he going to be OK?'

'It was just an allergic reaction. I say *just*; it was quite a bad one. We had to give him two shots of adrenalin and we've been monitoring him very closely. But he's back with us. I have to be honest, we were quite worried about him for a few minutes back there.' The cardiologist shook his head wearily and explained, 'New drugs. Can't always be sure how a patient's going to respond.'

'He wanted to try them,' Stella insisted. She was pale but dry-eyed. Holding everything in like a well-trained Russell. 'Said he'd give anything a try for a few more years. Now I don't know if we'll have a few more hours.'

'He's definitely better than he was but he's not out of the woods yet. We'll keep a very close eye on him. The next twenty-four hours are crucial.'

'OK, thanks for being so candid, Dr Malik.'

Touch and go. Oliver thought about all the things he should have said to his dad, all the things they could have done together if Russell & Co hadn't eaten up all their time. He wasn't going to be that kind of father, he was going to devote weekends and evenings and holidays to his kids. He was going to make time count. And, he was going to make what little time he had left with his father count too.

As if she understood what he was feeling, Victoria's hand crept into his, and her tenderness crept into his chest too. Just having her here gave him strength. He'd never known how it could feel to share a burden with someone. To be able to lean into them and feel the heavy weight lift, even if only for a short time. He hadn't known it was even possible to share joy too. But just watching her in the helicopter he'd been having as much fun as she was.

He walked his mother into the room and sat her down on one side of the bed, got a very worried-looking Victoria to sit in a chair across from Stella, and sat next to her, still holding her hand and not wanting to let go. He wondered if he needed to be checked out by the cardiologist too. His heart was pounding. He willed it to slow. Russells kept a tight control over themselves. He could do that. He was in charge now.

He let his mum fuss over his father for a few minutes. Pulling the duvet up to his chest, straightening the sheet, tidying the tray table. Her hands fluttered, busy. It reminded him of Victoria and the way she talked with her hands. It was amazing that even coming from completely different worlds, these two women were similar. When he saw his mum looking round for more fixing and fussing to do he stood, put his hands on her shoulders and said, 'Mum, you need to get some rest. You look exhausted.'

'I'm not going to leave him.' She was resolute.

'I always thought my stubborn streak was from Dad, but clearly I was wrong. Did you eat?'

As if to raise the stubborn stakes higher she crossed her arms. 'No. I'm not hungry.'

He smiled and shook his head. 'Neither of my parents want to eat anything. What am I going to do?'

'Phone Antoine.' Victoria's voice was low, as if she didn't want to intrude.

'What?'

Victoria spoke louder. 'Phone Antoine and get him to send over some of your favourite things. That might help get your parents' appetites back.' She made asking for help sound so easy. 'He knows you well enough to do this for you. Phone him.'

'No. I couldn't.'

'How many favours have you ever asked of anyone?' At the shake of his head she frowned. 'You Russells really do need to learn to ask for help. Phone your chef friend and ask him to deliver some food. He can only say no.'

Of course, Antoine didn't say anything except, *how quickly do you need it?* And soon enough a courier arrived with delicious-smelling meatballs and his mother's favourite lobster ravioli.

After making sure Eric was sleeping and safe they took the food through to the waiting area and had a feast. Oliver watched his mother's shoulders sag as she put her fork down. 'You can't look after Dad if you're exhausted. There's a relatives' room down the corridor, Mum. We just walked past it. I'll see if it's available and you can sleep there. I will call you if there's any change. I promise I'll stay here all night.'

'Me too,' Victoria said, slipping her arm around his waist and hugging him to her side.

He leaned against her, his heart filled with gratitude. 'You don't have to.'

'I know.' She put her palm to his jaw and smiled softly. 'But I want to.'

So, he settled his mother and came back to his father's room. His heart stuttered as he walked in and saw Victoria stroking his dad's hand. The repeated rush of affection wasn't what he'd expected when he'd planned this deal, nor the wealth of emotions she stirred in him. And he didn't know what to do about… any of it. He was lost in her, in this and in the swirling feelings about his father. He'd never *felt* so much as he had these last few days.

A nursing assistant wheeled a large chair into his father's room and gave them a duvet. 'Sorry there isn't any space for two big chairs, but you could take it in turns to get some shut-eye on this.'

They sat for a long time side by side, hands clasped together just watching Eric and listening to the whirs and clicks of the machines. His breathing was regular and the nursing staff seemed pleased that he was resting. When Oliver realized Victoria was sagging and drifting to sleep on his shoulder he kissed her cheek. 'Hey, sleepyhead. You can go home.'

'No. I'll stay here.'

'Then sleep on the chair.'

She shook her head, tendrils of her hair springing loose from its ponytail. 'You first. I'm fine.'

He loved that she was trying to stay awake for him but watching over his father was his job. 'I can't sleep. I'm exhausted, but wired. I'll watch him until the nurse makes her next check. Then I'll try sleeping.'

'OK.' She gave him a concerned smile that tugged deep in his chest and then she slid under the duvet. 'Wake me if anything happens. Or if you want to swap shifts.'

The nurses came and went. His father's vital signs were improving albeit slowly and eventually the pull of sleep was getting too much. Oliver went over and sat on the arm of the chair, strangely cold when Victoria wasn't close.

The way she'd held him on that street had made him realize he didn't have to face this alone, any of it. He had her, his mother, even his cousin to share some of the load. He just had to ask. Hell, that was an eye-opener.

She stirred, leaning her head against his thigh and he stroked her hair. Soon there was nothing but the sound of beeps and whooshes and the regular in-out snuffle of his dad's snores.

'There's enough room for you here,' Victoria whispered, as she shifted to one edge of the large cushioned chair. 'Slide on down.'

'I thought you were asleep.'

'Just thinking.' She lifted herself up and he slid into the chair, settling herself against him in the dark, the only light an eerie orange glow from the LED monitor lights. Having her here in his arms felt right. Good. He nuzzled the top of her head, inhaling the citrus shampoo smell and wondering how it was that he got hot just holding her.

He was acutely aware of the press of her body against his, the rise and fall of her breasts against his chest. Having her skin touch his made his whole body prickle with need. He wanted to make love to her right here.

That was clearly impossible, and he was officially just going to go insane with lust. But he did kiss her, because he couldn't not.

Soft and giving, the kiss filled his heart and he swore he felt their souls entwining until they were enmeshed and unbreakable. He regretted that he couldn't take her to bed in his Parisian apartment but this was the next best thing; she was here by his side when he needed her the most.

When she pulled away she looked blissful and he wished he could spend every day and all night exploring all the different kinds of kisses they could have. Then he remembered her phone call from earlier. 'Hey, you wanted to talk and I'm sorry we didn't get a chance before.'

She snuggled into his arms and breathed out on a smile he felt against his chest. 'It was nothing. I'm fine, just a wobble.'

'What brought that on?'

Her voice was low. 'Your mother and your cousin decided to pay me a visit today.'

'What? Together?'

'No.' She craned her neck from side to side so he started to massage the knots on one side of her neck. 'They both had their own agendas.'

'Which were what?'

'Andrew thinks everything's fake. The engagement, the ring, us. And conversely, your mother is far too invested in us as a couple. After they'd gone I had a horrible feeling this plan is going to completely backfire. I got spooked.'

If this blew up because of Andrew, Oliver was going to make him pay. 'He had no right coming to see you.'

'He said he was looking for someone. I think he's getting friendly with Peter.'

'Let him. Maybe it'll distract him from us.' But Oliver put two and two together. 'So after their visits you wanted to back out?'

'Yes.'

'Ah.' His gut knotted. He hadn't realized just how much he'd got used to her being around. The thought of her disappearing right now made his heart lurch. Was she still here because she felt sorry for him? Because she hadn't the heart to kick him when he was down? 'The Paris trip would have been awkward for you, then.'

He felt deflated that the surprise had been on false pretences. She'd spent the time there trying to find the opportunity to finish this. She had never actually answered his question about staying the night, after all.

'It was lovely. Really.' Her hand rested on the top of his thigh. 'It was a lovely idea.'

He closed his eyes as an inappropriate lust ricocheted through him. This was not the time, the place or the conversation for that. 'Do you still want to back out?'

She glanced over to his father and shrugged her shoulders minutely, as if it was all beyond her control. 'I want to help, Ollie.'

Which wasn't exactly the answer he'd been hoping for. But she wanted to stay and that was something.

Had the kisses meant nothing?

He knew they hadn't. She was scared of something – was it commitment? The possibility of being rejected again, like her ex had rejected her? Hell, Ollie controlled a feral urge to go around to that damned tailor shop and take the man outside. But then what? She'd still have those emotional scars. He just needed to keep building her trust.

His useless cousin and his mother weren't helping.

A whirring noise made her sit up quickly, jolting him backwards as she turned her head this way and that.

'What's that?' She shuddered, eyes darting from machine to machine.

'Sorry!' A nurse burst in, fiddled with his father's heart monitor pads. 'Happens sometimes if they get unstuck. No drama.'

Then she rushed out again.

Seemingly satisfied there was no emergency, Victoria settled back down. He felt the hard hammer of her heart against his chest as she shivered and said, 'God, I hate hospitals. I hate the smell. I hate the perpetual semi-darkness. The electronic sounds.'

It was a strange and strong reaction to something that was potentially life-saving. But then he remembered. 'The accident. I never thought.' It must have taken a lot for her to come here tonight and have those memories stirred up. 'How long were you in for?'

'Ten days.'

'Long time.'

'There were some internal injuries they had to deal with. And I was… recalcitrant, shall we say, about recovering.'

What was she saying? He read between the lines. 'You didn't want to get better?'

She shook her head. He tried to encourage her to say more, but she looked away.

He touched her chin and turned her to look at him again. He could see fear there as the memories bubbled up to the surface. 'Hey, I want to know. I want to know you, V.'

'Here? Now?' Her arms snaked round her chest. She was closing in on herself and she didn't have to.

He took hold of one hand and clasped it. 'You said earlier that I wasn't alone. Neither are you. I want to help and I think you need to vent it. Tell me.'

She took a deep breath and exhaled slowly. Grasping control. She spoke quietly to the dark, keeping her eyes fixed on a spot somewhere in the distance. In the past. Her heart thudded and her limbs tensed. And, for a woman who constantly moved, she was eerily still.

'It took me a long time to get over it. I was in the emergency department and they were working on Zoe right next to me. I don't know where Lily and Malie were. I can't remember… there are a lot of gaps.' Her hand went to her head as if she was trying to force out a memory. 'I remember bright lights, a lot of panic, people rushing and machines blaring. I heard the doctors say they couldn't save *her*. And in that moment, I knew I'd killed one of my friends. Can you imagine?'

He couldn't think of anything worse. 'It wasn't your fault.'

'I think I might have blacked out then, or maybe they'd put me under for surgery. But I woke up later in so much pain and not knowing who had survived and who hadn't. I was eighteen and didn't think my heart would ever recover, never mind my body.'

'What kind of surgery?'

'Some internal stuff. Bleeding, you know.' She shook her head as if her injuries weren't important. 'Zoe was thrown into the back of my seat and I was pushed forward into the steering wheel. They had to cut us out.'

Whoa. He sat up, his palms moving to gently cup her face. He wanted to rewind time and somehow be there, to stop her getting into that car, to stop the accident, to stop her pain. 'God, V. I can't even… Where did you get hurt?'

Although, he didn't have to ask. Every time they talked about the accident she subconsciously rubbed her stomach. He placed his palm on her belly and she pressed her hand over it, squeezing so hard he knew she was reliving that night again.

He scooped her into his arms and kissed her cheeks, her forehead, her mouth. 'You're so brave.'

'Not brave at all.' Her eyes welled with tears and she smudged them away. 'I wanted to hide away for so long, I couldn't bring myself to look my friends in the eye. But they came to see me, refused to give up on me. Cajoled me along.'

'I would hope so. Friends don't give up on each other. I would never—' He kissed her then, unable to stop himself. She looked so dejected and hurt and yet so vibrant and loveable.

She pulled away. 'You don't really know me.'

'I know enough. I know you would never willingly hurt anyone. That you still blame yourself for everything. That you put distance between yourself and others because you're scared you might get hurt.'

She thought about it for a moment. 'I – yes, I do.'

'You don't have to worry about that with me.'

'I know—' She stopped abruptly and swung round quickly as his dad turned over in bed then started snoring again. She gave Oliver a soft, sad smile. 'I just don't want to hurt you, or your parents.'

'You would never. Besides, I'm doing a fine job of that on my own. My mother tries too hard and I push her away, and my father wants me to live at the office. There's not a lot of affection going on.'

'I don't agree. You came back here with no hesitation, because you love them. Took control. Refused to crack.' Her eyebrows rose. 'You know, it is OK to crack.'

'No, it isn't. Not when people rely on you.' He kept his voice as low as he could and knew his words came out fast, but he couldn't stop them. There was something about Victoria that made him want to talk about the things that mattered. He knew she listened without judgement. 'You think my mother wanted to see me in tears? You think she isn't burdened enough without having to console her son?'

'I think you can all admit to being frightened right now.'

'That is not the Russell way, at least not for the men. That is not how I was brought up. We have to brush our emotions under the carpet, pretend everything is fine even though things are falling apart. Russells take control, not lose it. So, no, V, I cannot crack.'

Victoria sighed sadly. 'Your mum is aching for closeness, Ollie. She just wants to love you and I think she feels as if she's lost you and that's why she came to see me... to try to connect with you, through me. She told me she never wanted to send you away to school. She just wants to spend time with you. Before it's too late.'

'She didn't want to send me away? But she just patted me on the head and told me not to cry.' So why would she tell Victoria something different? Had his mother just gone along with what she thought was the right thing to do? Being a loyal Russell wife? Had she cried later? It explained a lot about his mother's more recent smothering; she wanted to make up for the days she'd lost when he was away at school.

Just being here, seeing his father so frail and his mother so anxious was a wake-up call. They needed to fix things before it was too late. 'They're not going to be around for ever. We need to work on our communication, right?'

'That will make her very happy. And you too, I think.' Victoria sighed, exhaustion nipping her features. 'You all know you love each other, you just have to show it.'

'I'll try. Hugging isn't the kind of thing we do freely in our house.'

'Then you should definitely do more of it. Did you know that it's scientifically proven that a twenty-second hug can reduce stress, lower blood pressure and increase happy hormones?'

He squeezed her against his side and kissed the top of her head. 'Now, that is sounding very attractive.'

She held him tightly and was quiet for a moment then said, very quietly, 'And you have to tell them you want out of Russell & Co.'

Dread wound through his gut immediately cancelling out the hug benefits. 'What?'

'For your own sake. You have to tell them how you feel about taking over the company.'

'And then what? I don't even know what I want to do.'

She smiled secretively. 'Your mum told me that your dad wanted to be an engineer.'

'No? That's a surprise. I did not know that.'

'But he followed the family line. Don't live your life with regret. Don't get caught up in duty without living your dreams too. And don't leave it until you have your family and babies because you'll feel like you have to give them security. If you're going to jump, Ollie, it has to be soon.'

Usually he thrived on time pressure but not this. 'I'll think about it. After the opening. Once things are settled down.'

'Don't leave it until it's too late.'

'My father's too sick for me to make any hasty decisions.' Even though the work gave him little satisfaction he couldn't walk away now. Things were too complicated. 'After New Year, maybe. It's always so busy until then.'

'Stop making excuses.' She twisted to look him straight in the eye. 'What are you scared of, Oliver Russell?'

'Scared?' His hackles rose. He wasn't scared of any damn thing. But he was blocked. He couldn't see past the looming pressure of taking the helm at Russell & Co. It felt like a heavy weight on his chest and sometimes he couldn't breathe when he thought about being stuck in that role for the rest of his working life. 'Making the wrong choice.'

She frowned. 'There is no wrong choice, apart from staying in a job you don't like just because of expectation. You can do this, Ollie. If you want. You have to live your best life, not the life they've groomed you for.'

He glanced over to make sure his father couldn't hear this, but Russell senior was still snoring. 'You don't understand what it's like. I've been training for this since the day I could hold a pencil. My father was keen for me to be as involved as possible, just the way he had been with his father. As soon as I was old enough, he had me working in the post room – we don't even have one of those anymore.' He'd never bared his soul to anyone like this before but Victoria made it possible to actually say these things. 'Times change.'

'People change too, Ollie. You could choose to do something that makes your heart sing. You need to walk away.'

She made it all sound so easy, but she wasn't the one doing the jumping or disappointing her family. But then again, she'd also been the one who'd stared into bleakness and made a choice to do something positive with her life.

No one had ever talked so intimately to him or about him before. No one had stood by him or hurt with him, either. Especially with a hatred of hospitals and for people she barely knew.

He stroked her hair, his chest full of light for her and worry for his family. He was hot and cold. Stressed to the max being here when he should have been ticking off his to-do list for the opening and yet didn't want to be anywhere else. The only thing keeping him together was Victoria.

He rested his chin gently on her head. Tucked her close. And closer. His body was alive and restless having her here, tortured by the press of her breasts, feeling her heat around him. Wishing he could feel her heat around him for real. His body prickled. She moved against him and the crackle of electricity between them sparked again.

'Later,' he whispered into her hair.

'Later.' She nodded and smiled sleepily. He watched her breathing became slow and regular.

I love you.

It hit him out of the blue. A thought and a feeling so intense he didn't know what to do with it. A hot golden glow in the centre of his chest. Strange and new.

And… he breathed in a difficult, ragged breath. It was too much. Unfamiliar. He didn't want it. Didn't want to depend on her, didn't want to feel this and then lose it in a few days' time. Didn't want to fall into the comfort and excitement and the happiness she gave to him and get lost in her.

Didn't want to walk away from it either. Fifty years? It hadn't even been fifty days.

Hell. How did you know?

How? He rubbed his forehead with the heel of his hand. What if he got it wrong?

What if she walked away like they'd agreed? It wasn't as if he could put this feeling into words for her. She had a plan. They had a deal. Until the first of December and no more. She didn't want the money or the helicopters or the celebrity. She didn't want marriage or kids, she'd been at pains to underline that.

She was already scared. And hell, so was he, now.

I love you.

The glow didn't dim. It flickered and shone and filled his chest.

And was the last thing he felt as the pull of sleep became too much to fight.

* * *

'He's going to be fine. He just needs to rest and build up his strength.'

'Oh, that's such good news.' Victoria exhaled the breath she'd been holding ever since the cardiologist had walked into the room for the morning ward round. It had been a very disrupted night. Not just because of the unfamiliar noises and constant interruptions from the nurses doing their checks, but also because of the closeness she'd shared with Oliver. Every time she prepared herself to let go, the connection between them tightened.

Stella clapped her hands. 'Did you hear the man, Eric? No more work talk. You have to focus on getting better.'

Oliver's dad was sitting in bed propped up by pillows. He needed a shave, his skin was sallow and he had huge bruises under his eyes, but he huffed weakly. 'Work talk makes me feel better.'

'Well, you're too old to work so we're going to start learning how to slow down a bit. I want more time with you, Eric, not less. We need to live to see Oliver's children. I'm going to pop out and buy some Sudoku books and I'm investigating tai chi classes for when we go home.' She picked up a glossy brochure and waved it at him. 'I found this in the relatives' room. It sounds like something we can do together. Victoria and Oliver are doing the fashion show and it's making them both happy, I can see it. It's time we did something that wasn't just work.'

Well, recognizing they needed to do more relaxing together was a good thing. But again, the mention of Oliver's children. Victoria took a deep breath and exhaled slowly. This wasn't about her, she reminded herself. It was about this family. They seemed to be taking on board the things she'd suggested.

Eric grimaced. 'Ollie, lad. Save me?'

'What did you teach me, Dad? Only enter into arguments you're going to win?'

'But tai chi? With a load of pensioners?' Eric grumbled, clearly feeling a little better. 'I'm going to go mad.'

'Well, you're going to go mad with...' Stella read from the brochure. 'Lower blood pressure, improved balance and enhanced sleep.'

'A good handle on my bank balance helps me sleep very well indeed.' The old man tutted. The thought of having to relax and retire making him seem much more determined to get better.

'It's time to let it go, Eric,' his wife said. 'Maybe you could do some of that tinkering in the shed like you used to do before we got married.'

'Tinkering?' The old man frowned. 'Don't know what you're talking about.'

'I know. It's a long time ago.' Stella smiled. 'Remember when you used to make things?'

'Dad used to make things?' Ollie jumped in, animated. 'What kind of things?'

'He made the cot you slept in when you were born and then...' Stella looked at her hands. 'We got too busy with the company.'

'It happens.' Ollie shrugged but he looked suddenly smitten with his dad. And also, kind of sad that he'd never met this other father who'd been happy making things. A cot? Victoria sighed... Where had they lost their way? When had they stopped paying attention to each other?

But in the end it didn't matter where they'd gone wrong, because they were finding their way back to each other now.

'There's a group of men in the village who run something called a Man Shed. They get together and do things for the local community... build play parks for the childcare centre.' Stella clutched her husband's hand. 'You'd enjoy that. Working with your hands again. Doing something nice for the children, like Ollie and Victoria are doing for her design students.'

'Man Shed?' Eric looked as if he was about to tut again, but he sat and thought and as he did his eyes glittered. 'Victoria, you have a lot to answer for.'

Oh, wow. Victoria couldn't hide her joy at seeing them talking like this, properly learning about each other after all this time. 'Sorry, not sorry, Mr Russell.'

Eric looked at his wife. 'I'll think about it.'

She patted his hand but didn't push. 'In the meantime, you can build your strength up with tai chi.'

Eric shook his head. 'Does it say anywhere that I have to be teetotal?'

'No. Nothing here.'

'Good. Ask the lovely nurse to bring me a gin.'

Ollie laughed. 'It's breakfast time, Dad.'

'It's five o'clock somewhere in the world.'

'We'll leave you to argue that one out with the medics. See you later.' Oliver pressed a kiss to his father's head and the old man looked up at him in surprise. Ollie then wrapped his mother in a hug. 'Be good. Don't argue. I'll be back later. I love you both.'

Victoria watched with a warm fuzzy feeling in her heart. He was trying. They were all trying.

They stepped outside, blinking into a snowy wonderland and Victoria took a deep breath. Being wrapped in Ollie all night had been wonderful, but she needed to face the day and her never-ending job list, and the confusion about where they stood now.

Having spent the night bundled up against him her body felt alive, relishing his every touch, his thigh against hers, the press of his body. The way he'd stroked her hair, her hand, her cheek. The soft kisses that were about giving and affection. The line they'd straddled but managed to keep a grip on.

Now, out here in the fresh air, she felt as if they were moving towards something more, something inevitable that would change her for ever. They walked through the frosted streets that were starting to fill up with work and school traffic. Her skin tingled. Her breathing came too fast.

Later, he'd said. And she'd agreed. Drunk on exhaustion and lust she'd agreed because she couldn't imagine not making love with him. But even now in the bright winter morning nothing had changed. She wanted this man. She gripped his hand. Anticipation wound through her until she felt like a coiled spring.

When they reached her front door he said, 'My father made my cot. I can't believe it.'

'I know. It's surprising, but lovely to know they cared so much. I'm so glad things are getting back on track for you all.'

He pressed his forehead to hers. 'I can't thank you enough, V. It's all because of you.'

'That's what friends are for, right?' Blinking hard, she looked away. All his family had needed was a gentle push.

'Friends. Sure. Definitely friends.' He smiled and tenderly smoothed down her hair. Something had changed between them. A seismic shift that had taken them from strangers to a deep every-level connection.

Later... they were edging closer to their middle of the night promise.

Later was now. Her insides fluttered. He looked dark and dangerous and delicious, his black coat and hair a sharp contrast to the silvery white-coated roofs and tree branches. She put her palm to his unshaven jaw. 'You must have so much to do. Your blood pressure must be off the scale. Ever thought about tai chi?'

He laughed and caught her gaze. 'My balance is age appropriate. And I'm not interested in sleeping when I go to bed, especially if you're anywhere nearby.'

His words stoked her need and she almost moaned as she stared up at him, lost in eyes so dark and misted with sex they bewitched her.

As if he felt the same coiled need as she did, he pulled her to him, his hand curving round the back of her neck. Somehow, they moved seamlessly from tenderness to desire but always there was so much emotion when it came to him.

His mouth was at her throat. 'Victoria Scott, you drive me crazy. I spent the whole night trying not to imagine you naked with me under that duvet.'

Oh, God. Her heart hammered and her body prickled with a longing that stripped her breath. There were so many reasons why they shouldn't take the next step, but it felt inevitable, fated. She wanted him. It was as simple and complicated as that.

She pushed herself against him, feeling the tight press of his body, wanting to feel his heat, his hardness. Wanting him inside her. 'I thought I was going to die if you didn't kiss me again.'

'God, you are amazing. I can't get enough of you,' he groaned as his fingers traced along her throat. His mouth moved up her neck to that soft place below her ear that had her curling with desire. She turned her head, desperate to kiss him but he moved away, just a fraction. And gave her a long, slow smile. Was he trying to drive her completely mad?

Unable to wait any longer she stood on tiptoes to meet his hungry gaze. 'Kiss me.'

'*God*. Victoria.' His mouth slid over hers and, as her balance was very definitely off-kilter when he was around, she fell deep into his kiss, still mesmerized at how one touch from Oliver could make her feel so much better. So alive, so desperate for more.

He pressed her hard against the door, his tongue sliding into her mouth, sending jolts of excitement through her. His fingers slid under her sweater and she writhed at the coolness, arching her back so he could fit his palm over her breast.

He trailed a kiss along her throat and whispered, 'I know a much better way to relax than tai chi. You want me to show you?'

Her body buzzed and burned. Yes. Yes, she did. She wanted him in her bed. The longer she spent with him, the more she wanted to be with him. Everything, every minute they'd spent together, all the getting to know each other, all the kisses, all the tender talks in the dark of night had led to this moment. She couldn't fight it. Didn't want to.

'Yes. Yes, please,' she managed through another hot and hungry kiss. She dragged her mouth from his and jammed her key into the lock, his lips on the back of her neck making her curl into him. She pressed her body back against his and felt the hard length of him. He wanted her.

She wanted him. There was no doubt. In fact, it was the only thing she was clear about. She couldn't think of anything she needed or wanted to do more than to take him to her bed.

She shoved the door open, her nerves a jumble, her hand trembling as she pulled him over the threshold. He turned her and pressed her up against the door. She grasped his shirt in her hand, started to undo a button. Two.

'Oliver.' It came out like a prayer. Maybe it was.

'You are so beautiful, my Victoria.' He stroked her cheek, then her throat and traced a fingertip down to the V of her breasts. Then his mouth went to where his finger had been and she gasped, wanting more and more and more.

Her fingers threaded through his hair and all rational thought fled her brain as his hand pushed up under her sweater and unclipped her bra.

Then reality crystallized and she pushed his hand away. 'Ollie—'

'What's the matter?' He was breathing hard and fast. 'Are you OK? Is this OK?'

'I… I have scars. I'm not as beautiful as you think I am.' But,

God, she wanted to believe she could be. She put her hand to her stomach wishing this could be different. Wishing she could be perfect for him. 'Not here.'

'I am so sorry you were hurt, V. And I wish, I really wish, I could have been there for you. I wish it hadn't happened at all.' He put his hand over her belly, over the gnarled skin. 'But there is nothing you could do or say that would make me believe you are anything but beautiful, inside and out.'

'But—'

He smothered her words with his kiss, one hand stroking her scars, the other cupping her face. He kissed and kissed and kissed her until she didn't know anything except that he really did believe she was beautiful.

'You are most amazing woman I have ever met,' he whispered. 'I've wanted to make love to you since the moment I set eyes on you.' His hand went to her heart. 'This is something, right? What we have? This is something.'

'It is.' She fought back tears. It was something precious and special. And time limited.

She knew she should have said a million things then, and one of them should have been about the consequences of those scars. But it would never be the right time to tell him and feel the hurt of rejection all over again.

God knew, she wished they had more hours, more days, more weeks together but he wanted her and she wanted him and this could be their only chance to grab something extraordinary.

So, when he asked, 'Do you want to go upstairs?'

The only possible reply was, 'How quickly can we get up there?'

* * *

Beautiful.

Her smile was one of satiated satisfaction, even while she slept. Her long, dark hair was fanned over her white pillow. Her soft body gilded in sunlight. She looked like a goddess. A queen.

His eyes lingered over the silvered scars on her belly that told the story of her nightmare and his heart contracted, shifting and making space for this amazing woman. She was a warrior. He smiled. His Victoria.

He'd never wanted to stay with a woman for long after sex but right now he couldn't think of a better way to spend his day than here in her bed, under her floral duvet.

What did all this mean?

He hadn't a damned clue. But it was something profound.

Too bad he'd received about a hundred messages from his PA and Andrew that needed answers like, two hours ago, and had to concentrate on that instead of this. Not her. Not *us*.

Wow. That thought blew his chest wide open.

He pressed a kiss to her head and tiptoed out of her bedroom, not wanting to wake her despite it being late morning. He needed time to reconcile what was going on in his life with this feeling in his heart. Needed time and space to do some clear thinking, because whenever he was with her his thoughts were only for her, when they should have been on his family, on his business, on everything except a fake fiancée who he'd grown very fond of.

Did he love her?

He tugged on his trousers, fastened his shirt, rattled at why he needed to get so damned deep all of a sudden. Those kind of questions hadn't ever bothered him before.

He jogged down the stairs and pulled open the front door. Once outside he saw that two stout and beautifully dressed Christmas trees were standing sentry at the main entrance of the new store. Delivery vans were parked up on the yellow lines and stacks of cardboard boxes lined the pavement. The rest of the stock was arriving. The deal was nearly done.

They only had a few days left.

And unless he could convince her to extend their deal, the clock was ticking.

CHAPTER SIXTEEN

THE NEXT WEEK WAS a blur of sleepless nights and hard work. Victoria felt as if she was fuelled by caffeine and nerves; half worrying about the fashion show, half worrying about Eric's recovery.

And always thinking about Oliver. What they'd shared that morning had been so precious and tender that it had fuelled her over the next few days. He'd kissed her scars and told her repeatedly that she was beautiful. She didn't know what it meant it for them but every time her thoughts strayed to him her heart hurt a little bit more.

Her fingers were sore from pinpricks from the last-minute alterations to the garments for the show and her head was pounding. Every part of her ached from bending down, reaching round, stretching across the mannequins, carrying the clothes over to the store, helping the girls.

They'd both known the next few days would be hectic. She'd thought – hoped – they may have bumped into each other at the store, but his PA had taken over the arrangements for the catwalk as he was too busy with everything else.

But every morning she texted him: How's Eric?

Every morning she received the same reply:

He said not to fuss. Mum sends her love. So do I. O xx

And every morning her heart shaped itself more and more to the family who were struggling to cope and trying not to show it.

One day to go and she finally got the news she wanted:

Dad's put on three kilograms. He's yelled at two nurses and bawled the cardiologist out. Safe to say he's much better and is allowed to come to the opening tomorrow. I would say he's being let out for good behaviour, but sadly, no. I think they'll be glad to wave him off.

She sent back:

I'm so pleased for him. And for you too. I can't wait. I'm so excited.

Did you get the email with the itinerary?

I did. It's perfect. Thank you. So much.

He'd given her such a gift. A chance to prove herself, a chance to chase her dreams. No, to grasp them.

My pleasure. Honestly. Are you ready?

Born ready!

V, I miss you.

Her heart had clenched tight at that. She imagined him cupping her face. Kissing her. Making love to her. With her. *I miss you too.*

She did. She missed him already and it wasn't over yet. She didn't want to think past the fashion show, for purely selfish reasons.

And now they were here. On the first floor of the Russell & Co Chelsea store. A long, raised runway extended before her, one end covered with dark-blue velvet curtains where the models would appear from. Rows of white seats had been placed either side of the catwalk. Portable floodlights were pointed towards the curtains.

Jasmine was fastening thick navy-blue bows to the chair backs and Nisha was putting pamphlets on each of the seats with shaking hands.

'It's just like a real catwalk, like at fashion week.' Nisha's voice was breathy and reverently low. 'I can't believe it.'

'Pinch yourself.' Victoria laughed. 'Then you'll believe it.' And just to show them – and in all honesty to show herself that she really wasn't dreaming – she pinched the skin on the back of her hand. 'How's it going backstage?'

Although, she didn't really have to ask, she knew full well: chaos. Loud. Giggling. The girls had asked their school friends to walk for them and their mothers were here too. There was a lot of oestrogen in there. A lot of laughter and nerves. Victoria had read them all the riot act about not getting make-up on the clothes and explained three times about the running order. No one seemed to be listening, everyone was high on adrenalin.

Just as it should be, then. A perfect day.

Apart from not having one tiny glimpse of Oliver Russell.

'All sorted.' Jasmine stood back to look at the chairs and nodded her approval. 'Just waiting for the male models to arrive. When did Oliver say they'd be here?'

Victoria eye-rolled at the over-familiarity. '*Mr Russell's* PA said they'd arrive at two to start at three.'

'It's two thirty.' Worry tainted Jas's young features. 'They're going to miss it.'

'There's still plenty of time.' Although Victoria conceded, the girl did have a point. They were going to be under a lot of pressure if they didn't turn up soon.

'Not if they need make-up and stuff.' Jasmine's face fell.

'It'll be fine.' Modelling a calm she didn't feel, Victoria patted the girl's arm. 'Don't worry.'

She walked over to the glass railing and looked down at the ground floor, trying to get a glimpse of that tall, dark and dangerous-to-her-heart man she'd grown so fond of. But he wasn't there, or at least she couldn't see him. But oh, what a successful day Russell & Co were having. Eric must be so proud.

The fairy lights on the ceiling had been lit, bathing the whole place in a soft, magical glow. The food stalls were packed out and delicious smells wafted towards her: garlic and ginger, apple and cinnamon, Christmas punch. A brass band played Christmas carols and people were standing around singing, some with snowflakes on their hair and coats.

'Oh, is it snowing? I hadn't realized.' She'd been stuck in here all day making final preparations.

Jasmine nodded. 'Yeah. Mum said it's thick and sticking. Snowball fights in the street later, right?'

'You're on.' Oliver's voice from behind made Victoria's heart dance. 'I hope you're a good shot.'

She turned to greet him, still off-balance whenever she saw him. He looked magnificent today in his dark grey suit and Russell & Co blue-and-white tie. His hair had been sleekly combed back which made him look taller and emphasized his eyes.

She'd been half hoping he'd come and find her, although she knew he'd be busy all day. And every part of her ached for his kiss, but she went for a smile instead. 'Hey, Mr Russell. How's everything?'

'Good. Better turn-out than I anticipated.' He grinned. 'Sorry I haven't been around, the media circus is bigger than we expected and I've been stuck doing interviews.'

'That's brilliant. The village is a hit.'

'It certainly is. There is one thing, though.' His genial expression changed, and he walked her away, out of earshot of her students.

Anxiety gripped her gut. 'What? Is it your dad?'

'No, he's in my office talking at the accountant. Got to feel sorry for the number-cruncher, right?' He ran his hands down his face. 'I'm really sorry, V. But they're stuck in traffic.'

'Who are?' Her heart thumped and pumped as if it was on steroids.

'The guys I hired for the runway. The male models.' His eyebrows rose in apology. 'This snowstorm has caused traffic chaos across town apparently and everything's backed up. They're not going to be here in time for the start.'

'What? No! I'm going first.' Jasmine had followed them and was eavesdropping, her hands to her mouth. 'They won't be here in time for my show?'

Victoria kept her voice level. *Find some calm.* 'Jasmine, this is a private conversation.'

But tears filled the girl's brown eyes as she dropped her hands in resignation. 'I guess that's that then. It was only a dream anyway. Stupid dream, too.'

'It is not a stupid dream, Jasmine. It's a fabulous one and we're going to fix this.' Victoria turned to Oliver, trying to keep the panic out of her tone. 'Can we get someone else to do it?'

He inhaled. 'Like who?'

'Nisha's brothers?' They all looked hopefully over the balcony and saw the long queue of people waiting at Aziz's stall.

Oliver shook his head. 'Unlikely.'

'Miss?' Nisha had now joined them and clearly sensed something wasn't right. 'What's happened?'

Victoria dug deep for what she hoped was a reassuring smile, even though she wasn't feeling reassured at all. 'The male models are caught up in traffic but don't worry, we'll work it out.'

'How, miss? How will we? Each of us needs at least one guy to walk. Mr Russell? What can we do?'

All heads turned to Ollie and Victoria immediately felt sorry for him. It wasn't his fault the weather gods hadn't come to the party. But he nodded and started to walk towards the escalator. 'I'll ask some of the staff from men's wear to come and help out. There must be someone who can do this.'

'Brilliant idea!' Victoria gave the girls a *see, I knew he'd fix this* look. Because she had every faith that he would. He'd go above and beyond for them. She knew that now. He would move heaven and earth for those he cared for.

Nisha called out to his retreating back. 'Make sure they're tall like you, sir. I haven't time to take anything up.'

He disappeared and Victoria sent the girls into the changing area to explain the problem to everyone else. Meanwhile, she paced. When she saw him coming down the escalator with a young man his height and almost his build, she almost kissed him.

Again.

That kissing thing was becoming a problem. The whole liking him thing was too. Because she did. Too much. But she didn't have time to focus too hard on it right now.

Ollie grinned as he stepped off the escalator and slapped the lad on his back. 'Tom's going to help. He's actually modelled before. So that's a win.'

'This is all a win. Really.' Victoria breathed out. This wasn't going to be a disaster. 'Fantastic. Thanks, Tom.'

'But…' Ollie shrugged. 'Everyone else is busy or flat out said no.'

'Well, thanks anyway. One is better than none. We'll have to rearrange…' She looked at the invited guests taking their seats next to the runway and changed her mind. 'No, we haven't time to rearrange anything. We'll just have to drop some of the clothes from the show. Shame, because Jasmine's are really something. I'll go break the news. Come on, Tom. Let's get you kitted out.'

She started to walk away. It would be OK. Showing some of their designs would be better than none. 'We just need to choose the best ones to show, that's all.'

'I'll do it.' The voice was resigned but determined.

She turned around to Ollie. 'You'll do what?'

'I'll walk for you.'

'No! No. You don't have to.'

He fell into step with her as they walked towards the changing area. 'This is my fault. I should have organized them to come earlier. I thought there'd be enough time.'

There was never going to be enough time, she knew that now. 'You didn't know it was going to snow.'

'Actually, I did.' He looked guilty. 'I read the weather forecast about a huge dumping of snow today. But I was only thinking about the impact it might have on customer numbers. I dropped the ball on the fashion show.'

'Then that's your karma. Come on, let's get you changed. This, I have got to see.'

★ ★ ★

Jasmine's squeals were almost deafening as she watched from the back of the stage as the first of the models stepped out from the curtain. 'Someone just took a photograph of my dress!'

'I know. I can see.' While Oliver got changed Victoria had slid next to Jasmine and peeked out at the packed seats. There was standing-room only now. On the front row someone she thought she recognized from the media had his eyes glued to the model walking down the runway, then jotted down notes on a tablet. A warm, bright feeling shone in the centre of Victoria's chest. 'That's fabulous. This is going to be so great for you, Jas.'

'Is that… is that the editor of *Vogue*?'

Oh. My. God. Victoria's breath stalled in her lungs. It was. No wonder he'd looked familiar. 'Um. Yes, it is. Front row.'

'How do I look?' Ollie tapped her on the shoulder. 'Be gentle. Lie if you need to.'

'Great!'

Although when he gazed down at the skull hoodie and safety-pinned trousers he didn't look as if he felt great at all. He grimaced and plucked at the hoodie. 'I am so far out of my comfort zone right now.'

'You look well peng.' She laughed at his expression. 'Do you know the editor of *Vogue*?'

'Not personally, but we sent out invitations to the editors of all the fashion magazines. A few RSVP'd. Some might want to interview the girls later, so make sure they stay a while after the show.'

She hadn't realized the extent of his help. 'I can't thank you enough for this. You've made their day. Life, actually. You've been approachable and encouraging and not enough people are like that.'

'Just look at them.' He grinned at Jasmine's excited face and Nisha's quiet little fist pump. 'I'm happy to do it. Even if I have to do this.'

And she knew he was. That helping her and her students had made him happy.

'Oh, God.' His smile wavered. 'Jasmine's calling me. It's my cue. Why did I offer to do this?'

'Because you're amazing.' She instinctively leaned forward to kiss him – because that was what she wanted to do. All. The. Time. But realized the girls were watching, so she patted his back instead. 'Off you go.'

'Just don't expect me to wiggle my way down the runway.'

'Break a leg.'

Break my heart.

She didn't have to watch to know he was a roaring success. The minute he stepped out onto the runway whistles and cheers erupted from the audience.

Time slowed. The bright lights blurred her vision, as if she was looking through a soft-focus lens. The noise seemed to retreat, and her eyes zeroed in on him as he did actually wiggle, making the audience cheer, and her heart flooded with warmth. She loved that he was willing to look ridiculous to help the girls. Loved that he'd done all this for her and for them. Loved the way he was smiling, the little bum wiggle he'd insisted he wasn't going to do.

Loved the way he'd kissed her on the top of her head in the same way he'd kissed the other people he cared for. Loved…

Oh, God. It hit her as she watched him take a dramatic bow that was so not what a model should do, but he got away with it because he was Oliver Freaking Russell. The guy with a big heart and the best kisses.

The hot sting of tears pricked her eyes.

She loved him.

Even though it was stupid, fairy-tale flipping madness to do so. Because, she couldn't have that damned fairy tale.

She pushed the tears away as she saw him walking back up the runway and found a smile. She couldn't let him see how she felt. The deal was ending in… oh, a few minutes.

He threw his arms around her and laughed. 'That was fun.'

'You were brilliant,' she managed through a thick throat. She just wanted more time.

'I know.' His laughter faded as he became serious, running his thumb over her lip. 'V—'

'Sir! Come on, you've got to get ready for the next one. And, miss! You need to tell us which dresses you want to show first,' Nisha interrupted, and Victoria sprang away from him. 'Right. Yes. Coming.'

'No rest for the wicked,' he growled in her ear as he pressed against her. The word *wicked* was delicious and dangerous and filled with a promise she couldn't keep. It was tempting to play with him right now. To allow herself to fall further under his spell. But.

She just couldn't.

'And here are the cavalry.' Giving her one last sexy misted look he raised his palms at two young men who were running into the changing area with calls of *sorry we're late!* and, *traffic was horrible!* Oliver wiped his forearm over his face. 'Saved from more righteous humiliation.'

Trying to keep her fraying nerves and shaking hands under

control, Victoria went to get her models ready for her collection, Her mind whirring with the revelation.

She loved him.

It was a full body blow. An actual physical ache.

She tried to concentrate on the now. On her clothes. On this wonderful opportunity. And not on him and a future that was looking pretty bleak right now.

The show was a hit. So much applause, so many people taking notes. She watched, biting her nails, from the edge of the stage. The bridesmaids' dresses received *oohs* and *aahs* and gradually her nerves started to dissipate. They liked her clothes. It wasn't polite clapping, it was encouraging and excited.

And then the model wearing her wedding dress stepped on to the runway and the noise stopped.

'What?' She looked from the model to Oliver who was standing close. Too close. 'What's the matter?'

'They love it. Can't you see? They love it.' He was staring at the dress. Just looking at it, his eyes soft, and then back at her. 'It's beautiful, V.'

It was. She peeked out again and saw people frantically scribbling, some dictating behind their hands into their phones. And too soon the last song started to play. It was the beginning and end of her dream. She blew out a long-held breath. 'I can't believe how well it's gone.'

'It's been amazing, miss,' Billie said, her large eyes glistening as she and the other two girls joined them for one last peek from behind the curtain. 'Thank you, so much.'

'Oh.' Victoria's heart swelled and a lump rose in her throat. She was going to say, *my pleasure*, because it absolutely was, but it was so much more than that. She was part of something that felt…

amazing, and well, a lot like a family. 'It wasn't really me, it was all Mr Russell's doing.'

'Thank you, Ollie,' Jasmine said with a very mischievous grin.

'Hey, I should be thanking you. Look at all those VIPs your show brought in. Now they're going to spend up large in my shop,' Ollie said, and Victoria could see that he was feeling the same punch of pride as she was and making a joke because he didn't know quite how to handle the praise, or the girls.

And that made her love him even more.

He called them all close. 'Right, you know what happens now?'

'No?' Nisha frowned.

'You go on that stage and you soak up all that applause. Go on, Jasmine, Nisha, Billie. I am so proud of you.' And he ushered them out to the sound of stamping feet and cheers.

'Thank you.' She could barely say the words to him. He'd done all this and she would for ever be grateful. The joy those girls were experiencing was multiplied a zillion times in her heart.

'You did this, Victoria. You. You've made their dreams come true. I just paid for the props, but you took their dreams and made them into real designers. I'm in awe. I just wish I could have done more.' His arm spiralled her waist as he pulled her against his hard body. 'It's your turn now.'

She wanted so much to curl into his arms and sink into the happy feeling buzzing in her chest. But she couldn't. Her heart cracked. She loved this man. So much for protecting herself. For playing the game. Because, hell, she was going to lose. 'Sorry? What?'

'Come on. For your bow.' He stepped onto the plinth and tugged her hand. 'Come on. They want to see you.'

She stepped back, her arm stretching as she kept a tight grip on his hand. 'No, I can't.'

'Yes, you can. You have to thank them for coming.' He gave her no choice but to follow him and they walked out to a sea of smiling faces.

Wow. Just wow. She breathed in. And again. So much noise. The lights hurt her eyes and it was easier to see the people at the back… Lily, waving and cheering as if Victoria had just won Designer of the Year. Oh, Lils! So lovely to see her smiling face.

The crowd was standing now and clapping as Victoria sashayed down the runway. They liked her designs. They were laughing and cheering for her, and it was infectious.

With her hand raised in a wave she turned to her right and scanned the audience and… gulped. Because with there in her line of vision were Andrew, Peter and Emilia deep in conversation. Ugh.

Peter looked furious, Andrew looked as if he'd just eaten something bitter and Emilia looked as if she'd backed the wrong horse.

This will show them I can move on. She gave Emilia a wink and walked to the end of the runway. Right in front of her, Ollie's mum and dad sat beaming and clapping. Stella looked transfixed, Eric looked weak but he was smiling. He seemed better, but not out of the woods yet. She nodded to them, a tiny part of her wishing this wasn't make-believe, wishing she wasn't lying to them.

'Hey.' Oliver stopped walking and squeezed her hand. 'You're amazing, Victoria Scott.'

'So are you. This has been an amazing day. Thank you. I don't know how I will ever repay you.'

He turned to her then and caught her chin in his fingers. The cheers and the clapping melted away and she looked at him. His eyes were glittering. Back in his suit he looked so handsome. So kind. So…

'Kiss me.' It was a command. Raw. A prayer she couldn't resist. Didn't want to.

His mouth was there, so close to hers. A last chance. One last grasp at something so good she didn't want to give it up. When he bent and moulded his lips to hers she gave herself to him.

This was no pretend kiss. This was real. This was her heart and her soul. Her gratitude and her desire. This was her love for him.

This was everything.

His hands framed her face, she wrapped her arms round his neck. Pulled him close. Felt the length of him crush against her.

I love you.

I love you.

Her heart felt as if it was turning in on itself.

Because this was goodbye.

Bright flashes of light in her face made her jump. She pulled back. The cheering was louder. The clapping deafening. People were stamping their feet.

Oh, no. God, what were they doing? She blinked. Twice. Tried to focus. She caught Lily's face, wrought with confusion. In the front row Stella looked completely smitten, as if the answer to all her problems was right there in that kiss. Even Eric was clapping.

'Congratulations,' Ollie said. 'I am so proud of you. They love you. Here's to your collection going viral.'

Viral. The photographers. She looked again at the crowd and gasped. Stella, Eric, Lily, even Andrew were all caught up in this. And if anything was mentioned anywhere in the media her parents and friends would be too.

But that was what they'd wanted, right? The Russells? Good PR.

This very public show of affection would rocket Oliver's company ratings. In truth, when it came down to it, she was just part of a damned good marketing campaign.

Her chest filled with pain. She'd wanted more time with him. Wanted to believe this amazing dream could be possible, but she absolutely couldn't do it anymore, couldn't lie to these people, couldn't pretend to anyone else that she was in a relationship with Oliver. Couldn't pretend to Oliver that she didn't want more than this.

Couldn't pretend to herself that she hadn't fallen deeply in love with a man who didn't know her deepest, most important secret. And couldn't bear to have them all looking at her like she was the answer, when she wasn't.

'That went down well.' As more flashes went off, Oliver leaned his forehead against hers, his breathing ragged, a smile on his lips. 'Once more for luck?'

She tried to swallow the lump in her throat away. 'For your PR?'

'For us.' His features softened as he looked at her with such warmth in his eyes. He actually thought it was real too. Wanted it to be. That was what made it worse.

'I... I have to go. Sorry. I can't do this anymore.' She let go of his hand and took a last bow then made her way back to the changing area, Lily's concerned expression at the forefront of her mind. She wasn't just hurting herself.

But Oliver was on her heels and he pulled her to face him. God, he was so beautiful it took her breath away. She couldn't quite believe she was doing this, any other fool would just hang on, but she had to.

'Vict—'

'Please. I can't...' She took a step back, and another. 'I can't breathe...'

Then she turned and ran through the changing area, found an exit door and thundered down the stairs, wanting to be far away from everyone. To collect her thoughts from the people who'd all bought in to her little deal with the devil.

She shoved open a heavy metal door and staggered outside into the cold night, finding herself outside the security entrance Oliver had taken her through that first day. Her heart tugged at the memory of that fateful meeting.

The thick layer of snow gave the street an eerie feel; making everything seem too bright and dampening the sound of footfall and cars. Too quiet when the noise in her head was deafening. She leaned against the wall and inhaled.

What was she going to do? People were going to see those photographs. Her friends and family. People were going to believe it was real. They would see how much she cared for him because her body language wouldn't lie. She'd pressed against him, wanted to feel him, wanted to hold him. For always.

It was real, to her. She'd fallen in love with him without a care for her own heart. She'd let herself fall, damn it, she'd enjoyed falling. She just had to... had to say the words...

'Victoria.' A voice behind her in the shadows.

'Ollie, please. I need a minute.' She fought the tears. Elation from her show and sadness at what she was about to do made her chest constrict tight.

'Vicki!' Louder now.

It wasn't Ollie. He'd never speak to her in that aggressive tone. She whirled round to find herself face to face with Andrew. Typical that he was the Russell who had followed her out and the last thing she needed was to see him gloating.

His eyes were intense. 'Running away?'

'No. I just needed to...' *Breathe.* She didn't need to explain. She clasped her hands together, felt the accusing point of the engagement ring diamond stab her thumb. 'What do you want, Andrew?'

'I want you to leave the Russells alone. Stop this game you're playing and step out of our lives.'

Even though he was demanding exactly what she was planning his words jabbed her like a knife point. 'And what if I don't? What if I love Oliver?'

'I'll tell them the truth.' He had Russell eyes but not the warmth and depth of his uncle's or cousin's.

Her heart kicked against her ribs. 'The truth about what?'

'You're stringing them along with your promises of a future, when we both know they'll never have grandchildren from you.' He leaned closer and she could smell alcohol on his breath. 'The Russell line will stop with Oliver and you know he wants more than that. He wants kids, Vicki. His parents are set on grandchildren to dote on. You need to be honest about that so they can, how shall I put it? Re-evaluate their choices. Maybe reconsider that ring.'

He looked lasciviously at her hand and she knew then that it must be worth a lot more than she'd thought.

So, he wanted to break this up so he could give the damned ring to his future wife? And provide beautiful Russell offspring which would slide him into the favourite stakes? But how did he know this private information about her? Who? Why?

Then it hit her like a physical blow in her scarred belly. 'Peter told you?'

'Just filled me in, you know. A friendly chat.'

She closed her eyes against the hot swell of tears. Blinked them back, because she sure as hell wasn't going to give him the satisfaction of knowing he'd ruffled her. 'I'm going to finish it anyway. Tonight. Then they'll never know. Please don't hurt them.'

His piggy eyes narrowed. 'You have until tomorrow.'

CHAPTER SEVENTEEN

SHE HADN'T COME BACK. She'd been gone for hours while he held the fort at the store doing interviews, herding the students, overseeing the rest of the festivities. Dealing with his parents' questions.

Meanwhile, she'd just disappeared.

And now he was caught up in more media nonsense. Someone from *#Garb* magazine had their mobile phone almost stuck up his nose as she threw questions at him about Victoria. And all he could think of was the way she'd looked so happy when the models were walking in her clothes. How she'd felt in his arms. The smile on the helicopter flight. The thick lightness in his chest when he thought about her at all – about all the good she'd done and the way she made him want to do good, do better too. And the way she'd looked so devastated after their kiss. Eventually, he held up his hands.

'Thank you, yes, I'll get her to contact you. Or you could message her though her website, victoriascottdesigns. I have to go.' Frustrated and – OK, yes, he admitted it – spooked by her running off, he pushed his way through the throng and back into the changing area.

There was no one there. It was late. Everyone had left and taken their things with them. Everyone, except Victoria.

Her dresses hung, slightly dishevelled, on a rack. The hangers had been stuffed in, leaving the clothes dangling at odd angles, people shoving them on in a hurry. He straightened them, mainly as something to do while he worked out his next step.

She'd run away from him.

He pulled out the wedding dress that had caused such a furore of response and his heart damned near cracked. As the model had walked down the catwalk he'd imagined Victoria wearing it. Walking towards him. In a church or something.

Damn. He tugged at his tie, loosening it, hoping to breathe better. But he didn't… couldn't, because the choked-up feeling was inside him. He was in too deep and she was sending him a huge message by leaving him on the runway like that.

But that kiss. It had been as if they'd been somewhere private. He had to find her but what the hell he was going to say to her he didn't know.

Outside, a cruel wind whipped the snow around his feet as he crunched towards her flat. Being near closing time now, the wine bar customers were starting to leave and every time they opened the door a chime of cheesy Christmas music filled the air. He could hear familiar squeals coming from up the road where Jasmine and the girls were having a snowball fight with Nisha's brothers. He peered over, hoping to see his Victoria amongst them. But no.

He guessed she wouldn't be in the bar but popped his head in anyway. The only people left were a drunk Father Christmas – *sans* long white beard – and an elf, fast asleep in the corner.

One of the bar staff – Sara with the cropped hair – raised her eyebrows when she saw him and then pointed her forefinger upwards. *She's upstairs.*

He pressed the buzzer to her flat and waited.

And waited. And pressed the buzzer again.

Then he scooped up snow, made a snowball and threw it up at her window. 'Victoria!'

And he waited. Concern prickled down his spine. This wasn't like her. She didn't do this. Although, she'd told him how she'd hidden way after the accident, so maybe retreating into herself when she was upset was her go-to.

That realization made everything suddenly seem worse. He threw another snowball and watched it crash against her studio window and disintegrate into a flurry of sleet raining down on his handmade Italian shoes, soaking them.

Just perfect.

Then suddenly there she was, standing in her doorway, haloed by the light behind her. Her eyes were red, and her face wet from tears. She was wearing pink pyjamas with reindeer on them. Despite the success of her show she didn't smile.

Heart lurching, he took a step forward and reached out to touch her cheek. 'What the hell, V? Are you OK?'

She batted his hand away. 'Look, Ollie—'

'You literally ran out on me. Left me hanging on that stage. What's the matter?'

She looked at her feet, at a spot over his shoulder. Anywhere but him. Her bottom lip wobbled. She pressed her lips together. Then said, 'Oh, Ollie. It's the first of December. We had a deal, right?'

'Ah.' He smiled and relief flooded through him. She actually thought it was over? His stomach started to unclench. That was all? She thought they had to call it a day, just because they'd said it would be so? An easy fix. 'So, we can make a new one.'

'No.' She looked as if her heart was about to break into a thousand pieces. 'I can't lie to them anymore. And all the press there, the photographs… there'll be a buzz about us in the media and people will be asking about me and about my parents, my friends.' Her hand went to her head. 'I didn't think this through at all.'

'Maybe, no one will report it.' Although chances of that happening were virtually nil. He'd made his PR team send out hundreds of press releases about the opening.

She showed him her phone. Photos of their clinch were already uploaded on Buzzfeed, the *Daily Mail*, gossip blogs, with cheesy soundbites that made him shudder:

Great Scott!

Heir to the Russell fortune is be-scott-ed with upcoming fashion designer.

Who is the woman who stole Russell heir's heart?

And more…

Eric Russell's mystery illness.

Russell & Co top boss struck down.

Eric Russell weak and frail…

God. Oliver pressed his fist to his forehead. This was a nightmare. He hadn't even thought about the way the press would intrude on his father too. His dad would be furious he'd been portrayed as weak.

Victoria's eyes glittered with hurt and anger. 'I mean, really? It's already happening. I don't want people digging around in my past. Lily's already upset about it. Although, I think that's more about me than this.' She brandished the phone at him again like a weapon she wanted to hurt him with.

He looked past her, up the stairs to her apartment. 'Lily's here?'

'No.' Victoria shook her head. 'She had to go back to Hawke's Cove straight after my show.'

Good. They'd have a chance to calm down in private then. He needed to explain about separating their private lives from their public ones. Her wobble was nothing to do with the way they felt about each other and everything about handling the stress of being in the spotlight. 'Can I come in?'

'I don't think that's a good idea.'

'V. Come on.' He put his palm on the doorframe to stop her closing the door in his face. 'It's a blip. People will have forgotten about it by tomorrow. We can get through this.'

'You can. You live your life out there all the time. I don't and I don't want to. I don't want people to know what I'm doing or what's happened to me in the past.'

'I'll fix it. I'll send out press releases tomorrow. I'll tell them—'

'What exactly? That I'm your fiancée? Because you know as well as I do that the backstory to that kiss isn't real. Our relationship isn't real, but now everyone – the whole damned world – thinks it is.' She wrapped her arms across her body. 'This is not something that even the great Oliver Russell can fix.'

'It is real. It can be real, V.' He touched a strand of her hair, let it run through his fingers, relishing the silk and the fresh scent. Not wanting to let her go. 'Let me try.'

'It's over, Ollie. All this pretence. Us. It's over.' She took a step back. Two. Until she'd retreated to the stairs leading up to her flat and sat. Her hand went out in front of her signalling him to keep his distance but every part of her body was keening towards him. If she was that desperate to get rid of him, she'd have shoved him and slammed the door already. Once again, she was saying one thing and her body was indicating something else. Even the sob in her throat gave her away.

'It's not pretence and you know it.' He went to her, knelt in front of her. 'The kisses, everything… Sure, it started out as some stupid game, I know. But those kisses were real, Victoria. The way we connect is real. Tell me. Tell me it's not real and I'll leave.'

He held his breath as she looked at him.

'It's real.' She shook her head, tears brimming in her eyes. 'But there are too many reasons why not, Ollie. We live in different worlds and have very different futures. Very different.' She sounded a little more determined now, as if she was talking herself into this. 'I'm sorry. Here's your ring.'

'No.' He wanted to rage at her. To tell her to stick her stupid decisions and to stay with him but that was the kind of thing his emotionally under-developed cousin would say. He struggled to stay calm because he got the feeling that she was on an edge here. But hell. He had emotion aplenty. 'Keep it.'

She squeezed Nana Norma's ring from her finger and held it out to him. A single tear edged over her lid and slid down her cheek. Her hand shook. 'Take it. *Please.*'

She actually meant it. She was really doing this. A heavy weight settled in his chest and spread through his body making everything hurt. The ring was the icing to this whole damned conversation. If she kept it they were still connected, right?

'First rule of gift-taking, V. You can't give it back. No returns, remember?'

'Maybe at the store.' She gave him a sorry smile at the reminder of when he'd given her the bolt of fabric. 'But this was your grandmother's. It's a Russell heirloom.'

'And now it's yours.' He looked down at the diamond in her palm. Light caught the precious stone making it sparkle but all he could see was a stretching darkness without her in his life.

'But your father...?' She shook her head.

'Is a logical and honourable man. He'll understand that a gift is a gift.'

'I'm glad he will, because I don't. They'll think I was only after your money or something. They'll think badly of me.'

'Never, Victoria. No one could ever think badly of you.'

'Oh, some people do.'

'Tell me their names and I'll go steal their pocket money.'

'And you would too.' She laughed softly, but her eyes were sad, her body language was resolute. She'd made up her mind.

So had he. He wanted her. He loved her. But he knew if he told her that she'd run up those stairs and lock him out of her life. She'd made a decision based on what she thought was the right thing to do. Well, so could he. 'I'm not leaving.'

'And I will not back down.' Her chin lifted. 'This has to finish. We agreed.'

'And we can un-agree. We're grown-ups, can't we talk about it?' OK, his emotions were rattling out of control. He felt a gaping chasm open up in his chest. 'What are you scared of, Victoria?'

She glared at him realizing he was throwing back at her the words she'd said to him that night at the hospital. 'Nothing.'

'So why are you giving this up? I know you feel for me the

way I do about you. Hell… I don't know what's going to happen, I don't have a crystal ball, but I want to try. I want us to try.'

'No, Ollie.' She looked at her toes.

'You're scared.'

Her head flew up and she locked eyes with him, vulnerability seeping from every pore. 'Yes. Yes, OK? I'm scared.'

'I won't hurt you. I promise.' He meant it too, more than anything he'd ever promised. He held her close to his heart. His everything. His Victoria.

'It's me. I'll do the hurting.' She shook her head, more tears threatening.

He couldn't believe she was willing to throw this away. 'So, you're scared and choosing to jump? What about living your best life?'

'This is the best I can have, OK?' Her expression changed from vulnerable to angry. Lashing out. She was like a trapped animal, attacking. 'And I happen to like my life.'

'We could have more. Bigger. Everything.'

'I don't need two helicopters.' She sighed, closing her eyes as if she was in pain. 'I just can't explain.'

There was a lot more to this and she wasn't making any efforts to tell him the truth. 'Can't? Or won't?'

She shook her head. 'It's not going to make a difference. This has to end. I never intended for it to get this deep. I wasn't thinking. I just got carried away. I…' She put her head in her hands.

'Do I not get a say in any of this?'

'Not if you're going to try to talk me out of my decision.' She lifted her head and held his gaze. One second. Two.

She was the most beautiful woman he'd ever met. Kind and funny and determined and driven. Everything he could ever want. He stroked her cheek. 'I want you, V.'

'Don't make this harder than it is, Ollie. We had a deal. I've honoured my part, now please honour yours.' She stood, slid past him and walked to the door.

He counted the steps, offering a deal to the devil with each footfall if she'd change her mind.

When she actually pulled the door open, he knew any hope was lost. But he did deals all the time. It was about compromise and priority. She was his number one. 'What can I do? How can I change your mind?'

'You won't.'

'Not even with this?' He tilted her face to his. Saw the confusion and the struggle, felt the tiniest bit of softening in her body. He wouldn't have kissed her if he thought she didn't want it, but she leaned in, straining towards him. He pressed his lips to hers.

She gasped, grabbing his coat lapels to pull him closer and moaning into his mouth. 'Oliver. Ollie.'

'I want you. You want me. I know you want me.' She just didn't want... what? He didn't understand. She couldn't explain. But whatever it was must have been so private or so dark she didn't want him to know. She was hurting and she couldn't tell him.

He hugged her against him, telling her with this kiss how much she meant to him. How he loved her. How they could make this work.

But he felt the wet of her tears on his face and he knew. She wasn't welcoming him back with this kiss, she was letting him go.

They stood there in her dimly lit corridor, holding on, gripping each other. Twenty seconds. More. He wanted to hold her for ever. If he'd known he'd fall for her like this, and so hard, he'd have never made that deal at all. Or made it for a hundred years.

When she pulled away her shoulders started to shake. She closed her eyes and controlled them. Then she put her palm to his chest. 'Goodbye, Oliver. Thank you for giving me the chance to be something different. Something special.'

'Oh, God, Victoria. You are.'

'So are you.' She nodded, completely in control now, which was a damned sight more than he could say about himself. Then she stepped aside and indicated for him to leave.

He stood out there for longer than he dared to think. Every part of him raging. Why would she do this? When they had a chance at something good?

Hell. What had he missed? Why didn't the jigsaw pieces fit? How did one particular woman have such an effect on his heart and his soul? Her taste was on his lips, her perfume on his hands. But it wasn't enough. He wanted the real her. For fifty years.

He'd never fallen in love before. Never opened himself up to the prospect of hurt. And now he knew why.

She didn't linger and watch him walk away. Didn't press her face to the window or run to him. She shut the door. Closed the chapter. Completed the deal.

And snapped his heart into a million pieces.

★ ★ ★

Victoria leaned against the closed door and lost the fight with her tears. She loved him and she'd pushed him away with no explanation.

But how do you do that? How do you say *stay with me when I can't give you what you want and need? Choose me. Choose no kids. Choose disappointing your parents.* She wasn't enough. She just wasn't. Sure, she'd tell him, and he'd be gentle, she knew that now. He wouldn't trample all over her heart the way Peter had done, but she didn't want him to make the wrong choice. And now he was gone. And she would never, ever fix her heart back together again.

She'd been so scared of being rejected she'd acted first. But it was better this way. A clean cut.

When her limbs finally stopped shaking she slowly climbed the stairs, her body aching from all the exhausting emotions of the day. First the high of her collection catwalk and now this.

She stumbled through to her studio and realized she'd left her clothes at the store. She'd ask Sara to go for her tomorrow and collect them. The last thing she wanted was to bump into Oliver and rub that raw wound. Her body felt broken. She felt like she was crumbling. She was broken.

She wandered through to her bedroom and slumped down on the bed. Tears running freely again now, she had no energy to stop them. The pain in her chest was so sharp she could barely catch her breath.

Her phone rang. Lily. Victoria snatched it up. 'Oh, Lils.'

'Is he there?' Her voice was gentle, as if she was talking to a treasured child.

'He was.' A sob almost stopped Victoria from speaking but

she managed to force the words out. 'Now he's gone. I told him to go.'

'Did you tell him the truth about the accident? Everything? Did you have a good talk?'

There'd been nothing *good* about it. It had broken her heart to make him go. 'I couldn't face another man looking at me with such disappointment and disgust.'

'Oh, honey. I'm so sorry that happened. But Oliver wouldn't treat you like that. I mean… did he?'

'No. He was lovely. Always lovely. And… I like him. I mean… a lot.' Truth was, she just wanted to run up the road after him and tell him she'd made a huge mistake. But she hadn't. She couldn't make the even bigger mistake of falling deeper for him and then having her heart broken even more later on. She wanted his babies… this wasn't about providing an heir for his family, this was about her deepest desires. The ones she'd thought she'd controlled, the ones she'd believed she'd come to terms with losing. But she hadn't. She wanted Oliver and wanted to a family. And she couldn't. 'Talk me down, please.'

But instead of hearing Lily's lovely voice she heard some beeps and Zoe and Malie appeared in little boxes on her screen. And oh, God she needed to see them. Needed the collective support, knowing they were there to hold her up. The Lost Hours, her friends were here for her.

'Hi' was all she could manage through the sobs and the lump in her throat.

'We saw. We know. We love you,' Malie said, her voice low and soft and comforting.

'You… you know I told him to leave? You know we broke up?'

Zoe shrugged. 'Your call. Whatever feels right, do it. We've got you.'

'You're a strong, brave, amazing woman. Heck, you're a going to be a world-famous designer after today's show.' Lily smiled her reassuring smile, although it was a little wobbly. 'You'll get through this. We'll get you through this.'

Victoria was so worried her friends would be upset about the kiss and the photos but here they were, looking out for her. 'I don't know. I think I love him. But it's too soon. I mean… stupid me.' She thought about the night they'd spent in the hospital, all wrapped up in each other, talking into the early hours. The way she'd opened her heart and he'd done the same. The connection between them that had tightened and tugged and bound them together. 'I'm not making any sense…'

'Hey.' Lily laughed, gently. 'It's OK, you're hurting. You don't have to make any sense at all.'

'I wish…' She sobbed. 'I wish I had said yes instead of pushing him away. I'm too scared.' She sniffed. 'I just don't want a rerun of Peter. Basically, I'm a coward.'

'You are not.' Zoe was always great at taking control and talking truths. 'You have faced so many challenges and you've overcome so much. You're freaking amazing.'

'I just wish I felt amazing instead of like a limp lettuce.' Victoria pulled a tissue from a box by her bed and wiped her face. 'OK. Tell me something happy. God, I'm always asking you that. Now I feel bad. It's like you're my happy fairies.'

Lily laughed. 'You did the same for me when Alistair absconded with my cash. I didn't think I'd ever get over that and… maybe I'm not quite there yet, but you girls made me feel better. Let me think… happy? Happy. Oh! Yes. It's Christmas soon. You'll be coming home to see us? Please say yes.'

Zoe's mouth tipped up at one corner. 'Hey, I know it won't be the same without me, but Malie's popping home for a few days, right? Three out of four, isn't bad.'

Malie nodded, but didn't say anything. Victoria knew that was because coming home was always difficult for her – with her brother gone she felt she had to be there once a year for her parents, but their relationship was strained.

Lily nodded too. 'I want to spoil you rotten. I'll feed you. You can be my official Christmas menu taster. Please come home.'

Home. Victoria hadn't thought of Hawke's Cove as her home for so long, but the pull of the familiar and comfort was too much to resist. She could retreat there and lick her wounds with people who loved her. She just wanted a hug. Lots of hugs. Lost Hours meetings in person. The comfort of her friends.

'To be honest I hadn't thought past today. But I'll book time off work and I'll come down for the silly season.' If she was going to get over Oliver Russell she couldn't do it on her own, she needed home and friends and love.

'And we can get silly on mulled wine together,' Malie said. 'And take the boat round to the cove and get very, very drunk on prosecco. And to hell with men.'

'Yes! To hell with…' Victoria couldn't say it. Because, despite how badly she and Lily had been treated in the past there were good men out there. Oliver was one of them. 'But… oh, you guys. I love him. I feel as if my heart is splitting in two.'

'I know. But your heart is big enough to cope. We love you, V. We've got you,' Malie said and Victoria knew that even if everything wasn't going to be all right, not for a long time, she'd be cocooned in her family's and friends' embraces. That would definitely make things a whole lot better.

'Thank you.' Victoria lay back on her pillow and the tears slid down her cheeks, soaking the linen underneath her.

She had her friends. She had her work, a job she loved and a dream that was starting to crystallize into something very exciting.

She just didn't have the one thing that mattered above everything else.

Oliver Russell.

CHAPTER EIGHTEEN

EVERYONE AROUND HIM WAS happy.

Yeah. It was Christmas. Big freaking deal. Oliver was in a fancy restaurant eating over-priced bland food with the top brass at Russell & Co. There was tinsel and glitter everywhere, as if someone had dumped a tonne of the stuff over the table. He'd been made to wear a stupid paper hat from one of the crackers and everyone had had too much to drink. Except him.

To make things a thousand times worse he'd been seated next to his cousin.

'Plans for Christmas?' Andrew asked as he swirled dark amber liquid around the bottom of a glass. His yellow paper hat had slid down over his forehead. He looked ridiculous. 'Going to your parents?'

'No. Haven't got time. Tomorrow's going to be the busiest day of the year, because every single man in this country leaves his shopping until Christmas Eve. On top of that Boxing Day sales start early. No point driving all the way out to Norfolk, only to have to drive all the way back again the same day.'

'Bah humbug,' Andrew growled.

'Probably.' Oliver bit back the string of curse words that leaped to his throat. His Christmas spirit had done a bunk the day Victoria had told him she didn't want to see him anymore and refused to even listen to sense or compromise. The last thing he wanted was to put on a brave face about Christmas. 'Don't know what all the fuss is about, to be honest.'

The only thing that would ever make him happy wasn't here. She'd disappeared again – OK, so he may have had a peek in The Landing last night and again tonight, just before he came to this shower of an event.

Andrew swirled and drank. 'So, you're staying in town? You want to get the hell out of here and find a decent bar?'

'No.' He wanted to curl up with Victoria. Kiss her. Undress her. *Fifty years.* He wanted that with her, he knew it now.

His cousin nudged him. 'Come on, Ol. We could find some women, get laid and then maybe we'll have a better chance for a happy Christmas.'

'You go. I'm going to bed.' Oliver scraped his chair back and stood.

'You are no fun.' Andrew shot at him. 'Don't tell me you're missing that Vicki woman.'

Oliver controlled his breathing. 'Victoria. She doesn't like Vicki.'

But she loved helping people. She didn't like inequality. She was funny and kind. She'd pushed him to make things better with his parents. She was passionate. She tasted like freedom and new chances. And she was gone.

He was having trouble dealing with that, to be honest. He'd never felt so damned alone. He hadn't even realized he'd been lonely but she made him feel… OK, stupid as it was, she made him feel whole. More than. Better. She just made him feel alive.

'You are well rid of her. I was on to her. She was taking you for a ride, Ol. Until I got wise and told her…' Andrew trailed off and looked back into the bottom of his now empty glass. Then shrugged. 'Oops.'

'What do you mean?' Oliver leaned in to his cousin, unable to hide the surprise and irritation from his tone. 'What the hell did you say to her?'

Andrew shrugged, eyes wide. 'Look, I just told her I knew her little secret.'

'What secret?' Oliver's heart rate escalated. He sat back in his chair. What had he missed?

'That she's barren. Infertile. Can't have kids. Can't progress the Russell line. She was stringing you along and you fell for it.'

'She can't what?' Oliver's mind went into overdrive, but the last piece of the jigsaw slotted into place. *I just can't explain*, she'd said. Because she believed she'd be rejected again, right? But… why hadn't she said anything? 'How do you know this, Andrew?'

'Her ex. Said she'd been tight-lipped about it when they were in the lovey-dove stage. Then, when they were starting to talk futures she dropped the bombshell.' He drained his glass. 'Can't have them. Turns out he did want them, so…'

Irritation turned to anger so raw and fresh it tightened Oliver's chest, snatched his breath. 'So… that Peter douchebag dumped her because of an accident that wasn't her fault?'

'Found someone else, so yeah.'

And she found them together. God. Peter had probably staged the whole damned thing too. Poor Victoria. The tightness sharpened and spread to his gut as he started to understand. 'And she thought I'd do the same.'

'She said she was going to end it anyway.'

Oh, God. And she'd had to deal with Andrew. Oliver imagined how that had gone down. And then hot on the heels of that thought he had another, worse... why had she been unable to tell him? Because she didn't trust him... was it him or every guy? Had she thought he was like Peter and that he'd run away at the sight of her scars and what they implied? Had he been that cold? The famous Russell ruthlessness in relationships as well as business?

But he'd let her go with barely a fight. So yes, she probably thought he was exactly like her ex. Oliver had let her go because he'd believed it was what she wanted.

He glared at his cousin. 'You didn't think to talk to me about it first?'

'I gave her time to come clean.' Andrew's hands went up in a submissive gesture. 'Let's just say I hurried it along before she got any more valuables out of you.'

'The ring?' Nausea whirled in Oliver's stomach as he started to understand his cousin's subtext. 'You want Nana Norma's ring?'

Andrew shrugged. 'It's as much mine as it is yours.'

'It's Victoria's now. I told her to keep it.'

Andrew's lip curled. 'Then you're more of a sucker than I thought you were.'

They were interrupted by goodbyes and handshakes with the rest of the Russell & Co staff. Oliver dug deep to find any semblance of Christmas cheer... and then just faked it until they'd all gone.

Then it was just him and Andrew. Oliver could barely hold back his anger at this whole situation. If Andrew hadn't threatened to out her then maybe she'd have stayed and eventually trusted Oliver enough to tell him. He wanted to deck his cousin right here in the restaurant. 'You should have stayed the hell out of my business.'

'I did you a favour, mate. You should be thanking me.'

'I should just floor you.' Oliver's temper flared and his hands formed tight fists. 'Why do you always ruin what I have? You're like a child. Jealous. You want to break my frickin' toys. Man...'

'You've got to fight for what you want, right?' Andrew glared at him. 'Can't have you throwing our inheritance away on that woman.'

'That woman happens to be someone I...' The pain in Oliver's chest tightened. He wasn't going to say that word to Andrew and somehow belittle it by have his cousin sneer at it. 'I admire Victoria a lot. What are you jealous of, Andrew? The fact I found someone like her?'

'I'm not jealous of you or anything you have or do. I don't care.' But everything about Andrew's demeanour belied his words.

'Not jealous of me coming here to clear up your mess? Not jealous of me being happy with someone for the first time in for ever? Not jealous... but you want to spoil it for me, right?' This did not feel good. Oliver knew they were better than this, but it needed to be said.

Anger flared red hot in his cousin's eyes, and he stood up, snarling, 'Why should you get everything? I worked hard for the Chelsea store and you're getting all the glory. You've always been tipped to be the Russell heir and you were just about to ruin it all with *her*. I did it for the sake of the company.'

'Ah. Now I understand. You want the Russell crown *and* the ring?' Looking up at his cousin but completely unintimidated by him, Oliver bit back what he really wanted to say. Thought he had, at least, but the words just rushed out of him. 'You know what? Take it. Take the whole damned business. I don't care. I don't want it and you obviously want nothing else. Have it. But do you know what'll happen? You'll blow it all up. You'll destroy what our parents and grandparents fought so hard to create, the way you destroyed me and Victoria. Because you just can't help yourself.'

'I won't destroy anything. You didn't have to come to Chelsea, I didn't want you here. You just wanted to show off.'

'Grow up, Andrew. We both know you needed help getting the store ready for opening. I get it, I do. It's a tough job. Maybe next time you should ask for help before we hit crisis point.' Oliver scraped his chair back and stood to meet his cousin eye to eye. 'If there is a next time.'

This was it. Oliver didn't want to do this anymore, so he turned to leave. But Andrew grabbed his arm. 'You don't tell me what to do.'

'I'm done here.' Oliver shrugged away.

'Don't turn your back on me,' Andrew's voice was low and dangerous.

'Have it. Have it all. Have Russell & Co.' Oliver turned and threw his hands in the air. 'You won't take advice. You just want, want, want. So good luck with the whole damn thing.'

'But—? What?' Something flashed in his cousin's eyes. Anger? Fear? 'It's mine? You don't want it?'

'It's yours.' Oliver just wanted to get the hell out.

'Wait!' Instead of the expected burn, Andrew closed his eyes. 'What?'

His cousin didn't speak for a few moments then, 'I… Damn. Ollie. I can't have it. You're right.'

'About?'

The anger whooshing out of him, Andrew slumped into his chair. 'I don't know what to do. I get lost in the details. I think I have… I don't know, some kind of attention problem, or focus issues. I don't know. It all came so easily to you, but I just stare at things and don't know what to do about them. My to-do list just gets longer and the panic sets in and then I do nothing.' Andrew breathed out. This admission was costing him, Oliver knew but he didn't care at all. 'I need help.'

'You figure? Not just with spreadsheets.'

'What can I do?'

His cousin was serious. He was actually asking for help. *Damn.* Ollie sat back down.

After everything, he couldn't walk away now. Victoria would never forgive him for not helping. Hell, she'd shown him the good you could do, the way you could lift someone up. It didn't take much, but by extending a helping hand you could change someone's life.

And he was family. Blood was blood and you did what you could, right? He wouldn't have been able to look his old man in the eye if he didn't offer a hand up to another Russell. Even after everything. He couldn't have Victoria, and even if Andrew had precipitated her departure, she'd been hell-bent on going. Because she thought Oliver would reject her if he knew the extent of her injuries?

Did she even know him?

But then people lashed out when they were hurting… it was a self-protection thing, Ollie understood. And who was he to put up a wall between him and a member of his family? He couldn't fix his relationship with Victoria, but he could take steps with his cousin.

He sighed. 'OK, Andy. We'll fix this. We'll get a mentor, someone who can walk you through things. We'll take it at your pace. We'll help you.'

'Yeah?'

'Yes. Because, unlike you, I believe in helping instead of hurting.' Victoria had shown him that too, he realized with a sharp stab. 'Maybe one day you could try that? Stop thinking about what you haven't got and think about what you have.'

'Like you, you mean?' Andrew ground out. 'You have everything a man could want. Fancy house. Great job. Billions in the bank. But you're pretty damned hard to be with.'

'Because you scared Victoria away.'

'You actually care about her?'

Oliver downed the last of his whisky. 'I do.'

'Damn.' Andrew shook his head. 'I'm sorry, man. I... I was in a bad place watching you come in over my head and take control. I was jealous of everything. And her ex, Peter... he told me that she couldn't have kids and I thought she was lying to you. To us all.'

'I don't know if I even want kids. But I do know that want her. That's the most definite I've been about anything in my life.' And now she'd gone. 'I want to talk to her about it, at least.'

'If she loved you the way she said she did, she'd have stayed, right?'

'When she believed all the Russell might was against her?' His cousin did not have a goddamned clue. But... wait... 'Roll back a bit. She what?'

'She said something like, *but what if I do love Oliver?*'

Oh God. Could this get any worse? Victoria loved him and the only person she happened to mention it to was his damned cousin? 'Ah, this is so screwed up.'

Andrew snorted. 'Well, you know how hard we Russells fight for things we want. Where is she now? What are you waiting for?'

Hell. Yes.

Victoria was the real deal. She was everything he hadn't even known he wanted. She filled the gaping hole in his chest with warmth and light and love. She gave him a fresh purpose and a new perspective. She made him want to be a better man. He wanted to be that man with her by his side.

And then he knew. Knew without a shadow of a doubt that he loved her. Adored her. That he wanted the next fifty years, fifty millennia with his Victoria.

For the first time in weeks he felt a flicker of hope. He wanted her and he had to show her she could entrust her heart to him. That he was not like her ex, that he'd love her not despite but *because* of what she'd been through. He had nothing but admiration for her. Oh… and love. Lots and lots of that.

He stood. 'I'm out of here.'

'What… where?' Andrew asked, his face contorted in confusion. 'What can I do to help? You want me to call her, say I was wrong?'

'No. Do not phone her. Ever.' Oliver didn't stop to explain more. He was going to do what his father had taught him – he was going to fight for a deal he believed in.

★ ★ ★

Victoria stepped out of the taxi that had brought her from the train station into Hawke's Cove, and breathed deeply.

Salt. Sea. Home. A pale December sun and clear skies. She breathed out. It was good to be here, even if just to get away from the claustrophobic rooms of her flat and the ever-present feeling that Oliver was literally a few yards away in his store and yet there might as well have been galaxies between them.

A squawking seagull circled overhead as she looked out to the choppy water. Over to the left was the imposing structure of Hawkesbury House, to the right were the little shops and houses that made up the seaside village where everyone knew everything.

No doubt they all knew about that kiss too. No doubt Mrs Whittaker would stop and ask her. Victoria would have been fresh gossip for a few days. She just hoped that now, three weeks later, the Hawke's Cove residents were too focused on Christmas to remember Victoria Scott's little front-page escapade.

She played with the ring that she'd transferred to her right hand because she hadn't the heart to take it off altogether. It was something physical to keep her connected to Oliver. Although, she had enough physical heartache that she doubted she'd ever forget him.

What would Nana Norma do? She'd hold her head up high and not give a damn about what other people thought.

But first, Victoria slid the ring from her finger and popped it into her purse. More for safekeeping than anything, but also because there were some questions she just didn't want to answer.

After dropping her bag off at home and dodging her parents' questions as to her wellbeing she meandered over to Lily's restaurant, The Sea Rose, and pushed open the door. The earthy scent of garlic and rosemary welcomed her, and she immediately felt… tearful. She was home.

'V!' Lily leaped out from the kitchen and wrapped her in a tight hug. 'There you are! One o'clock on the dot! It's so good to see you.'

Victoria's chest felt so tight she couldn't get any words out, so she hung on to her friend, squeezing the tears away. It was Christmas. She wasn't about to ruin that for Lily.

But her friend was too canny. She pulled away and held Victoria's shoulders, searching her face with a sad smile. 'It's OK, darling. It's OK. I've got you.'

'I thought I was done crying.' Victoria wiped her eyes with her fist. 'I was doing so well. I haven't cried for days. But… I'm glad to be home.'

'I've got a surprise that will make you feel a lot better. Come with me.' Lily took her hand and they walked out of the restaurant, down to the harbour. In the distance was the little rowboat they always 'borrowed' from Mr Michaels, who often caught them mid-steal and raised his fist, but never actually stopped them from doing it.

Victoria's heart jumped. Lily had promised her prosecco and peace and here it was. 'We're going to our bay? Now? Aren't you busy? It's Christmas Eve.'

'Never too busy for… Hey! Hey!' Lily whistled and shouted, and two heads suddenly popped up from inside the boat. 'A Lost Hours meeting!'

Heart jumping, Victoria peered towards the boat. A blonde head and a wildly curly one. And there tethered to the side of the harbour railings was Zoe's wheelchair. 'Oh. My. God. Zoe's here too?'

'Yes. She came for you.'

Her heart felt as if it was going to burst out of her chest. 'For… me?'

'Because of Oliver. And the kiss. And because we love you.'

They were all here simply because she was sad. Her lip wobbled and she struggled to hold back a sob. 'But… Zo's allergic to this place.'

Or, to her parents at least. Her chest constricted and she broke into a run. Lily whooped and ran along with her. 'Best surprise ever!'

'Oh. God. I am so happy to see you all.' Victoria jumped into the little rowboat and hugged her friends tight, not caring that the tears were flowing freely now. 'I can't believe you're here.'

'Hey. Can't have you being sad at Christmas. I'm just passing through, so we don't have much time.' Zoe held up a bottle of wine. 'Time enough for this, though. Let's get round to the bay and we can make a start. Jetlag's made me very, very thirsty.'

'Me too.' Malie held up some glasses. 'What are we waiting for?'

'Er… someone to row?' Lily, ever the sensible one, made Malie and Victoria clamber out of the boat again and push it into the water. It was a calm, clear afternoon and they were round at their secret cove in no time. They helped Zoe out of the boat, lit a small fire and sat around wrapped in blankets, chatting until the sun started to fade. It was the best Christmas gift she'd ever received.

'Thank you.' Victoria chinked her glass to her friends' flutes. 'For coming all this way for me. I know it isn't easy for you, Zo. Which makes it extra special.'

'Yes, well, you're going to have to entertain me while I'm here.' Zoe grinned. 'I'm not one for family reunions, but I do love you lots. So, tomorrow, after present-opening, can we meet for a drink or something? I'm going to need some *me* time.'

'Totally. I'm up for that,' Lily said. 'There's no way I'm going to let you all be here and not spend as much time with you as possible.'

'And we can plan when we're next going to get together like this. Like old times. No one understands me like you all do.' Victoria lay her head on Malie's shoulder enjoying the numbing effects of the alcohol. 'I want to come to Hawaii. Can you fit me in your suitcase?'

'Absolutely. Come! Please. I'll teach you how to surf properly. Then you can relax and do nothing in the afternoons and we can hit the bars in the evenings. It's hot all year round so it doesn't matter when you come. The sooner the better. You'd love it.'

It would be a distraction from everything. From Oliver. Who was still the first thing she thought about in the morning and the most consistent dream she had. But in that one they were happy and together. Victoria sighed. 'One day.'

Malie nodded. 'I have plenty of hot surfer mates, those dudes'll help to distract you, no problem.'

'Truth is, we were getting worried,' Lily said, turning to Victoria, suddenly serious. 'You did a lot of crying and then you went quiet. Too quiet.'

'It's the stupid season for me. The bar's been so busy and with all the orders for my dresses I'm a bit snowed under. I'm thinking of giving up the bar work and focusing solely on the dress designs, but then I'd have to find somewhere else to live and...' It had been struggle enough for her to put one foot in front of the other without thinking about moving house too. But she was starting to plan, so that was something.

'Have you seen him?' Lily's tone was gentle. It was inevitable they'd come round to this subject eventually.

'No. But that's not to say I haven't craned my neck out the window any time I thought he might be passing.'

'Thank God you're here, then.' Zoe stroked Victoria's arm. 'Your neck will thank you. I forgive you for not telling me about a fake engagement to a freaking billionaire. Almost.'

'I didn't know what to say, to be honest.'

'It looked like a very good kiss.' Malie smiled.

And so did Victoria, because it had been a very good kiss. Very good kisses indeed. 'Everything about him was amazing and I didn't explain… about me. About the accident, not properly. I never gave him a chance. *Us* a chance. God, I want to rewind that clock so much.'

'Maybe it's better in your head than it would be in reality.' Lily was always so rational. 'That's how it goes sometimes, right? They don't always live up to expectations.' And after what Lily's ex-fiancé did to her, she knew all about the difference between expectation and reality.

But Victoria imagined being naked and wrapped in Oliver's arms once more. 'I'll never know.'

'Did you see the press release in the paper about his dad?' Malie asked. 'Said something about a heart condition and new treatment and that he was recovering. That's good, right?'

'Eric's not going to let a bit of heart trouble keep him down.' Victoria wondered how he was coping with enforced tai chi and Sudoku and whether he'd been able to sneak out to his office and do some therapeutic spreadsheeting.

'What are you smiling at?' Lily asked.

'They are a lovely family. Even though he's growly on the TV, Eric's a pussycat really.' Victoria's throat suddenly swelled, and her voice croaked out the last two words. She didn't just miss Oliver she missed his whole freaking family.

Well, not Andrew, obviously.

'Oh-oh. I sense more tears.' Zoe poured more bubbles into Victoria's glass. 'Come on, V. Maybe it's time to start looking forward. Tell us about the amazing interest in your designs.'

'In a minute.' She was lost again in the memory of Oliver and it was painful and yet lovely at the same time. 'Did I tell you about riding in the helicopter to Paris?'

'Yes!' They all replied at the same time.

'A thousand times. Still not jealous.' Lily laughed. 'But I bet he didn't row you out to a secret cove and feed you bubbles.'

'No. Never.'

Zoe was right, it was time to look forward and to spend good times with her friends who'd come across the globe. For her. 'Only the very best people do that.'

'Always.' Malie grinned.

'To friendship. To the Lost Hours.' Zoe proposed the toast. 'To us.'

'To us.' Victoria looked through the flickering flames at her friends. They'd stood by each other through everything. When life had been bleak and the future felt out of reach, they'd cajoled and comforted. They'd been each other's strength when being strong had felt impossible. They'd crossed the world for her.

She didn't have Oliver and the future had certainly felt bleak for a while. But if nothing else, with these women by her side, she was going to have a happier Christmas.

★ ★ ★

It was almost dark as they dragged the boat up the beach back at Hawke's Cove and then settled Zoe into her wheelchair. Malie took control of steering but veered badly to the left. 'I'm not drunk, it's this sand.'

'Yeah, right. We believe you.' Lily laughed, her eyes dancing as she slid her arm into Victoria's and they all made their way towards the slipway. 'OK, who's coming to the pub for one more drink before I get back to work?'

'Me.' Victoria eyed the white building up ahead. 'Just one and then I have to get back before Mum and Dad go to Aunty Mary's for dinner and then Midnight Mass.'

'You're not going to join them? But it's your family tradition.'

'I'm mixing things up a bit this year.' Also known as avoiding her auntie's questions. She just wanted to wallow watching *Love, Actually* and possibly do a bit more crying over Oliver and what she'd thrown away. Oh-oh. Maybe the alcohol was going to her head.

'Hey. Dude alert.' Malie pointed to a lone figure standing at the top of the slipway, hands stuffed deep in his coat pockets. He was staring out at… at them. 'Tasty. Do you think he might want surfing lessons?'

Oh, God.

Victoria closed her eyes. Opened them again. Her chest felt as if it was collapsing in on itself. 'It's him.'

Zoe shielded the last rays of sun from her eyes and squinted. 'Who?'

'Oliver,' said Lily. Her voice sounded the way Victoria felt – cautious. Hopeful. Sad.

Despite herself, despite her friends, despite everything,

Victoria slipped her arm from Lily's and strode towards him. She couldn't stop herself. Didn't know what the hell she was going to say to him.

But she had to reach him, and fast.

CHAPTER NINETEEN

HE WAS HERE. IN sleepy Hawke's Cove on Christmas Eve. Victoria tried hard not to read a million messages into this and failed. Did he want her back? Was he here…?

'Victoria.' He nodded hello but didn't kiss her… not even her cheek.

Okaaaay. So, this wasn't going to be the grand reunion where they ran across the beach on a snowy Christmas Eve into each other's arms. Right. Too much *Love, Actually* made a girl believe in happy ever afters.

Maybe he was here with bad news? Her throat caught as her heart jumped. 'How's your dad? Is he OK?'

'He's actually much better.'

'I couldn't believe the way the press were so intrusive about his illness.' She walked towards a bench that looked out to sea and he came and sat next to her. They stared out, she didn't dare look at him and try to read his thoughts. But her heart jittered and she hoped. *Hoped.*

Oliver's hands were still in his pockets. He hadn't reached for her. 'Dad's used to handling that kind of thing. He sent out a press release saying he's had the doctors' sign-off and just has to rest up. He's getting stronger. But I'm not here about that.'

Hope rose as she turned to him. 'Oh?'

He gave her a small smile. She was relieved to see that he looked about as tired as she felt. Had he been having sleepless nights too? 'I have another deal for you, V.'

She daren't ask, but her body prickled with promise. 'Yes?'

'The thing is, ever since the catwalk show we've been inundated with orders and queries about your designs.'

Ah. He was here about that. Her shoulders sagged as if her hope bubble had literally been popped. 'I know. Your PA forwarded them. I'm working through them.'

'Good. I'd like to offer you space in the bridal shop. For your collections. A permanent place. Then we can help with the orders too.'

Whoa. Was he for real? She'd broken things off and he was still giving? 'I can't. It's not right.'

'What isn't?'

'You don't get to wave a magic Russell wand and give me my dreams on a plate.'

He frowned. 'I thought you wanted your clothes in a shop like ours?'

'I do. But I want to earn it, I want you to offer me the space because my designs are worthy and deserve to be there, not do it because you know me. I want to be good enough to be there.' It sounded churlish and ungrateful, but she didn't want to be his pity project.

He shrugged. 'I don't know anything about dress designs, I admit. But Marianne, the bridal store manager, can't keep up with the interest, especially when we don't have any of your stock. She insisted I talk to you about it. So, it's not my doing. I'm just the conduit.'

She bit her lip and thought. It wasn't just Oliver then. Other people believed in her. Hell, she knew that already, but she didn't… *believe* it. Could she do this? Could she grab this dream with both hands? 'I don't want any concessions. If they don't sell, then we reconsider. I want a proper contract.'

'I don't think that's going to be an issue. Russell & Co want to be exclusive and we'd aim to stock them in our global stores. Although, obviously you'd need to lawyer up to make sure the contract is to your benefit.'

'OK. Right.' Gone viral. Or global at least.

'Do we have a provisional deal?' He sounded like the true professional he was. Steady. Calm. Certain.

'Deal.' She didn't think she would be able to love him more, but she did. So much. So much it made her throat sore and her eyes sting. She missed him. She loved him.

She should have been elated. This was a chance in a million. A dream career in a beautiful space, but she would be at risk of seeing him every day. She would want him every day. And her heart would never heal. And yet she had to do it. 'You came all this way to tell me that? You could have sent an email.'

'I also wanted to tell you that I've taken a step back from the day-to-day running of the company and we're on the lookout for a new CEO.'

Oh, wow. 'You told your father?'

He nodded. 'You said we needed to communicate and be upfront. So, I told him I wasn't happy and wanted to do something else. I'll still be involved, but on a much smaller scale.'

'Good for you. I know that will have taken guts.'

'You know what he said? That he wished he'd done the same

thing years ago. He also said you were a bad influence on the Russells if you were going to make us all abandon the company and just have fun all the time. But he winked too, because he knows there are good people out there who could run the place better than we can.' Ollie's chest pumped. Proud of what they'd achieved. 'And I also know he loves you to pieces.'

'He's a good man.' She breathed out. 'I'm proud of you all, Ollie. And you decided to do what?'

He drew his eyes from hers and looked out at the ocean. Snowflakes fell all around them, settling on their shoulders, in their hair. 'I'm going to set up a trust to help less fortunate kids in the areas where our stores are. In inner cities the scope is huge. I'm constantly amazed at the disparity of wealth of people who live on the same street; at one end there's millionaire's row and at the other there's overcrowding and poverty. The Russell Trust will offer opportunities to those who need them, either working in our stores or business mentoring.'

Her heart soared at this news. He'd jumped. 'That's wonderful. I'm so proud of you.'

'You opened my eyes to what's possible You gave me the inspiration and courage to do it, V. You and those kids. I can't tell you how good it felt to see them on that stage, so help them chase their dreams.' So, OK altruism was a teeny bit selfish too. 'I'm going to need some help setting it up.'

'Of course. There are plenty of NGOs who could advise you.'

He swivelled to face her. 'I was hoping you might chip in too.'

'Me? I only know about my girls.'

'You see details I don't, V. You… Hell.' He ran his hand through his hair and shook his head. 'I'm not doing this right. This is not how I planned it would go.'

'Planned how?' What did he mean?

He took her hand in his. 'I want to do some good and I know the Trust will be a step towards that, but together we can be a tour de force. I want these kids to have a chance, to fulfil a dream. More, to be allowed to dream. Because even though I have everything I could possibly need, I never had the chance to do that. And you made it happen. You made me see beyond my world and opened up another one. One with you in it, front and centre. That's where I want you to stay, Victoria. In the centre of my life. To help me do this. To help me… well, live my best life.' He took her other hand in his, his eyes misted but… was there hope there too? 'V, you are the love of my life. You are everything I've been looking for and didn't even realize. I love y—'

'No.' She put her fingertips to his mouth suddenly all too aware of where this was going. She couldn't allow this to happen. *He loved her.* 'Don't. Please, don't.'

He wanted her in his life. He was offering her so much she couldn't take from him. It was too cruel to hear this, to know he loved her and to let him go a second time. It was going to be so much harder to walk away.

He shook his head. 'Let me finish. I love you—'

'Oh, Oliver.' The hot sting of tears burned her eyes. Her throat was rough and full. She had to tell him. She'd not trusted him enough to tell him her innermost secret, but he was a good man, he needed to know. She trusted he'd treat her gently at least. 'I'm so sorry. I don't want you to fall in love with lies, or things left unsaid. That's what happened with Peter.'

Oliver's lip curled at the mention of her ex's name, but she didn't move her fingers from his mouth in case he said more beautiful things that made her heart hurt. 'Please. Go back to London. I can't give you what you want and deserve. Oh, Ollie, I can't have babies. I can't do the family thing no matter how much I'd love to.'

And there was the sad reality; she wanted babies with Oliver. So much. Wanted her belly swelling with his child. Wanted a family with him. A future. It was so damned cruel she could barely breathe with the weight of it.

He took her fingers away from his mouth. 'I know.'

'How? Oh.' She realized she didn't need to ask. 'Andrew.'

Ollie nodded. 'Why didn't you tell me?'

'It was only a pretend relationship, right? But then things got serious and well… when is a good time to declare your inadequacies? It all got too much and then it got too late.' She blinked the tears back. 'I didn't want you to have make a choice between me and your family. I didn't want to put you in that situation. It isn't fair.'

'You are not inadequate. Clearly Peter is.' He squeezed her fingers gently. 'You win hands down, V. Every single time. I love you and that's all I care about.'

'But what about grandchildren? The family firm? It's what they want. What you will want too, given time. And I can't bear to see that disappointment in your eyes when it dawns on you that you wanted kids all along. I don't want to watch you leave, or hear you've got someone else.'

'Nothing is more important to me than you, Victoria Scott.'

'But what about your family line, passing down the Russell legacy?'

'What about my dreams, V? Of being with you? We can create a bigger legacy than just the Russell one. The Trust will give so many children a better future. What better legacy is there than that?'

A rogue tear slipped down her cheek. Then another. 'Don't you want to hold your own baby in your arms?'

'I want you, Victoria. I can't see further than that. I don't want more than that. If I have you in my life then I'll be the happiest man alive. And there might be options: adoption, fostering, surrogacy. Or maybe we'll just be us two together. A tour de force, right? This is just the beginning. You, me, that's all that matters, anything more will be icing. I love you, Victoria, with everything I am, everything I have.'

He kissed her then and she felt his words resonate through her body. He loved her.

He loved her and she believed him.

'I love you too, Oliver Russell.' She pressed her head against his and smiled. Snow was starting to fall and there was a definite feeling of magic in the air. All she needed now was to hear the tinkle of sleigh bells and she really would believe this was a dream. A perfect amazing dream. Come true.

He brushed the flakes from her hair and smiled. This time it was a little wary. As if he was nervous about something. Which was very un-Oliver-like. 'There is one more thing.'

'Oh, yes?'

'Third time lucky?'

'What? Oh?' Her heart danced as he got down on to one knee. Again. What was it about Oliver and benches and proposals? 'You're making a habit of this.'

'And I'll keep doing it until I get the right answer. Victoria. *My Victoria*, will you please do me the honour—'

'Yes!' She didn't even let him finish. 'Yes. Third time lucky indeed. Yes. Please, Ollie. I love you. I love you. I love you. So much.'

He stood and pulled her up from the bench and wrapped her into his arms. 'I'm the lucky one.'

He kissed her again and again and she let the wonderful feeling of hope and happiness swell through her. Maybe she was going to get the fairy tale after all. Or pretty damned close. When she finally opened her eyes, she saw the village Christmas tree lights shining, heard a group of carol singers somewhere near the beach.

'Happy Christmas, darling.' She snuggled against his chest. 'Our very first Christmas together.'

'Here's to fifty more.'

She pulled back from him and pretended to frown, because fifty years would be a wonderful innings after all. 'Only fifty?'

'Fifty million.' He laughed. 'A lifetime. For ever.'

* * *

Lost Hours. Lost Hours. Lost Hours. NOW!

After a Christmas morning with Oliver meeting her parents and brother, and wooing them as well as he'd wooed her, she needed to tell her friends her news.

Lily's text came back first:

Come to the restaurant, there's no one here but me.

Then Zoe's:

Thank God. I was starting to get desperate. I need to get out of here.

Then Malie's:

Give me five minutes.

Victoria bundled her gifts for them into a bag and ran down to The Sea Rose. After a round of 'Happy Christmases' they sat around their favourite table by the window with a good view of the harbour.

Zoe's question came first as she opened a bottle of Baileys that Lily handed to her. 'What the hell happened?'

Malie held out glasses one at a time as Zoe poured. 'Where is he?'

Lily put her hand on Victoria's arm and smiled softly, warily. 'Are you OK?'

'I'm fine. I'm more than fine actually.' Victoria sat up straight and took one of the glasses. 'He's back at the house.'

'And…?' Zoe's eyebrows rose.

With as much drama as she could muster Victoria took off her woolly glove and waggled Nana Norma's ring… back on the correct finger on her left hand. 'And he asked me to marry him!'

'Oh. My. God.' Eyes wide, Malie leaned over and held V's fingers so she could inspect the diamond. 'Wow. That's beautiful. Stunning. Obviously, you said—?'

'Did you tell him?' It was Lily. Always with the right questions, because she knew how important it was to Victoria that Oliver knew the truth.

Victoria smiled at the memory of him going down on one knee in the snow. 'I did. I told him I can't have children. Actually, he already knew because his stupid cousin told him two days ago. But he said it didn't matter. That I am the only thing that matters.'

Malie's hand went to her chest. 'Awww. That's… pretty epic.'

'Best damned thing I've ever had in my Christmas stocking.' Victoria held up her glass to chink with the others. 'Cheers!'

Lily chinked and smiled. 'That is so too much information.'

'So… we're aiming for an August wedding.' She thought about Stella's conversation all those weeks ago over dinner. *An August wedding. There's a chapel in the village.* That was a discussion they were going to have to handle with kid gloves. How to achieve what Victoria wanted and what the Russells expected? That was for another day.

She focused back on her three dearest friends. 'And I hope you'll be my bridesmaids.'

'Oh. My. God. It really is happening? Just like we planned all those years ago. Of course. Of course. Oh, yes!' Zoe reached over and wrapped her arms around Victoria and hugged her tight, then the others did the same until they were a jumble of limbs and smiles and laughter and tears.

Victoria wiped hers away, giggling. 'So, you have to promise to come back home for the hen do and then the wedding. I am not walking down that aisle without any of you. Understand?'

Zoe saluted. 'Yes, boss.'

And Victoria's heart gave a little leap because coming back to England was hard on Zoe and it was a big ask for her to do it again so soon.

'Maybe we could go to Ibiza for the hen party?' Malie gave a cheeky smile.

'Sounds like we have a lot of planning to do!' Lily grinned. 'Although, maybe we should go somewhere else? Ibiza has its own very special memories and we don't want to try to recreate them or we might be disappointed.'

'I do.' Zoe laughed and tapped her nose. 'But, obviously, I can't tell you what my specific memories are.'

And so the secret of Zoe's lost hours remained a mystery.

Then it was present time and they took it in turns to exchange Christmas gifts. The girls loved the dresses Victoria had made them from the fabric she'd returned to Betsy's to buy. The sea-themed one for Malie, the lacy one for Zoe, a lovely breezy summer dress for Lily, and individually designed hair clips all round. It was so good to see their faces, a little wind-chapped, noses red from the cold, eyes dancing. Smiling, laughing. Bolstering each other up, making Victoria's life just so much better because they were in it. God, she loved these women.

Then her phone rang. 'Oh. It's Ollie.' She covered the speaker with her hand and explained to her friends, 'I left him with my parents, poor guy. Hey, Ollie. I have some friends you need to meet. These women are the most important people in my life, apart from you. So, it's important you all get along. I'm switching to video mode.'

Then suddenly he was there on the screen and her body prickled with awareness.

Malie peered at the screen and grinned. 'Hey! Congratulations, Oliver. Heard a lot about you.'

'Thank you! I'm a very lucky guy.' He smiled. 'Hi, Malie. Hi, Zoe. Hey, Lily.'

'He knows our names?' Zoe shot with a confused but impressed expression.

Victoria grinned proudly. *That's my boy.* 'Of course he does.'

'I saw photos,' he explained. 'Plus, she talks about you non-stop. I can't wait to meet you all in person.'

'What about tonight?' Lily suggested. 'Come here to the

restaurant. I'd love to cook for you all and I've got some extra special Hawkesbury wine we could open.'

'Sure thing. Can't wait.' He nodded. Then he whispered, 'Hey, V. Did I pass?'

'With flying colours.' She smiled. 'Are you OK? Did you need something?'

'Your parents have taken the dog for a walk. They said they'd be a couple of hours. And your brother's at the pub. Which means… the house is empty.' He grinned with a wicked glint in his eyes that made her hot all over.

'Oh!' This was good news. 'That means we can—'

'Lalalalala. I do not want to hear about this.' Zoe stuck her fingers in her ears while Lily blushed and gave the thumbs up sign.

Malie's eyes widened. 'You'd better get gone, babe.'

She hugged them all to a chorus of goodbyes and then blew him a kiss. 'I'm on my way.'

'Great. I'll be waiting. Er… upstairs.' He smiled. So sexy. So damned perfect. All hers. 'But don't hurry, V. We have plenty of time. We have all the time in the world.'

ACKNOWLEDGEMENTS

This book might have my name on the cover but there are many people who have been instrumental in making it possible and who I'd like to thank from the bottom of my heart. Thank you to my Grandfather Bertie for always encouraging me to write, and pursue my dreams – sorry there isn't enough bird watching in this book! To my bonkers family for your endless support, for all birthdays and Christmas's you will be receiving this bloody brilliant book!

A huge thank you to my managers Jordan Johnson and Russell Eslamifar for believing in me and guiding me through this process with unwavering support, let's be honest the meetings about this book were always our favourite! And of course my literary agent: Amanda Harris, you're a superstar.

To my brilliant editor Becky Slorach for championing my novel and giving me the freedom to write the story and characters I've always dreamt of, you've been at the end of the phone 24/7 (seriously). Thank you to everyone at Mills & Boon and Harper Collins, in particular Kirsty Capes, Katie Barnes-Wallis, and Lily Capewell. Darling Lisa Milton, where do I start? We first met and I was clutching a glass of champagne at someone else's book launch imagining you giving me the chance of writing a book and... it happened.

To Lucy Truman and Kate Oakley for the wonderful illustration, the cover is simply divine. Louisa George, your talent has produced this and I am so proud.

Thank you to PG for enduring countless silent journeys with me whilst I was furiously writing, editing and re-editing. I love you. To AH for spending every night next to me in our dorm not complaining about me reading with a torch under the covers at school, I love you, bebé, here's to the next decade of friendship!

To my girlfriends who were my inspiration to write a story about female friendship and love, this book is dedicated to you all with love and admiration.

Finally, a humongous thank you to every reader who picked this up and has supported me along this crazy journey, I'm forever grateful and honoured.

If you loved **_Meet me in London_** read on
for an extract of Malie's story **_Meet me in_**
Hawaii from Georgia Toffolo and Mills & Boon

Coming Spring 2021

CHAPTER ONE

MALIE PUKUI CLOSED HER eyes and raised her head to the setting sun. She took a long, soothing breath and smoothed her corkscrew curls back from her face, holding her hands either side of her head as she bobbed on the surfboard and let the water lap around her knees. This was her favourite time of day. This and dawn. When it felt as though it was just her, her board and the beautiful ocean…

Peace. Calm. Tranquillity.

No expectations, no nothing.

Just me, she thought, *me and Koa, against the world*.

A bark from the deserted shoreline told her that wasn't quite true. She had Nalu, her four-legged friend and the surf school's honorary mascot with her. But he didn't encroach on this time.

She'd chosen this stretch of beach because it was secluded by the natural flora that had overtaken the public access long ago. It meant she was free to surf in peace, free to reconnect with her late brother and take time out from her full-on schedule.

There was no need to put on a front, no need to be anyone but herself.

She lowered her hands to her board and turned to look at Nalu now, playing in the swash, his tail wagging as he pranced back and forth.

'I'll be back soon,' she called out. And she would, really soon.

Just a few more minutes, one more perfect wave and she would paddle back in. She had a function to attend after all. A function that was important if her charity work was to grow and flourish like she hoped.

Still, she didn't feel ready to be that perfect face again. To smile and be polite, to laugh and be merry with those that held the purse strings and likely didn't do anything unless it rewarded them financially to do so. And she knew she had a mouth on her, that keeping it tight-lipped would be a challenge, but she'd do it if it meant she could help more people. People like her friend Zoe.

Now she smiled. The memory of seeing Zoe and her two other besties – Lils and Victoria – back in England last week. Learning of V's engagement, a real bona fide one, and not the pretend shebang it had started out as. It had been lovely and had certainly taken some of the sting out of Christmas with her parents.

One week back in Hawaii and the strain of it was still hanging over her like a cold she couldn't shake. And maybe that was the real reason she was sticking it out with the waves when she should be back at the apartment preening for tonight's cocktail party.

'Urgh!' She thrust forward on the board and paddled, her well-trained eye on the water now as she sought the right swell, duck-diving and paddling until she was forced to accept it was more about avoidance of her life than it was the perfect wave.

England persisted. Her parents. When would they just smile and approve? When would they be able to talk about Koa without filling her with guilt at being the one still here, and the one that didn't deserve to be?

Let it go, Malie.

It was as though her brother was in her head telling her to just chill, to enjoy the surf, the last for the night. And then she felt it, the familiar tug of the ocean beneath her; she could see the swell in the sea ahead, the perfect green wave. *Here it comes.*

She rose up and swivelled her legs beneath the water to turn her board. She lay forward, lifted her chin and paddled. A deep, outstretched motion tight with the board that had her gliding through the water. She checked the wave again, matched her speed and grinned wide. *Wait for it. Wait for it.*

Her board lifted with the sea. *Now.*

Up she popped. 'Thank you, Mother Nature!'

Nalu barked, frolicking into the water at her excited yell. This was why she surfed. This was why she couldn't give it up, not for her parents, not for anything. Harnessing the power of the ocean, the adrenalin rush of being propelled along, of getting it right and flicking the board this way and that… taking control.

She glided with the wave, heading into shore and already she knew, she just needed one more.

It wasn't like she'd spend *that* long getting ready anyway.

She turned and dropped down onto her board. The sun was settling on the horizon, beckoning her out, its orange glow stretching far and wide and mirrored in the sea. She fell forward and started to paddle, her eyes on the sun, her heart not ready to leave.

Nalu barked and her conscience pricked: *You're going to be late.*

She ignored it. It was just one more ride.

She stopped paddling, the lull in the waves giving her time to sit and ponder, to take in the beauty before her.

The geographic gap fell away and she could just as easily be sitting on her board back in Devon, in Hawke's Cove. Sunsets were much the same when you were staring out at the never-ending sea.

A longing came over her, an ache she couldn't quite shift – if only she were back in the Cove. If only things were different.

It would always be home to her. Even if it wasn't the right place for her anymore. She couldn't be trapped by it again, by her parents and their fears, their disapproval of her surfing, their pain over Koa's death. Hawaii gave her the freedom that she needed, and she was so grateful to her godfather for giving her the job at his surf school.

And she loved it, really loved it. She got to surf all day, teaching others about the magic of the ocean, the power of the wave, the freedom.

As though sensing her mood lift, the waves started to swell before her.

Maybe one day her parents would accept her. She swivelled her board around. Maybe one day she could return.

She dropped forward, felt the rush of the ocean beneath her, behind her, as familiar as her own heartbeat. No, she would never give this up. And until her parents could accept it was a part of her, she would just stay away.

Crazy when she considered that it was them who had given her this addiction, the surf school they'd run once-upon-a-time being her home from home as a child. But that had all been before the unimaginable had happened, the—

Her thoughts quit, there was movement in the sea ahead, Nalu was in the water, barking. The sound was sharp, incessant, like the rise of an alarm.

What the—

'H-help… Help…'

The yell sounded male, an accompanying spluttering the unmistakable sound of a person taking on water. The lifeguard in Malie had her scanning the water, the hairs prickling at her nape.

The sea, the shore, was shrouded in darkness and she squinted into it as her eyes adjusted from the sunset. How long had she rocked out here for? How long had she sat—

Oh goodness, no.

She caught a glimpse of someone in the water, their strokes hurried, panicked. She could no longer make out Nalu, but they were definitely in trouble. Either side of them the waves were breaking, the perceived stillness of the water in which they swam telling her the person was caught in a rip current and instinctively fighting for shore.

'Don't fight it,' she yelled. 'Go with it!'

She was already paddling for them, her head raised and eyes trained on their position. They didn't seem to hear her and she cursed, yelled again, 'Hey, over here!'

The waves were picking up, getting bigger, but it worked in her favour, propelling her closer until she was almost parallel to the person.

'Swim to me!' she yelled, one hand waving at him to come her way.

Finally he saw her, his eyes wide as he flicked his hair off his face and continued to strike for shore. He was going nowhere and if anything, he was struggling more, fear making his strokes ineffective and sending him under.

'You can't fight the current.' It was difficult to stay close to him now as each wave urged her into shore, but she couldn't let it. She had to stay with him. 'You need to get out of it, come towards me.'

She could see the disbelief on his face, knew the look of fear well. He wasn't coming out. She was going in.

'It won't take you under, I promise.'

He shook his head, his mouth filling with water as he gasped.

'If you can't swim to me, float on your back, go with it and I'll get you.'

It was as though he wasn't listening now, just propelling his arms forward in a jagged front crawl that was too exhausting to watch, let alone deliver.

She cursed under her breath and thought quickly.

She couldn't enter the current where she was, she'd only get swept away from him, but she needed to get him on her board before he lost his ability to stay afloat.

'Please, trust me, stay calm, float, I'm going to come and get you…'

She kept shouting back to him, explaining what she was doing, not knowing whether he could hear or if he was even paying attention. People often didn't when they were in a life-threatening situation. But maintaining that contact was crucial to getting him through this.

She paddled into the current closer to shore and let it take her.

'Grab on,' she ordered as she approached, slipping her own body off the board but keeping one arm over it as she helped him take hold. 'Now grip it.'

She wrapped her arm around his back which was so broad she had to pull away from the board a little and push her hip into his back to keep him up. 'We're just going to go with it for now.'

She spoke close to his ear, certain he'd hear her, even over his ragged breaths, and she wondered at how much water he'd taken on, whether he was even lucid enough to stay with her.

Nalu barked from outside the rip current, swimming to keep pace with them; he wasn't silly enough to join them, like Malie he was waiting for the strength of the current to ease, enough that she could power them both out of it.

If the guy had just done as she'd asked… But then what on earth had he been doing in the first place? Swimming where there was no lifeguard and at this time of day, without the knowledge it took to understand the water.

Foolish, foolish, fool.

And she'd tell him as much just as soon as they had dry land beneath their feet.

She felt the tug of the water start to ease and kicked out, each strike of her legs taking them further into safety.

He was bigger than her, muscular too, and… in a shirt? Who goes swimming in an actual *shirt*?

'Thank you,' he suddenly blurted, his voice rasping as he leaned forward to rake one hand over his face and look to her.

'You want to thank me,' she said, looking to the shoreline, 'you can help swim us back in.'

It was a short, snappy retort, but then, he'd been an absolute idiot and he wasn't dead, so he could pull his weight.

It worked to get them in quicker and as their feet hit the sand, she slid the board away so that he could crawl up the beach. She walked up behind him, the board hooked under her arm. He turned onto his back, his eyes closed as he laid one hand on his chest, the other by his side. He dragged in a shaky breath, then another.

She dropped her board down and stood over him, aware that she was staring but unable to look away. She was relieved he was

OK, angry that he'd been a fool but now that he was on dry land and not spluttering up half the ocean, she was struck by just how good-looking he was.

Considering that she dealt with ripped surfer dudes day in, day out, some novice in the sea shouldn't really be touting this much appeal.

'Hey, you OK?' she asked.

His lashes fluttered as he gave a choked hum – they were thick, dark, almost feminine, if not for the fact they fanned cheeks that looked like they'd been chiselled from granite.

'What the hell were you thinking?'

He wet his lips, lips that made her think of kissing. It was an impulsive reaction, it wasn't rational. She'd just rescued him, for God's sake. But they were so full, full yet firm, a flush of colour in his otherwise pale and cleanshaven face.

Was it the ordeal that made him so pale, or was it just the light of the moon? Either way, it gave him a sexy vamp-like edge, a total contrast to the tanned Adonises she was used to. Perhaps that was why she found him uniquely appealing. And then his throat bobbed as he swallowed, the move drawing her eye lower... and oh my, would her stomach just quit its fluttering.

He opened his eyes and the fluttering became a full-on typhoon. It was too dark to determine their colour, but his eyes met her own with an intensity that took her breath away. He swept his hair off his face unveiling an angled brow that gave a surety to his features, a confidence that belied his fear of seconds ago.

'I'm sorry I got you caught up in that.'

His voice rasped and her body positively purred over it. Was that how he always sounded, or was that just the effect of the sea?

He was English too; a Londoner, if she were to guess.

Well, English or not, hot-vamp or not, you should be rollicking him, not standing here drooling like a sex-starved nymph.

Where's your good sense, Malie?

Back out in the sea, it would appear…

Could this day get any worse?

When Todd Masters pulled himself up the beach on his hands and knees, thanks to his jelly-like legs that had refused to support his weight, he'd hoped he could feign passing out and she would just leave him to it. Let him regather his wits and his pride alone. If only…

Someone up there was clearly having a laugh at his expense today. First his father had refused to accept his help which had resulted in a phone call from hell, and then he'd tried to save a dog from drowning only to find himself the one in need – *in need?* He was *never* the one in need.

And now his rescuer was mad, real mad, judging by her silhouette that showed her hands were fisted on her hips.

'Never mind sorry,' she erupted – *definitely* mad. 'You could have got yourself killed.'

He let his head loll back, his eyes closed again, like he could somehow magic away the whole situation. He'd been an idiot and he'd likely put her in danger too. It had been foolish, reckless, stupid even, and to his horror, he could feel a foreign surge of heat creeping into his cheeks.

Beside him there was a swoosh as she dropped to her knees, a soft curse falling from her lips as her hand fell to his chest. Her palm was warm despite the clinging wet fabric of his shirt.

He couldn't peep, if he did, he knew the blush – *a blush, for goodness' sake* – would spread. And he was trying to force it back. He didn't blush, he didn't get embarrassed and he sure as hell didn't need help. He was always the one to give help. And yet… the sea water swishing around in his gut, currently threatening to make a reappearance, and the way his knees almost knocked told him he'd definitely needed that help.

'Hey.' Her hand pressed into his chest. 'Hey.'

Still he didn't react.

'Hey!' There was nothing soft about it now, her palm was hard, urgent as it shoved at him. 'Are you OK?'

He took hold of her wrist before she could shake the sea water out of him and gave a laugh. Not that he really felt like laughing. And that made it a nervous laugh and he hadn't produced one of those since… well, for ever.

'I'm OK, save for my ego. That's taken a hit.'

He opened his eyes to look up at her and the whole world seemed to stop. For the briefest moment, all he saw were a pair of piercing eyes only a foot away, close enough to feel her harried breath mingle with his. They were cat-like, so dark as they glittered at him, captivating him, and he had the ridiculous notion that he was drowning all over again… until they narrowed and flashed with another surge of rage.

'Your ego is the last thing you should be worrying about.' She pushed off him, rocking back on her heels. 'What on earth did you think you were doing out there?'

It wasn't just her eyes. It was the angle to her cheekbones, her perfect almond-shaped face and lips that were plump in spite of their tight, grim line.

He swallowed. He really needed to get a handle on this situation. He felt unsteady, rocked to his core, and now he wasn't so sure whether that was from his near-drowning or her.

'Are you going to answer me?' She fisted her hands back on her hips and continued to loom, the angle drawing his eyes to her chest, the narrow slant to her waist, and swell to her hips... and he wasn't overheating with pure shame anymore.

He scrambled up onto his elbows with a cough and she scuttled back, just a little, but the space was good, really good. It gave him the clarity he needed, to drag in air that wasn't tainted by her coconut sea scent.

'I'm really sorry.'

'Wading straight into a rip current and refusing to listen to a single instruction I gave you.'

'Hey, I listened.' He raised a hand to ward off the onslaught of her words. 'I just couldn't understand why you wanted me to do that.'

She shook her head so fiercely droplets of sea water fired at him, her mass of hair already springing up into corkscrew curls as they released her fury on him. 'You *never* try and swim against it, no one can beat it.'

'I just wanted to get back to shore before the riptide pulled me under.'

She laughed. The sound sudden, unexpected and glorious. At least she wasn't livid now. 'For your information, you were caught in a rip current, and no one gets dragged under by it, you get swept out.'

'OK.' He said it slowly. 'That's not what I've seen on the TV.'

'This is real life. So in future, you get caught like that, you do as

335

I say and you either swim parallel to shore, or you go with it until you feel the pull soften. *Then* you get out of it *before* attempting to swim to shore. Understood?'

Understood? He couldn't remember the last time someone had spoken to him in such a way and he had the ridiculous urge to roll his eyes. 'Yes, Mum.'

'This isn't funny, dude.'

'I didn't say it was.' But she'd just called him *dude* and now he really did want to laugh. How interesting it was to be stripped of his identity and just be one of the masses again, or the dudes, as she put it.

She was studying him intently and he realized too late that his amusement certainly wasn't amusing her. He tried to straighten his face, to look serious. Was there another lecture brewing?

'You could have died out there,' she admonished but it was softer now.

'Yes, I got that much, thank you.'

'Unless that was your intention?' She frowned and swept an eye over his length: shirt, chino shorts, socks… at least he'd had the foresight to toe off his trainers and drop his mobile in them before running in. 'It's not normal to go swimming dressed for dinner.'

'Look, I was trying to rescue a dog.'

'*A dog?* You ran in the water where there's no lifeguard, the light is almost gone, to rescue a dog?'

She didn't sound like she believed him. Great, did she now think he'd put himself in danger intentionally? His amusement morphed back into embarrassment just as swiftly. This was getting better and better. Where was the dog anyhow? He started to scan the beach and then a thought occurred to him.

'Hang on, *you* were way out in the water when I got here, *you'd* gone in with no lifeguard, limited light... *yada yada yada*.'

She lifted her chin. 'I know what I'm doing, plus I'm a qualified lifeguard.'

'Oh, so you can rescue yourself when in difficulty, yes?' He'd swear she was the one blushing now, and even if she wasn't, it suited him to think she was. 'That's a cracking skill.'

She shook her head and shoved at his chest. 'I wouldn't have swum into the rip current for a start.'

'No, I got that loud and clear.' He looked back to the sea, to where he'd been making an idiot of himself minutes before and frowned. 'Not that I understand how you spot one in the first place.'

She turned to look at the water too. 'You see that channel you were in; you see how the waves are breaking either side, but that strip looks calm, virtually still...?'

He shifted higher onto his elbows and looked to where she motioned with her hand. 'Yes.'

Her eyes came back to him, sharp, direct. '*That* is a rip current.'

'Got it,' he hurried out, which he did, and he would certainly remember it in future. 'But at the time I was more focused on the dog that—'

As if on cue, said dog trotted up and like his rescuer shook off his hair, showering Todd in another layer of sea water. Only this time the effect wasn't quite as appealing.

'It was this one as it happens.' He nodded his head in its direction and noted how the hound looked far too innocent and in no way in need of rescuing at all. The dog gave a sharp bark in agreement, or to rattle him further – he couldn't decide.

'Nalu?' She still didn't sound convinced.

'Na-who?' He stared at the dog like he could blame it for everything that had gone wrong that day.

'Nalu…' She leaned over and ruffled its great big head. 'He belongs to the surf school further down the coast.'

'He does?'

'Yup and that's why he's called Nalu, it's Hawaiian for wave or surf.'

'Very apt.' He knew he sounded disgruntled, but he couldn't help it. If it hadn't been for Nalu, he wouldn't have made such a complete fool of himself. 'I take it he knows all about rip wotsits then?'

She laughed again, the sound even lighter and easy now. 'Yup.'

Nalu gave a little snort and plonked himself down.

It really was time to bring an end to the whole emasculating experience, but the idea of just walking away from her was worse than enduring it.

Instead he found himself asking, 'Well, now that I know Naa-luu is safe and I certainly am, because of you, how about a drink to say thank you?'

Her eyes widened. 'A drink?'

'Yes… you know one of those things people do for fun?'

She nibbled her bottom lip, a move he found strangely contrary to the confidence she projected both in and out of the water.

'I can't, I already have plans.' She glanced at her watch and gave a curse under her breath. 'And I'm going to be late.'

She looked back to him as she shot to her feet. 'Will you be OK getting home?'

Her obvious concern was sweet and frustrating – *no, humiliating*

– at the same time. It would probably be better all round if they never saw one another again. His ego certainly thought so.

'I'll be fine, my place isn't far.'

She hesitated, leaning on one foot then the other. 'OK. But if you want to swim, maybe stick to the more common areas next time. This section doesn't get many visitors with it being so overgrown.'

'That's what made it perfect.'

Her eyes narrowed and he knew she was trying to suss out his reasoning.

'Well, next time, maybe just avoid the water and the acts of heroism.'

'You're on, I'll leave those to you.' He laughed as he said it, expecting her to take that as her cue to leave. Instead she went back to chewing her lip as Nalu trotted around to sit at her feet.

'You can stop worrying, you know, I'm not about to go back in.'

'Of course, yeah…' she glanced away and then back to him. 'I'll see you around… come on, Nalu.'

Then she was off, ducking to grab her board on the way and jogging into the foliage that bordered the beach. He was left with his ego in pieces but a strange excitement thrumming through his veins. The come down of the adrenalin, he supposed, only he had a feeling it wasn't just that…

And he hadn't even caught her name.

He knew where she came to surf, though… if ever he wanted to engineer a future meet-up…

'You need to move,' he suddenly heard from the foliage, not that he could make her out. 'The tide is about to take your designer trainers out.'

He shot up, she was right, the water was already lapping at his toes.

He launched himself at his shoes, his wet and sandy clothes making the entire move awkward and her soft giggle trickled through the air, tailing off as she went further into the greenery.

He found himself smiling down at the footwear now in his hands. *Smiling?!*

He could have died and instead of reeling from it, he was grinning like a fool.

He pulled his phone out of his shoes and checked his home screen, cursing when he saw the time.

No more grinning now, she wasn't the only one about to be late.

Meet
me in
Hawaii

by

Georgia Toffolo

The gorgeous new romance
coming Spring 2021

PRE-ORDER NOW

MILLS & BOON

THE HEART OF ROMANCE

Keep in touch with...

Georgia Toffolo

Follow:

f ToffTalks

◎ Georgiatoffolo

𝕏 @ToffTalks

For all the latest book news from Georgia, sign up to the newsletter: **b.link/ToffNewsletter**

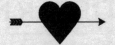

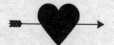